Praise for Julie Benson

"This is a heartwarming story about beating the odds to find joy and love."

—*RT Book Reviews* on *Roping the Rancher*

"Benson takes the reality TV world and bends it around in this charming contemporary romance."

—*RT Book Reviews* on *Bet on a Cowboy*

"This is definitely recommended... I'll be getting my hands on Julie Benson's next book very soon."

—*Goodreads* on *Big City Cowboy*

Praise for Kathleen O'Brien

"O'Brien has penned a complex novel that manages to skillfully weave together several different plot points.... A fantastic read!"

—*RT Book Reviews* on *The Secrets of Bell River*

"Darkly gothic and disturbing, *Happily Never After* is a thrill ride reminiscent of V.C. Andrews's *Flowers in the Attic*, with the added appeal of a robust romance and an unnerving mystery that will leave you guessing until the very end. Quite simply, you must say 'I do!' to this book."

—*RT Book Reviews*

"If you're looking for a fabulous read, reach for a Kathleen O'Brien book. You can't go wrong."

—Catherine Anderson, *New York Times* bestselling author

HOME ON THE RANCH:
COLORADO RESCUE

———— ✕ ————

JULIE BENSON
KATHLEEN O'BRIEN

**Previously published as *Roping the Rancher*
and *Betting on the Cowboy***

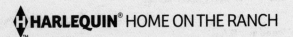

ISBN-13: 978-1-335-50714-3

Home on the Ranch: Colorado Rescue
Copyright © 2018 by Harlequin Books S.A.

First published as Roping the Rancher by
Harlequin Books in 2014 and
Betting on the Cowboy by Harlequin Books
in 2013.

The publisher acknowledges the copyright
holders of the individual works as follows:

Roping the Rancher
Copyright © 2014 by Julie Benson

Betting on the Cowboy
Copyright © 2013 by Kathleen O'Brien

Printed in U.S.A.

HARLEQUIN®
www.Harlequin.com

CONTENTS

An avid daydreamer since childhood, **Julie Benson** always loved creating stories. After graduating from the University of Texas at Dallas with a degree in sociology, she worked as case manager before having her children: three boys. Many years later she started pursuing a writing career to challenge her mind and save her sanity. Now she writes full-time in Dallas, where she lives with her husband, their sons, two lovable black dogs, two guinea pigs, a turtle and a fish. When she finds a little quiet time, which isn't often, she enjoys making jewelry and reading a good book.

Books by Julie Benson

Harlequin American Romance

Big City Cowboy
Bet on a Cowboy
The Rancher and the Vet
Roping the Rancher
Cowboy in the Making

Visit the Author Profile page at Harlequin.com for more titles.

ROPING THE RANCHER

JULIE BENSON

For Sue Casteel, and the other volunteers and staff at Equest Therapeutic Horsemanship in Wylie, Texas, without whom this book couldn't have been written. The amazing work you do changes lives for the better.

Chapter 1

"I don't care how good the therapy is supposed to be. There is no way I'm letting you get on a horse," Stacy Michaels said to her younger brother when they left his neurologist's office.

"This isn't about me. It's about Dad, isn't it?"

"Of course it is." Stacy punched the elevator down button with so much force she chipped her fingernail.

"Dad died filming a movie stunt. This is a therapy program," Ryan insisted.

Since he'd been only a few months old at the time, he knew nothing about their father's death other than what he'd been told. While an eleven-year-old Stacy had been in the movie as well and witnessed the entire event. Even now, almost sixteen years later, some nights she still woke drenched in sweat from the nightmares.

The months before her dad's accident had been the

best time in Stacy's life. She smiled at the memories
of working with him on the movie and how she soaked
up every drop of attention he poured on her. The image
of him beaming when he told everyone within earshot
how she was a chip off the old block and that one day
she'd be a star flashed in her mind.

Her life had been perfect.

Then a week before filming ended, her father, playing a fifteenth-century knight, was shooting the big
battle scene against her character's kidnappers. When
his mount became spooked by the special effects, her
father fell and the horse trampled him to death, with
Stacy a few feet away.

Now her brother wanted her to give the okay for him
to become a patient of a therapeutic horse program. Not
as long as she was his guardian.

"There has to be another option."

"You heard what Dr. Chapman said. We've tried
everything else. This is my best shot to walk without
this damned walker," Ryan said, as he struggled to
maneuver onto the elevator.

A year ago Ryan had been driving when a man
walked out onto the street from between two parked
cars. Unable to avoid the man, Ryan hit him and then
barreled head-on into a telephone phone pole. The man
nearly died. Both of Ryan's legs were crushed and he'd
sustained a brain injury that left him with control and
balance issues. Despite two surgeries and countless
hours of physical therapy, he still needed a walker. The
investigation cleared Ryan of any wrongdoing, but he'd
still carried a fair share of guilt over what happened.

Stacy stared at her brother, his eyes filled with determination and, more importantly, hope. Her breath

caught in her throat. She hadn't seen that emotion in his gaze for months. He deserved every chance to get his life back to what it had been, but how could she let him get on a horse? "I don't know."

"Please, you've got to let me try this. Whatever the risk, for me it's worth it."

She told herself he wouldn't be racing around hell-for-leather on a movie set with cannons booming around him like their father had been. From what Dr. Chapman said, the horse Ryan rode for therapy would be walking or at most trotting around an arena with multiple volunteers to ensure nothing went wrong. She glanced at her brother. He was so young. How could she deny him this chance to get his life back? "You win."

"You're the best."

"And don't you forget it."

Once in the car Ryan stuck his nose in the program brochures the doctor had given them, occasionally tossing out information. "Most of the programs have spring sessions starting this time of year. That means I can start right away. In ten weeks I could be ditching my walker."

"Where's the closest one?" Stacy asked, her mind starting to work on how she'd carve time out of her schedule to accommodate his therapy sessions.

Then a thought hit her. Her next movie, *The Women of Spring Creek Ranch,* was scheduled to start shooting next week in Estes Park, Colorado.

Unless she figured out a way to be in two places at once, she had a problem.

"Mom, Ryan had another appointment with the neurologist this afternoon. You told me you'd be there."

Stacy fought to keep her voice level despite her growing irritation as she walked into the living room of her mother's recently redecorated Malibu beach house.

"I went out to lunch with some friends and lost track of time."

More likely she lost track of how many cosmos she'd had, and based on her bleary-eyed gaze, smeared mascara and rumpled blouse and slacks, she had passed out the minute she got home.

Which was exactly why Ryan had asked Stacy to sue for guardianship. They'd both hoped Andrea losing custody of her son would be the wake-up call she needed to pull herself together. So far that hadn't been the case.

"I know I should've been there, but I've had so many doctor appointments of my own." Andrea, a passenger in the car with Ryan, had broken her arm. She'd also received minor cuts to her face and neck, for which she'd insisted on plastic surgery to repair. She'd also attended biweekly sessions with her therapist to cope with the emotional trauma. "I couldn't bear facing another doctor. Plus, you're so much better dealing with Ryan's problems than I am."

Same old story. Her mom couldn't cope so she bailed on her son.

Stacy sank onto the couch beside her mother, took a deep breath and recounted the details from Ryan's doctor appointment.

"I don't know if that's a good idea considering what happened to your father." Andrea's voice broke. "I still miss him so much. How could God have taken him when he always took care of me?"

The accident that killed Stacy's father was the first

blow that sent Andrea's world spinning. Her mother had taken to her bed. If it hadn't been for their nanny, Stacy didn't know what would've happened to her and Ryan. Molly had been the one she clung to when she woke from nightmares. When she skinned her knee, she ran to Molly who hugged her and dried her tears.

Stacy's life changed even more when the movie she filmed with her father opened a year later. Critics raved not only about Jason Michaels's performance, but Stacy's, as well. Talk shows wanted to interview her. Directors sent scripts to her father's agent for consideration. The next thing Stacy knew, she had a full-time job.

Her focus changed from studying for her weekly spelling test to preparing for her next audition. Six months later she landed a role on what turned out to be an Emmy-award-winning series, *The Kids Run the Place,* that ran for ten years. Looking back now, she realized being on that show saved her life. The cast became more of a family than her own had ever been. She'd often pretended her TV parents were her real parents. One day she even begged Sophia Granger, her TV mom, to take her home with her.

Don't think about that now. Concentrate on Ryan's problem, and getting Mom to see he needs her.

"The doctor thinks the therapeutic sports riding will improve Ryan's muscle control and balance," Stacy said, summarizing the information she'd read on the internet. The horse's rhythmic movement was what helped people. To control and direct the horse the patient had to master his own body. The skills learned on horseback then carried over into the patient's everyday life. "The risk of something going wrong is minuscule."

Maybe if she said the words enough she'd believe them, too. "Ryan wants this chance at a normal life."

"I trust you to decide what's best. I don't know what I'd do without you to take care of things."

Maybe you'd have to face reality for a change and be the parent.

Resisting the urge to massage her aching temples, Stacy counted to ten, trying to dredge up more patience, because all she wanted to do was shake her mother and scream for her to snap out of it. Not that doing so would do any good. Her mother would only burst into tears and ask how her daughter could say that to her when she was still dealing with the pain caused by her injuries and her recent separation from husband number three.

Grant had turned out to be prime marriage material. Three months ago he claimed his wife's physical and emotional problems from the car accident were draining him creatively, and the negative energy was affecting his auditions, costing him roles. Then he moved out.

"I start filming next week. I was hoping you could go with Ryan to therapy."

Stacy reached into her purse, pulled out the list of programs and held the paper out to her mother. "The doctor highlighted the ones he thought were the best."

Her mother scanned the information. "These are all out of town. I can't go anywhere. Grant and I are meeting tomorrow to talk about reconciling." Her mother's blue eyes sparkled, as she toyed with a strand of golden hair, highlighted perfectly and often to cover the gray. "He says he misses me. That his life is so empty without me."

Stacy wanted to laugh at her mother's naïveté. More likely Grant missed his bills being paid and the lifestyle he'd become accustomed to living with Andrea. Life had to be less pleasant for him when he had to actually earn a living.

"That's wonderful that he's willing to talk about a reconciliation, but Ryan needs—"

"I still can't believe Grant moved out." Tears pooled in Andrea's eyes. "I thought we'd be together forever. That he'd take care of me."

Maybe you should learn to take care of yourself. That way you wouldn't end up devastated when a man lets you down.

The biting words sat perched on Stacy's tongue. While it would feel cathartic to confront her mom, dealing with the emotional meltdown afterward wasn't worth it.

Andrea glanced at the therapy information again. "It says here therapy is once a week. Couldn't you hop on a quick flight, go to therapy with Ryan and then fly right back to the set?"

Stacy swallowed hard. She wouldn't be here banging her head against the wall trying to get Andrea to help out if the problem were that easily fixed. "I can't be gone for an entire day every week."

Her mom frowned and crossed her arms over her chest. "I certainly can't be locked into weekly appointments. I have to be here to work on my marriage. That and healing physically from the accident have to be my top priorities."

"This is exactly why Ryan doesn't think you care about him."

"That's not fair. I love my son. I just need to concentrate on myself right now. That's what my therapist says. Until I do that I don't have anything to give to anyone else."

Life had dealt her mother some tough hits, but that didn't give her the right to crawl in her shell and forget about her son.

"I need to do this movie. Finances are tight."

Andrea waived a delicate manicured hand through the air. "You're just like your father, always worrying about money. He was always a sky is falling type, too."

Stacy sighed, and clasped her hands on her lap. Andrea received a generous settlement when Stacy's father died, but she lived as though the money would never run out. How many times would they have to go over budget basics before her mother understood? Apparently at least once more. "Your expenses have to be less than your income. Since your divorce from Allan, that hasn't been the case. We had to liquidate a lot of your investments in the divorce settlement."

Her mother bit her lip. For a second she looked older than her years, and Stacy's heart tightened. "I wish I'd listened to you about asking him to sign a prenup. I was just so scared that if I did he'd say I didn't trust him, and he'd leave me."

Which he did anyway. While a broken engagement would've been tough on her mother, it would have been less financially painful than a messy divorce. Why couldn't her mother see that?

Because she's so desperate for love.

"Mom, you have to stick to the budget we made out. You can't just disregard—"

"Don't start lecturing me about how I spent too much money redecorating the house before Grant and

I got married." Andrea folded her hands, which were still young-looking, thanks to weekly deep moisturizing treatments, on her lap. "I don't regret spending a penny of that money. I wanted him to feel like this was his house. Part of the reason my marriage with Allan failed was he felt like he was living in your father's shadow."

"I'm trying to explain why you need to make some changes. If insurance pays for Ryan's therapy at all, it'll reimburse us. I can't afford to lose out on work right now."

Especially when I'm the only working member of the family, and it's been a while since I had a hit movie or series.

Her mother frowned. Tears filled her eyes again. "I'm sorry we've been such a burden to you."

No. Andrea's "poor me" routine wouldn't work today. She refused to feel guilty. This was all about Ryan and what he needed. "We're a family, and family helps each other out."

But shouldn't the flow go both ways?

"Grant and I might still be able to make our marriage work." Her mother's lips trembled, and her voice broke. "I don't know if I can survive another divorce. Stacy, you have to help me. You've got to give me this chance. Can't you see if they can work the shooting schedule around Ryan's therapy?"

"I was lucky to get this role. Half of the actresses in Hollywood wanted it."

"Nonsense. That woman owes you," her mother said, a sneer on her face as she referred to Maggie Sullivan McAlister, the creator and director of *The Women of Spring Creek Ranch*.

"No one gave me the part. I *earned* it."

"After what she did on that dreadful reality dating show, she's lucky you didn't sue her for every penny she had. I still can't believe that cowboy chose the plain Jane director over you."

Stacy only agreed to be a bachelorette on *Finding Mrs. Right* because she'd been between jobs. Never once had she considered letting her heart get involved with the bachelor. She hadn't been foolish enough to believe a reality show relationship would last longer than the latest fashion fad. For her, the show had been a job like any other TV show. A vehicle to getting a series of her own.

"I got over that ages ago." Now if only other people would quit bringing the subject up, she could forget about it, too. "If I ask Maggie to shoot around Ryan's therapy I risk her giving the role to someone else. Mom, please go with Ryan so I can do this movie."

There, she'd put it all on the line. She told her mother exactly what she needed. Stacy held her breath, and prayed this once her mother would pull up her mom panties and be the parent.

"Grant and I need time to work out our problems. Then I can go with Ryan for therapy. Surely waiting a month or two won't make that much difference."

So much for Andrea stepping up and doing the right thing by putting her children first.

"He shouldn't have to wait until it's convenient for us." Ryan deserved this chance, and apparently she was the only one willing to make it happen.

As a child, whenever she asked her mom to play a game or read a book to her, the response had always been, "In a minute." Or, "Not now." Or, "Ask the nanny." That taught Stacy a valuable lesson. Asking for something led to disappointment. When she learned to quit asking, she avoided that pain.

Harnessing her anger, Stacy mumbled something about how she'd take care of Ryan's therapy, said good-bye to Andrea and stumbled out of the house. Once inside her car, she dropped her head to the steering wheel and cried.

A minute later Stacy dried her tears and told herself to snap out of it. A pity party never helped. All it did was wreck a girl's makeup, and leave her with red, puffy eyes. There had to be a solution. All she had to do was find it.

Later that afternoon as Stacy sat in her cozy Hollywood condo, she faced the truth. She could either do the movie or she could give her brother a chance to recover.

There would always be another movie. Maybe not as wonderful a role as the lead in *The Women of Spring Creek Ranch,* but losing the job wouldn't kill her career. Of course she'd have to solve her cash-flow problem. She'd call her agent and ask him to get her any work he could find to bring in some quick money without requiring a long commitment. Commercials. Voice-over work, whatever, as long as the job paid. Her career would be fine.

Provided Maggie understood. Otherwise Stacy could find herself blacklisted with every director in town. Her hand shook as she picked up her cell phone. "Maggie, I hate to do this, but I've got to drop out of the movie. My brother needs physical therapy. It's a ten-week program, and right now I need to be with him. I can't be on location for a movie and get him to his therapy sessions."

"While I'm disappointed we won't get to work together, I understand. Family has to come first."

Such a simple concept. How come her mother couldn't grasp it? "The doctor says his best chance to walk again is a therapeutic horse program."

"That's the therapy where patients ride horses, isn't it?"

"It is."

"One of the things about a small town is anything happens and everyone knows about it," Maggie said. "You're not going to believe this, but Colt Montgomery, a war vet, opened a program like that on his ranch a while ago. It's a couple miles down the road from where we'll be filming at Twin Creeks."

The image of the stereotypical crotchety rancher in the old Westerns popped into Stacy's mind. The one who preferred his horse's company to people. Who cared if it was Rooster Cogburn running the program if he helped Ryan?

"The program's new, and I don't know anything about it," Maggie continued, "but if it's an option for your brother, you might be able to arrange his therapy around our shooting schedule."

Who would've thought she and Stacy would work together after how things had gone between them on the reality show *Finding Mrs. Right*? Stacy bit her lip, trying to control her emotions at Maggie's unexpected kindness. Her mother wouldn't help, but here was someone, barely an acquaintance, who was willing to do what she could to alleviate her problem. Tears blurred her vision. "You'd do that?"

"You could pop over to the Rocking M Ranch for a therapy session during your downtime. If your brother's doctor thinks the program will work, I'm willing to give it a try. The name of Colt's program is Healing Horses."

"Maggie, I can't tell you how much I appreciate this, especially considering what I said to you and Griffin during the finale."

Stacy had been one of the bachelorettes on the show competing for the heart of a Colorado cowboy, Griffin McAlister. Because of that opportunity she'd received a deal for her own reality show. However, things had been contingent on her getting a marriage proposal and the free publicity that went along with the engagement ring as the "winner" of *Finding Mrs. Right*. Never one to leave situations to chance and sensing Griffin was as enthusiastic about marital bliss as she was, Stacy approached him with a deal. He'd propose. They'd play the happy couple during the post-show appearances, and then quietly break up. She'd say they parted amicably, and he'd do likewise. They'd fulfill their contracts, get the free publicity to help their careers and come out without a scratch to their images. A win-win situation all around.

But things hadn't gone as planned. Instead, Griffin and Maggie fell in love and he proposed to the director instead during the live finale. At the time all Stacy saw was her latest career opportunity flying out the window and she'd been brutal in her anger.

"I owe you an apology, too," Maggie said. "I couldn't talk to you at the audition with everyone else around, but I want to tell you that now. I know people say 'we didn't plan this, it just happened' all the time, but that really was the case with me and Griffin. The more we worked together, the more we got to know each other, and we fell in love."

"I think you were the only one who got to see the real man," Stacy said. When she was with Griffin on a date she'd sensed he was holding back, that he was treating the show like a job, too. Looking back now she saw that fact even more. He hadn't been shocked by her business proposition. His only concern had been whether he could trust her to keep quiet about their deal. Once she'd answered that question, he'd agreed. In fact he'd appeared almost relieved, but then he'd pulled the rug out from under her at the finale.

"I'm hoping Healing Horses will work for Ryan because I'd love to work with you. I think this project is going to be amazing."

As she told Maggie she'd talk to Ryan's doctor and call her no later than tomorrow with an answer, hope and determination blossomed inside of Stacy.

With a little luck Ryan would get his therapy and she could make the movie. Another win-win situation. Hopefully this one would work out better than the last one.

Chapter 2

Boring. Calm. Uneventful. Ordinary. The words once made Colt Montgomery go stir-crazy, but since coming home from Afghanistan, they sounded pretty damned good. Of course, raising a teenage daughter on his own meant he didn't use those words in conjunction with his life very often, but he kept hoping.

Everywhere he went in town people and life seemed the same, and yet he wasn't. Life in Afghanistan consisted of endless monotony and preparation, interrupted with bouts of sheer terror. He spent a good portion of his day wondering if someone he was there to help would turn on him with an AK-47. Then one day he was home.

Going to a war zone changed a man in ways few could understand, but he was one of the lucky ones. He'd come home with all his body parts. Except for some minor scars and an occasional nightmare, he returned unscathed, but then he hadn't been there for his full tour, either.

Once home, he struggled with what to do with his life. While he loved being a parent, he needed more than raising his daughter and being a rancher. Then he heard from one of his buddies, Dan, who'd lost a leg in Afghanistan. His doctor recommended an equestrian sports therapy program, but there wasn't one near him. After that email, Colt discovered the purpose he craved in creating Healing Horses.

He'd gone through a seven-week training course to become a registered instructor. Then he started training horses and found local physical therapists willing to donate their time to recommend activities and work with clients when necessary.

When Colt finally was able to open the doors to Healing Horses, Dan was the program's first patient.

Footsteps tapped across the wooden floor outside his office. He looked up from the stack of bills due on his desk to see his daughter walk in, and his heart ached.

He'd come so close to losing her when he was in Afghanistan, and all because of his selfishness. When her mother ran off with a computer repairman and died a month later in a car accident, he should've quit the National Guard Reserves. He'd known getting deployed was a possibility, but he never really thought it would happen. So much for long shots.

When he'd been shipped to Afghanistan, his younger brother came to Colorado to stay with Jess. Reed, a bachelor, made more than a few mistakes, and Jess ran away. What could have happened to her, now that gave Colt real nightmares. Pimps. Drug dealers.

General crazies waiting to prey on a naive fourteen-year-old. He thanked God every day that Reed and Avery, now Reed's wife, found Jess at the Denver airport before she got into any serious trouble.

Jess's running away had been a hard kick to the head for Colt. This time he got the message. She was the most important thing in his life and it was high time he proved it. So he asked for a hardship discharge, left the National Guard Reserves and returned to Estes Park.

Looking at her now standing in his office, he realized every day she looked more like her mother. Same petite frame, long chestnut hair and warm coffee-colored eyes as her mother. Jess was the constant reminder of how young and in love he'd once been. Sometimes he looked at her and tried to find bits of himself. Today he didn't have any trouble finding a similarity. Her chin pointed at him in stubborn defiance she inherited from him. He braced himself for whatever hand grenade she was about to throw his way.

"Cody Simmons asked me out to a movie on Saturday. Can I go?"

He closed his eyes for a second to regroup. Times like these he missed having her mother around to tell him whether or not he was being too much of a hard-ass. "As in out for a date, asked you out?"

"The word *date* was never mentioned."

"I'm not falling for that one again." She'd burned him with technicalities more than once before he learned to choose his words very carefully and scrutinize every one of hers for land mines. "Would you be going with a group of friends?"

"Not exactly, but—"

"Then it's a date, and the answer is no."

Cody was a good kid. He was an honor student, worked part-time at the Cinemaplex and was a pretty good bronc rider in the junior rodeo circuit, but none of that mattered to Colt. Just thinking about Jess dating shoved his panic into overdrive, especially since he knew what seventeen-year-old boys were like. Basically a bundle of hormones fantasizing about sex every thirty seconds. He hadn't been much older than Cody when he and Lynn started having sex. By graduation she'd been pregnant and they were planning a quickie wedding.

No way did he want history repeating itself with his daughter.

"Your 'no dating until I'm sixteen' rule is so old-fashioned."

"Then you better go get your bonnet, missy."

Three more months were all he had before he started greeting boys at the door with a shotgun and giving them his own version of the Spanish Inquisition before he let them out the door with his daughter. He now understood why man invented the chastity belt.

"All my friends have been dating since they were fifteen. What difference will a few months make?"

"What difference will it make to wait?"

She crossed her arms over her chest, shifted her weight onto one foot and glared at him. Such determination and strength, and yet so much hurt behind those beautiful brown eyes. How could a mother walk out on such a wonderful child?

Leaving him, he got. He and Lynn had troubles from the moment the ink dried on their marriage license. She wanted so much that he couldn't give her. Bright lights, the big city, adventure. Being a military wife and later a rancher's wife weren't what she had in mind.

If only he'd known that earlier, but they'd been high-school sweethearts who swore the love they felt would last forever. They were too young and foolish to know what they didn't know. He wondered now if their relationship would've run its course sooner if Lynn hadn't gotten pregnant.

But then he wouldn't have Jess, and he wouldn't trade being her father for anything. She was the only good thing that came out of his marriage.

"You don't understand what it's like being the only one who can't date. I'll become a social outcast."

He bit his lip to keep from laughing at her woeful my-life-is-over look and drama queen voice. To a teenage girl everything turned into a Greek tragedy. Life with her was like walking a tightrope. One misstep, either with being too strict or too permissive, could lead to a big fall.

"In a couple of days everyone will forget that your hard-ass dad won't let you date."

"If I say no, Cody will probably ask another girl to go with him."

Good. All the better.

Instead, Colt said, "If he really likes you, he'll wait until you turn sixteen."

"Guys have needs—"

"What the hell do you know about that?"

His blood pressure approaching stroke levels, he prayed his daughter wasn't talking about the kind of needs he knew about all too well. His ate him up so bad sometimes he couldn't sleep at night. Hell, he couldn't remember the last time he'd gotten laid. Sure he'd taken the edge off, but that wasn't the same as being with a woman. Sometimes holding one, losing himself in her warm curves and pretending they cared about each other was the only thing that would ease the ache.

For about five minutes when he'd first returned from Afghanistan, he considered dating. Then he remembered what it was like living in the small town he grew up in where gossiping was a town sport. The last thing he wanted was people talking about his love life and his teenage daughter hearing the stories.

On top of that, a casual relationship, in a lot of ways, sounded worse to him than no relationship at all, but he refused to have any other kind. One disastrous marriage was enough.

"Guys have fragile egos," Jess said, easing his panic somewhat. "Getting turned down for a date is hard on their self-esteem. He'll find someone who can go out with him."

"She's not my concern."

"I know. I am."

"That's right." ·

"Just because you don't have a life, doesn't mean I can't have one."

Ouch. He'd died and gone to hell, and this conversation was his punishment. "I've got a life."

But her words got him thinking. What did he have other than Jess? A brother and sister-in-law. The ranch he grew up on. His therapy program, Healing Horses. Was that enough? It had to be right now. He couldn't handle anything else. Definitely not dating and the emotional pitfalls that went along with trying to maintain a romantic relationship. Life with a teenager was exhausting enough.

"A monk has a more exciting life than you do," his daughter said. "You've got work. That's not the same. What're you going to do when I go to college in two years? I don't want you to end up being one of those weird old men who lives alone and talks to himself all day long."

Apparently he hadn't been the only one wondering what his life would be like when Jess went off to college. Part of him dreaded her leaving, while a piece of him looked forward to the freedom he'd have. For as long as he could remember responsibilities ruled his life. From the time he and Reed were strong enough to lift a saddle his father had worked his sons harder than any ranch hand. As the big brother, he'd watched out for Reed. Colt had stepped in to defuse things once their mother, the family peacemaker and punching bag, died. Then at eighteen he'd found himself in the military responsible for a wife with a baby on the way.

An empty nest and the chance to figure out what he wanted to do with the rest of his life sounded pretty good right now.

"Your life shouldn't stop because you've got me to raise."

"It hasn't." He picked up the top bill and scanned the paper, hoping his daughter would take the hint that he was done discussing her dating and his.

"Why don't you trust me?" Jess accused. "I thought you'd forgiven me for running away."

Jess's quiet words and the clear pain in her expressive brown eyes hit Colt hard like a kick from an angry mule. He replaced the bill on the stack. "I have. I know if you're ever that upset again, you'll come to me, and we'll work things out. I don't want you to ever be afraid to tell me anything."

Unlike how he and Reed had been with their father, who they tried every trick to avoid. The old man was as likely to greet a simple good morning from his sons with a slap upside the head as a smile, and there was never a way to predict which they'd get or change the outcome. "I trust you. It's the boys that scare the hell out of me."

"We'd just being going to a movie."

He'd told himself he wouldn't be the hard liner his father had been. He wouldn't drive his daughter away. The last thing he wanted her thinking was that he didn't trust her. He sighed. Time to cowboy up and prove the fact. "I'll compromise. Make it a double date, and you can go."

His daughter charged around his desk, flung her arms around him and squeezed him tight. "I won't let you down," she whispered in his ear and kissed him on the cheek. Then with one last grin, she headed for the door as Nannette McAlister, his assistant at Healing Horses, strolled in. "You'll never guess what happened. Dad said I could go out on a double date this Friday."

"You finally wore him down, huh?" Nannette was the kind of mother every child should have. She loved and encouraged her three children, and their friends were always welcome in the McAlister home. All she wanted was for them to be happy. His brother had found that out firsthand.

Since Reed married Avery, Nannette's youngest and only daughter, he and Jess had been enveloped in the family fold, as well.

"I'm putting my full trust in my daughter," Colt said

to Nannette to emphasize his point with Jess. "She promised she won't let me down."

Jess shook her head. "I'm leaving before he changes his mind."

"Smart girl."

"I take after my father," Jess said before she dashed off.

"How's the morning going?" Nannette asked once she'd settled at her desk, and started booting up her computer.

"Better now that Jess is gone. This dating stuff is going to kill me."

The older woman smiled knowingly. "I feel your pain. Raising Avery gave me more gray hairs than her brothers combined. I know it doesn't seem like it sometimes, but you will survive having a teenage daughter."

"Thank goodness you keep reminding me of that."

When Nannette heard about him turning the Rocking M into a horse-therapy ranch, she'd immediately volunteered to help with bookkeeping. Then when they started classes, she'd assumed scheduling duties, as well. Taking the money he'd gotten from the grant Healing Horses received three months ago to hire Nannette McAlister had been the smartest thing he'd ever done.

When her computer finished booting up, she punched some keys and said, "We received another client application." The hum of the printer filled the office. Nannette grabbed the paper, scanned the application and froze. "This can't be the same Stacy Michaels."

"I need a little context, Nannette. So far you aren't making a lot of sense."

She walked across the room and handed him the paper. "Stacy Michaels was one of the finalists when Griffin was on that ridiculous dating show."

Colt had wondered what kind of woman went on a show like that and fought with a pack of women to win the "love" of a man they'd just met.

A woman whose moral compass didn't point due north, that's who.

From the little bit he saw of the show, he remembered flighty, beautiful women with long legs and short form-fitting skirts that almost showed the good china. Great to look at, but no substance. Women who'd looked down their more-often-than-not surgically altered noses at just about everyone.

After glancing at the application, he said, "It doesn't matter if it's the same woman or not because she wants to sign her brother up for the spring therapeutic sports riding session. It's already started and it's full." He picked up his phone and punched in the number listed on the application. The sultry feminine voice that answered could get a rise out of a man two months after he was dead and buried. His pulse rate shot up like a rodeo bull out of the shoot as he asked to speak to Stacy Michaels.

"This is Stacy."

He shifted in his desk chair. Lord, he'd been alone too long if a woman's voice over the phone could get his imagination and motor running this fast.

"Hello? You still there?"

"Yeah. This Colt Montgomery. I run Healing Horses. I received the paperwork for your brother." He explained about the problem with the class she registered Ryan for. "You'll need to sign him up for our fall class."

"That won't work. I'm in the area to film a movie with Maggie McAlister. In fact, she was the one who recommended your program. I was hoping we could work my brother's therapy session around my shooting schedule. I could just pop over from Twin Creeks, deal with his therapy and then head right back."

Pop over? Did she think Healing Horses worked like the drive-through lane at McDonald's?

"Mr. Montgomery, I'm in a bind here. I can't lose this movie opportunity, but I have to get my brother into therapy. There has to be something we can do."

He'd heard about Maggie filming a movie on Twin Creeks. Since becoming parents, she and Griffin had started a production company and were trying to do more projects at the family ranch when their reality show *The Next Rodeo Star* was on hiatus. Considering that, Stacy probably was the same woman who'd been one of Griffin's bachelorettes.

He shook his head. His gut told him this woman would be trouble. Stacy was probably a high-maintenance city actress who had people catering to her every whim. That was the last thing he needed, but they weren't talking about her needing therapy. They were talking about her brother.

The application indicated her brother Ryan had been in a car accident a little over a year ago. He'd suffered a traumatic brain injury that left him with impaired gross and fine motor skills as well memory problems. He'd been through two surgeries to correct his crushed legs. Despite that and extensive physical therapy, he still required a walker and struggled with balance and control issues. The kid was only seventeen.

If he told Stacy no, would she make her brother wait to get therapy until she finished her movie? He refused to be responsible for a kid not getting the therapy he needed. "We offer private classes. 'Course that's more expensive."

"Great. Sign Ryan up for that instead."

Not how much more expensive? Must be nice to not have to worry about money. Now him, he pinched pennies until they cried uncle, but he'd do whatever he needed to in order to make Healing Horses work without having the program's needs financially impact Jess's life or her college plans.

"When would you like his therapy to start?" he asked as he jotted down the changes on Ryan's paperwork.

"We'll be in Estes Park Thursday. If he could start therapy next week that would be great. Having private sessions will work better than Ryan being part of a class anyway. I'm going to do everything I can to avoid shooting conflicts, but sometimes my schedule changes at the last minute. I'm hoping you can be a little flexible."

He could see it now, calls with her saying something had come up and she needed to reschedule. Showing up late for appointments because whatever she had been doing ran long. He intended to set her straight up front. "Since we're a new program, our physical therapist and instructors have other jobs. Rescheduling a session isn't easy."

"I'll try my best to avoid any conflicts."

Once he ended the call, Nannette asked, "Was it the same Stacy Michaels?"

"Since she's an actress, I'm pretty sure she's the one you met. I need you to schedule private sessions for her brother. She said they'll be getting into town the end of this week. She'd like his therapy to start next week." He rubbed the back of his neck, where an ache had settled. "Is she as bad as she sounded on the phone? Because she sounded like an arrogant, high-maintenance, huge pain-in-the-butt celebrity."

"When she showed up at the ranch she looked like she was dressed for some fancy New York City cocktail party. She had on this skimpy, skintight dress and these strappy little heels. In Colorado. In December."

His stomach dropped. "What about her attitude?"

"I'm not sure we got to see who she really was. Hardly anything that happened on *Finding Mrs. Right* was real. There were scripts and discussions about what would make good TV. Everything everyone said and did was for the cameras. Her being here will be different. There won't be any cameras. This is real life. Plus, she's not the patient. Her brother is."

"She sounds like someone who creates chaos wherever she goes. We can't let her upset our routine. A big part of our program is having structure and order."

"That's the spirit. You were in the military. Keep her in line."

Of course Nannette, the spokesperson for the United Optimists of America, would think that. He'd been to Afghanistan and faced the possibility of dying on a daily basis, but women? No man could keep one in line.

* * *

Stacy had forgotten how beautiful Estes Park was. Even though she wasn't really a back-to-nature kind of gal or the outdoorsy type, the scenery called to her.

The Rocky Mountains stood guard around the small town of Estes Park, almost cradling its inhabitants. That reassuring and enduring presence resonated with Stacy. Something about the wide-open spaces eased the tightness in her chest and stilled her restlessness. The last time she was here she discovered how much slower-paced life was. That had been a huge headache for her. Now it felt as if that was exactly what she needed.

So far settling in had gone smoother than she anticipated. She and Ryan had unpacked and stocked their cabin with food and other staples. They'd met with the school, seen to his registration and he started his first day of classes yesterday. She'd met with Maggie and gotten the shooting schedule so she could schedule Ryan's therapy sessions once they had his initial assessment.

"Now that you've had two days of school, are you sure you want to go Estes Park High? It's not too late for me to get a tutor for you."

"I'm cool with going to school here."

Maybe he wanted a change. Since his accident, Ryan's relationship with his friends was strained. Because he couldn't keep up physically, his friends had moved on. Maybe meeting new people who weren't comparing him to how he used to be would help him come back out of his shell.

"I've actually met a couple of kids. One of them is

the daughter of the guy who runs the therapy program. She's in one of my elective classes. Her name is Jess."

So Rooster had a daughter. "What's she like?"

"She's nice. She said she knows what it feels like to be a little different than everyone else."

"What's she mean by that?"

Ryan shrugged. "The kids here aren't as worried about how much money a guy's family has. They're more real."

His phone dinged indicating he had a text. He scanned the message. "It was from Mom. She said she might join us next week. Can you believe it? Does she really think I'll buy that? Next she'll tell me to write a letter to Santa at Christmas." Ryan chucked. "I'd probably get better results from the letter."

"At least she's trying." More like Andrea was saying the right thing. Their mother talked a good game and tossed out big promises. Follow-through proved to be an entirely different matter. "She might surprise us." But only if Grant moved back into the house and agreed to come with her. Otherwise Andrea wouldn't leave California, but Stacy bit her tongue to keep from mentioning that.

"When are you going to quit giving her more chances? She doesn't deserve it."

For Ryan's sake she kept banging her head against the wall in attempt to get Andrea to change. A teenager needed the guidance and love of a parent. He'd changed so much over the past years. Some of it was just normal teenage-attitude stuff, but she knew some of the differences were because of their mother. Every time she disappointed Ryan, every time she put her needs above his, Stacy saw a little part of her brother die inside.

"She's going through a tough time." She regretted her words the minute she uttered them. How could she have been so thoughtless to Ryan when he'd faced far worse than Andrea? "Not like what you're going through, but she's not as strong as you are."

"She's a selfish bitch who doesn't care about anyone but the husband of the month."

Out of the mouths of angry teenagers often came the harsh truth.

Part of her considered talking to him about how families should forgive and love each other no matter what, but she lacked the energy for a battle. Especially when he was right. She'd tried so hard to make up for Andrea's shortcoming so Ryan wouldn't grow up feeling unloved, but there was only so much she could do.

No matter how hard she tried, she wasn't his mother.

Ryan glanced out the window. "Are you sure you know where we're going? I think we went past this barn a little while ago."

Stacy flashed him a bright smile. "I've got everything under control."

No way would she admit she didn't have a clue where they were. She'd never hear the end of it because Ryan had suggested they print a copy of the directions before they left the cabin. Since they were running late, she'd brushed him off saying they'd be fine with her GPS app on her phone. Unfortunately she'd forgotten how spotty Wi-Fi could be in the Rocky Mountains, forcing her to rely on her memory.

"That's your too-big smile. It means you're lying because you're afraid if you tell me the truth, I'll be upset."

"I don't do that."

"You do it all the time. I'm not a kid. I don't need you protecting me."

They'd both grown up too fast. She'd hoped to save him from some of that, but life had a way of refusing to go along with a person's plan.

"Okay, you win. I admit it. We're lost." She spotted a small ranch house in the distance to the left. "I'll head for that house and ask for directions." Then she pointedly stared at her younger brother.

He stared back. His right eyebrow rose and he smiled.

"Are you going to say it?"

His grin widened. "Say what?"

"I'm not going to have an 'I told you' so hanging over my head. Let's just get it over with."

"But it's more fun to torture you this way." His smile faded and he picked at a frayed spot in his jeans. "I know you don't think this horse-therapy stuff is a good idea, but I researched it a lot. I think it could really help me."

Right after the car accident, Ryan's attitude amazed her. He'd been so full of hope. He swore he'd regain full use of his legs no matter what he had to endure. He'd remained positive during his first surgery and the countless hours of physical therapy. Then the doctors recommended another surgery. When he failed to see much improvement after the second operation, something inside Ryan withered.

He quit going out with friends. Though he hadn't said so, she suspected being with them only reinforced what he couldn't do. He argued with her about attending physical therapy.

"I'm tired of doctor and therapy appointments controlling my life. I want to be normal again. I want to hang out with friends, go out on a date or spend the whole day in school without getting pulled for an appointment. This sports riding program is my best bet to have that. I know you're scared because of what happened to dad, but I'll be okay. Everything I read about the program says falls are rare."

But they do occur. She could handle anything but something happening to Ryan again. He was all she had. Her only family. The only one who cared about what happened to her.

No, that wasn't true. Andrea cared about her, but only because if something happened to Stacy, who would pick up the pieces of her life when it inevitably fell apart?

"I'm praying you're right."

They came around a curve and a loud pop echoed around them. The car pulled hard to the left. Stacy clutched the steering wheel, pulled her foot off the gas and struggled to maintain control. Her sweaty palms slipped on the steering wheel.

"Slow down!" Ryan screamed.

"We're fine." She flashed him a quick smile, hoping to ease his fears and stave off a full-blown panic attack. His fingers dug into the armrest. His breathing grew rapid and shallow. "Breathe slow and deep."

She'd veered into the other lane. She turned hard right. Too hard. The car spun. Ryan's screams reverberated through the car as they headed for the ditch.

Images blurred around Stacy. Her hands grew numb, and then seconds later the car stopped.

"God, no! Not again!" Ryan screamed.

Thank you, Lord. He's yelling. That means he can't be hurt too badly.

Her heart thundering in her chest, her body shaking, Stacy grabbed her brother's arm and squeezed. "Look at me, Ryan. Are you hurt anywhere?" His gaze locked on hers, and he shook his head. "Breathe with me."

She inhaled deeply and held her breath for a second before slowly exhaling. She did that for a minute or two until his breathing matched hers and the panic receded from his eyes. "I'm sorry. I think we blew a tire." She squeezed his hand again before letting go. "You handled that so well."

"No, I didn't. I screamed like a little girl."

"Don't be so hard on yourself. Remember how bad the attack was the first time you got in a car after the accident? You've come so far since then, but that doesn't mean that sometimes you won't get thrown for a loop."

A chorus of moos and clomping hooves on the pavement around them drew Stacy's attention. Not only had they gone off the road into a ditch, but they'd run into a barbed wire fence, taking a good section of it out. Cows making the most of the damaged fence made a break for it and wandered all over the road.

Now what? She put the car into Reverse and tried to back out of the ditch, but the tires spun in the soft ground. They clearly weren't going anywhere.

"I'll go for help."

"What about the cows? We can't leave them all over the road. They'll cause an accident."

She drew the line at worrying about the cows. They'd have to fend for themselves. If they were smart enough to get on the road, they were smart enough to find their way off again. "I bet animals get on the road around here all the time. People are used to watching out for them."

"This is a tourist town. What if someone from out of town comes along? They could get hurt because we…"

Ryan's voice broke. Stacy reached out and laid her hand over her brother's, but he pulled away. This scene was hitting a little too close to home for him. His breathing accelerated again. His pupils dilated.

"Okay. Don't worry." She patted his arm. "Maybe if I lay on the horn they'll move."

The horn's harsh blare hurt her ears, but the cows were apparently hearing impaired because they didn't even twitch. She laid on the horn for a good thirty seconds this time. Nothing.

"Got any suggestions on how to get them to move?"

"Sure. We studied roping cows and ranching in school just last week." Ryan laughed and the tension left his features.

"Smart-ass." Stacy chuckled. This was the brother she loved so much. The one she feared might soon become smothered by his physical limitations.

She glanced at her watch. They were already late for Ryan's appointment. "I could call someone, but we don't have time to wait. We're already running late." How hard could it be to get the cows off the road? "I should be able to take care of this. In one episode of *The Kids Run the Place,* we went for a vacation on a dude ranch. We had a cattle-drive scene."

"That was when you were thirteen. Can you even remember anything from that far back?"

"Gee, I don't know. They say the memory goes the closer you get to thirty. In a couple of years I probably won't even be able to remember who you are." She opened the car door. "Stay here while I get the cows moving. You've been through enough today."

"I'll help."

No way would she risk him getting hurt. They'd pressed their luck enough for one day. "I've got it. There aren't many of them."

"Just because my legs don't work like they used to doesn't mean I can't do something."

So often since the accident she'd felt she lacked the skills to deal with Ryan. At times she had to be mother, cheerleader and therapist. Being a substitute parent to a teenager had been tough enough before his accident.

"I don't know—"

"It doesn't matter what you say. I'm coming."

She thought about pulling rank. With a teenager? They'd only end up having a huge fight and he'd do what he wanted to anyway. "You can help me holler at them, but stay close to the car."

Then she climbed out of the sedan, retrieved his walker from the backseat and handed it to him when he opened the passenger door.

Lost and now chasing cows off the road. Great start to the day. Could things get any worse?

Stacy moved toward the animals. Waiving her arms, she yelled, "Go! Get out of here!"

Joining in the effort, Ryan waved his left arm and shouted along with her.

Of the cows on the road, only one lifted her head and turned in Stacy's direction. Then the animal returned to munching on grass, without moving an inch. She searched her memory for how the cowboy at the dude ranch kept the cows moving. He'd sauntered up to them full of confidence and authority, slapped a lasso against his thigh and hollered at them. Trying her best to imitate the cowboy's swagger, she moved forward, yelling, "Ya," and slapped her thigh.

"Watch out, Stacy."

She glanced over her shoulder toward her brother and her right foot landed in something mushy. "Ugh!" Her foot slid. Her balance waivered and she felt herself falling. Her backside landed hard against the paved road, but that wasn't the worst part. The unmistakable sour smell of manure wafted around her.

"Are you okay?" Ryan asked.

Really? He had to ask? She was sitting in the middle of cow pie. Of course she wasn't okay. "I'll live."

Though her shoes were goners and probably her jeans, too. She glanced at her favorite pair of shoes, leopard print Louis V stilettos ruined with cow poop, and the dam holding her emotions in check sprang a gigantic leak. Tears stung her eyes. She was so damned tired of being strong, of taking care of everything and everyone around her. Of smiling for the world when all she wanted to say was to hell with it.

The whine of a motor sounded around her. Not a car, but some smaller recreational vehicle. She closed her eyes. A moment later when the noise stopped she opened her eyes to find a hand in front of her face.

"Looks like you could use some help."

Stacy's gaze traveled from the hand—not a well manicured hand like the actors she worked with, but one of a man who worked hard for his living, rough and tanned—to find a tall golden-haired man dressed in faded jeans and a Western plaid shirt standing beside a three-wheeler with a small cart. She grimaced. The only thing worse than falling in a cow pie was having a cowboy with an incredible body sculpted by hard work and piercing blue eyes witness her embarrassment.

"No, I'm good. Just thought I'd sit here and reconnect with nature."

"At least you haven't lost your sense of humor."

Her heart fluttered at the twinkle in his sky-blue gaze. Oh, my. He wasn't even close to her type, but this cowboy definitely had something, and every cell in her body knew it.

Chapter 3

When Stacy placed her hand in his, the calluses on his fingers brushed her wrists. She almost gasped when excitement rippled down her spine. That is, once she recognized the emotion, which was hard to do considering she couldn't remember the last time she'd felt anything resembling interest in a man. Once she could speak, she joked, "Good thing, because my pride's sure shot."

"I bet it'll recover."

Her reaction to the cowboy was out of whack. A born and bred California girl, she'd been attracted to well-built surfer types. Something about their daring, how they challenged those giant waves drew her. Maybe because she'd always been so cautious, but then she'd realized all they cared about was catching the next wave.

She'd dated a few actors she'd worked with over the

years. A movie pulled them together, but those relationships never worked. Actors had a way of slipping into their characters almost 24/7 during a film. When filming ended and she came to know who he really was, she often realized she'd been more attracted to the character he'd been playing than the real man.

A few times she dated businessmen, but they became frustrated with the travel and long absences associated with her job, but cowboy guy here? The rugged outdoorsman type never even showed up on her radar. So what about this cowboy got her all hot and bothered?

There was something about his eyes. Clear and blue, they shone with mischief and determination definitely, but something else. The look of an old soul haunted his gaze for brief flashes.

That combination in his steely gaze told her this man would be trouble. No doubt about it.

When the woman at his feet clasped her delicate hand in his, their gazes locked and his breath hitched. Blond hair. Blue eyes that sparkled like a mountain spring under the morning sun. A woman who could look this pretty while sprawled in manure had to be trouble.

He glanced between her and the teenager waiting by the car. A teenage boy who needed a walker. His stomach tightened. Unless Colt missed his guess, Stacy and her brother Ryan had arrived.

He'd expected her to be beautiful because all the bachelorettes on *Finding Mrs. Right* had been knockouts, but he'd expected more California high-maintenance style. Not a woman with natural, understated makeup wearing jeans. Granted they were fancy designer ones with sparkly things instead of sturdy rivets and she had on stiltlike heels, but he wouldn't have pegged her for a Hollywood actress.

After he helped her stand, he reached into his back pocket, pulled out a bandana and handed the cloth to her. "It's not much, but this will let you wipe off a little. I'm Colt Montgomery. Are you by chance Stacy and Ryan?"

"A little worse for the wear, but that's us." She laughed. The rich sound raced up his spine.

Colt strolled to where the teenager stood at the edge of the road, and shook hands with the kid. This he knew how to deal with. "How about you help me get these knuckle-headed animals back where they belong?"

For a minute the kid's eyes widened with surprise before he masked the emotion, but before he could respond his sister piped in. "I don't think that's a good idea."

The first thing Healing Horses needed to work on was getting Ryan's sister to quit treating the kid as if he would shatter right before her eyes.

"I wouldn't ask if he couldn't handle it."

"You don't know him. I do." She crumpled his red bandana in her fist. "Plus, these cows are huge. What if one of them charges?"

"A car heading straight for them won't budge these things, and you're worried they'd suddenly get the gumption to charge?" He shook his head. City folks and their harebrained notions. "These aren't the bulls that run in Pamplona."

"I don't know. A couple of them look like they could be troublemakers." One of the cows raised its head and turned toward her. She pointed at the animal. "That one's been giving me the evil eye. I think she has it in for me. Can you personally vouch for her character?"

Her attempt at humor almost made him smile. Almost. This woman appeared to have more than one trick up her sleeve to disarm a man, but then what did he expect from an actress? She could pretend to be anyone she wanted to.

Ignoring Stacy and her pretty blue eyes that he suspected could see straight inside him, he turned to Ryan. "What do you say, sport? You up for this?"

"Just tell me what to do."

"Wait a minute. Are you sure that's a good idea, Ryan?" Stacy stepped forward, but then stopped and smiled at her brother. "Be careful."

"Ryan, you head over there to the opening in the fence. Stand right beside it and make sure the cows don't make a last-minute break for it." Colt knew once he got the animals that far, they weren't likely to find the energy to go anywhere. "They probably won't. It's more likely they'll get all bunched up. If that happens just swat them on the rear to speed them up."

"Got it."

Ryan clutched his walker and tried to find a level spot. Once he did that, he moved his walker and stepped. He repeated the process again. Colt glanced at Stacy. Her gaze locked on her brother as she stood there, her body rigid, her hands clasped in front of her, nibbling on her lower lips. *She wants to help, but she knows he needs to do this on his own. Maybe there's hope for her.*

A couple of steps later Ryan wobbled. Colt glanced again at Stacy. When she stepped forward he shook his head and she froze, concern clouding her beautiful features. Sweat beaded on Ryan's face as he worked his way out of the ditch to the hole in the fence. Once there, Colt walked up to the ring leader and slapped the cow on the hind quarters. "Move!"

In fewer than five minutes he had all the cows back in the pasture. That job done, he tugged the fence until it and Stacy's rental car created a temporary barrier. "This should hold them until Charlie can fix the fence." Colt strolled to his three-wheeler, crawled on and then glanced back at the pair. "Ryan, hop on the back with me. Stacy, ride in wagon and hold the walker."

Ryan headed toward him, but Stacy stood rooted in her spot glaring at him. "Why do I have to ride in the cart?"

"Your butt's covered in manure."

"Ryan, won't you switch—"

"I'm not having manure all over my seat."

She appealed to her brother again.

"Sorry, sis. I'm siding with Colt on this one."

Hands on her hips, she said, "You've got to be kidding?"

"It's either the wagon or walk," Colt replied.

She shook her head, dropped her hands off her hips and walked toward the wagon. "Men."

When Stacy arrived at the Rocking M Ranch she found herself thankful that the jolting ride over in the cart hadn't loosened her teeth.

They stopped in front of a mocha-colored wood-and-brick house with trees that stood guard around the structure. The house, while not huge, wasn't too small, either, and was in pristine condition. When they reached the front porch, she discovered a rocking chair. She could envision Colt's long frame seated there as he surveyed the beautiful land around him.

This wasn't a house. It was a home.

Once inside the living room, Colt turned to Ryan. "You can hang out here while I show your sister where to clean up. Then we'll head for the barn and I'll show you around. We've got a few things to take care of before your first session, like picking out a horse for you."

"Shouldn't I be there for that?"

"He's seventeen. He'll be fine." Colt motioned for her to follow him. "I'd let you use my daughter's room, but you know how teenagers are about their privacy."

At the mention of his daughter, she glanced at his left hand. No wedding ring, but then a lot of guys, especially ones who worked with their hands, didn't wear one. "Ryan said he met your daughter at school. How old is she?"

"Almost sixteen. I've got three months until D-Day."

"Huh? I don't get it."

"She gets to date and drive when she turns sixteen in three months."

"You look tough. I bet you can survive it. I did with Ryan. I'm not saying it'll be easy, but it can be done."

"Guys are different."

She thought about his comment. In some ways she'd had it easier with Ryan. Guys didn't get pregnant. They weren't victims of date rape. There were a hundred other horrors parents of teenage girls had to worry about.

At the end of the upstairs hallway Colt opened the door and stepped aside for her to enter. Stacy walked into the room and stared. Never in her life had she seen such a neat, well-organized bedroom. Not a speck of dust lay on any of the large rustic furniture. The bed was not only made, but there wasn't a wrinkle anywhere on the dark brown comforter. No clothes on the floor. No shoes for someone to trip over. Not even any change tossed on the nightstand by the massive bed. "Either your wife spends all her waking time cleaning or you've got an amazing maid."

"I'm not married, and you're looking at the maid."

That explained the no ring. Was he divorced? A widower? Whatever his situation, between that and being a war vet, the man probably carried more baggage than a 747. She didn't want to know.

She craved average and uncomplicated.

Knowing about a person's life led to attachments and caring, which led to emotional entanglements, responsibilities and expectations. All of which usually ended up with her getting disappointed. She thought about her past relationships. Whenever she started having expectations or wanted more out of the relationship, her boyfriends suddenly stopped calling.

She and Colt had a business arrangement. He was to help Ryan overcome his physical disabilities. Period.

But she couldn't miss the similarity of their situations. She was raising a teenage boy and half the time she felt clueless. While he was raising his daughter alone, and from his comments, she suspected he often felt out of his league, too. Men and women saw the world differently, and no matter how she tried, they couldn't really stand in each other's shoes.

She could imagine how much harder it would be for a guy to raise a teenage girl alone. Dealing with female hormones and emotions which caused bigger ups and downs than an amusement-park roller coaster, her developing body *and* the sex talk issues. The man must be made of titanium.

"You need something to wear while your clothes are in the washer." He walked to his closet door. Inside were neatly folded shirts, organized by color, even the plaid ones, stacked on metal closet organizer shelves. He selected one. Then he grabbed a pair of jeans and a belt and handed the items to her.

She stared at him. He was easily six-two and solidly built. "You're kidding, right? Have you looked at me?"

A slow grin spread across his face, as his gaze scanned her from head to toe. And not a quick look, but a slow inspection that let him take his time to check out all the assets. She, who was used to guys staring at her as if they could see through to her underwear all the time in auditions and on the set, blushed at the intensity in this man's gaze.

"What in particular am I supposed to notice?" His low, husky voice slid over her, making her tingle. Really? Tingle? Men didn't make her do that. What was up with her reaction to this guy? He wasn't even close to her type. He was too strong. Too imposing. Just plain too much.

But there was something about him. An honesty and a confidence she found compelling. *He's real. What a woman saw was what she'd get.*

Stop it. He's the last thing you need right now.

She cleared her throat. "I'm built a little bit different than you are."

"Thank the good Lord for that."

She pinned him with her best no-nonsense, we're-not-going-anywhere-on-a-personal-level stare. "These will be huge on me. I'm not sure your belt has a hole tight enough to keep the jeans from falling off. Doesn't your daughter have something I could borrow?"

"I can't loan you anything of Jess's without written permission. My luck, whatever I gave you would turn out to be her favorite pants. You'd fall in another cow pie or snag them on something in the barn, and I'd be a dead man."

His words said with a straight face and a tinge of fear rippling in his voice made her smile. Humor? What an odd, but not unpleasant, combination with his take-charge attitude.

"You're afraid of a sixteen-year-old girl?" she teased back.

"Damn right. You were that age once. Don't you remember what you were like with your clothes then?"

"What was I thinking?" At that age she'd been on a hit TV series. Her image had been everything, and yes, she'd been fanatical about her clothes.

"A smart man knows when not to press his luck." He took the clothes from her and placed them on his enormous bed. Then he pointed to the door opposite the closet. "There's the bathroom. The towels are in the linen closet and the soap's in the shower. My robe's on the back of the bathroom door. Try the clothes or put on the robe. I don't care which."

Then he told her where to find the washer and dryer, and said to join him and Ryan when she could. He was out the door before she could even comment.

Stacy found Colt's bathroom in the same pristinely clean and organized fashion as his bedroom. After she washed up, she grabbed the forest-green terrycloth bathrobe off the hook and slipped the garment on. An earthy smell mixed with a spicy scent flowed over her as if the man had wrapped her in his strong arms.

Not good.

Wearing his robe was way too intimate. She smoothed her hand down the fluffy fabric. How could she feel a connection with a man by putting on his bathrobe? It was silly, but in slipping into the garment, she felt exactly that—connected.

A vision of Colt, strong and confident, standing in this room, wearing this same garment filled her vision. While the robe reached her ankles, the garment would hit him just below the knees. She could see him, the robe gaping to reveal his muscled chest, standing in front of the sink shaving that stern chin of his. Then she saw his clear blue eyes focused on her as a woman in this room.

Wrong move. Afraid of the ache pulsing in her body, she scooped up her dirty clothes and headed for the bedroom door. She had to get out of his room. Intent on escape, she flung open the door and almost barreled into a dark-haired teenager with caramel-colored eyes, a Chihuahua clutched in her arms. Except for her strong chin, she looked nothing like her father.

She must be the exact image of her mother.

"Are you Jess?" After the teen nodded, Stacy continued to introduce herself. "I'm Ryan's sister. Thanks for showing him the ropes at school."

"He told me about the movie you're making. I can't wait to see it in the theater. Maggie said I can be an extra in a couple of scenes."

Not knowing what else to say, Stacy said, "Cute dog. What's its name?"

"Thor."

"That's an interesting choice for a name."

"I know. It drives people crazy." Jess tossed Stacy a saucy grin. "You were one of the finalists when Griffin was on *Finding Mrs. Right*."

"That was me."

"Getting dumped on national TV had to suck."

Sure did. Thanks for bringing up the pleasant subject. Being on that show and some comment about the disastrous finale would end up on her tombstone. Some bad decisions kept on giving. "It wasn't a lot of fun. For a while I was the punch line to some pretty nasty jokes."

"It hurts when you get made fun of for someone else's choices."

She knows because she's been there. The words to ask what had happened with Jess sat perched on her tongue. No, she wouldn't ask. No attachments, remember? She was only here for ten weeks. Get in. Do the job. Get Ryan the help he needs and get out.

"Luckily there's a new scandal every five minutes in Hollywood, so everyone moved on pretty quickly."

"Dad sent me to see if you need anything."

"I'm good, but thanks for asking." Stacy nodded toward the wadded clothes in her hands. "I was just going to put these in the washer. I'm not sure I can salvage them, but I'm going to try."

"I heard about your fall. The first thing I learned when we moved here was to always watch where I step."

"I could've used that info earlier," Stacy joked as she followed the teenager downstairs to the utility room where they tossed her clothes into the washer. "I'm a little taller than you are, but I could also use something to wear. Maybe some sweatpants and a T-shirt? Your dad said he couldn't loan me anything of yours without written permission."

"He knows better than to mess with my clothes. One time I put a load of my stuff in the washer before I left for school. He came along and put them in the dryer. I didn't talk to him for a week after my favorite jeans shrank so much I looked like I was ready for a flood."

"That hurts. A shirt can be replaced. That's easy, but jeans?"

"I know. It's about impossible to find a pair that fit right and look good."

Stacy nodded in feminine understanding. "Guys don't get that."

"Especially a cowboy. Any pair of Wranglers is fine with them." Together they headed upstairs again. When Jess opened the door, Stacy realized looks weren't the only way this girl differed from her father. Clothes, books and papers littered every surface. Obviously she hadn't inherited her father's neat-freak tendencies.

After digging through her dresser, Jess pulled out a pair of gray knit yoga-style pants and a plain white T-shirt. "These should work and don't worry about getting them back to me right away. I only wear them to sleep in."

"Thanks. I want to see how Ryan's doing, and I can't go to the barn in a bathrobe." Jess handed her the clothing. "Your dad said I could put on a pair of his jeans and one of his shirts."

Jess laughed. "Sure, that would work. The pants would end up around your ankles."

"That's what I said." Stacy shook her head. "His solution was to hand me one of his belts."

"My dad's a great guy, but sometimes he's such a *guy*."

That was one thing Colt Montgomery was. All man.

In the barn, Ryan leaned on his walker and looked at Colt. The haunted look in the teen's gaze reached out to Colt, reminding him of the look he used to see in Reed's eyes at that age. This kid had seen way too much and been hurt a time or two.

"Thanks for telling my sister to lighten up. She's gotten a little overprotective since my accident."

"I picked up on her being the worrier type, but I bet it's only while she's awake."

Ryan smiled, and some of the tension left his face. His shoulders relaxed, too. "She's always watched out for me. Our dad died when I was a baby and our mom's worthless. It was just the two of us."

Like him and Reed. Two kids clinging to each other through the storms of life that tossed them around. Now her protectiveness made sense.

"That's why we went to court to get her named my guardian."

Colt wondered about why she'd legally taken on the parent role with her brother when he read the application. That told him a lot. How many sisters would do that? She could've turned eighteen, moved out of the house and went on with her life without giving her brother much thought. She could've left him to fend for himself.

Like he'd done with Reed.

Until recently, Colt hadn't known how bad things had been for his brother after he left home and enlisted. One night things got so bad Reed nearly beat their old man to death. Then damned if the bastard didn't want to press charges for assault. If it hadn't been for Nannette's husband, Ben, Reed would've been arrested for assault. Ben McAlister had been one damn fine man. He'd been there for Reed when Colt hadn't been.

Unlike him, Stacy stuck around for her brother.

"She's especially concerned about me doing this therapy," Ryan continued. "Our father was thrown from a horse on a movie set. That was how he died."

"And she's letting you get on a horse? How did you talk her into that?"

"It wasn't easy, but she knows this is my best chance to walk on my own again."

Still, that took guts on her part. Then he thought about the movie Maggie was making, *The Women of Spring Creek Ranch*. "The movie she's starring in is about female ranchers. Won't she have to ride a horse for the movie?"

"She said none of her scenes have anything to do with horses." Ryan's hands tightened on the walker handles. "Do you think you can help me get rid of this thing?"

"A local physical therapist and I went over your doctor's report to develop activities geared toward your physical issues. I can't promise you'll get rid of that thing by the end of your sessions, but I know we can help you."

"I bet you're wondering why I'm here, cause you see people who are so worse off than me."

"Everyone has the right to get the most he can out of his life. We help whoever needs us whether it's a little or a lot." He motioned for Ryan to follow him. The tap-scrape of the walker echoed through the barn. "Being a teenager is tough enough without having to deal with medical issues. What were you into before the accident?"

"I ran track and played basketball. My friends and I used to rock climb a lot."

The unsaid words hung in the air between them. *And now they do, and I can't.*

"I have a couple of good buddies who were hurt in Afghanistan. It's a tough adjustment. It changed their lives completely."

Being there changed mine, too. Just not in the same way.

"I'll give you the fifty-cent tour," he said to Ryan. "We'll get some of the busy work out of the way. Then you can have your first session tomorrow."

Colt led Ryan into the tack room in the center of the barn where the shelves were stacked with helmets. He handed one to the teenager. "Try this on."

"I'm seventeen and have to use a walker. Now you want me to wear this? Dork of the month calendar, here I come."

The kid still had spirit. Good. That would work in his favor. "Sorry. It's the rules. Every rider wears one."

Ryan tossed on the helmet and snapped the chin strap. "If a picture of me in this thing ends up on Facebook, I'll kick your ass."

Colt laughed. "Fair enough." Then he checked the fit. Two tries later, and they had the right one. "Our next step is picking out a horse for you. How tall are you? About five-eleven?"

"I guess."

"I think you and Chance will get along well. Come on. I'll introduce you." They walked through the barn to the horse's stall. The animal sauntered over and pressed his nose against the window bars. Colt rubbed the animal's head. "You ever been on a horse before?"

Ryan shook his head and moved closer to the stall. "Can I touch him?"

Colt nodded, and explained what the therapy would entail. "You two are going to become good friends. You'll be working on using your body to direct Chance. That will help you regain control of your own body."

"Ryan, where are you?" Stacy called out.

"Over here," Ryan responded.

"We're in the first row of horse stalls."

A minute later she joined them, but she shied away from the stall door, keeping as close to the larger open area as possible. "I see Jess loaned you some clothes." Ones a bit too small for her. His daughter's knit pants and T-shirt molded to Stacy's lush figure, leaving no doubt about her feminine curves. A body like hers could make a man break out in a cold sweat and damned if Colt wasn't doing just that.

"This is Chance," Ryan said as he stroked the gelding's head. "Colt thinks he and I will do well together."

Stacy leaned forward and glanced in the stall. "He seems nice, but isn't he awfully big? What about another horse? A smaller one?"

She had the nerve to question his judgment about horses? That hit a sore spot. "We may be a new program, but we *have* done this before. Ryan's not our first client."

"I didn't mean to offend you or criticize the program. This is all new to us, and I have some questions. Maybe you could set aside some time to talk with me about my concerns."

"Send me an email and I'll answer them the best I

can." Stacy might have let her brother sign up for the therapy, but her watching him mount a horse wasn't going to be easy. Colt's job was to make sure she didn't interfere with his program or Ryan's therapy. Somehow he didn't think that would be simple, either.

"I'd rather talk in person, especially since I'm here right now."

Colt glanced at his watch. "Ryan and I are done here, and I've got to get ready for my group class, so let's see how tomorrow goes. If you still have questions after Ryan's first session then we'll talk."

As Colt walked away he couldn't help but think that Ryan's sister was a worrier, and no doubt about it, the woman was trouble.

When Stacy and Ryan returned to Healing Horses the next afternoon for his first therapy session, the coffee she downed at lunch to perk up churned in her stomach, leaving her queasy. For the past twenty-four hours she kept telling herself Ryan would be okay. That nothing would go wrong, but doing so failed to keep her nightmares in check. They started out with her as a child with her father. Then a giant horse materialized. Its enormous hooves crushed her father before her eyes. Fog floated in as she raced to him. By the time she reached his body, she found herself kneeling over Ryan.

She wished Colt had been willing to talk to her about her concerns before Ryan started therapy, but he'd fobbed her off instead. That made her even more edgy.

As they made their way toward the barn, Ryan

glanced at her, his eyes filled with concern. Now she'd done it.

"Are you going to be okay? I know how hard this is for you, but I'm not going to be doing any crazy stunts on the horse. The most I'll be doing is walking around trying to get Chance to go from one side of the ring to the other. If things get really wild I might stop somewhere and throw some bean bags at a target."

He shouldn't have to worry about you. Pretend you're in a movie. Slip into the role of a big sister who's sure everything will be fine and doesn't have a care in the world.

'Course it might take a performance worthy of an Academy Award, but she'd give it a try. "Sounds pretty tame, almost boring." She smiled and tried to relax her shoulders. She was hunching them again. "It's not so much that I'm worried about you. I'm just tired because we ran so long shooting yesterday."

At least that part was true.

"Colt's going to be mad that we're late."

"I couldn't help it. The director switched the shooting schedule on me."

By the time they reached the barn, she'd managed to get her nerves under control, at least outwardly.

Colt met them inside the door, his arms crossed over his broad chest, a frown darkening his handsome features. "You're late."

Ryan glared at her. "I told you he'd be mad."

"It won't happen again." If she could help it.

Colt led them to a small room with a battered leather couch, an equally beat-up fridge and a TV. "Here's the family waiting room. Ryan will be back in about an hour."

"You expect me to stay here? I want to be there during his therapy."

"That's not a good idea."

"I don't need you there to hold my hand, Stacy."

No, Ryan didn't. This wasn't about what he needed. Despite knowing that, she couldn't stem her concerns now that she was here.

She ignored her brother's comment and addressed Colt instead. "I didn't read anything in the material you gave me that said I can't be present during the session."

"Most people take my word for it when I've said it's better if they wait here."

Everyone else hadn't watched their father get trampled to death. "I'm not most people. Now we can stand here wasting more of everyone's time or we can get on with Ryan's therapy. Which is it going to be?"

"We'll give it a try, but there better not be any trouble."

When they reached the mounting block area in the barn, Colt introduced them to Nikki, the young woman who would be the leader for the session, and her friend Sarah, who'd act as the sidewalker. Then Ryan clip-clopped up the steps to stand on the block. When Nikki led the massive horse, saddled and ready to go in front of him, Stacy started chewing on her lip. She knew from her research what everyone's job was, but that failed to ease her anxieties.

From the information she'd read on Healing Horses, she knew Colt was a registered instructor. That meant he ran the session and worked with a physical therapist to create a program suited to Ryan's needs. He was trained. Certified. Regulated. But the others helping with the session were volunteers.

The leader's responsibility was the horse. This volunteer maintained the horse's pace and kept the animal calm. The sidewalker's role was to help the client with balance. But Stacy couldn't let go of the fact that they were volunteers. How much experience did this skinny cowgirl have? She was only a couple of inches taller than Stacy's own five foot six, and couldn't be more than twenty-one. "Colt, excuse me. Can I talk to you for a minute?"

Was that squeaky, panicked voice hers?

He stalked over. "First of all, calm down. If your voice gets any higher only dogs will hear it." He nodded toward the horse. "If you get upset and agitated Chance will sense that."

"Then maybe he's not the right horse for Ryan. I know I mentioned this yesterday and you weren't concerned, but he seems even bigger out here than he did in his stall yesterday. Don't you think Ryan might need a smaller horse?"

The bigger the horse, the more damage he could do if something went wrong.

Colt shifted his stance and stiffened. "Chance is the right size. Ryan's a big kid."

"What about your leader? Is she capable of controlling an animal that size? How much experience does she have?"

"Nikki is a champion barrel racer. She's been around horses all her life. There isn't one in the state that she can't handle."

"Why is there only one sidewalker?" Often clients had two people to focus on them, help interpret instructions and provide physical and emotional support.

Instead of answering her, Colt walked to Nikki and

whispered something. Then the woman led Chance away. When he stalked to Stacy, determination filled his gaze. He closed the distance between them in two long angry strides.

"We need to talk." Colt clasped her upper arm and tried to lead her away. When she attempted to pull away, he stopped, leaned down and whispered in her ear. "We can do this one of two ways. You can come with me of your own free will, or I can toss you over my shoulder. Which is it gonna be?"

"You wouldn't."

"Try me."

Chapter 4

Colt knew he needed to nip the situation with Stacy in the bud right quick. This first session would set the tone for every one to come. With Stacy more jittery than a mama bear with her first cub, they'd never get around to helping Ryan.

Stacy stared at him for a minute with hard determination and he thought she might defy him. That might not be a bad thing. The thought of getting his hands on those great curves of hers did have a certain appeal and could end up being the bright spot in his day.

"Lead the way," she conceded at last, leaving him a bit disappointed.

Once they rounded the corner out of sight and earshot of Ryan and Sarah, Colt said "I want to make some things clear. Once the horse is in front of the mounting ramp, the therapy session's started. Other people talk-

ing confuses the animal. The leader and Ryan should
be the only one giving commands."

"What if—"

"No, what-ifs. Those are the rules. It's for everyone's safety. When you're around the horse, you need
to remain calm, quiet and not make any sudden movements. It can make a horse shy or kick out."

"I admit I'm a little nervous."

"You'd have to take a Xanax to get down to nervous."

"I wasn't that bad."

He crossed his arms over his chest, leaned back on
one heel and tossed her a she-had-to-be-kidding look.

"Okay, maybe I was getting a little overly—" She
paused, obviously trying to find the right word.

"Panic stricken? Paranoid?"

"I'll dial it down. I'll really try."

The pain in her voice took the wind right out of
his sails. This had to be so hard for her. He'd forgotten what she'd gone through with her father. Only a
complete ass would be this harsh on a woman in this
situation. "I know this is tough for you. Ryan told me
what happened to your father. How a horse trampled
him to death on a movie set. What you're feeling is
understandable."

She paled and her shoulders hunched, leaving her
looking vulnerable and small. Almost alone against the
world. "Everything I read about programs like yours
says falls are rare, but they do happen. I can't get that
out of my head."

"Ryan's got more physical control than most of our
clients. He's got better chances of getting hit by lightning than falling off a horse. What happened to your
father won't happen here."

"My head knows that, but my heart can't let go of my fear. He's all I've got."

That he could understand. While she wasn't Ryan's parent, she and Ryan had that kind of relationship. What if he'd seen a loved one get trampled to death and then someone wanted to put Jess on a horse? "It's hard, but you can't let the past and your fears affect Ryan's therapy. Go to the waiting room. Turn on the TV and forget about what's going on. It'll be better for everyone. You included."

She stiffened. Her back ramrod straight, her gaze tossed daggers at him. He'd sure hit a nerve. It was almost as if what he said made her mad. As if he'd called her weak, and now she was out to prove she could handle this, but danged if she wasn't even prettier with her dander up.

"He's my brother. I'm his guardian. It's my job to watch out for his best interests and to ask questions."

So much for the understanding, soft approach. "You're getting in the way."

"You can't make me leave."

"We know what we're doing."

"Then you shouldn't have a problem with me asking a couple of questions because you can explain your actions with sound reasoning."

The woman had grit. He had to give her that. Normally he admired that trait, but right now her tenacity had given him one monster-size headache. "I'm willing to talk about your concerns, either before or after the session."

"But what if something comes up during the therapy?"

"I'll deal with anything that comes up. That's my

job. If you can't follow my rules, find another program for Ryan." They both knew there wasn't another therapy option that would allow her to continue working on the movie. "Now what's it gonna be?"

Defeat crossed her delicate features. "I'll be quiet. I promise, and I'll keep my questions until after the session is over."

Damn. He felt like the playground bully who'd chased the prettiest girl in class, knocked her down and left her with a skinned knee. "I'll give you one more shot."

After they returned to the mounting area where Ryan and Sarah waited, he motioned for Nikki to return with Chance. Before Colt could get them moving toward the ring, Stacy's voice stopped him. "Are you sure Ryan doesn't need two sidewalkers for safety purposes?"

"So much for being quiet." He glanced at his watch. "That lasted less than two minutes."

"His therapy hasn't started."

"One sidewalker is plenty." He motioned Nikki to keep coming.

Chance sensing Stacy's anxiety tossed his head and she jumped back. "I don't think this is the right horse for Ryan. The animal seems awfully nervous."

Knowing he needed to get control of the session and eliminate the problem, he stormed toward Stacy. "I warned you."

"What are you doing?" Eyes wide, she stepped back.

He took a minute to calm down before answering. Then in a measured voice he said, "You being here isn't good for anyone. Not the horse. Not Ryan, and certainly not you."

That pretty little chin of hers pointed at him in defiance. "I'm not leaving."

When he'd closed the distance between them, he lifted her into his arms and slung her over his shoulder. Damn she was tiny, barely weighing more than his favorite saddle. She pounded on his back, but he barely noticed. A mosquito had a bigger bite. "Chance is a calm horse. It's you who's making him act like he is. Hell, you're making everyone nervous."

"Put me down. You can't do this."

"Seems I can." He continued walking. When she squirmed in his arms, he tightened his grip around her shapely legs and then swatted her on her tight little butt. "Settle down. I don't want to drop you."

"That's exactly why you should put me down. That and the fact that you don't have any right to do this." She went limp in his arms, though anger still rang out in her voice, loud and clear. "Why is it you keep telling me what to do? You are the most arrogant, presumptuous man I've ever met."

"My ranch. My rules." He stomped out of the barn and through the arena toward a small grassy area with a picnic table. He deposited her on the other side of the short fence. "Stay here and keep quiet. If you don't, the next step is locking you in the tack room. Understand?"

She wobbled and grabbed the fence post for support. Then she looked up at him with what he could only describe as terror in her eyes. "Tell me Ryan will be okay and that nothing bad will happen."

Her voice, soft and scared, reached inside him and squeezed. He placed his hand over hers. When heat shot through him with more force than a bull bent on ridding himself of a rodeo rider, he pulled back. "We know what we're doing. This is a different situation than a movie set. I won't let anything happen to Ryan."

The trust in her eyes almost bowled him over. He refused to let her vulnerability get to him. She was an actress. Who knew how much of what he saw was real and how much was a show staged to get her way? "Stay here and be quiet. If you can't handle that go to your car or the waiting room."

"But what if—"

"You take care of the problem or I will, and you won't like my solution. I guarantee it."

For the next hour, Stacy rode a roller coaster of emotions as she stood on the grassy area outside the arena and watched Ryan work to control his body and direct the horse around. A few times he'd wobble in the saddle making her hold her breath and clutch the bench underneath her, but he quickly stabilized.

At those times, Colt never even flinched. Just looking at him, all arrogant and confident, sent irritation coursing through her system. She wasn't sure what to make of him. First of all, he'd gone all caveman on her and thrown her over his shoulder, making her angrier than she could ever remember being.

But she wasn't sure who she was madder at—him or her.

Admit it. You liked having a strong man's arms wrapped around you.

She scoffed at the idea. Being a take-charge guy was one thing, but Colt took that to the extreme. How dare the man tell her what was best for her brother? He hadn't been with Ryan through all the surgeries and physical therapy. Colt hadn't seen how the lack of progress destroyed his spirit. She knew her brother better than anyone and what was best for him.

But as Ryan's therapy session progressed, she found herself admitting Colt appeared to know what he was doing. He offered suggestions on ways Ryan could improve his control and balance. He complimented her brother on what he did well.

After the session ended and they stood back in the barn after Ryan dismounted, Stacy found herself more than a little shaken, and not just because of her concern for her brother. She wasn't sure how to process the emotions Colt aroused in her.

Forget about Colt and concentrate on the fact that Ryan had survived his first therapy session without incident. Now she had to lay the groundwork for the future ones.

"Ryan, help Nikki and Sarah groom Chance and put away his gear."

Her brother glanced between her and Colt. "You aren't going to kill each other, are you?"

"All I want to do is talk to her," Colt replied in an even voice.

Ryan turned to her as if waiting for her confirmation. "Go. Colt's right. We need to discuss some things."

Once the others left she spun around to face Colt, her anger returning. "Don't you ever manhandle me again like you did today."

"I owe you an apology."

Talk about a shot out of the blue. She hadn't expected that at all. She figured he wasn't a guy used to having his authority, his rules or his decisions questioned. After all, he was ex-military. Weren't they all about structure, order and following the status quo?

When did men, even non-military ones, ever admit their mistakes? *And you've had so much experience with men,* a little voice inside her taunted. At least the actors and male directors she worked with over the years never admitted their mistakes, but men outside of the entertainment industry? She admitted the data was a little sparse.

"I'm usually a pretty even-tempered guy, but I was so all-fired mad I couldn't see straight." He ran his long fingers through his sun-kissed blond hair. "And obviously I wasn't thinking clearly."

That made two of them. "I have to ask questions. I'm responsible for Ryan. I have to watch out for him."

"You're worried about him falling. I get that, but you don't understand. What you were doing increased the risk of that very thing happening."

His words hit her like a hard punch to the stomach. Had she really done that? The thought left her weak. She clasped her hands in front of her to keep them from shaking.

"So where do we go from here? I have to be with him."

"It would be better for you both if you weren't there."

"Let me rephrase that. I *will* be here while he's going through his sessions."

"I'll make a deal with you. I'll train you like any other volunteer. If you pass the muster and agree to follow the rules like everyone else, I'll let you be Ryan's sidewalker. That should give you a greater sense of control."

No. She couldn't do that. Horses were huge, unpredictable, and the thought of being that close to one left her shaking in her Louis V's. "I can't do that. I wouldn't be any good. Just the thought of being near a horse makes me physically ill."

"A person's fear over something is usually worse than facing it. Being in a war zone taught me that. You can do this."

The faith and certainty shining in his eyes bolstered her courage. When had anyone believed in her other than to think she could pull off a role convincingly?

She would do this for Ryan. Then she could be there with him. She could support him and understand what he was going through. "I'll do it."

"So we're clear, you'll have to follow the same rules as any other volunteer. That means I'm the boss and you do what I say, no questions asked."

She nodded. "When can we start?"

"When do you have a day off from shooting?"

"Saturday."

"I'll see you here at eight. Don't be late." He pointed to her fancy high heels. "And get some decent boots."

A few days after his run-in with Stacy, Colt picked Jess up from school and she asked if she could go to Halligan's that night. "A bunch of the kids are meeting there to listen to Maroon Peak Pass. I really want to go. Not only because my friends are going, but I want to support Emma."

Jess met the band's lead singer and guitarist while volunteering at the Estes Park animal shelter, where Emma worked as the volunteer coordinator. "Is Cody one of the kids that'll be there?"

She shrugged. "I didn't ask, and I don't care."

His throat tightened. "Did something happen on your date?"

"He seemed like such a great guy, but he was a bore."

That he could handle. "I wish I could say that would be the last boring date you'll go on, but it won't be."

"You mean I have to kiss a lot of frogs before I find a prince, kind of thing?"

"You kissed him?"

"No." She drew out the word so it sounded more like *no-ah.* Translation: Dad, you're being such a jerk. "All he did was talk about himself and how great he was. Why would I kiss him after a date like that?"

She was growing up so fast in some ways and still so young in others. "You think you could make time to have dinner there with your old man before you meet your friends?"

The remainder of Stacy's first week in Estes Park passed by uneventfully after Ryan's therapy. Amazingly, Ryan loved Estes Park High School. He'd come home talking about the kids he'd met and was actually excited. He said it was almost freeing not having anyone know what he'd been like before the accident. His life was a blank slate now and he could make it whatever he wanted.

"Everyone says there's a great band playing at Halligan's tonight," he said the minute he climbed into the car after school.

"What kind of band? Country, I'm guessing."

He nodded.

"Since when are you interested in country-and-western music?"

"I don't care about the music. I just want to hang out."

"I can drop you off. What time do you want to go?"

"I was hoping you'd go with me. You could use some fun, you know."

"Okay. What's up? No teenager wants to go to hear a band with his sister. Even one as cool and wonderful as I am."

"Don't go, then. Sit home alone. What do I care?"

Then the reason for his request hit her. How could she have been so stupid? Ryan wanted to fit in. He'd already bought a closet full of Wranglers and ditched his fancy sneakers for cowboy boots. She bet he was uneasy about going alone. He wanted her there as a safety net. "You're right. I do need to get out. How about we go for dinner and then stay to hear the band?"

An hour or so later after she'd cleaned up and changed, she and Ryan walked into Halligan's Bar and Grill to find the restaurant packed.

The last time she'd been in town, she'd kept to herself. Since her lodgings possessed a kitchen she'd hidden out there, living on whatever she could throw together or ordering from whatever places delivered, but this time was different. She couldn't crawl into her cave. Not when Ryan wanted to belong so much.

Heads turned as they walked in. Stacy smoothed a hand over her blouse.

"I told you you'd be overdressed." Ryan warned her that Halligan's wasn't like the restaurants and clubs she went to in L.A. She'd stubbornly told him she was who she was and she wasn't about to change. Now she wished she'd reconsidered.

Halligan's was a Wranglers, cowboy boots and cotton shirt type of place, and whether you were a man or woman that was the dress code. Dressed in a burgundy silk blouse, designer jeans and stilettos, she stuck out like a dandelion in a clover field.

The place had a down home kind of charm with its Formica-topped tables, neon beer signs and wood floors. Families sat at some of the tables. Friends at others. Some people shot pool or tossed darts in one of the game rooms. The stage and dance floor took up one end of the restaurant. The tantalizing smell of fried food wafted through the air, making her stomach growl. How long had it been since she'd had anything fried?

Definitely not since she starred in *The Kids Run the Place*. The producers had been sticklers about her weight. Once her mother found that out she'd instituted daily weigh-ins and kept a log of every bit of food that went into Stacy's mouth.

When she asked for a table for two, the perky little cowgirl hostess informed them it would be about an hour before she could get them a table. Stacy turned to her brother. "How about we go home, grab something to eat and come back to hear the band?"

"I guess so," Ryan answered, disappointment filling his voice.

As they turned to leave, someone called his name. "Hey, there's Jess and her dad." Without even asking if she minded, he maneuvered his walker around the tables toward them, leaving Stacy no choice but to follow.

She hadn't seen Colt since Ryan's therapy, and wasn't prepared for how at ease and how handsome he looked. Tomorrow when she met him for her volunteer training she'd be ready, but not now.

"We just ordered, but you can join us. Can't they, Dad?" Jess said.

Colt nodded as he shifted in his chair. "Sure." His tight tone told Stacy he wasn't any happier about this than she was.

"Great," Ryan said, and plopped his long body into the chair beside Jess.

"We don't want to intrude," Stacy said in a last-ditch attempt to get out of the situation, but her brother and Jess were already in a deep discussion about the merits of tonight's band.

"It's a lost cause. They aren't listening." Colt slid the remaining chair away from the table. "If I promise to be good and not to throw you over my shoulder again, will you have a seat?"

I don't want you to be good. I want to feel your arms around me again.

Where had that thought come from?

Stacy no sooner sat down when Jess and Ryan stood. "We're going to play darts. Text me when my food comes. I'll come get it. Ryan can order his food in the game room." Then the teenagers left before she or Colt could protest.

Once alone silence settled around her and Colt. She toyed with the plastic menu. Talk about awkward. The last time she had a first date hadn't been this uncomfortable. That's the problem. With the teenagers gone this felt like a date. Not good. She needed to get out of here quick.

Since Ryan had found Jess to hang around with, Stacy could go home and curl up on the couch to watch a movie. That's what she should do, but somehow the idea sounded much better earlier. Now her plans sounded—pathetic.

"I'm going to leave. I can pick up Ryan later."

Coward.

Yup.

Colt's hand covered hers when she tried to push away from the table. The simple contact sent shivers through her. They both jerked away as if they'd touched a hot stove. When was the last time she felt this kind of excitement with a man?

Way too long.

His blue gaze locked on her. "You can't leave me here to eat alone. First Jess dumps me and now you want to. A man's ego can only take so much." He had the most soul searching eyes. They could strip a girl defenseless in seconds. "Stay."

Her mouth went dry. Her heart rate skyrocketed.

"All right. I'll make the sacrifice so you don't have to sit here alone." She picked up the menu, thankful that her hands didn't shake.

"Who's your friend, Colt?"

The waitress, a curvy blonde in jeans so tight it was a wonder she could walk, strutted up to their table. She eyed Colt as if she was a five-year-old birthday girl and he was one of her presents.

"Jenna, this is Stacy Michaels. Her brother, Ryan, and Jess are friends from school."

"I thought you looked familiar. You were one of the finalists in that dating show Griffin McAlister was on."

Here we go diving headfirst into the most embarrassing experience of my life.

"I was."

"Were you the one who caused the horse to bolt and left Griffin in the hospital or were you the one who threatened to sue him at the finale?"

While what she'd done was embarrassing, at least

Stacy's actions hadn't landed Griffin in the hospital and temporarily paralyzed. She should have expected to encounter some resentment toward her because of what she'd done to one of the town's favorite sons, but the animosity still caught her off guard. She plastered an I-refuse-to-let-your-insult-get-under-my-skin smile on her face.

"It really doesn't matter," Colt interjected. "That's in the past. Everyone's moved on. In fact, she's got the lead role in the new movie Maggie's filming."

Stacy stared. He defended her?

"That's so like you, Colt. You're always one of the first ones to say forgive and forget." Jenna smiled at Colt. Could this chick lay it on any thicker? And he didn't even seem to notice the woman drooling over him.

The waitress's grin disappeared when her gaze focused on Stacy. "What makes a woman go on a dating show? I mean, to compete with other women for a guy that you've just met and let the whole world watch? That doesn't seem the best way to find a man."

No kidding, and any woman who thought it was needed serious psychotherapy. There was a reason why those relationships rarely lasted. They weren't based on things that mattered like shared values and respect. Those bedrocks kept a couple together through life's ups and downs. But what could she say to little miss cowgirl?

Avoid the issue. That's what she'd do.

"You know, Jenna, as wonderful as it is chatting with you, with the crowd in here tonight you've got to be incredibly busy. I don't want to monopolize your time, so I'll give you my order so you can be on your way. I'll have a veggie wrap."

"A veggie wrap?" Colt scoffed. "You need some meat on your bones. You look like a strong wind would blow you over. Halligan's is known for their burgers." Colt turned to the waitress. "Get her a buffalo burger instead."

What was it with this guy telling her what she should or shouldn't do? She'd been taking care of herself since she was eleven. "I ordered a veggie wrap because that's what I want. I don't eat red meat."

"Any fries or onion rings to go with that?" Jenna asked.

Stacy bet Halligan's had killer fries. Probably crunchy on the outside and all warm on the inside and the thought of onion rings left her weak. "No, thanks."

"Don't tell me. You don't eat fried food, either," Colt said.

"As a matter of fact, I don't." While the business had loosened up about actresses' weight— Melissa McCarthy winning an Outstanding Lead Actress in a Comedy Series Emmy was groundbreaking—the rule still was the more a woman weighed, the fewer scripts crossed her agent's desk.

Jenna jotted down Stacy's order on her little pad and then glanced longingly at Colt. "Are you staying to dance tonight? I get off at nine."

"I haven't planned that far in advance. I know it doesn't look like it right now, but I'm here spending time with Jess. She and Stacy's brother are playing darts."

"How's she doing? A girl needs that strong female presence in her life, especially when she's a teenager."

Jenna's eyes widened as if she'd realized how what she'd said could be taken as a criticism of Colt's parenting skills. "Not that you aren't doing a great job as a parent. It's just sometimes a girl needs to talk to another woman."

"Luckily Jess has Avery for that."

Stacy perked up at his comment. Who was Avery? His girlfriend? An unfamiliar emotion she refused to label jealousy snaked through her.

It's none of your business who he's dating.

Someone from another table called the waitress. After Jenna promised to check back with Colt later and reminded him to "holler" if he needed anything, she sashayed off.

Once they were alone again, Stacy said, "Thanks for saying something when she started in on the dating show stuff. It gets old having to explain that I'm over what happened. I don't know why everyone thinks I'm carrying a torch for Griffin."

"Since you brought it up, why did you go on that show?"

Stacy leaned toward him. "I'll be honest with you, but you can't ever tell anyone."

"You can trust me to keep your secrets."

The joking tone in his deep voice contrasted with the sincerity shining in his eyes. The breath caught in her throat. What would it be like to have someone to share her deepest dreams and fears with? Someone who after he heard all that, still cared for her.

Big wrong turn.

Time to fix her mistake before she went much further down this road and ended up in another ditch. Ignoring the feelings he brought to life inside her, she said, "I was between jobs, and needed to jump-start my career. I don't care what they tell the media, no one goes on a dating show expecting to fall in love and have the relationship last. It's all about creating a career or advancing one."

She traced circles in the condensation on her water glass. "My plan was to get some valuable TV exposure so I could get a network interested in giving me my own reality show. The good news was I did that. The bad news was my show was a miserable failure."

"I don't get the fascination with reality shows. Why would people want to watch other people living their lives rather than going out and living their own?"

"I guess some of the allure is because people can be part of lives they could never have. You know the rich and famous or the wild and crazy stuff. That and we've become a voyeuristic society."

"Did you always want to be an actress?"

His question hit her right between the eyes, startling her, mainly because she'd never thought about it before. Had she ever really had the opportunity to choose her career? "Jeez, this is starting to feel like you're interviewing me for an article."

"I'm just curious. I really want to know."

Genuine interest? In her as a real person? It had been so long since she'd experienced that.

Stacy explained how she'd fallen into her career when her father recommended her for a role in his last movie. "Spending that time with my dad was so wonderful. Then he died." She bit her lip to control the ache unfurling inside her heart. "After that, I got the chance to do the series *The Kids Run the Place,* and I had a career."

"I remember that show. It was great. You starred in that?"

She nodded. After the series took off she never had the chance to step back and decide if acting was what she wanted to do with her life. "My mom was in charge of my career then. I didn't have much choice. I was the family breadwinner."

"That's a lot for a kid to handle."

By then she wasn't a kid anymore. She smiled at the strong man across from her. "Your turn to be in the hot seat. What made you start the therapy program?"

How long had it been since she'd sat with some-one and talked in something more than sound bites? Really shared something personal and real about her-self? When was the last time someone, especially a man, made her want to talk about herself, and she'd felt genuine interest in his life? More importantly, how long had it been since a man had showed a real inter-est in her as a person?

Not good.

Don't look in his eyes and you'll be okay. It's his eyes that get a girl.

A man was the last thing she needed in her life right now. Not with her mother on the constant verge of a nervous breakdown, her career needing another seri-ous boost to refill the family coffers, and a brother in physical therapy. She couldn't care about anyone else now. That would send her right over the edge.

Too bad she felt so wonderful talking with Colt, being honest. Sharing. Because she couldn't afford the luxury of feeling anything for him.

Chapter 5

Colt hadn't been thrilled when Jess invited Stacy and Ryan to join them for dinner, not after how the first therapy session went. The woman had him alternating between wanting to throttle her and scoop her up in his arms. And not just to haul her off. When he'd told her how her behavior could get Ryan hurt, she'd looked so vulnerable and frightened. Anyone who loved another person as much as she loved her brother had to possess a good heart. He'd wanted to hold her and ease her fear. He longed to tell her everything would be okay because he'd make sure of it.

That thought scared the hell out of him.

But now that they'd started talking, he found himself having a good time and she appeared genuinely interested in what made him start Healing Horses. "A buddy of mine got hurt pretty bad in Afghanistan. His doctor recommended a horse-therapy program, but there wasn't one close to where he lived. I figured I had the barn, the land and horses. Why not do some good with them?"

"Was it bad in Afghanistan?"

His tour was the last thing he wanted to talk about. He tried hard to put that part of his life behind him. "You know how you get tired of everyone asking about when you were on *Finding Mrs. Right?*" She nodded. "That's how Afghanistan is for me."

Jenna arrived with their food before Stacy could respond. The waitress again asked if he'd thought any more about his plans. He mumbled something about he still wasn't sure and she said she'd check with him after her shift ended.

"Are you going to take our waitress up on her offer?" Stacy asked.

"What offer?"

"Come on. You can't be that clueless. She so wants to jump your bones."

"Jenna? No. You're wrong. I've known her forever. There's nothing between us. I've never thought of her in that way." The thought of dating a woman who'd trailed after him and her brother didn't feel right. Kind of like kissing your sister. If he'd had one.

"You may not have, but I can guarantee she has."

"The one woman, or rather young lady in my life is sometimes more than I can handle right now. Add to that getting Healing Horses off the ground, and I've got enough responsibilities to keep me on the edge of insanity. Which reminds me, I need to text Jess that her food's here."

Grateful for the task, he pulled out his phone and

sent the message. A minute later, his daughter arrived, scooped up her plate and left again.

"I understand. It's hard being responsible for a child of the opposite sex. I try my best to understand things from Ryan's perspective, but no matter how hard I try I can't stand in his shoes."

"That's for sure." Clothes, menstrual cycles, dating. Enough to drive a father screaming into the night. "I think you've got the easier deal. Guys are simple. Women are complicated."

"You've got to be kidding? Guys are easy? You don't want to talk about anything, especially your feelings. You just get mad. With Ryan sometimes I think the only way I could figure him out was if I was a mind reader."

"That sure would come in handy."

They continued talking about the kids while they finished eating, and when the band started warming up, Jess and Ryan made their way back to the table. "We're going to sit with some friends and listen to the band. Are you two sticking around or will you be coming back to pick us up?"

"I thought we'd come and sit by you two," Colt said with a straight face. When horror crossed his daughter's face, he chuckled. Sometimes it was just too easy to pull her chain.

"Dad, you wouldn't?"

"'Course not. Though the thought of torturing you like that does sound fun." He turned to Stacy. "Want to stick around and listen to the band for a while?"

"Might as well. All I'd do otherwise is go back to the cabin and watch TV until I had to pick Ryan up."

Once seated at a table around the dance floor, Colt

noticed Travis Carpenter kept eyeing Stacy like a stallion watched the mares in the next pasture. Carpenter's behavior shouldn't have bothered him, but it did. Probably if it were anyone else he wouldn't care.

You are so full of it, and you know it.

Carpenter had been a blowhard from the day he strutted into Colt's kindergarten class. Though he'd been shorter than most of their classmates, even then he'd possessed enough ego for the entire class. Seemed from then on they competed over everything. Who could run faster, who could get the better score on a test, who could get the prettiest girl in the class to go out with him. Colt won that contest in high school when Lynn dumped Travis to go out with him, putting them on the outs for good.

Now Colt sat here at a table with Stacy, not knowing what to say or do with Travis watching the whole embarrassing display. What did he expect when hadn't been on a date in over sixteen years?

When the hell had he started thinking of this as a date? Damn. He should've left when they finished eating and come back to pick up Jess. He still could. A smart man worked to fix his mistakes before they bit him on the ass.

"Eight o'clock is gonna come awfully early—"

"Hey, little lady," Carpenter said as he materialized beside their table and introduced himself. "Since Montgomery here isn't asking you to dance, how about you and I take a turn around the floor?"

Stacy lifted her feet and pointed to her strappy little high heels and pouted. "Unfortunately, I didn't wear my dancing shoes tonight. Maybe next time."

"It's a slow one. All you need to do is hang on to me."

Travis swayed slightly. Colt glanced at the man's eyes to confirm his suspicions. Yup, he'd had too much to drink. "The lady said not tonight."

"Stay out of this, Montgomery. This is between me and the lady here, and I didn't hear the word *no*." Travis stepped closer. "I didn't realize it until I got up close. You're the actress that was on that show with Griffin."

Stacy nodded and smiled, but it wasn't an open, heartfelt one like he'd received earlier. This smile failed to make her eyes sparkle. "That's me, and apparently my only claim to fame."

"McAlister was an idiot to let you go, especially for that plain mouse he married. If you've still got a hankering for a cowboy I'm up for the job."

Colt shook his head. What woman wouldn't be thrilled with that offer? Protective feelings surged within him again. What was it about this woman that brought that out in him? "Go home and sleep it off, Carpenter."

"I don't hear her complaining."

"Gentlemen, dial back the testosterone," Stacy teased, in an obvious attempt to ease the brewing tension. "It's getting a little deep in here."

Carpenter clasped Stacy's hand and tried to coax her to stand. "Come on. How about that dance?"

Stacy glanced between him and Carpenter, concern furrowing her brow. "One dance, but that's it."

"You don't have to dance with him."

Stacy smiled and waved him off. Once on the dance floor, Carpenter's meaty hand slid around her waist and he pulled her against him. Too close. Stacy playfully swatted his arm and tried to put some distance between them. Colt scooted forward in his chair, waiting to see the other man's response. Then the man's hand slid to Stacy's rear, cupping and then squeezing her feminine curves.

Colt vaulted out of his chair and headed for the couple. As he approached, Stacy grabbed Carpenter's hand and attempted to remove it. "Get your hands off my butt."

"Come on, honey. You're a Hollywood actress. Don't play modest," Carpenter responded.

"That's it. We're done." When she turned to leave, Carpenter refused to release her. If anything, he tightened his grip.

"You promised me a dance."

Colt closed the distance between them in two long strides. "Let her go."

Travis glared at him over Stacy's shoulder. "You gonna make me?"

"This isn't about you and me. The lady asked you to let her go."

Stacy tried again to break free, but Carpenter only smiled. "You promised me a dance, and it's not over yet."

"Yes, it is." Stacy stomped down on Carpenter's foot with her pointy little heel and elbowed him in the ribs.

After Stacy broke free, Carpenter lunged toward her, but Colt stepped in front of her. The other man lowered his shoulder and barreled into him, sending him careening into a table. Couples scrambled to get out of the way. Women shrieked.

White-hot rage darkening Carpenter's features, he reached for Colt again, but Stacy grabbed his arm. "Stop it!"

"Dad, are you okay?" Colt cringed when he heard his daughter's voice as he struggled to free himself from the overturned furniture. Before he could, Carpenter hauled him to his feet. Having reached the limit of his patience with talking to the drunk, Colt managed to turn around and get Carpenter into a control hold.

The drunk kicked and thrashed around, trying to get loose. "Montgomery, I'm going to take you apart."

Carpenter's boot connected with another table, sending it tumbling over. Glassware shattering against the wooden floor added to the chaos. "Settle down, and I'll let you go."

A shrill whistle cut through the chaos, followed by Mick Halligan's harsh voice. "This damned well better stop right now. You two go to neutral corners and park it. I've called the police, and you can bet your sweet ass I'm pressing charges." Then Mick glanced at the band. "Show's over. Let's have some music."

As Colt sat at the table waiting for the police to arrive, he couldn't believe he'd gotten into a bar fight with his daughter around to witness his stupidity. Great example he'd set for Jess, he thought as he rubbed his aching jaw, but when Carpenter put his hands on Stacy he couldn't think about anything but helping her.

And look where it got him? Waiting to see if he'd get thrown in jail.

"Jess, I don't want you thinking using physical force to solve problems is the right thing to do."

"Dad, you don't need to make this a teachable moment. Mr. Carpenter was crazy out of control. His hands were all over Stacy. I mean, he was grabbing her ass."

"You saw that, huh?" Stacy asked, blushing.

"I did, too." Ryan turned to Colt. "If you hadn't done

something, I was going to. Someone had to show that bastard he couldn't treat my sister like that."

At least he'd kept Ryan from having to defend his sister. Even drunk, Travis would've pounded Ryan into the floor.

"I think you did the right thing helping Stacy. It wasn't your fault he threw the first punch. After that you were just defending yourself," Jess continued.

But would the police see it that way? Where had his military training gone? He should've assessed the situation and the risk before he acted, but when Travis started pawing Stacy, all he wanted to do was protect her.

A few minutes later the front door swung open and in stalked what looked like half of the Estes Park police force. Chief Parson immediately talked with Mick. After a short discussion, the chief told his officers to get statements from the patrons. Then Parsons headed straight for their table.

"Can we talk about this somewhere other than in front of my daughter?" Colt asked when the lawman reached them.

Of course, since Jess witnessed the whole scene, he was trying to close the window after the house was full of flies.

"I agree. These youngsters don't need to hear this." The chief moved a few feet away with Colt and Stacy. Then Parsons said, "I hear this ruckus started because two men were arguing over you."

Stacy stiffened, crossed her arms over her chest as her eyes flashed fire at the lawman. "That's right. I turned on my feminine wiles and stirred both men into such a frenzy they ended up brawling over me."

"This isn't Los Angeles. You might be some fancy star there, but that doesn't mean a thing to me, so don't get smart with me, Missy."

"Then show me some respect, and don't assume I did something wrong."

Colt bit his lip to keep from smiling. It sure was easier to appreciate her stubborn feistiness from this side of the conversation.

"Fair enough," Parsons acknowledged. "Tell me what happened."

"We were sitting at a table—"

"I want to hear this from her, Colt," Parsons snapped.

Stacy detailed how when she and Ryan arrived tonight the wait for a table was almost an hour and how Jess had invited them to join their table. "The kids wanted to stay for the band, but didn't want to actually be seen with us. You know how teenagers are." The lawman nodded. "Colt and I sat at a table where we could keep an eye on Jess and Ryan. When Travis came over it was obvious he'd had too much to drink. He asked me to dance, and I politely declined. He wouldn't take no for an answer and got confrontational. I decided the best way to get rid of him was to humor him, but once we got on the dance floor his hands were all over me. When I tried to leave he wouldn't let me go."

"That's when you stepped in?" Parsons asked Colt.

"He was manhandling her. I told him to let her go."

"None of this was Colt's fault," Stacy continued. "If Travis had let me leave the dance floor when I wanted to, the fight wouldn't have happened. He threw the first punch."

The chief shook his head. "Travis doesn't surprise

me. He's always been a little long on temper and short on common sense, but you, Colt? This isn't like you at all."

No kidding.

"I don't have any choice but to haul you and Carpenter in to get your statements and sort this out." The lawman rubbed the back of his neck. "Mick's pretty pissed about the damage. He wants both your heads, and Carpenter's hollering for you to be arrested for assault. I should let both of you cool your asses in a cell for the night. That would fix your wagons."

"Travis deserves to go to jail. He started all this, but not Colt. He's done nothing wrong. All he did was help me." Stacy's voice rose in pitch as her anger boiled over. "If he hadn't stepped in who knows what I would've had to do to get Travis to back off. You didn't see the look in his eyes. I guess the lesson here is the next time a man takes liberties with a woman, the men around here shouldn't offer help because it could land them in jail."

"Jack, cut me a break. I'm here with Jess, for God's sake." Colt's voice and gaze pleaded with the chief.

"Even more reason to toss you in jail. You should set a better example for your daughter." Chief Parsons shook his head. "If I don't haul you in every hothead in town will think he can use his fists to settle a problem."

"If you arrest Colt, I'll contact my lawyer immediately and the press. I'm sure TMZ would love to do a story on this."

"Is that a threat?" Parsons asked.

"It's a statement of fact."

Colt placed his hand on her arm, pulling her attention from the lawman. A shudder rippled through him.

"It won't come to me getting arrested. I'll go to the station and get this sorted out. What I need from you is to take Jess home. Stay with her until I get there." He had to get Stacy out of here before she made a scene. This was his home and he had to live here once she returned to California. "Please?"

She nodded, thankfully picking up on his unspoken plea. "But if charges are filed, I want to know."

On the way back to Colt's house with Ryan and Jess, Stacy tried to minimize the situation. She explained how Colt agreed to go to the police station to give a formal statement. She chose her words carefully and emphasize that he hadn't been arrested.

By the time they arrived at the house exhaustion set in. Even the kids looked weary. When they mumbled something about waiting up for Colt, Stacy said, "Taking statements and sorting things out could take a while. It's silly for us to wait up. You can get all the details in the morning, Jess." When the teenager looked as if she wanted to protest, Stacy added, "Ryan can crash here on the couch and I'm going to sleep in the chair. I'm exhausted."

"If you're sure I don't need to worry about Dad."

They'd finally hit the problem. How could she have failed to realize how concerned Jess was? The girl hid her emotions well. "I promise there's nothing to lose sleep over."

She'd call in favors and threaten to blast the story from coast to coast if she had to in order to keep Colt out of jail.

Some of the panic left Jess's gaze. "Ryan can use the guest room."

"Great." He turned to Stacy. "Then you can take the couch."

After the teenagers headed upstairs, Stacy turned on the TV and curled up on the couch. What a night. She still couldn't believe Colt defended her. Not once, but twice. For once in her life someone stepped up and handled something for her.

His actions still left her a little tingly inside. True gentlemen, especially in her business, were as rare as an exotic dancer with real breasts.

The little voice inside her said she was being foolish. She'd watched enough Westerns to know about the cowboy code and protecting womanhood at all costs. Plus, Colt was a military man. Didn't they all have that black-and-white sense of right and wrong ingrained in them during basic training? That's what brought about his actions tonight. He wasn't standing up for her because he cared for her. He would've done the same thing for any woman.

But what if he'd stood up for *her?*

No, she refused to think about that possibility. If she considered dating anyone, he'd be someone who'd never been married before. He definitely wouldn't have children, much less a teenager. He'd probably be a man who was in the entertainment industry. One who could understand the demands of her career. One who would be comfortable accompanying her to movie premiers or the Academy Awards. She couldn't see Colt putting up with the red carpet pomp and circumstance.

But she kept coming back to how he'd stood up for her. She'd felt protected and safe. Something she hadn't felt since her father died. And what did he get for his efforts? He got hauled off to jail.

A couple of hours later, cowboy boots clicking across the wood floor woke her. She opened her eyes to find Colt towering over her.

"Thanks for staying with Jess."

"I'm not sure if I told you, but thank you for that what you did tonight. If I didn't seem grateful, it was because I was a shocked."

"I didn't mean to scare you. I'm not usually the kind of guy who gets into a bar fight."

"It wasn't that. I was surprised because you stepped in. I've learned to be pretty self-sufficient over the years.

"That doesn't say much about the people in your life." He sank into the chair to her right and pinched the bridge of his nose.

That was for sure. "I'm sorry helping me got you into trouble."

"Do you stir up this much trouble everywhere you go, or am I just lucky?"

He turned toward her, and she noticed his swollen and cut lip. "You're hurt."

He shrugged. "When Travis landed that sucker punch, his damn college ring cut me."

"You should put some ice on it to keep the swelling down."

She jumped off the couch, took a couple of steps and realized she had no idea where the kitchen was located. "Where's the kitchen?"

"I don't need any ice. I'm fine."

That he was. Absolutely fine with a capital *F*.

"At least let me clean the blood off and put some antiseptic on your cut." She reached into her purse sitting on the floor, pulled out her little first aid kit and located a foil packet with an antiseptic wipe. When she stood beside him, she leaned over and dabbed the white square to the cut that started on his lip and extended about an inch onto his chin. His spicy scent floated over her, igniting her senses. The stillness in the house created an intimacy she hadn't felt in a long time. "I feel like I should be doing more to make this right. If I had handled things better with Travis... I should've been able to get rid of him. What can I do to make this right?"

His crystal blue gaze darkened. "You could kiss my sore lip and make it all better."

At first she thought he was joking, but then she looked into his eyes. No mistaking the desire shining there. Blood pounded in her ears. She shouldn't kiss him. She knew that, but she wanted to. Desperately. She wanted his arms around her. She wanted to pretend he'd protected her because he cared. That he cared about *her*.

Common sense told her to jump off the couch and run as fast and as far from Colt as possible.

Instead, she leaned forward and touched her lips to his jaw. Then she kissed him lightly on his lips.

Chapter 6

Colt tossed out the "kiss and make it all better" comment expecting Stacy to toss a joke right back at him or put him in his place. His heart nearly stopped when she didn't do either of those things. Instead her lips covered his, and his body shifted into overdrive.

Her hands clutched his shirt and he wrapped his arms around her tiny frame. Her sweet floral scent floated over him. He felt alive. The need to be closer to her overwhelmed him. He missed having a connection with a woman. Sure he had friends and his brother, but there was something about having a woman in his life. They saw things, they understood on a different level, offered a comfort a man couldn't find anywhere else. A soft place to fall.

"Better?"

"My lip's better, but certain other parts ache like crazy."

He lifted her onto his lap. His hands framed her face as he kissed her. He could lose himself in her so easily. She slipped her hand under his shirt, warm and searching. His breath hitched. Her seeking fingers brushed over one of his scars. "What happened here?"

"I got hurt."

"No kidding. It's a scar. Did you get it in Afghanistan?"

He didn't want to remember how Sanders had been blown apart and pieces of his buddy's bones had slashed through his chest. To distract both of them, he nibbled on the sensitive skin below her ear. Her groan rippled through him.

"Never mind." She leaned forward and kissed his puckered flesh. His hands buried in her hair, the silky texture teasing his fingers as heat blasted through him. Unable to bear more of her tender exploration for fear of embarrassing himself, he pulled her face to his.

His lips covered hers again, hungry and almost desperate. Her hands fisted in his shirt as she clung to him. Through a haze, he heard a door creak upstairs, followed by the click of dog nails and the slap of bare feet on the wooden floor. The sexual fog surrounding him evaporated. He lifted Stacy off him and dumped her on the couch. Her hair mussed from his hands, her skin flushed from his touch, her hands shook as she adjusted her blouse. Much longer and her shirt would've been on the floor.

How could he have forgotten his daughter and her younger brother slept upstairs? The woman, her intoxicating kisses and her magic hands could make a man forget to breathe.

A minute later Jess stumbled into the living room,

her dog Thor trotting behind her. She glanced between him and Stacy.

He was busted. How the hell was he going to get out of this mess?

Stacy wanted to run for the front door the minute she saw Jess, but running would only make her look guiltier. Nothing to do but straighten out her big girl panties, or in this case her twisted blouse, and bluff her way through the situation. That was it. She was an actress. She'd pretend nothing happened. Play it cool, and Jess wouldn't realize a thing.

Right. Even Meryl Streep couldn't pull off that performance.

Jess glanced between her father and Stacy. A knowing grin spread across the teenager's face. "I guess I interrupted something."

"No, I just got home," Colt muttered as he shifted his stance like a kid caught in a lie.

"I was asleep on the couch. I woke up when the front door closed. I'm a light sleeper. Then I wanted to talk to your dad about what happened at the police station, so we were sitting here talking."

So much for playing it cool. Shut up, Stacy. You're rambling and making the situation worse.

"I'd have to be blind to believe that bunch of BS."

Stacy cringed and refused to meet Jess's gaze.

Great acting job.

"What was or wasn't going on here is none of your business." When Jess opened her mouth to say something else, Colt shook his head. "Don't push me. My patience is wearing thin."

"I can't believe this, Dad. After the lecture on dating

you gave me the other day? I guess this is one of those 'Do as I say, not as I do' moments." Then she walked over to her father, kissed him on the cheek and darted out of the room, her dog trotting behind her.

"I didn't think there was anything more embarrassing than my parents catching me making out with my first girlfriend. I was wrong."

"I can't believe—" Stacy paused, wanting desperately to fan her heated face. *I can't believe we acted like a couple of horny teenagers.* "You're right about that."

He shoved his hands in his jean's pocket and shuffled his feet. She stood, not knowing quite what to do now. Finally she said, "I'll wake Ryan so we can go home."

"Let him sleep. Not point in closing this door now that the horse has gotten out of the barn. You can either sleep here on the couch, or I can bring Ryan home when he wakes up."

This time she listened to her common sense. "Dropping him off tomorrow would be great."

As Stacy parked by the Healing Horses barn, she told herself she could do this. She could face her fear of horses. Then she almost laughed. Today facing Colt seemed scarier than facing a horse.

She'd kissed him last night. Not he kissed her. Well, not at first anyway. No, she'd been the aggressor.

How would she face him? Pretend last night never happened.

Like you pretended nothing happened when Jess caught you two making out? Because that worked so well.

When she walked into the barn, instead of finding

Colt, she discovered Jess. *Please don't let her bring up the other night.* "Where's your dad? He agreed to train me to be a sidewalker so I can help with Ryan's therapy. I don't want him thinking I'm late."

"Yeah, that's one of his pet peeves." Jess crossed her arms over her chest, and Stacy braced herself and resisted the urge to squirm. This was not good. "What are your intentions with my dad?"

She'd known whatever Jess had been going to say would be something she didn't want to hear, but never in her wildest nightmares had Stacy's thoughts gone to "What are your intentions?"

Beam me up, Scottie. Where was a good Chief Engineer with a transporter when a girl needed one?

Stacy's tongue stuck to the roof of her dry mouth and her mind raced to come up with a plausible answer. Intentions? As in for the future? Damned if she knew. While she might not know that, she'd sure known what her objective had been last night. She wanted to get hot and heavy with Colt.

She couldn't exactly tell his daughter that.

Honesty. They say it's the best policy. She could tell Jess the truth about the future at least. "I'm not sure what's going on between your father and me. We're so different, but when you and Ryan were in the game room last night we talked. I enjoyed his company. He's a nice guy, but we barely know each other."

"That's not what it looked like in the living room."

"It's not—"

"I'm not stupid. You two were getting pretty cozy."

Anyone over the age of five could've figured that out. "I won't lie to you. We were kissing, but that was it."

Only because you showed up.

"He hasn't dated anyone since my mom died almost three years ago."

"Her death had to be hard on you both."

"You have no idea. You can't tell him I told you, but I think you need to know. My mom didn't like it when Dad was in the military. She said she was sick of moving all the time. So he left the Air Force, joined the National Guard Reserves and we moved back here where he grew up."

"But he went to Afghanistan recently, didn't he?"

Jess said he'd been in the National Guard Reserves until a year ago. "Him joining the Reserves was their compromise, but Mom wasn't happy with that, either, or with living here. Then one day she left me a note. She said she was in love with someone else. She said she was sorry to leave me, but she had to take this chance to be happy. She hurt Dad so bad. He tried not to let me see, but I could tell. He was different. I don't know how to explain it."

Colt's wife had an affair and ran off with her lover?

Stacy's heart cracked for both the teenager and the man. The woman had left not only her husband—from what she'd seen at Halligan's, a wonderful, caring man—but her child, as well? A daughter who needed her, who loved her, who counted on her mother to be there for her. Didn't she have any idea of the pain and trauma that caused?

Jess stood there, her arms crossed over her chest, her brown eyes hard as she fought to hold back her tears.

I thought my mother was bad, but she at least stuck around. The woman was a fool and didn't deserve Jess and Colt. She'd been given two precious gifts, and she'd thrown them away with the wrapping paper.

"It wasn't your fault she left."

"I know that." Tears sparkled in Jess's eyes. She bit her lower lip. "The last thing I ever said to her was what a terrible mother she was and that I hated her. Then she died in a car accident."

Jess would never have the chance to take back those angry words. She'd never be able to repair her relationship with her mother, or even find closure. Such a huge burden for such a young woman.

The crack in Stacy's heart widened as Jess's pain reached out to her. She wrapped her arms around the teen, but Jess stiffened and pulled away. "I know you feel guilty about what you said to your mother, but I'm sure she knew it was the anger talking—anger you had every right to feel, by the way—but you've got to let it go."

"But how?" Tears now rolled down Jess's pale cheek.

Damn Jess's mother. How could she do this to her child? How could she choose a lover over this wonderful young woman? "I wish I could tell you. All I can say is that my mother and I haven't always gotten along, but she knows I love her. I'm sure your mom knew that, too. Focus on the good memories you have of her, of the special times you had together." *Please, Lord, let there be some good ones this dear girl can hold on to.* "Your mom wouldn't want you to be feeling guilty. You've got to forgive yourself for what you said. Don't let what happened between you rule the rest of your life."

Like my mother's ruling mine.

No. Don't think about that. Focus on Jess.

Jess swiped her sleeve over her eyes. "Because of what happened with my mom, I'm a little protective of my dad. That's why I asked about what's going on between the two of you. I don't want him getting hurt again."

Which was exactly what Stacy would do if she and Colt got involved. There was no avoiding it since she was only here for a few weeks. On top of that, she couldn't handle a romantic relationship. Hers invariably ended badly, and she was barely staying sane dealing with her current responsibilities. Even if they agreed up front to keep things casual and fun, she wouldn't risk them getting attached—either her to them or them to her. She refused to leave him and Jess like his wife had.

"You're a pretty great young lady. Your dad's lucky to have you."

"Yes, he is, and if you hurt him, you'll answer to me. Got it?"

"Message received. I have no intention of hurting your dad. We come from such different worlds. All I can ever see between us is friendship."

Chapter 7

Colt walked into the barn and heard the tail end of his daughter's conversation with Stacy. *The last thing I ever said to her was what a terrible mother she was and that I hated her. Then she died in a car accident.*

His daughter's words sliced through him. He'd never known about Jess's last conversation with her mother. She'd been carrying so much guilt, and he'd been clueless. He almost charged forward, but then Stacy's words stopped him. *It wasn't your fault she left.* He could tell Jess all day long not to feel guilty, but she needed to hear that from someone else.

As he listened to Stacy talk to Jess he realized for someone who lived in Hollywood where honesty and being real could be deadly to a career, Stacy did a damn fine job dealing with Jess. Unless this was an

Oscar-worthy performance, Stacy truly cared about his daughter.

He and his daughter had both kept secrets. The day before Lynn died she'd called him, too. Things weren't going so well with her lover now that they were playing house. She thought she'd made a mistake. Could she come home?

His first reaction had been to tell her hell, no, he wouldn't take her back, but then he thought about Jess, and he changed his mind. Instead he told Lynn he'd think about what she said and call her in a couple of days, but he never got the chance.

He'd often wondered if he'd told her she could come home would she still be alive. Even if their relationship hadn't worked out, Jess would have her mother. His fear of getting hurt again, of looking like a fool robbed his daughter of that opportunity.

And now she was protecting him.

All I can ever see between us is friendship.

His male pride stung knowing that Stacy could so easily dump him into friends-only status, but that was for the best. Considering what Lynn leaving had done to Jess, he wasn't sure he ever wanted to bring another woman into her life. Maybe once she went off to college he could find someone to share some time with, but not now. He wouldn't risk Jess getting attached and getting hurt if his relationship fell apart.

If Jess wasn't attached to Stacy before today, she probably was now.

He shut the barn door hard enough to alert Jess and Stacy to his presence. "You ready to get started on your training?"

"Absolutely." Stacy posed and pointed to her boots. "See, I remembered to get boots."

Gazing at her standing there in jeans, a simple white blouse and cowboy boots—not fancy ones with lots of color and handwork like he'd expect her to wear, but simple sturdy ones—got his motor running. She looked so blasted cute and proud of herself. Standing there before him she looked so right here, her bright smile lighting up the barn.

Keeping his mind on business was so much easier when she wore fancy rhinestone jeans, an expensive silk blouse and those skinny little heels. Then it was easy to remember she belonged in California. Now, not so much.

He smiled at the memory of the strappy heels she'd worn. Those weren't so bad. They had a way of making her hips sway in a way that mesmerized a man. He swallowed hard.

"It's good to know you can follow directions."

Her bright smile faded, and damned if he didn't feel as if he'd stolen a kid's Halloween candy.

"I think she looks great," Jess said. Then her cell phone rang. When his daughter stepped away to answer the call, he and Stacy stared at each other for a minute, before he said, "You ready to get started?"

"No, but let's get going anyway."

"Ryan's on the phone," Jess said when she returned. "He and I talked about the volunteer work I do at Aunt Avery's shelter, and he wants to go with me for my shift today. Is that okay with you, Stacy?"

"It's fine with me if your dad doesn't mind waiting to start my training until I get Ryan and drop him off."

"You don't need to take him to the shelter. My aunt's picking me up, and we'll just swing by and get him."

After Jess went outside to wait for her aunt, Colt said, "We'll work with Babe. She's a sweet little Haflinger cross pony we use with young riders."

"I'm not sure I can do this. I couldn't sleep last night because of the nightmares."

"I think it was Mark Twain who said, 'Courage isn't the absence of fear, but the mastery of it.' We'll start slow." He led her down the row of stalls. "Weird noises, or loud, excited voices can make the horses nervous. Keep your movements slow and deliberate."

They stopped at a stall about halfway down a long hall. "Hey, Babe. Come here and show Stacy what a sweet girl you are."

The pony trotted over to the bars. He rubbed the golden animal's head. "There isn't a horse that doesn't like having its head caressed. Come here and give it a try."

Stacy shook her head, her eyes wide, her chest rising and falling with her rapid breathing. He stepped away from the horse and moved closer to Stacy. "Relax. Breathe with me."

His gaze locked with hers as he breathed deeply and evenly, until she started calming down. "She's still in the stall. The bars on the door and windows are sturdy, and I'm here. Nothing is going to happen."

"You promise?"

The words hung between them. He couldn't do anything but nod. Hell, he could barely breathe.

She turned away from him and inched forward toward the stall. He scooted closer, needing to offer support. Her delicate fragrance teased his senses. She always smelled like the bouquet of spring flowers his mom used to put in a recycled can vase he made her in first grade art class. He leaned closer and whispered in her ear. "Talk to her."

"Hi." She reached out, her hand shaking. The horse whinnied, and she jumped back, bumping into him. His arms wrapped around her waist to steady her. Physical awareness slammed into him, strong and potent.

He released her as if he'd grabbed a barbed wire fence. *Get yourself under control. You're not a horny teenager.*

No, just horny.

Abstinence was going to kill him.

Lord, don't think about that.

What was he doing? Oh, yeah, getting her comfortable with the pony. "Babe was just saying hello. See how her ears are forward, but relaxed?"

"If you say so."

"That just means she's interested in what's in front of her. You're someone new and she's curious. There's nothing to be afraid of."

At least for her. Him, he wasn't so sure of. His body was running hotter than a thoroughbred after a mile run. "Talk to her like you would a friend."

She inched forward, a look on her face as though she was heading to the dentist for a root canal, but damn, the woman had guts. For him that was far more intoxicating than her beauty. Looks faded. Character lasted.

"Hi, Babe. I'm Stacy. Go easy on me. I'm a little nervous." This time when she reached out, she rubbed Babe's forehead. The animal leaned into her, and she relaxed.

"See, she won't bite your arm off."

"That's good to know."

"If you're good to a horse, he'll be your friend for life. They're pretty easy to please."

Just like me.

He reached into his back pocket and pulled out a carrot. "Give her this."

Stacy stared over her shoulder at him. "I don't know. You sure she won't bite?"

Babe wouldn't, but he wasn't so sure about him. The urge to nibble on that spot on her graceful neck where her pulse throbbed as fast as hummingbird wings nearly overwhelmed him.

Instead, he placed the vegetable in her hand and then covered her hand with his. He stood beside her as they held the treat out to Babe, who snatched up the carrot.

"If you're anxious about working with a horse, it never hurts to bring a treat."

"I'll stop at the grocery store on my way home."

He let go of her hand, and stepped away. Friends. Remember? That's what she wanted to be. That's where he needed her to stay—safely in the friendship zone. He cleared his throat and returned to why she'd come today—her training. "Because of your issues, we won't have you do anything to get the horse ready for the lessons. I'll take care of that. I want you to feel comfortable around the animals, but your job during therapy will be to help Ryan with his balance and reinforce instructions. You'll walk beside Ryan. If you sense he's struggling with his balance, you place a hand on his ankle or his belt until he's steadier."

Before he could say anything further, her phone rang. She grabbed her cell out of her back pocket. "I should check and make sure it's not Ryan."

Colt nodded. "We'll take a short break."

Maybe then he could cool off. He almost laughed. Cool off? Only if he took a second cold shower.

Stacy's heart sank when she glanced at her phone after Colt walked away. Her mother. She considered letting the call go to voice mail, but Andrea would keep calling until she answered. Better to deal with whatever molehill her mother had turned into Mount Everest as quickly as possible. "Mom, this isn't a good time. Can I call you back later tonight?"

"This can't wait." Her mother's high-pitched, frantic voice jumped across the phone line. Stacy closed her eyes and sighed. Nothing ever could with Andrea.

"There's water all over the garage. I don't know what's wrong or what to do."

"Can't Grant help you take care of it?"

"He's at a friend's running lines to prepare for the audition he has on Monday. I can't bother him. He needs to focus all his energy on that. You have to help me. Now the water's starting to come into the den. It's going to flood the whole house. I know it. It's going to ruin all the furniture. What should I do?"

"First of all, you need to shut off the water. Get a screwdriver and a wrench. The box to shut off the water is in front of the house by the sidewalk. Use the screwdriver to take the lid off the water box. Then use the wrench to turn the brass knob—"

"I can't do that." Andrea's voice skipped up another level in pitch. Stacy guessed one notch from hysterical. "I don't know where the tools are or what a wrench looks like. I need someone to help me. You've got to do something!"

How could any person be so helpless?

"Mother, there's nothing I can do from here in Colorado."

"Don't yell at me!"

She wasn't yelling. Her mom always accused Stacy of that when she didn't do exactly what Andrea wanted or became the least bit forceful. Stacy counted to ten and vowed to keep her voice emotionless. "Ask one of the neighbors to help you shut off the water. If you can't find one of them, call the plumber. Tell him you can't shut off the water and you need him to come to the house as soon as possible."

She refused to think about what an emergency "drop everything and come right now" fee would be as Colt returned. "I've got to go."

"I don't know where the plumber's number is."

"I'll send it to you." Then she ended the call before her mother could ask her to call the plumber for her. After she texted the phone number to Andrea, she turned off her phone's ringer and shoved it in her back pocket.

"Problems?" Colt asked.

Just the same old, same old. My mother can't cope with the smallest problems and wants me to take care of everything.

"My mom's got water all over the garage, and expects me to fix everything for her from here."

"All she needs to do is shut off the water and call a plumber."

"That's what I told her, but from the way she reacted you'd think I asked her to build a nuclear reactor." Stacy rubbed her temples in an attempt to ease her pounding headache.

Her phone vibrated in her pocket. Her mother would have deal with the problem on her own.

"Your butt's buzzing."

"I know. At least I'll get a good minimassage from all her calls."

"You aren't going to answer?"

Guilt tickled her conscience. She could give the plumber a quick call, but then irritation kicked in. Her mother could make a simple phone call and deal with the plumber. "No, I'm not going to talk to her right now."

"Good for you. Sometimes you have to be tough. If I did everything for my daughter she'd never learn to stand on her own. Sounds like your mom needs to deal with the water problem or learn to swim."

His validating words lifted the brick off her chest. She wasn't being the worst daughter ever by expecting her mother to deal with this problem. "You're absolutely right. Thank you." Her phone vibrated again. "What's next on the training schedule?"

"Now comes the big test. We're going into the stall. I'll get Babe bridled and then you'll lead her to the arena."

Her stomach plummeted. "You said all I'd have to do was walk beside and help Ryan."

"Which means you will actually *have to stand beside* the horse." He started to walk toward the stall, then stopped and glanced over his shoulder at her. She couldn't move.

"You want me to go in a closed space with a horse?"

His gaze softened as he returned to her. When he stopped in front of her she couldn't breathe. The confidence in his eyes reached out to her. Confidence in her, but not in the way Andrea looked at her as though she'd do whatever needed to be done. The look in Colt's eyes was different. He believed in *her*.

"Trust me. I won't let anything happen to you."

This time when he headed toward Babe's stall, she followed. Once inside, she scooted to a corner as far away from the pony as possible.

"You stay there until you feel comfortable. There's nothing to worry about. Babe's a sweet girl." He patted the animal's neck. "I can't believe you're starring in a movie about women who own a horse ranch. Won't your fear of horses be a problem?"

"I was worried about that until I read the script. My character doesn't have any scenes where she needs to ride. Of course things can change, but when I auditioned for the role, I told Maggie about my issues. She said she didn't think it would be a problem, but if it was, we'd work through it."

"That's another reason why you need to get more comfortable around horses. Your character will be more believable if you don't break into a cold sweat when a horse is within ten feet of you."

"I'm not sweating."

"Liar."

"You're such a gentleman."

"Have you forgotten about how I came to your defense at Halligan's?"

"That was then. This is now."

He nodded toward her and smiled. "That's better. See, you're almost next to Babe and you're still breathing."

She hadn't realized that as they'd talked, she'd

moved closer to him, and thus, to the horse. The man could make a nun feel comfortable in a strip club.

He slipped the bridle on as he explained important things she needed to know about horses. Never stand directly behind one. Don't duck under the animal's neck. Go around him so he's not startled. "The best place to stand is by the horse's shoulder where you both can see each other."

She started to relax. The horse seemed pretty calm.

"When you're leading a horse, make sure *you're* the leader. You move first. The horse follows you." Then he held out a rope to her. "Here's the keys."

She wasn't sure she was ready for this, but if she couldn't get near a horse, she couldn't be part of Ryan's therapy. Needing Colt's reassurance that she could do this, her gaze sought his.

"Trust me. I won't let anything happen to you."

Her heart tripped. Heaven help her, but she believed him. That's the kind of man he was. When he gave his word, it meant something. Not like most of the people in her life. In her life? She had a handful of friends, but would they be there for her if she asked? More like she had close colleagues, and in her business, a promise meant something could be counted on unless things changed or a better deal came along.

Hand shaking, she took the rope from him. "What do I do now?"

"Start walking to the stall door. She'll follow."

You can do this. Don't let fear rule you.

Muttering the phrases like a mantra, she started walking. The pony fell in step behind her.

"You're doing great."

Colt kept offering encouragement, and she made it through the stall door. As they walked down the hallway to the arena, the pony's hooves clicked on the cement floor like a drumbeat. A sense of accomplishment bolted through her as they left the barn and entered the arena. Her breath came out in a soft rush. She glanced at Colt. "I did it."

"You sure did." The pride in his eyes drilled into her. The man made her feel as if she could do anything.

For the next hour they worked together. She led Babe around the arena and Colt gave instructions as he would during a therapy session. They talked about various situations that could come up.

"I'm feeling comfortable with Babe, but what about Chance? He's so huge."

"We screen our horses and they go through training, too. People don't realize, only one out of fifteen horses works for a program like this. What I'm trying to say is, the animals in my program are the safest horses a person can be around."

She'd take his word for it.

As they walked back to the barn, Colt said, "If you really want to understand what Ryan's going through and get over your fear, you should get on a horse. You'd realize what great animals they are." He opened the arena gate for her to lead Babe through. "You and I could go riding some day."

"Riding?"

"More like walking through the national park like the tourists do. We could make an afternoon of it. Stop along the way and have a picnic."

She froze. As if him asking her to go riding hadn't

thrown her enough, he'd gone on to explain. He couldn't be doing what she thought he was doing. She knew that, but had to ask. "Are you asking me out on a date?"

Chapter 8

Colt hadn't meant to ask Stacy out. The words asking her to go riding jumped out before he considered what he was saying. He almost winced. Obviously he'd botched the invitation, since she wasn't sure he'd asked her out, but now that he had, maybe it wasn't such a bad thing.

He'd been strung tighter than a barbed wire fence since he'd kissed her. Hell, since they'd met he found himself thinking about her at the oddest times—sitting in the carpool lane waiting to pick Jess up or while he tried to write grant proposals. The fantasies were getting so bad this morning he'd taken a cold shower to get his body under control.

He needed to get her out of his system. If he spent time with her, got to know her, he'd see she wasn't any different than he expected—a fancy city woman. He'd see she'd never be happy in his life. He'd see how much her career meant to her and how much she loved California. Then she'd quit driving him insane. He would be able to stop dreaming about her. He'd quit imagining what it would be like to make love to her.

"I don't think us going out would be a good idea."

From the look of almost horror splashed across her face now, he wished he could take back what he'd said. In an effort to salvage his tattered pride he said, "Did you hear me mention the word *date?*"

"No."

"I offered to help you get over your fear so you could understand your brother's therapy better and because it would help you do a better job in your movie. Think of it as research." He couldn't believe he'd said those words with a straight face. God ought to be striking him with lightning for that whopper.

"Since my character doesn't need to ride a horse or even sit on one in this movie, I think I can call it good with what I've done today."

"Not even if I put you on a horse that's so old she couldn't do more than walk if I lit a fire under her? It can't get much safer than that."

"I'll pass."

"Chicken?"

"Absolutely. The closest I'm getting to a horse is being Ryan's sidewalker."

That was probably for the best. He'd finish her training. They'd see each other around town and at Ryan's therapy. Fine with him.

That night Colt sat at the kitchen table with Jess and tried to find the words to talk to her about what she'd confided in Stacy earlier. Damn, parenting was hard work and seemed to get more difficult as she grew up. He'd thought figuring out why she was crying as a baby was tough? That didn't come close to talking to her about sex, dating and her mother running off on them. They'd discussed her mother leaving before, but when Jess said she was fine and understood her mother leaving wasn't her fault, he left things at that.

Because he hadn't really wanted to deal with the truth and her pain. Or his. But he couldn't do that any longer.

Never one to go around the fence when he could open the gate, he decided on the direct approach. "I heard what you said to Stacy about the last conversation you had with your mom. Why didn't you tell me about it?"

"You were eavesdropping?"

"No. I came into the barn to meet her for our training session and heard you talking. I was going to let you know I was there, but then I heard what she said and stopped. She said pretty much what I would've. I figured you needed to hear that from someone else. Your mom knew you loved her. If she were here, she'd tell you she knew you didn't mean what you said. She wouldn't want you feeling guilty over it."

"You really think so?"

"Absolutely."

"I was so mad at her, and I never got the chance to take back what I said."

"Stacy was right. You've got to let it go."

"Why did she have to leave town? If she'd stayed here…"

Jess's words trailed off, but he knew what his daughter had been about to say. *If she'd stayed here she would still be alive.*

If he'd said Lynn could come back that day she might still be alive, too, but that's something he'd have to live with. He wouldn't burden his daughter with that. "I'll be honest. I think she was searching for something and she didn't think she could find it here." His hand covered his daughter's smaller one. She laced her fingers with his and held on so tight his fingers started to go numb. "I don't want you thinking it was your fault she left."

Lynn wanted the freedom she'd have had if she hadn't gotten married so young and had a baby right away.

He never felt as if their decision caused him to miss out on life. He'd already decided to go into the Air Force and getting married didn't change that. Lynn had felt differently. She'd planned on going to college. When she tried attending later when Jess was a toddler, juggling motherhood, classes and studying with a husband who wasn't always around proved too much for her. He'd mentioned her trying again a few years later when Jess went to elementary school, but Lynn hadn't been interested.

"Your mom left me. I truly believe when she was more settled, she'd have asked you to live with her if you'd wanted to." He wasn't really sure about that, but his daughter needed to hear the words, and he figured God would forgive him for that lie. "Then you would've had the opportunity to tell her you didn't mean what you'd said. Fate took that chance away from you."

"I miss her so much some times, especially when

I hear friends talking about all the stuff they do with their moms."

Nothing he could do could ever change that. There were events in a girl's life she wanted to share with her mother—picking out a prom dress, planning a wedding, the birth of her first child—and Jess would have to navigate those milestones without her mother's guidance. He recalled Reed telling him while he was in Afghanistan how he'd taken Jess shopping for a dress for the Spring Fling. The experience still gave his brother nightmares, and he'd been forced to call Avery in as a reinforcement. That's the best Jess would ever have—stand-ins for her mom.

That's what angered him most about Lynn's leaving, what she'd left her daughter alone to deal with.

"I wish I could tell you that will get easier, but I'm not sure it will. Things will happen in your life, and you'll wish your mom was there to share them with you."

"I'm just so glad I have you."

"But it's not the same," he said. "When you're missing your mom, it's okay to talk to me about it."

"I know it hurts you to talk about her."

He'd tried to keep his daughter from seeing how much, but apparently he hadn't done as good a job as he thought. "I don't need you to protect me. It's not your job. I loved your mom. She was a big part of my life. We had some wonderful times together and the best thing we ever did was create you. I don't want to erase that part of my life. Got it?"

He needed to let go, too. Of his anger at Lynn for leaving him with such an awful mess to clean up. Of his guilt for the fact that she'd been so unhappy with him she'd felt the need to leave town and had gotten herself killed. Of his grief over the death of the love of his youth.

"Now since we're talking about you feeling the need to protect me, what were you thinking when you asked Stacy what was going on between her and I?"

"You haven't dated in forever."

When she emphasized the last word he cringed. "That's right. Dinosaurs roamed the Earth when your mom and I were dating."

"You're a great guy, but Stacy's used to Hollywood actors."

Ouch. When his daughter thought he couldn't compete with the guys Stacy normally dated that really hurt. "While I get to get to give your dates the third degree, you are to stay out of my love life."

"What love—"

"Don't even say it."

He didn't need to hear his fifteen-year-old daughter say he didn't have a love life. He knew the fact all too well.

Despite the success of her training session a few days earlier, Stacy's nerves started getting the best of her as she drove to Healing Horses.

"You don't have to do this, you know," Ryan said, his face etched with concern for her.

She released her death grip on the steering wheel and flashed him a tight smile. "I want to."

"No, you don't. I can tell because that's your too-big smile again."

"You're seriously making me doubt my skills as an actress." He was right. She hadn't wanted to, but that wasn't the only thing she was nervous about. She wasn't sure how to deal with Colt now. Ever since he'd kissed her she didn't know what was going on between them, and the other day only ratcheted up the attraction between them.

"You're great on a movie set, but not so hot at hiding your feelings in real life."

"I want to be there for your therapy sessions."

"You mean in a way other than from the opposite side of the fence or hanging over Colt's shoulder?"

She glared at her brother. "You're never going to let me forget that, are you?"

Ryan laughed. "You've got to admit it. That was funny when he picked you up. You should have seen the look on your face. Talk about looking weirded out."

"It wasn't so hilarious from my perspective." Being in Colt's arms brought a variety of emotions to life along with her outrage—excitement, desire, longing. A whole lot of longing. The feelings had only grown stronger when they worked together the other day. If he hadn't looked at her with such confidence it would've been easier to stay detached. If he hadn't been so patient and so damned understanding. Dealing with him as the overbearing, take-charge Neanderthal man was much simpler. And safer.

She cleared her throat and turned to Ryan. "I think this will be good for me. In an odd way, the training and dealing with my fear of horses is helping me deal with Dad's death."

More than the years of therapy ever had. Little bits and pieces of the days before her dad's accident had started coming back to her. Snippets of conversations between the director and her father about whether or not he should let a stuntman do the scene. Her dad had argued that he could handle the stunt. The director had expressed his concern, and her dad had countered with the realism would enhance his performance.

"It had to be tough being there when Dad died. I wish I'd gotten to know him."

Over the years she'd tried to share her memories of their father with Ryan, but it wasn't the same as him having his own. As she turned into the Healing Horses driveway, she said, "You're a lot like him, and not just in looks. You've got his easy way with people, his charm. You've got his good heart."

At least before the accident squelched that wonderful part of Ryan's personality. Since they'd arrived in Colorado, she'd seen sparks of that person returning.

As she parked her car, her stomach tightened. What had Colt said? *Courage isn't the absence of fear, but the mastery of it.*

She kept telling herself that as they prepared for Ryan's therapy. When she and Ryan stood on the mounting block as Colt led Chance in, her heart pounded almost painfully as the large animal approached. Colt's gaze locked with hers. The confidence in her she'd seen there the other day blazed there now. *He believes in me. He thinks I can do this.*

Her courage bolstered, she fought down her urge to run. Colt's words rang in her ears. *The animals in my program are the safest horses a person can be around.* Chance didn't even glance her way as Colt and the animal stood in front of them. "You okay?"

She nodded, too afraid to say anything.

While he stood by the horse's head, Colt said,

"Stacy, help Ryan get his foot in the stirrup. His upper body is strong. He can take it from there."

She nodded again, but said nothing, not wanting to do anything to confuse Chance. Once Ryan was mounted, Colt led Chance forward, away from the mounting area and headed toward the arena. From her training she knew her job was to walk beside the horse. She wouldn't need to do anything other than to watch for Ryan having balancing problems. If that occurred, she was to place her hand on his boot near his ankle. That would offer him extra stability. If that wasn't enough she could move her arms across his thigh and grasp the front edge of the saddle.

For the next hour she walked beside her brother. The slight changes in his control and balance as they progressed through the session amazed her. After working in the arena for a while, they stopped by an area containing what looked like a bean bag game kids might play at a birthday party.

Colt handed Ryan bean bags and told him which hole in the board to aim for. Ryan had to work on maintaining control of Chance as he threw bags at the target. Though he struggled with keeping Chance still on his first attempts, Colt offered suggestions and Ryan quickly improved. When a bean bag finally sailed through the designated spot, Stacy bit her lip to keep from cheering. Not only because of her brother's accomplishment, but from the pride shining on his face.

If only Andrea could see what a different this therapy was making for Ryan.

You can't get blood out of a turnip. Or manufacture love where the capacity for the emotion didn't exist. Sure, Andrea had been married three times, but the desperate need to be taken care of, not real love, fueled her actions.

The thought barreled through Stacy. Had she ever been in love? Maybe like her mother she didn't possess the ability to truly love that way.

No, she loved Ryan. But what about loving a man? She shook herself mentally and focused her attention to Ryan through the remainder of the session. When they returned to the barn, Jess met them. She smiled at Ryan. "You're doing great. You must've been a cowboy in a past life."

"Thanks. You want to help me groom Chance?"

Once Ryan dismounted, he and Jess led Chance back to his stall and Stacy couldn't contain her excitement any longer. "I did it, Colt. I walked beside that huge horse, and eventually I wasn't so scared."

"I'm shocked that you were able to be quiet for that long."

"Do you overwhelm all your volunteers with this much gratitude and praise? Would it be so hard to toss me a bone? To say I did a good job?"

He shifted his stance, his scuffed cowboy boots kicked up dust with his movements. "You did a damned fine job. I'm duly impressed."

His words thrilled her as much as an Academy Award nomination would.

"I could tell how hard it was for you to keep quiet, especially when Ryan hit the right spot in the target that first time."

"That was pretty cool," Ryan said as he and Jess returned.

She glanced at Jess and then at Colt. "How about it? You two want to go out to dinner celebrate our success—Ryan's improvement and my first session as a sidewalker? My treat."

"We've got plans. We're having dinner at my brother's house tonight," Colt replied.

"I bet Uncle Reed and Aunt Avery wouldn't mind if Stacy and Ryan came, too," Jess added.

"No, that's all right," Stacy murmured. "We can do it some other time."

But Jess wasn't listening. She'd already pulled out her cell phone and dialed.

"You wouldn't mind if my friend Ryan—the guy who came with me to volunteer at the shelter the other day—and his sister came to dinner with us tonight, would you?" Jess rattled on about Stacy being afraid of horses and how her dad talked her into becoming a sidewalker. "Ryan's therapy's going great, and Stacy survived her first time volunteering, so she asked us to celebrate."

Stacy cringed. Somehow when Jess said it that way, Stacy felt pathetic and alone. As if she had no one to share good news with other than Colt and his daughter.

And you think you do?

A minute later, Jess ended her call and Stacy said, "I appreciate you wanting to include us, Jess, but you have to call your aunt back. We're not going to horn in on a family event. We can celebrate some other time."

"It's cool. Aunt Avery said she's been meaning to ask you and Ryan over. She said you two met when you were here before."

Stacy cringed. She hadn't made the best impression with Griffin's family. She'd been a stuck-up pain in the ass, who hadn't cared about anything but advancing her career.

"Thank you, but no." She might be pathetic, but she still had some pride.

"If Jess's aunt is okay with it, what's the big deal?" Ryan asked.

"We weren't invited."

Then Jess and Ryan started talking at once trying to convince her to change her mind. When she remained adamant, Ryan said he didn't care what she did, but he was going.

A shrill whistle cut through the chatter. She and the teenagers turned to Colt, who stood there, feet braced, arms crossed over his broad chest in full take-charge mode. "We'll pick you up at seven." When Stacy started to protest, he held up a hand and stepped closer. The man had a presence that could make a girl swoon. "Don't make me throw you over my shoulder to get you there."

Stacy pointed her chin at him in defiance. "I won't let you in the house."

"I will," Ryan tossed out.

"Traitor," she snapped at him, without taking her gaze off Colt. "You wouldn't do that again."

"Wanna bet?"

No. She knew she'd lose. "We'll see you at seven."

By six forty-five Stacy considered telling Ryan she was coming down with a cold, the flu, the plague or whatever other disease she could think of to avoid going to dinner. She'd changed her clothes three times. Everything she owned seemed so—California Hollywood. After her last meeting with Avery and the incident at Halligan's she didn't want to look as if she was putting on airs.

The first time she'd stayed in Estes Park she'd been so concerned about her career and looking good for the cameras that she never treated anyone like… She paused. She hadn't really given anyone here much thought, but things were different now.

Because of Colt. She didn't want to embarrass him tonight with his family.

Settling on a simple cobalt knit top and jeans, she added her favorite chunky silver necklace and earrings and glanced in the mirror. *I'm as ready as I'll ever be.*

When she answered the door after the doorbell rang a couple of minutes before seven, her breath caught in her throat. There stood Colt looking way too fine in dark jeans and a tan shirt that highlighted his golden skin and hair.

His heated gaze scanned her from head to toe. The appreciative male grin that he flashed her bolstered her courage. A pleasant flush spread through her. "You look great, Stacy."

"So do you."

Lord this was awkward. *That's because it feels like a date.*

Anxious to blast that thought out of her mind, she called out, "Ryan, hurry up. Colt's here."

Footsteps pounded overhead and then down the stairs. A minute later, the three of them headed out the door. Once in the car, Ryan and Jess talked nonstop in the backseat. Unable to stand the silence between her and Colt any longer she asked, "How long have your brother and Avery been married?"

"Since early December, but they've known each other their whole lives. They were high school sweethearts until Reed left for Stanford." Colt told her how his brother came from California to stay with Jess when he'd been deployed. "Jess got sentenced to community service at Avery's animal shelter for vandalism—"

"In my defense, I didn't actually participate in the spray painting," Jess explained. "Some friends of mine, who're no longer my friends, I might add, did the vandalism. Then they ran off and left me to take the fall."

Now Jess taking Ryan under her wing made more sense. Her mother ran off, then died. Her father was deployed to Afghanistan, and her friends bailed on her leaving her to take the rap for their vandalism. Yup, the girl understood what it felt like to be on the outside.

"The good news was," Jess continued, "because of a shelter policy, Uncle Reed had to volunteer with me. That's how he and Avery got back together."

Family. Jess's affection for her uncle and his wife rippled through her voice.

Colt, his daughter and brother obviously had the give and take true families possessed. When Stacy visited Estes Park before, she'd envied Griffin's relationship with his family. He had a home filled with love and people who supported him. When he defied the network and proposed to Maggie on the finale, his family and the community rallied around him. They hadn't left him standing alone to fight the battle. Now, since Colt's brother had married Avery McAlister, he and Jess had been enveloped in the McAlister clan, as well.

As they walked from the parking lot to Avery and Reed's apartment, Stacy tried to quell her nervousness. What was the big deal? It was just a simple dinner at someone's house. At someone's house that she hadn't made the best first impression on.

When Avery answered the door, Stacy was amazed

at how the woman, with only a bit of lip gloss and mascara, dressed in scrubs and scuffed tennis shoes, could look as though she belonged on the cover of a magazine. "Come on in. I just got home. We had some abandoned kittens come in to the shelter right before I left. We couldn't find their mother, so I get to spend the night feeding them every two hours."

"Sounds like fun," Colt joked.

"The joys of having a wife who brings her work home." A tall, dark-haired man and the scraggliest dog Stacy had ever seen tagging after him joined them. The man wrapped his arms around Avery, and then introduced himself as Colt's brother.

She'd never guess they were related, much less brothers. Except for their height, Colt and Reed Montgomery had nothing in common physically.

"Do you need any help with the kittens?" Jess asked. "If you do, I could spend the night and help out."

"You can help me with their next feeding before you leave," Avery said.

"Reed, the timer went off, so I took the lasagna out of the oven." Nannette McAlister strolled out of the kitchen. "Everything's on the table so we're ready to eat."

Griffin's mother was here? Now Stacy wished she'd pulled the "I'm sick" routine. When she'd met Nannette, the older woman made no secret of the fact that not only didn't she approve of her son going on the reality dating show, she didn't think much of the bachelorettes, either.

Could this night get any worse?

In a lame attempt to ease the tension she felt, Stacy said, "Thank you for letting us join you. I hope it hasn't caused too much trouble." Her words sounded as awkward as she felt. She nodded toward Mrs. McAlister. "It's good to see you again."

The older woman nodded and mumbled a polite greeting in return. As everyone moved into the small dining room conversations swirled around Stacy. Once Ryan sat, she took his walker, pushed it into the nearby corner and then settled into her chair in between him and Colt. She felt herself pulling inward as she tried to come up with an excuse to leave once they finished eating. Coming from a small family who never ate dinner together, sitting down with a total of seven people overwhelmed her.

"Your adventures at Halligan's the other night are the talk of the town, big brother. Did you really get into a bar fight with Travis Carpenter?"

Stacy cringed. The night just got worse.

Chapter 9

Colt wanted to jump across the table and punch his brother. Didn't Reed realize how uncomfortable this conversation would make Stacy feel?

Since they arrived, Stacy had changed. Instead of the fearless, say-what's-on-her-mind woman he knew, she'd become quiet. Almost as if she wanted to blend in with the furniture.

Now his jackass brother brought up the night at Halligan's. Beside him he almost felt Stacy pulling away even further. He didn't know where she'd gone, but she wasn't here with them. At least not the feisty woman he knew.

"Thanks for bringing that up, Reed, because I haven't been embarrassed enough by everyone in town asking me about the fight."

His brother flashed him a stupid grin. "Glad to help

out. What happened? Getting into a bar fight isn't your style."

Before he could answer, Jess spoke, her young face scrunched up with revulsion. "You should've seen it. Mr. Carpenter's hands were all over Stacy."

"We don't need to rehash all the gory details," Colt said, hoping everyone would take the hint and move on to another topic.

"So you played the knight in shining armor coming to a lady's rescue. Now that seems like you," Reed said.

Yeah, he was a regular white knight. One who charged in before he thought about the consequences or the fact that his daughter was watching.

Out of the corner of his eye he spotted Stacy, her posture all rigid, her back looking as if it had been glued to the chair. "Anyone see the Rockies game yesterday? Looks like they might have a good season this year."

"What Carpenter was doing must have been bad because Colt's the kind of guy who follows the rules no matter what. Nothing riles him. He's got more patience than anyone I know," Avery said, ignoring his obvious attempt to change the subject. Getting this group to move on to a different subject would be as easy as a getting a bull out of a pasture full of cows.

"How awful for you, Stacy."

Stacy's eyes widened as if she couldn't believe someone was talking to her. "The man had more arms than an octopus. It might not have been so bad if he hadn't been drunk."

"It's about time someone knocked some sense into that man," Nannette added. "Travis always has been too big for his britches. That's his father's fault. Travis is the youngest. He's got four older sisters. His father was so glad to finally have a boy he treated his son like his diapers didn't stink."

Reed laughed. "He'd sure be different if he'd had a mother like you."

"You're right about that. Mom never tolerated any of us putting on airs," Avery said. "I'd heard when Travis drinks his manners evaporate."

"That's a nice way to put it," Stacy said, her body relaxing some as the topic moved away from their actions at the bar, focusing on Carpenter instead. "Travis wouldn't let me leave the dance floor."

Nannette gaze filled with compassion and concern when she turned to Stacy. "How frightening. Thank goodness Colt was there to step in."

"And what thanks did he get? He got hauled off to jail." Stacy turned to him, and the fire blazing in her clear blue eyes told Colt the feisty woman he knew had returned.

"It turned out okay. Having to listen to a lecture from Chief Parsons was the worst part. Other than that, I had to pay a fine and for part of the damages at Halligan's."

"That's not fair. You didn't start the fight," Ryan said.

"I'll talk to Chief Parsons. You did nothing wrong." Stacy shook her head. "I knew I should've contacted my attorney that night. If I had this wouldn't have happened."

"It's no big deal." He wanted to forget the night ever happened, and not only because of the fight. "As far as I'm concerned the matter's over."

"I'll reimburse you for the fine and whatever the damages were."

"It's already taken care of." He didn't need her seeing to his responsibilities. He'd gotten into the fight. He'd man up and take the consequences.

"That's the least I can do since you were defending me."

"There's no need."

"I don't want what happened taking money away from Healing Horses or from other necessities. It's not easy surviving on one income."

He winced. What did she think? That he was a charity case? "I do all right."

"I didn't say you weren't. At least let me pay half."

"No."

"Why won't you let me help you?"

Her words stopped him cold, her offer both thrilling and ticking him off. Anger kicked in both at her for wanting to help and at him for being pleased that she had. "I don't need the help."

"Is Healing Horses having money problems?" Reed's voice startled Colt. He pulled his gaze away from Stacy.

Five sets of eyes trained on him and Stacy.

He'd forgotten everyone else. For a few minutes there had been no one around but Stacy. The woman made him lose all common sense. She lit a fire in him like no other woman. Not even his wife. No woman ever made him so out-and-out frustrated, or made him want her so much.

After a deep breath and counting to ten, he said, "Healing Horses is doing fine. The spring classes are full. We just got another grant. If I get real lucky at an auction I should be able to pick up a few more horses."

"I'm going to one this weekend," Avery said. "We received an anonymous donation to purchase horses to keep them from going to meat packers."

"What?" Stacy and Ryan gasped in unison.

"Horse meat is a delicacy in some places in Europe. Meat packers will buy unwanted horses here and ship the meat overseas."

"How can people do that?" Ryan's voice filled with horror. "Horses are such beautiful animals."

"I know. With the donation we'll buy as many horses as we can. Then we'll find adoptive homes for them."

"I never knew this kind of thing happened. How awful." Stacy glanced at Avery. "How can I help? Can I make a donation to the shelter?"

"I'll always take money, or you could come with us to the auction and bid on horses yourself. If you, Colt and I all bid that would help keep the prices up and knock out a lot of the meat packers. They want to get the horses dirt cheap."

"I should update the website to let people know how they can help, and that the shelter will have horses available for adoption," Reed said.

"I'll send out something on Facebook," Jess added. "Ryan, you can help me with that. I'll also do a blog on the subject for the shelter."

They thankfully spent the rest of the meal discussing Healing Horses, Avery's work at the shelter and Reed's business. All safe topics. Stacy opened up and talked about Maggie's movie and her role. "People are calling the movie a female *Bonanza* for the twenty-first century. If it does well at the box office, who knows, it could lead to a series."

"I think Maggie's movie will be a blockbuster. Everybody's always talking about how great cowboys are, how they're the backbone of the West and all that kind of stuff, but nobody ever shows how strong the women are here," Jess said.

Avery nodded toward her mom. "Look at Mom. She's a perfect example of that."

"I've had a lot of help running my ranch from my kids." Nannette, beaming from her daughter's compliment, turned toward Stacy. "I know you've done both movies and series. Which do you prefer, Stacy?"

"Movies are great, but a series means getting to stay in one place and money coming in consistently. Those things have a big appeal now that Ryan's living with me."

"That's what Maggie says. She and Griffin love doing *The Next Rodeo Cowboy,* but once my granddaughter is school age, they don't want to do all that traveling."

"Then we'll have to hope the movie is a huge success, and Maggie gets the chance to direct the series," Avery said.

"They could film it here," Reed added. "Now that would be a boost to the local economy."

After dinner, Jess and Ryan took Avery's laptop and went to the living room to work on getting the word out about the auction on social media. When Avery and Nannette started clearing the table, Stacy picked up her plate and Colt's. Then he picked up some glasses.

"While I appreciate your willingness to help, Colt, my kitchen's not that big," Avery said. "And if you help clean up, then Reed will feel like he has to help. Then we'll be tripping over each other like puppies trying to get to their mom at feeding time."

"She's right," Reed said. "You can help me update the website."

Colt glanced at Stacy, trying to sense if she felt comfortable being left alone. Then he shook himself mentally. What was he worried about? This was Nannette and Avery.

"Go," Stacy said, as if reading his mind. How did she do that?

As he and Reed walked through the apartment to his brother's office, Reed asked, "Are things really okay with Healing Horses? If you need money, RJ Industries can give you another grant."

"I don't need my baby brother bailing me out."

"Think of it as me paying you back for helping me reach adulthood. Hell, if it hadn't been for you either Dad would've killed me, or I'd be in jail for killing him."

When his brother settled in at his desk, Colt sank into the wing chair in the corner of the room. "Damn, Reed. Getting into that fight with Carpenter scared the daylights out of me. With our history and the way Dad was—"

"You are nothing like that bastard."

"You didn't see me at Halligan's. I'm not sure I've ever been that mad."

"He started the fight. You didn't go out looking for one. Remember how our old man used to do that?" Anger filled Reed's gaze, but the emotion was different now. No, it wasn't exactly anger. More regret and resignation. "Some days I would look at him and know it was going to be a rough one. The look that he was spoiling for a fight was in his eyes. We're not like that."

Certainty rang out in Reed's voice, and Colt knew he was right. Despite his fight with Carpenter, he wasn't like his father. That didn't mean the feelings Stacy stirred up in him that night didn't leave him shaking in his boots. "Thanks. I needed to hear that. How did we turn out okay when he was such a dick?"

"I had you and the McAlisters' house to escape to. You had Lynn."

Wow. The words knocked Colt harder than an angry bull. Sure, he'd loved his wife, but had part of her allure been her family? Its stability, the calm that radiated her household? Lynn's house became his shelter amid the storm of his life. Had he used Lynn as an escape? Had that been another reason why they didn't make it?

What did it matter now? No use in feeling guilty when he couldn't change anything.

"Dinner was interesting. Stacy really gets under your skin." Reed pulled up the shelter's website. "I wondered what was going on between you two when I heard about what happened at Halligan's. I've never seen a woman light a fire under you like Stacy did when the two of you were arguing about her paying your fine. Not even Lynn got you that riled up."

His brother didn't know the half of it. Not that Colt planned on admitting the fact.

Play dumb.

"There's nothing between me and Stacy."

Reed laughed, and not just a little chuckle. No. A full out belly laugh. "How could you say that with a straight face?'"

Discipline learned from years in the military.

But he couldn't deny it. Stacy annoyed him more than any woman he'd ever met, and yet he admired her. Her spunk, her fortitude. The courage it took her to get anywhere near a horse after one killed her father. He liked how she spoke her mind. He thought of their earlier discussion tonight. No doubt about it, a man knew what she was thinking because she held nothing in.

Lynn had been the opposite. She never said what she thought, preferring instead to let him guess. Usually wrong. No, she held everything in and then one day she'd blast him out of the water with how mad she was. That's what happened with their marriage. He'd sensed for a while that she was unhappy and brought up the subject a couple of times. She smiled and said nothing was wrong. He'd known better, but hadn't wanted to push. To tell the truth, he hadn't wanted to know how bad things were. Then one day she waltzed in, said she'd been miserable for years and left. No talking about it. No giving him a chance to change. She'd given up on him.

He couldn't see Stacy giving up on anything or anyone.

"I think it's great that you're interested in a woman. It's about time you came back among the living male population."

He stared at Reed. "What's that supposed to mean?"

"You've been a monk since Lynn left. Is that what you really want? To spend the rest of your life alone?"

The last thing Colt needed was someone else to worry about, and that's what happened with relationships. All he wanted was a calm, boring life, without any further entanglements. He needed a romantic relationship like a farmer needed to milk a bull. Plus he

had Jess to consider. He couldn't risk bringing someone into her life who might leave her. She'd dealt with
so much in her life. She couldn't handle any more loss
and Stacy would leave.

"I'm happy for you and Avery, but I'm already a
onetime loser. That was enough for me. Only an idiot
with a track record like mine would go there again."

"Who said anything about marriage? Go out on a
date."

"I'm not sure I remember what to do. I only dated
one girl before I started dating Lynn and that was when
I was sixteen."

"Suffering from performance anxiety?"

After the other night? No way. His body remembered exactly how to react to a woman and what to do
with one. That was the problem.

"Things have changed a whole helluva lot since
then," he said.

"Just go out and have some fun. Go to dinner. A
movie, whatever. Anything but taking her to a family
dinner." Reed shook his head. "What were you thinking?"

"It wasn't my idea. It was my daughter's."

How did a guy just date and have fun? If there
wasn't any chemistry with a woman he might as well
go out with his buddies instead. If there was a spark between them, then how did he keep from wanting more?
No thanks. Dating sounded like a recipe for disaster.

"I don't know why we're talking about this. Stacy's
only going to be around for a few weeks. Once her
brother's done with therapy and she finishes the movie
she'll hightail it back to L.A."

"That's perfect. You can have a good time with both

of you knowing nothing else can come of it. That's a great way for you to get your feet wet."

"What about Jess? She got attached to Avery pretty quick when you two started dating. What if she does the same with Stacy? I don't know if she could take getting close to Stacy and then having her leave."

"If you're worried about Jess dealing with it, talk with her."

"Talk with my teenage daughter about my dating a woman? That's just what I need."

"You're thinking too much. Jess knows Stacy isn't sticking around, right?" Colt nodded. "Then it shouldn't be a problem. Trust me on this. What harm could having a little fun do?"

Somehow Colt didn't think things would be that simple.

"You don't have to help clean up, Stacy," Avery said once Colt and Reed left. "You're a guest. Mom and I can handle it."

She didn't want to be a guest.

When she'd said how Travis wouldn't let her leave the dance floor, both women understood what she'd felt. Compassion had filled their eyes, and Nannette had shown a mother's concern. Would Andrea have cared if she knew what happened at Halligan's? Really cared about her and how scared she'd been? Something told Stacy all Andrea would've been more concerned about was how to turn what happened into a publicity op.

Her heart skipped a beat. She wanted to belong.

"Helping will give me a chance to apologize to both

of you for the way I acted the last time I was in town," Stacy said as she followed the women into the kitchen.

"No hard feelings." Nannette carried plates to the sink. "Griffin was as much to blame for what happened on that show as anyone else."

"You're right about that," Avery added. "If he'd told Maggie he loved her before the finale, things would've been so much better."

"He wasn't ready to admit that then." Nannette turned to Stacy, a glint in her eye as if she were about to share a secret. "My children can be a little hard-headed."

"Mom, I'm right here."

"I know you are, dear." Nannette kissed her daughter on the cheek. "I love you, but you know I'm right."

Love filled the small kitchen as it had at the dinner. Deep. Constant. Unfailing. Stacy looked away.

"I wasn't being hardheaded. I was being cautious with Reed." Avery pointed to the stove. "Would you hand me that pot, Stacy?"

She nodded and retrieved the item. "I'm glad things worked out for Griffin and Maggie. When I've seen them together on the set they seem very happy. Now that's the only way to find love on a reality show and have it last."

"I was right," Avery said, a huge grin on her face. "I never thought you were on that silly show expecting to find love."

"How anyone who watches that show can expect couples to stay together longer than the time it takes to boil water is beyond me," Nannette added.

"You'd be surprised how many people believe that's

really why I went on the show." She explained about how she'd needed to revive her career.

"You've changed since you were here before," Avery said.

Lately, she felt as if that was a lifetime ago. "My life's different than it was then." When she'd met Avery and Nannette her career had been everything. Andrea's second husband had taken her to the cleaners, and she'd turned to retail therapy to cope. The money flew out faster than the Concord, and Andrea started having trouble paying her bills. Feeling the added financial pressure to supplement her mother's finances to keep a roof over Ryan's head, Stacy needed the steady income a series offered. Then Ryan had the accident and he moved in with her. Things like that changed a woman fast. "*I* was different then."

"What do you think of Colt?" Nannette asked as she wiped the kitchen counter.

What a complicated question.

No, it wasn't. The answer was simple. *He's wonderful. Honest, dependable and sexier than a man had a right to be.*

"He's a great father, and he's helping Ryan so much. The work he does at Healing Horses has amazed me. He's really making a difference in people's lives."

"That's not an answer to the question. I asked what *you* thought of *him*." Nannette's knowing gaze drilled into Stacy.

Too bad. That's my story, and I'm sticking to it.

"He's a good man. I was thankful he was there at Halligan's."

"He got that from his mother. She was a good woman." Nannette shook her head. "I still can't believe we didn't know what hell those boys went through after their mother died."

Avery explained how Colt and Reed's mother died after falling down the stairs when Colt was twelve. Before her death, their mother shielded her sons from her husband's temper and his fists as much as she could. "Reed told me Colt could let a lot of what their dad said and did slide, but Reed always argued with their father. That made things worse. Colt was the one who calmed the disagreements down or stepped in when things got really bad between Reed and his dad. Reed swears Colt kept the two of them from killing each other."

The strength of character it took to survive what life dumped on Colt astounded her. No wonder he protected Jess so fiercely, and no wonder he'd been so appalled by getting into a fight. An abusive father, an unfaithful wife, a tour in Afghanistan where who knows what horrors he'd witnessed, and none of that broke him. The fact that he still possessed a kindness, a gentleness, spoke of his nature, and now she understood why his eyes sometimes held the look of an old soul.

She'd started falling down a slippery slope with Colt. She couldn't help admire him, but she couldn't think about what it would be like to have a man of such strength, such courage in her life. She couldn't imagine him as a soft place to fall when life left her battered and bruised, because if she did, it would be so easy to fall in love with Colt.

And that she refused to do.

Chapter 10

After cleaning the kitchen everyone congregated in the living room where the teenagers had started playing video games with Colt and Reed watching.

"I hate to be the one to end the party, but I had an early-morning shoot today, and it's catching up with me."

Ryan and Jess paused their game and started complaining.

"Do we have to leave? It's Friday night…"

"It's only ten o'clock."

"To avoid an inevitable heated discussion or pulling rank, I'll take Stacy home," Colt said.

Then Nannette said she would drop the teenagers off when she left. That settled, he and Stacy headed for the car.

After two minutes of silence in the car, Colt turned to her. "Did something happen in the kitchen?"

"We just talked girl talk while we cleaned up. Nothing major."

Nothing other than I realized how easily I could get attached to you and your family and had a mini panic attack.

Heady and dangerous stuff. The night had been eye-opening and exhausting. Being part of the Montgomery/McAlister clan had been overwhelming and wonderful, but now came time to face reality again. While she could enjoy belonging for the night, that was all she could have. She had a life and responsibilities. Ones that didn't mesh with life in Colorado.

"I'm sorry Reed brought up what happened at Halligan's. I know it made you uncomfortable. He was so busy getting his digs in at me, he didn't see that."

"I wish you'd let me pay for your fines."

"We closed that discussion."

No, he had. She decided not to push the issue. She could always make an anonymous donation to Healing Horses to balance the scales with him when her finances leveled out.

"You don't have to go to the auction."

"Ryan sounded so excited about going. I'd hate to disappoint him."

"Just because you don't go doesn't mean he can't tag along with me and Jess."

"I really shouldn't go. I haven't had a chance to learn the changes in my lines for tomorrow night's shoot." Who was she trying to convince, him or her? Tonight had taught her a lesson. Friendship with Colt wouldn't be easy. Or satisfying. It was like trying to eat half a cookie. The little taste only left her wanting the whole treat.

"I understand. Work has to come first. I'll have Jess text Ryan about picking him up. You'll have the day to yourself."

As she jumped out of Colt's truck she realized she'd made the sensible choice deciding not to attend the auction. No use pressing her face against the store window when she couldn't afford to buy anything. Doing that only made her ache for what she couldn't have, but if she'd made the right decision, how come she felt so lousy?

After the dinner at Avery and Reed's, Stacy flipped a switch inside her head. She refused to get attached to Colt and Jess.

Instead of chatting and joking with him before the session started, she helped Ryan prepare. At first Colt appeared confused by her reserved attitude and tried to tease her out of it. He tried so hard to get her to talk to him. He'd even gone so far as to ask her why she'd changed. She'd fobbed him off with a lame comment about having a lot on her mind. The wounded look in his soft gaze nearly did her in, but eventually he quit trying, and that left her feeling even worse. What had she expected? That he'd fling her over his shoulder, carry her off and demand she tell him what was going on?

Despite days of rain putting them behind schedule, Stacy was pleased with how the movie was going. Colt had been right. Becoming more comfortable around horses improved her performance. She felt more at ease and identified with her character better, resulting in what she felt was her best work.

Now to catch up and avoid added financial costs,

Maggie lengthened their filming hours, leaving Stacy with little time for anything other than work and Ryan's therapy. That meant they didn't go into town much and helped her avoid running into Colt.

The only good thing to occur over the past few weeks was the amazing physical progress Ryan had made. His balance and control of his legs improved enough that for short periods of time he'd traded the walker for a cane. The hope was with continued horsemanship and physical therapy and a lot of hard work he could eventually get rid of the walker completely.

Remembering what she'd learned about Colt from Avery and Nannette strengthened her resolve to keep her promise to Jess. About keeping her and Colt's relationship on the friendship level, but oh, how the man invaded her dreams, and not in a friendship way.

This morning she woke up from a doozie. In this one instead of Jess interrupting them the night of the fight at Halligan's, she and Colt continued their romantic play. They explored each other's bodies until they both lay naked together on the couch. Just as he'd been about to enter her fevered flesh, Stacy woke up, disappointed and aching.

To top off her day, the shoot had run long, forcing her to call Colt to ask if they could push back Ryan's therapy a half an hour. After a lecture about this being her one free pass and she'd better not ask to reschedule again, he agreed. If she hurried, she'd have time to grab takeout for her and Ryan. They could sit, eat and catch up before they headed to Colt's. They hadn't done much of that lately.

"Stacy, I need to talk to you in my office before you leave," Maggie called out.

"Sure thing. I'll be there in a minute." So much for getting to sit and eat with Ryan before his therapy. She pulled out her phone and texted her brother to make some mac and cheese or something for his dinner because she was running way late.

Maggie and Griffin lived in a simple wood-and-brick, ranch-style house they'd just built on the far edge of Twin Creeks Ranch. When she'd settled into the wing chair across from Maggie's desk, the director slid script pages across the smooth walnut surface. "We've had to make some changes to the scene where Brandon's character notifies you that the bank is threatening to foreclose on his ranch."

Script changes happened all the time, but the director never called an actor into the office to discuss them unless the alterations were substantial, or she thought the actor would balk at the modifications.

Stacy's hands shook as she picked up the papers and scanned the sheets. Instead of informing her in the living room, they'd changed the scene to outdoors. She was to be working on the ranch, on a horse when her boyfriend rides up on a four-wheeler.

"I hate to do this to you, knowing what happened to your dad, and especially since we talked about this before filming, but the scene has so much more impact this way."

Stacy nodded, her entire body numb as she tried to absorb the shock. Walking beside a horse to help Ryan in his therapy sessions was one thing. Crawling on top of one was something else entirely.

"If you absolutely can't get on a horse, we can use a stunt woman and editing can mix those shots with close-ups of you."

Stacy clasped her hands together in her lap to keep them still. She was being silly. All she had to do was sit on the horse and then dismount when she saw her boyfriend arriving. Simple, but her mind couldn't help but dredge up memories of the shoot with her father so long ago. Cannons blasted. Horses reared. Her father tumbled to the ground. She pinched her eyes shut and tried to shove aside her memories. An image of Colt smiling at her with pride when she'd accepted the lead rope from him came to her.

"I'd prefer not to do the scene that way, but if we have to we can." Maggie's calm voice pulled Stacy back.

Volunteering at Healing Horses had taught her she had nothing to fear. This was a different movie. This wouldn't be a battle scene with loud noises and gun blasts. She could do this.

"I'm willing to try, but can I ask for a couple of things?"

"Anything."

"Can we keep the crew to a minimum?"

Maggie nodded.

What else did she need to be able to pull this off? Colt.

"I'd like Colt Montgomery to be there, and for him to pick the horse for me to ride. He trained me to be a volunteer in his therapy program." He wouldn't let anything happen to her. "I'd also like him to talk to the crew about what can make a horse skittish. That's why my dad died. The loud noises spooked the horse."

"I think that's a great idea. I can call Colt tonight."

No, she needed to ask him to do this. She needed to see in his eyes that he knew she could handle this.

She needed his calm reassurance that he would keep her safe. "I'll see him in a little while at Ryan's therapy. I'll ask him."

"The plan is to shoot the scene on Saturday."

Stacy nodded. Today was Thursday. Part of her wished she had more time to prepare, but then she'd only have more time to worry. Colt would make sure nothing went wrong.

If he agreed to help her. As she left Maggie's office and headed to her car Stacy nibbled on her lower lip. How could she ask him to do this for her when she'd all but ignored him lately? Especially when he'd looked at her so often with that old-soul look filling his gaze?

I hadn't wanted to hurt him, but I've done just that.

And now she planned on asking for his help. She'd be lucky if he'd even talk to her.

Ryan's therapy sessions had become torture for Colt. He'd missed Stacy. Talking with her. Joking around. Just being with her. He hadn't realized how much he looked forward to seeing her each week until their relationship changed after the dinner at Reed and Avery's house. He'd replayed the night over in his head, but no matter how hard he tried, he couldn't figure out what could've spooked her.

Part of him wanted to know what happened, what caused her to shut down on him. When he'd asked a couple of weeks ago, she'd out-and-out lied and told him nothing was wrong, confusing him even more. Her open and honest nature was one of the things he admired about her. Why would she start pulling punches now? Common sense told him to quit digging, because sometimes it was better not knowing, but he couldn't let go.

Today was even worse. Not only did she seem distant, she appeared as skittish as a new foal. Ryan's session dragged on, but Colt managed to get through it. When they reached the barn, Jess stood waiting. She and Ryan had become almost inseparable, and whenever he had therapy she met him and together they groomed Chance.

When Colt turned to leave, anxious to escape the tension surrounding him and Stacy, she said, "Could we talk for a minute?"

He froze at the sound of her voice. "I take it this means you're talking to me again."

She nodded. "I'm sorry. Our shooting schedule's been grueling lately. I've been tired and haven't been myself."

The silence he could take, but not the lying. He expected better of her. He was done playing games and pussy footing around the situation. "That's crap and we both know it. What's really going on? Do I have BO or bad breath?"

She smiled at his teasing. She had the best smile.

"Can we just forget it and go back to being friends?"

Having her in his life as a friend was better than this damned polite-acquaintances crap. If that was true, then how come his stomach fell when she'd said the words? "I didn't know we'd stopped being friends."

"Good. I'm glad that's settled." Stacy shifted her stance and her head bobbed up and down like a bobble-head doll. What was going on? "I was also wondering if your offer to go riding was still open."

Something was up. It didn't take a rocket scientist to

know that. This time he had to know. "What changed your mind?"

Guilt flashed in her expressive eyes. "I need your help."

His heart sank like a rock tossed into a pond, sending ripples of disappointment through him. He'd been silly to think Stacy changed her mind because she wanted to be with him. Instead she'd asked to go back to the way things were because she needed something from him, and that hurt like a kick in the teeth from an angry stallion.

That's what had kept him and Lynn together so long. She'd needed him. She'd never been on her own. She went from being her parents' daughter to his wife. He took care of everything. As a baby, when Jess got fussy, he spent hours rocking her because Lynn got impatient and frustrated. When Lynn became unhappy with her job at the real-estate management company when a new manager took over, he took on extra work as a hand at Charlie Logan's ranch so she could quit. Then after she'd left him, she'd wanted to come home because she needed someone to take care of her again.

But Stacy's actions hurt even more because she'd always been so open with him.

"Maggie gave me a script change today. I've got to sit on a horse for a scene. I told her I could do it, but now I'm not so sure, and I certainly don't want the first time I get on a horse to be the day we're filming the scene."

He thought about telling Stacy he couldn't help her. That's what he should do.

He couldn't fret about her. He had his daughter to worry about and a therapy program that could financially fall apart at any time. He needed more responsibility like he needed a hole in his work boots.

"I'd like you to talk to the crew. Tell them how to act around horses and what makes them skittish. I know I'm asking a lot, but would you select the horse for me to ride?" Fear darkened her eyes to the color of a cold mountain spring, but she stubbornly pointed her delicate chin in the air as if she refused to let her emotions get the best of her.

All he wanted to do was take her in his arms and hold her until the fear went away.

"I can pick out your horse. The rest will take time away from my work here."

"I'll pay you for your time." She inched closer. Her subtle floral scent swirled around him bringing with it memories of when he'd held her. "I know what happened to my dad was a fluke, just one of those weird times when everything goes wrong and someone gets hurt, but I'm so scared. The real reason I want you to be there when we shoot the scene is I'd feel so much better if you were there. I know you won't let anything happen to me. I don't trust anyone but you to keep me safe. Please."

Damn. She had to go and say that.

I don't trust anyone but you to keep me safe.

How could he say no to that? Only a complete ass would turn her down knowing what had happened to her father and how scared she had to be.

"Okay. When's the shoot?"

She flung herself at him, throwing her arms around him, and hugged him. Her dynamite curves pressed up against him. At that moment, with the happy hormones blasting through his system she could've asked him to lasso the moon for her and damned if he wouldn't have said yes.

"Great. The shoot's on Saturday. Could we get together tomorrow for the riding lesson?"

"Sure. We can start with walking around the corral and then head out on one of the tourist trails."

The little voice inside him called him every kind of fool, and said he'd just made a big mistake, but what the hell? He'd made so many in his life. What did one more matter?

Chapter 11

When Stacy arrived at Colt's ranch the next day, she found him in the corral saddling a horse the color of her favorite Starbucks drink, a caramel macchiato. Another equally large sable-colored animal stood already saddled nearby. The sight of Colt, all Western male goodness, his biceps flexing as he lifted the saddle and placed it on the horse sent her pulse as high as the elevation.

You promised Jess there wouldn't be anything between you and Colt but friendship.

That didn't mean she couldn't appreciate his obvious assets, and the man possessed those in spades.

He was so a part of the land around him, so real, so solid, and not just in a physical sense. When was the last time she'd had someone in her life she could count on? Someone she could call on in the middle of the night, who'd actually answer the phone?

Not since her father died.

She had friends, most of them actresses in the business, but she doubted any of them would be there for her, and the men in her life had come and gone. They got tired of playing second to her career, and her mother and brother for her attention and time.

Colt hadn't been so easy to drive away. Though Lord knows she'd tried. She glanced at the gray clouds as she walked to the corral. "The weather forecast said there's a chance of rain today."

"It's supposed to hold off until tonight."

"That's not what the weatherman on channel eight said."

"You're just using that as an excuse not to go riding."

Of course she was. She'd told Maggie she'd try because she wanted to do what was best for the movie, and while she acted confident when she'd asked Colt for his help the other day, the closer she came to getting up on a horse, the better the idea of letting a stunt woman handle the situation sounded.

"Are you chickening out?"

His taunt stung. She'd never been one to shy away from a challenge or let someone down, and that's what she'd do to Maggie if she backed out now. She'd have to find a stunt woman which would delay the movie further when filming was already behind schedule. That cost the production company money.

"I don't want to get rained on, that's all."

He chuckled. The deep rich sound tickled her senses. The man had the infuriating habit of calling bull whenever she tried to slide something past him. "Next thing you'll be telling me is that the grass is orange." He patted the horse on the neck. "Come over and meet Bess."

"That's the horse you expect me to ride? She's huge."

"In this case, size really doesn't matter. She's the sweetest, most even-tempered horse we've got, and she's practically geriatric, but she's still got her looks. Don't you, girl?"

The horse whinnied in response. Stacy smiled. The man had a way about him.

"I hope time is as easy on my looks as it's been to Bess. She's still beautiful." The horse possessed a graceful beauty. Hopefully her heart matched her looks.

Stacy opened the corral gate and forced herself to step inside. A gust of wind sent a cloud of dust swirling around her.

It's an omen. The universe is trying to tell me something.

"You'll be fine. Tourists do this all the time. Most of them city slickers like you who've never been on a horse."

"Do I look that scared?"

"Like you're about to shoot the rapids in a barrel." He motioned her to come closer. "I'll hold Bess steady. Grab the saddle horn and put your left foot in the stirrup. Then push off with your right foot and pull yourself into the saddle."

"Why do I think that's not going to be as easy as it sounds?"

"Again, tourists manage this all the time. Half of them not in anywhere the shape you are."

He thought she was in shape? He'd noticed? The heat of her blush crept down her neck.

Remember, just friends.

Oh, but being more could be so much fun.

Trying to focus she grabbed the saddle horn, and after a minute of struggling she managed to get her boot in the stirrup. Then she pulled. She went up, and then came right back down. "I knew getting in the saddle wasn't as easy as you made it sound."

"Try again."

She did, with similar results, except for this time when she started to come back down, his hand cupped her butt and propelled her upward. She glanced down at him from her lofty perch. "Cheap way to cop a feel."

This time he blushed. "Was it as good for you as it was for me?"

It sure was.

She loved how he made her laugh. Why did it feel as though she did so little of that when she was home? Then she glanced down at him. She'd sworn he was joking, and yet, she sensed in a way he wasn't.

Because of his eyes. She knew desire when she saw it in a man's gaze, and her body responded. Heat charged through her, awakening places inside her that had been dormant for so long.

Then Bess nudged him and the spell broke.

She glanced at the mountains around her. Such evidence of endurance. A constant presence. So much like the man beside her.

"How's the view from up there?"

Colt's question made her realize where she was. She waited for panic to slam into her, but the emotion never came. "I'm on a horse, and I'm in one piece."

He smiled at her and she swore she now saw pride in his gaze. "You sure are."

"The view from up here's amazing."

"It's pretty fine from where I stand, too."

Men often told her she was beautiful, but there was something different about Colt's compliments. Maybe because his felt more genuine, and he seemed to admire her as a person. For who she was on the inside.

"Why sir, you'll send a girl's head spinning with pretty words like that," she teased, feeling desperate to break the attraction pulling them together.

She'd told Jess there wouldn't be anything but friendship between them. The words had tumbled out of her easy enough. Too bad following through was turning out to be tougher than she expected.

He mounted his horse and turned to her. "I'll lead the way. Bess knows to follow. Tap her flanks with your heels and she'll follow Jax here."

A twinge of fear rippled through her when Bess shifted under her. "Tell me again how tourists do this all the time and how safe this is."

"We haven't lost a city slicker around here in years. You'll be fine." He flashed her a confident you-can-do-this smile. "If you get scared or want to come back, just say so."

Determined not to let fear rule her, she mumbled a quick prayer and nudged Bess forward. For the first fifteen minutes or so of the ride Stacy gripped the reins so tight her fingers went numb, but the farther they rode, the more she relaxed.

As the ranch faded from view, the foliage grew denser and mountains enveloped them. The stillness surrounded her. The last time she'd been in Colorado she'd missed the city. Its entertainment, its hectic pace with nonstop activity, but not this time. Now she found a peace here her soul craved.

She hadn't realized how much caring for Ryan and

dealing with Andrea had weighed on her until she'd gotten out from under some of the pressure. While her mother could still call, the distance kept Andrea from being able to expect Stacy to "pop over" as her mother would say, and deal with every imagined tragedy.

And Colt had worked wonders with Ryan. Her brother was happier than she'd ever seen him. He talked about friends and socialized more since they'd arrived in Estes Park than he had in the entire time since his accident. His grades had improved and he'd started talking about attending college again.

How could she go back to that bleak life? How could she cope with being that strong again and taking care of everything alone?

Soon she'd have to find a way to do just that, but until then she refused to think about what was to come. Instead she'd concentrate on finishing the movie and enjoying her time here. She deserved that.

After an hour or so of riding, they came upon a clearing. Memories stirred within Colt as he stared at the remnants of a fort he and Reed had built as kids. Their hideout. The fortress where they'd gone to escape their father and his tirades.

Here they'd read books, played cards, or just hung out in the quiet. They could forget for a while and be kids.

He stopped and glanced over his shoulder at Stacy. "I'm ready for lunch. How about you?"

"I'm amazed how hungry I am."

After he dismounted, he walked to where Stacy waited, still seated on Bess. "You need help getting down?"

She shook her head. "Let me try. I would like you to hold her steady, though."

As he stood beside her, his hands on Bess, he said, "Do you realize how far you've come?"

She beamed down at him. "I think I can really do that scene now. Thanks to you."

"You did all the hard work."

"I understand now how the horse therapy helps. There's something about riding that is freeing."

"These programs can help so many people. Ones with mental disabilities. People like Ryan with physical injuries. It's also helping vets who suffer from PTSD." Stacy waited while he retrieved the blanket he'd tied behind his saddle. Then he shook out the old wool and placed it on the ground. He told her to get settled while he returned to Jax and grabbed his saddlebags containing their lunch.

"You're making such a difference for so many people."

When he turned the sight of Stacy sitting under a canopy of Aspen trees, her face bright, her eyes sparkling nearly bowled him over. She looked so at ease, so right sitting here on his land. Maybe this hadn't been such a good idea. He'd better find some self-control real quick.

As he sat on the far edge of the blanket and placed the leather bags between them, she said, "Thank you for helping me prepare for the scene."

He unpacked their simple picnic and handed Stacy a sandwich. "It's egg salad. I figured that was safe. I know you don't eat red meat, but I wasn't sure about chicken or turkey."

"Thanks for remembering. For the record, I do eat

chicken and turkey." She took a bite. "This is good. What restaurant did you get the food from?"

"Now I'm insulted. I made lunch."

"Wow. A man who can cook and keeps a house clean enough it could pass the white glove test. How is it that some smart woman hasn't snatched you up?"

"Maybe I just haven't found one I wanted to let grab me."

Until you.

Unable to resist, he leaned over and kissed Stacy. Lightly at first, but when she responded, he couldn't help but deepen the contact.

Thunder rumbled in the distance, and Stacy practically jumped away from him. "We shouldn't have done that."

"If you're waiting for an apology, you're not going to get one."

More thunder rolled toward them. "Still sticking with your weather prediction?" Stacy teased, easing the tension inside him, but not the physical ache.

He glanced at the sky. The dark clouds on the horizon would be rolling in soon. "We need to head back." He scooped up the remnants of their lunch, shoved everything in his saddlebags and stood. Briefly he considered holding out his hand to help Stacy up, but changed his mind. The less they touched the better.

Ten minutes later, the sprinkles started. The temperature, which had been warm and pleasant when they headed out on the trail, dropped at least twenty degrees when the front moved in. The wind picked up, now coming in from the north.

"I thought you said the rain was supposed to hold off," Stacy chided.

"Guess it's a good thing I'm not a weatherman. Take the path coming up on your right. It'll get us back to the ranch quicker."

Then the heavens opened up, drenching them. He glanced back at Stacy. Worry lined her forehead. "Bess is used to walking in weather like this. She's sure-footed, so there's nothing to fret over. We'll be back to the ranch in a few minutes."

Stacy patted the horse's neck. "I trust her. I don't think I'll ever be someone who wants to dash around on a horse hell-for-leather—isn't that the expression?"

He nodded, unable to speak. The rain had soaked through her clothes. Her pale blue T-shirt left almost nothing to the imagination, outlining her lacy bra. The cold had hardened her nipples. His body hardened in response.

"But I could see her and I taking a leisurely afternoon stroll every once and a while."

Sure she was more than easy on the eyes and her body could keep a man busy for months exploring every exciting inch of her, but those things weren't what he found most intoxicating. Her grit. Her tenacity. The way she never let anything get the best of her. He couldn't help but admire her. She'd faced her worst fear. She wasn't some dainty little thing that folded when a strong wind blasted her. Those things drew him like a stallion to his favorite mare.

When they reached the ranch, he dismounted and turned to Stacy. As he helped her off her horse, he said, "You know where my room is. Go inside, dry off and get warmed up. I'll see to the horses."

"No, you're cold and wet, too. I can help. Just tell me what to do."

They led the horses into the barn and down the first row of stalls. "Bess's is the third one down."

While she took Bess, he put Jax in his stall and removed his saddle and bridle. After he set the items in the aisle, he joined Stacy to help with the other horse. "Do you remember where the tack room is?"

"Is that the room where you keep all the horse gear? Where it's all neatly arranged by the horse's name?" He nodded, and Stacy continued. "Has anyone ever mentioned you take organization to a whole new level?"

"You wouldn't say that if you had to spend ten minutes finding the right bridle." He handed her the bridle and told her Jax's was outside his stall. "While you put those away, I'll see to the saddles." *And work on getting my hormones back under control before I dry my clothes from the inside out.*

Five minutes later they sloshed into his house. By the time they reached Colt's room, Stacy knew what it felt like to be a Popsicle. She'd never been so cold in her entire life. She wrapped her arms around her middle, not only for warmth but because her shirt had become completely see-through. At least she'd put on her best ice-blue Victoria's Secret bra today. She'd be even more embarrassed if she was wearing some industrial white thing.

"My bathrobe's still hanging on the bathroom door. When you get that on, toss out your clothes. I'll change out here."

Standing in his bedroom, his presence overwhelmed her. His wet shirt revealed the definition of his rock-hard abs and broad shoulders. His jeans molded to his strong thighs and she refused to think about what else they revealed. So much for being cold. Not a problem now. She practically ran into the bathroom, slamming the door behind her, wincing at the harsh sound.

As she peeled off her soggy clothes her imagination went crazy. All she could think about was Colt a few feet away shedding his clothes, revealing those amazing abs and everything else. Her jeans hit the floor with a thwack and she reached for his robe. She'd thought the last time she slipped into this garment it was intimate. Today was past intimate.

She'd tried so hard to stay away from Colt. To keep from feeling anything for him, but how could she when he'd done so much for Ryan since they'd arrived? He'd given her brother that steady male presence he craved. Ryan had changed so much since they arrived. Not only had he improved physically, going from needing a walker to occasionally only needing a cane, but he'd grown in confidence.

But Colt had helped her in so many ways, too. She enjoyed his company and how he made her laugh. He kept her from taking life too seriously, from becoming overwhelmed. She didn't feel as if she had to always be strong when she was with him, and now, after she'd basically ignored him for weeks, he helped her overcome her fear of horses.

Over a few short weeks, he'd become a part of her life, and she feared she was falling in love with him.

No.

She couldn't. Loving someone started out all sunshine and butterflies, but her relationships never lasted. Loving led to being vulnerable, to disappointment, to unfulfilled expectations and responsibilities.

A knock on the bathroom door broke through her thoughts. "You got those wet clothes off yet?"

After mumbling something like an apology for taking so long, she scooped up her clothes, opened the door and tossed them out. While he went to throw their clothes in the dryer, she located a hair dryer. When she finished with that task, she sat on the toilet. What else could she do to avoid facing Colt? The two of them together with her dressed in his robe? Not a good idea.

A knock sounded on the door again. "You okay in there?"

Startled, she slid off the toilet and landed on the floor with a thud and a squeal, banging her hip in the process.

The door burst open and Colt filled the space. "What happened? Are you all right?"

"Just call me Grace."

He rushed forward to assist her, but she held up a hand to stop him. Once on her feet she took a couple of steps, but his robe tangled around her legs. She reached to free the material, lost her balance and she tumbled smack into Colt. His arms wrapped around her, steadying her.

Desire coursed through her. Lightning crackled closer outside as the storm moved in, mirroring the one brewing inside her.

Her hands cupped his cheeks, his rough stubble scratching her palms as she pulled his face down to hers. Her lips covered his, searching, asking, pleading.

She wanted to feel. She wanted to care. She wanted this man.

More than she'd ever wanted anything in her life. For however long she could have him, even if it was only for the afternoon.

Colt deepened the kiss. As he pressed against her

she felt the evidence of his desire. Her hands fumbled
with the buttons of his shirt, needing to explore more
of him. "I can't do this."

He pulled away, confusion and disappointment flaring in his gaze. "I understand."

"No. It's not what you're thinking. I want you. I can't
get these damned buttons undone."

His beaming masculine smile sent a new rush of
passion coursing through her. "Let me see what I can
do."

Unlike her, he made quick work of the task. Then
she slid his shirt off. Her hands caressed his firm flesh.
Who needed a gym if hard work could do this for a
man's body? Her lips found his again.

His callused hand slipped inside the robe, knead-
ing her breast, sending fire racing through her. She
moaned. The hoarse sound filled with need and longing startled her as the soft fabric slid down her body.
Lightning cracked outside and thunder rumbled toward
them. "A storm's rolled in."

"And not just outside. You're cold." He scooped her
into his arms and carried her to the bed. "Scoot under
the covers."

She slid between the sheets and then glanced at him
towering beside her. Scars dotted his magnificent chest,
but only added to his appeal. Testaments to his courage.

"Undress for me. I want to see you."

"You're so bossy."

"I'm sorry," she stammered, and clutched the blanket up around her chin.

"Nothing to apologize for. No one pushes you

around. I like knowing exactly what you want. I don't have to guess what you're thinking."

"Then strip."

"Yes, ma'am."

His fingers shook as he unbuckled his belt, and slowly lowered his zipper. His gaze locked on hers as he slid his jeans past his hips, revealing himself to her. The sight of him, strong, proud and pulsing with desire for her, fueled her need. An image of him like this, except wearing his cowboy hat, flashed in her mind. He looked so damned sexy in that hat. She'd have to ask him to pose like that for her. More thunder rattled around them. Or was that her heart?

Colt thought he'd come right then and there when Stacy told him to strip. As he kicked off his jeans, she licked her lips, and he closed his eyes, trying to harness his control before he embarrassed himself. Warms hands clasped his heated flesh as her lips moved over his chest.

For a moment he lost himself to his emotions, his desire. The fever built inside him, threatening to burn him to cinders. He needed her in his arms. He yanked back the blankets and practically pounced on her.

It had been so long, and making love had never been like this. Frenzied. Consuming. Real. He had to slow down, but he couldn't.

He suckled her breast while his hands found her heated core. Her moans echoed through him, fueling his ardor, driving him to heights he never knew existed. As he caressed her, her hands clutched his shoulders. Her teeth nipped at his neck.

"You're so beautiful, and not just on the outside."
He kissed her, his tongue mating with hers.

He felt the waves rock through her as she reached
her peak. Her nails dug into his shoulders. "Now. I
want you inside me now."

He stilled. Birth control. He didn't have anything.
"I didn't plan for this. It's been so long." He swallowed hard and told himself not to babble. "I don't
have a condom."

"It's your lucky day." She kissed him lightly and
smiled. The smile of a satisfied woman. Then she
crawled out of bed. As he stared at her beautiful body
displayed for him, he couldn't follow her train of
thought.

*That's because there isn't a drop of blood left going
to your brain.*

She found her purse on a chair, dug around inside
and retrieved a foil packet. "I have one."

A man had to love a woman who was prepared.

The thought ricocheted through him. Did he love
Stacy? He admired her. Lusted after her big-time. Appreciated her spunk, but love?

Then her frenzied hands were on him again, and he
forgot everything but her. His hands teased her sensitive flesh, needing to ignite her passion, but she shoved
him down on the bed and straddled him.

As she situated herself on his heated flesh, he rev-
eled in the pleasure coursing through him. They moved
together. He stared up into her gorgeous face, reveling
in the passion returning to expressive eyes. Passion for
him. Clear and mesmerizing. His gaze locked with hers
as he caressed her, bringing her to another peak. Only

then did he let go. Wave after wave crashed over him, breaking him and somehow putting him back together.

What had he done?

He'd connected with a woman on a level he never knew possible. Had he also made the biggest mistake of his life?

Don't go there. Savor this. Don't think beyond now.

While the storm inside them had subsided, the one outside hadn't. Lightning continued to slash across the sky and thunder rumbled around them.

He felt more content than he had in years. Being with Stacy felt right. The question was, where did they go from here? He cared for her, but he refused to examine his nagging thoughts about love. Right now his life couldn't take any more upheaval. Jess and his therapy program had to be his top concerns. The most he could offer Stacy was a casual relationship, but would that offend her? Make her think she was good enough to sleep with, but not worth any type of commitment?

Casual relationship. The phrase rubbed him the wrong way. He wasn't the love-'em-and-leave-'em type, and that's exactly what it felt like he was doing.

Thunder rumbled outside. He lay there fulfilled and content, Stacy's gentle curves nestled against him, heating him up all over again, and knew they should talk about what happened between them. Hell, they should've talked about where things were headed before they tumbled into bed, but he figured better late than never.

"I guess we just became more than friends," he joked, not knowing how else to bring up the subject.

"You heard that comment?"

"That and a little more. Thanks for what you said to Jess. I had no idea she was carrying around so much guilt over her mom. She and I had a great talk about everything after that. She really opened up to me, and we cleared the air about some things."

"She loves you so much."

He shook his head. "I still can't believe she asked you what your intentions were. I said while I appreciated the concern, that's not her job. I'm an adult and can take care of myself."

He failed to mention how damned embarrassing her conversation had been. No man should have to discuss his love life, or lack thereof, with his teenage daughter.

"I don't want you getting the wrong impression about what happened between us," Stacy said as she slid away from him. "I don't want you thinking I'm expecting anything from you. I'm usually not so impulsive. Not that I didn't enjoy what happened, I did. It was amazing, but there can't be anything other than something casual between us. Our lives are so different. We don't even live in the same state."

He noticed whenever she was nervous she talked a mile a minute. Good to know he wasn't the only one feeling uneasy.

"I wasn't about to get down on one knee, if that's what you were thinking." His words came out with a bite rather than as a lighthearted joke as he intended. Hadn't she said exactly what he'd been thinking? So why was his pride bruised? "We're both adults. We enjoy each other's company. There's nothing wrong with that."

"Except we're both responsible for a teenager."

What kind of example are we setting? The words hung unspoken between them, and where did they go from here?

Sleeping with each other once? They might be able to keep that from Jess and Ryan. Carrying off an affair? No way.

What were they going to do?

Lightning cracked close, too close, and before the light faded the deafening roar of thunder shook the walls. Colt jumped out of bed. "Damn. That hit something."

"Are you sure?"

He didn't answer, but scooped up his jeans off the floor where he'd dropped them beside the bed earlier. He shrugged them on and moved to the window. "The barn's on fire! I've got to get the horses out."

Then he bolted out the door.

Stacy leaped out of bed, her heart and mind racing. She dug through her purse again and located her phone. As she dashed through the house to retrieve her clothes from the dryer, she called 911. She explained the situation to the dispatcher and asked the woman to send the fire department. That done, Stacy dressed and ran outside after Colt.

The driving rain pelted her skin soaking her again as she raced for the barn. Flames licked at the back side of the structure's roof. At least it was the area farthest away from the horses. The barn door stood open. She darted inside. Horses' panicked shrieks filled the air. Smoke stung her nose and lungs. The gray haze burned her eyes.

As she ran toward the stalls, she scanned the area for Colt, finding him down the first row. "What can I do?"

"Get out. It's not safe in here."

"I'm not leaving you alone to deal with this. I won't let these animals die." *Or you.*

Something could fall on him. The smoke could get to him and no one would ever know. She refused to think about what else could happen.

Colt yanked open a stall door and Babe charged out. "Go away, Stacy. Call 911."

"I already did." She grabbed his arm. "We don't have time to argue. Tell me what to do, damn it."

"Open stall doors. The horses should get out on their own. If one won't I'll take care of it."

She nodded. "I'll get the other row."

He grabbed her hand. "You sure?"

She nodded and squeezed his hand before she ran off toward the other stalls. Wood being consumed crackled around them. Sweat poured down her face, blurring her vision as the heat increased. She pulled open a stall door, jumped back, watched the horse race out and moved on. Her breathing grew labored as she moved down the row.

When the last horse was free, Stacy ran back to where she'd left Colt. "Colt, are you done? Where are you?"

A horse's shrill screech of a panic cut through the fire's roar. "Go. I'll follow in a minute."

She hesitated at the far end of the row. No, she wouldn't leave until he went with her. As she ran down the aisle toward him she saw him struggling with a huge black horse. The animal pulled the rope from Colt's grasp and reared.

"Colt!"

Stacy's screams reverberated around her. All she could see was her father being crushed under a similar massive animal's hooves.

History was repeating itself.

Chapter 12

No. Stacy refused to let this happen again. She'd been too young to prevent her father from dying, but she *would* save Colt.

The horse's hooves pounded his chest, knocking him to his knees. His arms covered his head as he fought to stand. The animal reared again.

"No!" Stacy screamed as she waved her arms and ran. "Colt, tell me what to do."

In the few seconds it took her to reach him, he'd managed to stand and was pulling his bandana out of his back pocket. Then he grabbed the horse's lead rope and handed it to her. "Talk to him and hold on. If I can get his eyes covered, he should calm down."

"Hey, big boy. It's okay. I know you're scared. My dad used to sing to me when I was afraid." The words to *Put On a Happy Face* from one of her father's favorite musical, *Bye Bye Birdie,* flowed out of her, calming both her and the horse. The animal stopped pulling against her. His movements grew less frantic, until he calmed enough for Colt to tie the bandana around his eyes.

Then Colt took the rope from her. "Let's get the hell out of here."

Sirens screamed in the distance as Colt, with Stacy beside him, led the horse out of the barn to discover the storm had moved on. Rain sprinkled his skin as he opened the corral for the animal to join the other horses nervously milling around. Then everything hit him at once. How reckless she'd been. How he could've lost her, and how without her he'd more than likely be dead right now. He reached out and his soot-covered hands cupped her face as he kissed her lightly. Then he leaned his forehead against hers.

"Thank you for not following directions. If you'd listened to me and left when I told you to, I'd be dead."

He kissed her again and then interlocked his hand with hers to still their shaking. Fate could be brutally fickle and had a way of making a man see what really mattered in life.

"I wasn't going to let what happened to my dad happen to you."

She hadn't left him. She'd fought with him. The city woman, hotshot actress who when she'd arrived had been afraid to be near a horse, had battled a fire and her fear to not only to help save every animal, but him, as well.

"Are you okay? The horse kicked you in the chest."

"I'll be bruised and sore tomorrow, but I suspect the whole thing looked worse to you than it actually was." He looked toward the barn, as the firefighters worked to control the flames still licking at the barn. "I'd never have gotten all the horses out in time if you hadn't helped. You have got to be the strongest woman I've ever met. Damn woman, you're amazing."

"Tell me you have insurance," Stacy said as she, too, stared at the scorched barn, the firefighters having gotten the blaze under control.

"I do, but I've got a huge deductible. That was one of the ways I cut operating costs so I could get the program up and running sooner." He rubbed his forehead as his mind raced to list the things he'd need to do over the next few days. Call his insurance agent. Double-check his list of the barn's contents. Find someone to stable his horses until the barn was inhabitable again.

"I bet the community and anyone who's gone through your program will help you come up with the deductible. We can have a fund-raiser to raise the cash and replace anything insurance won't cover. Bring a bridle and help Healing Horses rebuild."

We. He liked the sound of that.

"That's a great idea."

"I'll work on jotting down some ideas. I can talk to Nannette to see what she thinks."

Had Lynn ever been this much a partner in his life and what mattered to him? He mentally shook himself. He had to stop thinking about his wife. She was dead and gone. That marriage was in the past. He'd told Stacy not to let what happened with her father affect her now. He needed to do the same. He had to let go of Lynn, of his anger and his disappointment. No more. He was done viewing the world though the haze

of his failed marriage. He was finished keeping everyone at arm's length.

Starting with Stacy. What a woman. She made him
feel like he wasn't alone, looked like a first-class diamond and was just as tough.

He wouldn't find a better woman if he searched for
the rest of his life. His heart expanded. He'd fallen in
love with Stacy. No doubt about it. As he listened to her
spin ideas for the fund-raising event, he didn't know
where his relationship with her would go, but he'd hold
on to her for as long as she was here and enjoy the ride.

The next morning when Colt arrived at the Twin Creeks
movie set along with Jess and Ryan, Stacy met them
near the barn. Seeing her dressed in Wranglers that
showed off her great curves, cowboy boots, her blond
hair pulled back in a ponytail, a cowboy hat perched
on her head sent a jolt through him. At first, he almost
didn't recognize her, but damn she looked fine. Almost
as good as she had in his bed yesterday afternoon.

All he wanted to do was put his arms around her and
tell her how lonely his bed had been last night without
her there with him.

How did other people juggle having a love life
and being a single parent? Someone ought to write a
manual. After Stacy greeted Jess and her brother, she
glanced at him, mumbled a greeting and blushed the
prettiest shade of pink. At least he wasn't the only one
who wasn't sure how to handle things this morning.

"You two are going to be bored," Stacy said to Ryan
and Jess. "Making movies isn't as glamorous as everything thinks. It's a lot of doing the same scene over
and over again."

"Maggie said she could use us as extras in the scene

that you're filming after you finish this one," Jess said, her young face beaming with excitement.

"Do you know where Maggie is?" Ryan asked. "She said to check in with her when we got here and she'd tell us what we're going to be doing."

Stacy pointed toward the trailer off to her right. "She should be in there double-checking things for the shoot."

Once the kids left, Colt considered bringing up what happened between them yesterday, but what could he say? That he was confused as hell about their relationship, had no idea how to handle things between them now and did she have any suggestions?

When the awkward silence stretched as he stood there like a scared school boy, Stacy finally said, "You don't have to be here. I'm sure with the fire yesterday you have important things to take care of. Since Maggie agreed to let me ride Bess, I'll be all right."

The day before friends and neighbors started arriving with horse trailers to move his animals even before the firefighters put out the fire. "The most important things are done. We got the horses moved yesterday, and I already talked to the insurance agent this morning. He'll be out this afternoon to look at the damage and start working on the claim. Until he does that, there's not much I can do."

"If you're sure."

Her words said one thing, but the uncertainty in her gaze told him something else. He brushed his knuckles across her cheek. "I promised I'd be here for you, and I'm a man of my word."

"That's what I was hoping you'd say. I know everything will be okay, but I'm still edgy. Having you here makes me feel so much better. Safer."

This woman had invaded his life, every nook and cranny. Quickly, thoroughly and with surprising force. The thought rippled through him leaving him stunned.

The catch was she wouldn't stick around. Ryan's ten-week therapy had only a couple of sessions left. The movie was set to finish shooting a week after that.

Their days were numbered.

Before he figured out how to respond, Maggie called for everyone's attention. "We're set to start." She motioned for Colt to come forward. "Everyone here knows what happened to Stacy's father. Because of that, we're taking extra precautions. She and I thought it would be a good idea if we went over a few horse basics before we started shooting."

Colt spent the next few minutes going over the fundamentals with the crew. No loud noises. No sudden unexpected moves. If the horse started pawing the ground or seemed at all nervous, he'd let Maggie know, and they'd stop filming until he figured out what the issue was. Maggie said Colt didn't need to consult with her. If he felt they needed to take a break, he was to call cut. His job was to remain focused on Stacy and ensure her safety.

After talking to the crew, he led Bess to the pasture fence and helped Stacy mount. "I'm so glad Maggie was okay with me riding my BFF here." Stacy leaned down and patted the horse's neck. "Good thing you still have your looks, girlfriend. Most actresses your age aren't so lucky."

"You two are quite a pair."

She flashed him a weak smile.

The woman and the horse had a lot in common. Both beautiful, sturdy stock, dependable and made of steel, but with a heart of pure marshmallow—all sweet and soft.

"You'll be fine, but I'm right over there if you need me. You ready?"

She nodded, and he placed his hands over her as they clutched the reins so tight her knuckles whitened. Her grip relaxed under his. "All set."

He squeezed her hand one more time. "Thata girl."

Then Colt joined Maggie and the camera crew. That way he'd remain close to Stacy and the action, but wouldn't risk getting in the shots.

Maggie called for action. Stacy nudged Bess with her heels and the pair started walking along the fence. The actor in the scene rode in from the west on a three-wheeler, stopping a few feet away, jumped off the vehicle and made his way to Stacy where he helped her dismount. Then they talked while they walked toward the barn with Stacy leading Bess.

Simple.

Stacy relaxed once Maggie called cut. While her performance had been mediocre at best, she was thrilled she made it through the first take with nothing going wrong. When Maggie approached, Stacy said, "That was awful, but now I've got my nerves under control, I'll do better on the next take."

"It's okay. I expected you to be little uptight to start. We're not going to rush this." Maggie wrapped her arm around Stacy's shoulders. "Are you doing all right? We can take a break if you need to."

"I'm fine. Let's give it another try."

A few takes later Maggie claimed she had what she

was looking for, but she wanted to try a different spin on the scene before she called it good. She wanted one more take with Brandon upping the emotion a little and showing more anger. Stacy sat on Bess watching the actor approach in the three-wheeler. As he came closer she waited for him to slow down. He didn't. If anything he accelerated. Her stomach tightened. Bess shifted nervously under her, as if the animal also sensed something was wrong.

"Get out of the way!" Brandon shouted. "The accelerator's stuck."

Stacy tugged on Bess's reins, trying to turn the horse away from the fence. They had to get out of the way. Voices screaming orders created an indiscernible chaos pounding in her head. She couldn't think. Couldn't remember anything Colt told her about controlling a horse.

"Toss me the reins and grab the saddle horn."

Colt.

The death grip on her heart loosened as she followed his instructions. He grabbed the reins and led her and Bess away.

Brandon jumped off the three-wheeler, but the vehicle barreled forward, crashing into the fence near where she and Bess had been. The sound of metal colliding with wood and concerned voices echoed in Stacy's ears.

She glanced at Colt, and started shaking. The situation could have gone so differently if he hadn't been there. Bless that take-charge attitude of his. He'd known she needed help before she could even call out to him.

His hands slipped around her waist, strong and

warm, comforting her as he helped her off Bess. "I didn't know what to do. I couldn't remember anything you told me about how to tell a horse where to go."

She leaned into him, her head resting on his strong chest. The hammering of his heart pounded against her cheek. "You're safe now."

"Thanks to you."

The crew rushed forward to help Brandon, who was unhurt except for a few scrapes to his arms. Slowly the noises quieted, and then Stacy heard Ryan's screams.

Brandon's mishap triggered Ryan's memories of his accident. Her gaze searched for Ryan, finding him huddled against the barn. When Jess approached him, he shoved away from his friend almost knocking her down. Stacy raced toward him, but the closer she got, the more he looked as if he would bolt. "Ryan, it's me, Stacy."

She wrapped her arms around him, trying to comfort him and still his shaking, but he broke free. His eyes glazed over, he looked like a cornered animal. She moved toward him, but he backed away.

"Watch out!"

"Ryan, look at me," Stacy begged.

She thought he'd gotten past this. His nightmares had subsided. He'd been so happy lately, almost back to his old self, but here they were with him lost inside his head, reliving the tormenting images of his accident.

Stacy glanced over her shoulder to find Colt. Her gaze locked with his, pleading with him to help her. "He won't let me touch him. What can I do?"

"Nothing." Colt inched forward. "Hey, buddy. I'm here." He moved forward another step. "Talk to me, Ryan."

"No! Get out of the way!"

The vacant look in his gaze told Stacy he wasn't really seeing anyone or anything around him, only the past.

"Ryan, look at me. Talk to me. It's Colt."

Colt continued to inch closer until he stood in front of Ryan. The pain and guilt etched on her brother's face broke her heart. "Officer, I didn't see him. I swear."

Touching Ryan's shoulder, Colt said, "It's okay, Ryan."

Colt encircled her brother in his strong embrace. Ryan shoved against him, but couldn't break free. "It was so awful. He came out of nowhere. I didn't mean to hit him."

"I know."

"It was so awful. He almost died." Sobs erupted from Ryan. His head rested on Colt's broad chest. "I heard from him the other day. He'll never walk again. I'm getting better. I might even walk on my own again. I don't have any right to be doing this well while he's in a wheelchair for the rest of his life."

"I get it. I feel the same way a lot of days. Some of my buddies didn't come home. Some lost arms or legs, but not me. I came home in one piece. Why did I when they didn't?"

"How do you live with it?"

She hadn't realized Ryan kept in contact with the man he hit, or that he carried enough blame for a lifetime. No matter how much she sympathized or wanted to understand, she couldn't comprehend how he felt over what happened. But Colt understood because a similar survivor's guilt gnawed at him.

"I try to live my life in a way that honors them. I try to make a difference."

Stacy stared at the two men in front of her as emotions crashed over her, almost bringing her to her knees with their force.

Two men capable of such incredible compassion yet forged of iron.

And she loved both of them more than she dreamed possible.

Her knees threatened to buckle under her as the realization slammed into her. How had she let this happen? Andrea fell in love every five minutes, but Stacy knew better than to give her heart away.

Over the years she'd wondered if she ever loved any of her boyfriends. Now she knew that she hadn't.

A cowboy who lived in Colorado? Why did it have to be a man like that when she finally fell in love? She thought her mother picked the wrong men? Like mother, like daughter.

Maggie joined her. "Colt's amazing. He seems good with Ryan."

Too bad he was so wrong for her in so many ways because Maggie was right. "He understands Ryan and what he's going through in a way I never could."

"After this afternoon's events, I've decided to use the last take of the scene with you and Brandon. We'll call it a day and pick up tomorrow."

"You had a full day scheduled. Stopping now will cost you a lot of money." Stacy glanced at Ryan. He appeared much calmer. His fidgeting had ceased, and his face looked more relaxed as he and Colt stood near the barn talking. That's what Ryan needed right now—time with a man who understood what he was going through. She told Maggie to hold off on letting everyone go until she talked to Colt and Ryan.

"How about you two get out of here?" Stacy said when she joined them by the barn.

"You need Colt here for the scene," Ryan said, his eyes clearer than when she'd spoken with him before.

"We're calling that scene good, so I'll be fine. Get out of here. Do some guy stuff."

As she stared at Colt, she prayed he received her silent message. *Get Ryan out of here. Talk to him. Help him cope with what he's feeling.*

He caught her gaze over her brother's shoulder, and nodded in understanding. How could he know her better in such a short time than friends she'd known for years?

"Ryan, I could use your help sorting through the equipment in the barn to see what's salvageable and what needs to be replaced."

"That sounds a lot better than being an extra in the movie. I only agreed to it because Jess asked me to."

They talked to Jess and decided since she still wanted to be in the movie that Stacy would bring her home later. Once the guys left, the rest of the Stacy's day proved uneventful. They filmed another scene around the ranch, a get-together with the area ranchers with Jess as an extra. With that done, Maggie wrapped up early for the day.

When Stacy dropped Jess off, she found Colt in the rocking chair on the porch. "What're you doing out here?"

"Enjoying the quiet and the sunset." He stood. "Ryan is playing video games and the noise was getting to me."

She glanced over her shoulder and gasped at the beauty before her. The setting sun was just dipping behind the mountains, darkening them. A fiery glow spread across the sky. "It's beautiful. I could sit here for hours."

"I do some of my best thinking in this chair."

"I can see why. Something about being here has cleared my head in a lot of ways." Since coming here she'd taken a long, hard look at her life and found it lacking, except for her relationship with her brother. The thought reminded her of why she'd come. "Thanks for all you did for Ryan today. How's he doing?"

As she followed Colt inside he asked her to stay for dinner and then said, "He's doing better. We took inventory here to see what we could salvage. After that we went to Twin Creeks to check on the horses. There's something about working with a horse that calms a person. That kid's been holding a lot in. He knows how much your mother dumps on you and he doesn't want to do the same thing."

Once in the kitchen she sat at the table and tried to process what he'd said. "I had no idea he was thinking that."

This was the kind of kitchen she'd dreamed of having, cozy and warm. The kind of room a family congregated in at the end of the day to reconnect and share their lives. Truly share. Where everyone listened because they cared about each other.

"We spent a lot of time talking about the accident. He's beating himself up for not anticipating someone could walk out from between the parked cars. He thinks if he'd been a better driver, he could've avoided hitting the man. He keeps replaying the scene in his mind trying to figure out what he could've done differently."

"He's being too hard on himself. The police investigated and saw no reason to charge him. They determined he'd done nothing wrong."

"He knows that, but it doesn't make him feel any less guilty because he's walking and the guy he hit isn't."

"Like you feel guilty because you came home and friends you served with didn't?" He nodded, and pain flickered in his gaze. "How do I help him deal with what he's feeling?"

"You can't. He's got to come to terms with it."

"Have you?"

"Some days, I think so. Then others I'm sure I haven't even started. That's how it'll be for Ryan. It would help if he didn't spend so much time alone. That gives him too much time to think. He says you've been putting in long hours on the set."

"I can't help it. Filming is behind and Maggie's worried about money. She says we've got to wrap up on time."

"Don't get your dander up. I wasn't criticizing, merely stating facts, and I've got a solution. He can come here after school."

"This isn't your problem. I'll figure something out. I could ask Maggie if Ryan could come to the set after school."

"Why do that when I've offered a better solution? Let me help."

His words, said with a good amount of irritation in his voice, made her think. Why hadn't she just been thankful for his offer instead of insisting she could take care of everything on her own?

In her experience whenever anyone offered help there were strings attached. They wanted something from her. Either that or they failed to follow through. Look at Andrea. How many times had she promised to be there for her children only to have "something come up?"

But Colt was different. "I guess I'm a little out of practice accepting help. Thank you."

How could she ever repay him for everything he'd done for her? Worse yet, how would she ever be able to walk away from him?

A few days later as Colt stood inside the front door of Halligan's with Stacy beside him, greeting people as they arrived for the fund-raiser to help Healing Horses cover the insurance deductible, he marveled at the changes in his life. Ryan and Jess had settled into a routine. Their friendship seemed to be a stabilizing force in both their lives. After he picked them up from school, they sat in the kitchen doing homework. Then they either worked with the horses or played video games until dinner. If Stacy finished shooting in time, she joined them and the four of them sat together, ate and discussed the day's events.

Like countless other families.

After dinner he and Stacy either snuggled on the couch to watch TV or sat on the porch in their rocking chairs. He smiled thinking of how Stacy had hugged him when she showed up to find the chair he'd bought her next to his on the porch.

He was happier than he'd been in years. Stacy had

slipped into his life and turned it upside down, but in a good way. He enjoyed being with her, even though he spent the majority of his time trying to figure out a way to get her alone. Not that it had gotten him anything other than a few minutes here and there to share a few kisses and some heated necking.

Lord help him. How was he ever going to let her walk out of his life?

She'd helped him in so many ways. This fund-raiser was another perfect example. Without him even asking, Stacy organized the event with Nannette's help. The pair met with Nannette's daughter-in-law Elizabeth, a former New York City advertising executive who now ran a local ad agency, to design posters and put them up around town. Then Stacy talked to Avery's friend Emma and asked Maroon Peak Pass to play for the event.

"Thanks for doing all this. I'm surprised Mick agreed to let me in the place. He's still mad at me for the fight with Carpenter."

"You'll have to thank Nannette for that. She's the one who sweet-talked him and promised there wouldn't be any trouble. She even talked to Travis and told him if he came within fifty feet of Halligan's tonight, he'd answer to her."

Colt laughed. "That would put the fear of God into any man. Even Carpenter isn't foolish enough to cross Nannette."

"No kidding. I think we should send her to Washington. She'd have the nation's problems fixed in a week."

"Now that would shake things up."

He shifted his stance, their conversation oddly trivial and awkward after everything they'd been through.

"Great idea, having this fund-raiser," Brian, an old friend of Reed's and one of the city's Board of Trustees, said when he walked through the front door. "What you do for the disabled in the area is so important to the community."

Colt introduced Stacy. "This was her idea. She did all the work. I just showed up."

"I heard you helped Colt get the horses out when the barn caught fire."

"I did what anyone would have done," Stacy replied.

Not every woman would've charged in. Would Lynn have risked her life to save his? More than likely she'd have called 911, and told him to forget about the horses and save himself.

Not Stacy. She dived in and helped. She stood by his side.

"She did more than that." Colt explained how the horse had kicked him and Stacy had calmed the animal enough for him to cover its eyes and lead him out. "Without her, I might have died in that fire."

"Who would've thought a fancy city-girl actress like you had that much gumption in her?" Brian's voice pulled Colt away from his thoughts.

"I'll take that as a compliment," Stacy said with a huge grin on her face.

"Why wouldn't you since that's what it was?" Brian glanced at her, confusion clouding his plain features. "You're all right."

"She certainly is," Colt said.

And he'd fallen for her. He hadn't even known Cupid was in town, much less seen the arrow heading his way.

Chapter 13

Brian's simple statement and the admiration shining in Colt's gaze set off a ripple of pride in Stacy. Tonight was different than the last time she'd been in Halligan's. No whispers and pointed glances shot her way. No questions about her time on *Finding Mrs. Right* and how she felt being tossed over on national TV. Instead she'd received compliments for her quick thinking and bravery. She felt as if she belonged.

Even when Griffin and Maggie walked in that feeling didn't change. How could she be uncomfortable around them when her heart had never been involved? Her pride? Sure, but never her heart. When he'd proposed to Maggie at the finale she'd been more worried about her career and upset over looking like a fool. Never once during their dates did her heart flutter when Griffin looked at her. He never made her want more out of life. Like Colt did.

"Thanks for coming out tonight to support Healing Horses," Colt said.

"We're family. Where else would we be?" Griffin replied and slapped his friend on the back.

They have no idea how lucky they are. What a gift having a family like theirs is.

Maggie turned to her. "How's your brother doing? I feel so awful about what happened."

"I think him melting down was a blessing in disguise. I didn't know that Ryan had been in contact with the man from the accident. Now that's out in the open, and we can deal with what he's feeling. He had a session with a psychologist and that's helped, too."

"Two more days of shooting. Can you believe it?"

She flinched at Maggie's statement. Not tonight. She didn't want to think about leaving.

"I didn't know you were that close to being done with the movie." Beside her she swore Colt stiffened.

"All we've got is one more scene to film, and based on how great yesterday's rushes were, we should breeze right through that," Maggie continued.

Colt's hawklike gaze zeroed in on Stacy and she resisted the urge to squirm. "Do you know when you're leaving?"

Ask me to stay. Tell me you can't bear the thought of me leaving you.

"Originally Ryan and I thought we'd fly back next week, but I don't have to be back in L.A. until I start shooting my next movie in six weeks."

"You could stick around for a while."

Colt's comment wasn't exactly what she hoped to hear, but it was something. What harm would there be in staying a few weeks longer? She could take some time for herself and unwind. When was the last time she'd done that? Plus, the extra break from Andrea would be another benefit, but more importantly she would have more time with Colt to see what developed between them. "I could use a vacation. I could take time to do all the touristy type things I keep hearing everyone talk about before I head back."

"I bet you could use some time off. That director of yours is a slave driver," Griffin added, only to have his wife swat him on the arm.

"I'd be happy to play tour guide," Colt offered. "We could start with the tour of The Stanley Hotel. They filmed *The Shining* miniseries there."

"Spring break's in a couple of weeks. The transition would be easier for Ryan then. He wouldn't have to miss any school."

That's not why you want to stay, and you know it.

No, but the rationalization sounded like the perfect one for public consumption. That way if things didn't work out with Colt she had a way to salvage her pride.

"Colt, the band would like you to say something before they start playing," Nannette said as she joined them.

While Colt stood on stage, Stacy and Nannette sat at a back table. "Thanks, everyone, for coming tonight to support Healing Horses. That's one thing I've always loved about this community, how everyone pulls together when someone's in need."

"I've got to say, you've surprised me," Nannette said. "The girl that showed up at my ranch never would've taken the time to do what you've done for Colt by organizing this."

"Colt's done so much for Ryan, it's the least I can do."

He's done so much for me.

She heard him talking about his work with Healing Horses and a thought popped into her head. He mends people.

He'd done that with Ryan. He'd mended her as well, and she hadn't even known she needed putting back together. Because of him, she didn't feel alone for the first time since her father died. Colt had taken some of the weight off her shoulders by helping with Ryan. He'd given her a safe place to unwind at the end of the day. A person to confide in, bounce ideas off of, someone to sit and be with if she didn't feel like talking. He'd been the first person in her life in so long who had given more than he'd taken.

She thought of the two of them sitting in rockers on the front porch. A sunset never looked more beautiful than it did from her spot in the comfortable oak rocker he'd bought for her and placed on his front porch beside his. She could see herself sitting there with him in her old age. The realization rippled through her leaving her weak. She bit her lip.

She loved the man with all her heart, but loving someone wasn't always enough to make a relationship work in the real world.

"There's more to what's going on with you and Colt, and we both know it." The older woman's knowing eyes stared through her.

The words that she and Colt were just friends stuck in her throat. She wouldn't lie to Nannette, and even if she did, the older woman would see it for what her words were—a big, stinky pile of cow manure.

"Movie sets are funny places, almost a world of its own. The cast, crew and the people we come in contact with become a family of sorts. At least during filming." Then shooting wrapped up. People said they'd keep in touch, but Stacy discovered that to be one of those polite phrases individuals spouted with all sincerity but failed to follow through on. Or, they commented on each other's Facebook posts or tweets, and occasionally texted each other, but that wasn't really being involved in someone's life. "Unfortunately, a lot of the relationships forged on the set fade once the movie's done."

What if her relationship with Colt was one that grew out of close proximity and shared emotional events—Ryan's therapy, facing her fear of horses, Colt's barn fire and Jess's revelations about her mother—but it lacked the substance to last?

"Colt cares about you. I see it in his eyes when he watches you when you're not looking."

But did he care enough to try to make things work between them? Enough to tackle the issues keeping them apart, like the fact that they lived in two different states? "I'm not so sure."

"You'll never know if you don't give it a chance."

"It's not that simple. My life is in California. That's where my mom lives. That's where my career is."

"Sometimes what we think is important is really just noise keeping us from hearing that little voice inside telling us what we really want our life to be about."

Noise? The clatter in her life was deafening. Colt quieted some of the din for her. He had a way of cutting to the heart of the matter.

He'd shown her what life could be like when there was give and take. Like yesterday. Andrea had called during the lunch break. She didn't know what to do.

As if she ever did. Things weren't going as well as her mother hoped since Grant moved back. He'd been coming home late, and when Andrea questioned him about his whereabouts, he accused her of not trusting him. Her mother went on to say Grant often wasn't answering his cell when she tried to call him and he seemed distant. Then Andrea tearfully added she couldn't wait for Stacy to come home.

Stacy knew the signs, having seen them time and time again with her mother's other relationships. Andrea latched on to a man, but then became so fearful of losing him she clung to him with a desperation that drove him away.

Not once did her mother ask about how the movie was going. Nor did she ask about Ryan and if the therapy had produced any results. Unlike Colt who always asked about her day and actually cared what she said.

Stacy stared at Nannette. Strong, capable and nurturing. So unlike Andrea. *Too bad we don't get to choose our family.*

"It's not that simple. I have Ryan to think of, and my mother's had a difficult life. Her marriage is on the rocks—"

"Life's hard for everyone."

Stacy froze, afraid she'd offended Nannette. What was she thinking? Nannette was a widow and a cancer survivor. "I'm sorry. That was thoughtless of me to say after everything you've gone through. Unfortunately, my mom doesn't possess your strength. She relies on me so much."

The older woman placed her hand over Stacy's. "You're not your mother's keeper. She's a grown woman. You've got the right to live your own life. That's part of a parent's job—to let go."

That sounded wonderful, but how did she get Andrea to see the fact?

She glanced at Colt on the stage. "I want to thank Maroon Peak Pass for playing tonight. Now I've yammered on too long, so I'll get out of the way for them to take over." Colt turned to Emma and said something before he left the stage.

A minute later when he stood beside Stacy, he nodded toward Nannette and asked the older woman to excuse them. Then he slipped his hand in Stacy's, and her heart tripped. "Dance with me. We didn't get to do that the last time we were here."

"There are things I need to check on—"

"I'm here to see to things. You two go on," Nannette said, a bold matchmaker smile on her face.

"We've had a request for a slow one to start off the night, so grab your honey and come out on the dance floor," Emma announced.

Colt leaned down and whispered in Stacy's ear. "I need you in my arms."

A shudder rippled through her as his heated breath fanned over her skin. How could she resist his husky plea and heated gaze, especially when she wanted him to hold her, too?

As she followed him onto the dance floor she told herself that tonight she'd forget about everything but Colt. When his hands slid around her waist, she leaned into him, savoring the feel of him. His strength seeped into her. If only she could bottle that feeling and take it home with her to use when dealing with Andrea left her weak and feeling drained.

"Not being able to have you in my arms has been killing me."

She'd missed him holding her. They'd seen each other every day since Ryan started going to Colt's house after school. The four of them ate dinner together most nights. If shooting ran late, Colt kept something warm for her and then he kept her company while she ate, but they hadn't been alone.

"Kids, even teenagers, definitely complicate things, don't they?"

"I'm just glad they had plans with friends tonight so we could have some time alone."

Stacy laughed and glanced at the couples around them on the dance floor. "I don't know what your definition of alone is, but this isn't mine."

"We could sneak out."

"Of a fund-raiser for your program? Not likely, or in good taste."

"So when would it be okay for us to cut out? And keep in mind the movie the kids are at ends at ten-forty."

Just the thought of being with him again made her all tingly inside, but making love with him was the last thing she should do when she was leaving soon. What she needed to do was wind things down with him or decide where they went from here.

What if she brought up the idea of them continuing to see each other and he smiled, said no, thanks, but wished her luck? But wasn't that what she wanted when she first became involved with him? No strings attached? She'd wanted things in her life—like a mother who acted like a parent—but fate never cooperated. Great time for fortune to turn the tables on her and grant her wish.

Bits and pieces of her and Colt's discussion after they'd made love flitted through her mind. She'd been up front with him. *There can't be anything other than something casual between us.* Then he'd echoed her sentiments saying they were both adults and could enjoy each other's company. She still saw his smile when he added that there wasn't anything wrong with that. Not exactly the response of a man who wanted a more permanent relationship.

When she'd uttered those words she'd believed them, that she'd be happy with a casual relationship. She wanted more, but couldn't have it. There wasn't a lot of work for an actress in a small Rocky Mountain town of eight thousand people. Plus, her mother was counting on her coming back. How could she bail on her mother with Andrea's marriage on the rocks again?

She'd been a fool to think she could be content with something that paltry. Leaving him was going to be like leaving a part of herself behind. How could she go back to the barren wasteland that had been her life now that she'd seen what life could be like with a true partner to share it with?

She leaned closer to Colt and kissed him. She wanted this one last night to last forever and she wanted that one last time with him. "I think we could leave at ten without causing too much gossip."

Normally Colt enjoyed socializing with his friends and neighbors, but not tonight. By the time he checked his watch for the tenth time since Stacy told him she figured they could leave at ten, he thought he'd go crazy. Nine-forty-five. How could time pass so slowly?

"Quit checking the time. People are going to think you don't want to be here."

He leaned forward to whisper in her ear. "They'd be right because I'd rather be home alone with you."

"Then go on stage. Thank everyone one more time for coming and let's get out of here."

"Yes, ma'am."

He forced himself to stroll up on stage and talk for a full minute before he told everyone to enjoy the rest of the night.

As he and Stacy headed for the front door, he chatted with anyone who stopped him along the way instead of shoving them aside and making a break for the door.

By the time he and Stacy walked into his house five minutes later, his jeans had become more than a bit uncomfortable. No sooner had they walked in the front door than he scooped Stacy into his arms and headed upstairs.

"This is much better than the last time you carried me off."

"You've got to admit you were a pain in the ass then."

"You sure know how to sweet-talk a girl."

He stopped on the stairs and kissed her long and hard, like a man who thought he was drowning and she was the lifeline he'd just latched on to. "I'm a little out of practice."

"You could have fooled me." She slid her hand inside his shirt. Her nails skimmed over his skin sending pleasure bursting through him. He raced up the remaining stairs and into his bedroom.

He tried to swallow the lump in his throat as he placed her on his bed, but the damned thing wouldn't budge. Earlier when Maggie announced the film only had two more days until they wrapped up, he'd wanted to grab Stacy and kiss her until she agreed to stay, because he couldn't bear the thought of her leaving.

Then she'd changed her mind, deciding to stick around for a little longer. He'd gotten a reprieve.

Now he needed to make the most of his time with her.

She held out her arms to him and as he joined her, he forgot everything but her and the pleasure they could find in each other's arms.

Two days later when Maggie called cut, pride over her accomplishment washed over Stacy. Seeing life here through Colt's eyes, becoming a part of Ryan's therapy team had given her insight into her character. Drawing on those things and the connections she now felt to the land and the people around her elevated her performance. No doubt about it, she'd done her best work ever in this movie.

"Filming on *The Women of Spring Creek Ranch* is done! Can you believe it?"

Maggie went on to thank the cast and crew for all their hard work. When everyone started leaving, Maggie approached Stacy and asked to speak to her alone. "The early buzz about the movie is better than I could've ever hoped for. Don't tell anyone, but John Hammond and I are developing a script for a pilot to pitch to the network."

A little flutter raced through Stacy. Hammond had

developed more than a few top-rated shows over the years. His latest remained solidly in the top ten ratingswise.

No, she refused to hope. People pitched series all the time and only the tiniest fraction made it to filming a pilot. An even smaller portion got on the air.

"That's wonderful. I know how much it would mean to you to shoot a series here."

"The traveling isn't a problem now because Michaela can come with us, but this is home."

Yes, it was.

"We both know how tough it is to get a series on the air, but I wanted to mention it to you so you could think about it. I can't see anyone else in your role, Stacy. When we get the script done, can I send it to you?"

"Of course."

"Having a bankable star on board would definitely help our pitch with the network."

Maggie's comment shook Stacy. Three months ago she'd struggled to get auditions for A status roles and now she was considered "bankable" enough to impress the network. The entertainment industry could make a girl lightheaded from that quick a climb.

Then the implications of Maggie doing a series sank in and sent thoughts spinning through Stacy's head. A series meant a consistent income. The stability of being in one place, being able to have a predictable home life without worrying about location shoots.

And this series would be shot in Estes Park and eliminate the long-distance relationship factor for her and Colt. Not that he'd given her any indication that he wanted anything more than a casual relationship with her, but that could change in the next few weeks.

Despite knowing she shouldn't hope because that's how she got hurt, Stacy found herself doing just that as she returned to her trailer. Maybe this once fate would cut her a break.

Once inside her trailer, Stacy pulled out her duffel bag to pack up her personal items. She lifted the intricate silver frame containing the picture one of the crew had snapped of her and her father dressed in fifteenth-century finery their first day on the movie set. Her finger traced the surface. What would her father think of Colt? She liked to think he would approve. That he'd say as long as Colt made her happy and was there for her he was pleased. As she placed the photo in her bag, she couldn't help but think how different her life would've been if her father had lived.

Andrea would have someone else to rely on, and I would have had my freedom years ago.

As she packed up her makeup, her cell phone caught her eye. She had three missed calls from her mother and three corresponding voice mails waiting. She massaged the knot in her neck and wondered what her mother wanted now.

She listened to the first message. "Grant doesn't love me. He's having an affair with a young actress. He filed for divorce."

Her mother's voice grew more frantic in the next message. "Why haven't you called me? I need you, Stacy. I always thought you'd be there for me no matter what. That I could count on you."

Stacy's hands shook as she listened to the last message. "I don't know how I can live without Grant. If I'm gone when you get home, please explain things to Ryan."

Gone? She hadn't heard her mother sound that desperate in years. Since Allan, her second husband, left her. Andrea couldn't be thinking of what it sounded like. Her mother wouldn't commit suicide, would she? Her hand trembling, Stacy punched in Andrea's number and prayed she wasn't too late. The phone rang. Once. Twice. Three times before her mother answered.

"Stacy? Why didn't you call sooner?"

"I'm sorry. We were wrapping up filming, and I didn't have my phone with me."

"I can't bear losing Grant." Andrea's voice broke. "I don't do well living alone."

"You'll get through this. It won't be easy, but you can do it."

"I miss your father so much. I want to be with him again." By the time Andrea finished her sentence, her words had started to slur.

"Mom, have you taken something?"

"A couple of Xanax. I'm so tired."

Panic, hot and sharp, bolted through Stacy. "How many did you take?"

"Only a couple."

Buzzing sounded in Stacy's ears. Her mind started to spin. The weight she'd been carrying since her father died crushed her. She started shaking. A chill spread through her as something inside her broke. Maybe if she got cold enough, numb enough, she wouldn't hurt. She didn't want to feel anything because the agony squeezing her heart right now was going to kill her.

"I'm almost positive I didn't take more than a couple."

Andrea's voice pulled Stacy out of her haze. She had to find someone to stay with her mom until she got there. "Don't take any more pills and don't drink any alcohol. I'm going to call Bethany to take you to the hospital and I'll be on the first flight I can get."

"Okay. I can't wait until you come home, Stacy. You'll help me, won't you?"

After she reassured her mother, Stacy called Bethany, Andrea's best friend, who promised she'd get her to the hospital and stay with her until Stacy arrived. Then she booked seats for her and Ryan on the first flight from Denver to L.A., and texted her brother that she was leaving to pick him up at school. Minutes later when he climbed into the car, she updated him on the situation with their mother. "So we're heading home sooner than we planned."

"I should've talked to you about this before now, but I'm not going back."

She struggled to absorb the blows he'd delivered. She wasn't strong enough to fight him right now. Not when she was concerned about her mother. Not when she was being torn apart over having to leave Colt.

"Our mother's on the verge of suicide. If you don't come back it might push her over the edge."

"She won't kill herself. She's too selfish to do that."

"Are you willing to take the risk? I'm not." When he remained stubbornly silent, she said, "We're all the family she has. That's where our home is."

The words rang hollow in her ears. Home? California didn't feel much like home anymore. No, she definitely couldn't call it home anymore.

Because Colt wasn't there.

She couldn't think about that now. If she thought about leaving Colt she'd fall apart.

"That's not where my life is. I'm happy here. I've

got more friends, hell, better friends, than I ever had in California." He crossed his arms over his chest, and his hard green eyes flared with teenage defiance. "I'll ask Colt if I could move in with him and Jess. She and I have talked about it. She thinks her dad will be fine with the idea."

"He won't agree to it if I'm not okay with it," she tossed back.

"I'll go to court and get emancipated. Since I'll be eighteen in ten months it shouldn't be a big deal."

"Why are you doing this?" She loved him so much and had practically raised him. Couldn't Ryan see how he was destroying her?

"Why are you rushing back to her? What's she ever done for us other than give birth to us?"

"She's our mother. We're family and sometimes being part of a family requires making sacrifices."

"But we're always the ones doing the sacrificing." He stared out the window. Though he sat beside her in the passenger seat, he felt so far away. "I'll do whatever I have to so I can stay here. I have the right to be happy. I won't go back."

For the majority of Ryan's life she'd told herself she'd wanted her brother to have choices she never had, but now that he could choose to stay in Estes Park when she couldn't, jealousy mixed with white-hot anger tore her apart. Granted Andrea wouldn't ever win parent of the year, but didn't they both owe her something? They couldn't leave her to fall apart.

Stacy didn't have time for a knock-down, drag-out fight with him, especially one she wasn't strong enough to survive. Ryan had to go back to California with her because she couldn't cope with Andrea and her problems alone. She needed someone to listen, someone who understood what she was going through, someone to hold her together, but how could she convince Ryan?

She probably couldn't, but Colt could. She pulled into the nearest parking lot, turned around and headed for Colt's ranch. "We'll see what Colt has to say about this."

"I'm coming. Hold on," Colt called out as he made his way to the front door. "Quit ringing the blasted doorbell. You're giving me a headache."

He yanked open the door and found Stacy standing there, her face drawn, her arms crossed over her chest, fire blazing in her eyes. "You've got to talk to Ryan. My mom's threatening to commit suicide, and he's in the car refusing to go back to California with me. He thinks he can move in here with you and Jess. Tell him he can't live here."

His head spun from the verbal assault she'd just hurled at him. Her mother threatened to commit suicide? What the hell had happened? Then add Ryan with his teenage dander up and no wonder she was spitting mad. Considering their moods, he bet neither one of them was listening to the other. It's a wonder they arrived at the ranch in one piece. He walked past Stacy, strode over to the car and rapped on the passenger window.

Ryan rolled down the window. Attitude and teenage defiance rolled off him in waves. "What?"

"Join Jess in the kitchen."

When the teenager opened his mouth, Colt shook his head. "Don't say anything. We'll work this out, but you and your sister need to calm down first."

Ryan got out of the car, slammed the door hard enough to make Colt's teeth rattle and stormed up to the house. He clomped past his sister leaning on his cane without even looking in her direction.

"Wait a minute. Come back here," Stacy yelled at her brother.

"Let him go."

Stacy clutched his arms. Her nails dug into his skin. "Tell him he can't move in here. Tell him it's his duty to come with me."

"We need to talk first. Tell me what happened."

She told him about her mother's voice mails and their conversation. The more he listened, the angrier he became at her mother. Lord. What kind of woman leaves a message for her daughter saying she's going to commit suicide and blames it on her child for not "being there" for her? The woman could teach Catholic nuns a thing or two about imposing guilt on others.

Knowing his anger wouldn't help Stacy, he stuffed the emotion down. Though he wanted to scoop her into his arms, hold her and tell her everything would be all right, he knew that wasn't what she needed right now, either. She was wound too tight and holding on by a thread. Her gaze held the same glazed and frenzied look he'd seen in green soldiers' eyes the first time they came under fire.

Remaining factual and detached was the best way to go. That and helping her sort through what to do. So instead of holding her, he clasped her hand and led her into the living room where he settled onto the couch and patted the spot beside him. She shook her head, refusing to sit and started pacing instead.

"I'm so tired of holding what little family I have

together. When my dad died, my mother crawled into a hole. Ryan was so little then. On the nanny's day off Andrea let him cry in his crib. I was the one who went to him. Later, I was the one he ran to when he fell down. Not our mother. She was too busy trying to snag a husband or keep one the one she'd caught."

"You raised him."

"That's why his wanting to stay here hurts so bad. I can't lose him. He's all I have."

You have me. The words almost jumped out, but now wasn't the time to talk about how he felt. She had enough to think about with Ryan and her mom. He refused to add to her emotional turmoil. "This isn't what you want to hear, but you can't force Ryan to go back to California."

Her expressive face tightened with anger as she circled his living room. "You're right. I don't want to hear that."

"I won't lie to you to make you feel better because that won't do you any good. If you push him too hard you risk making him even more determined. He'll do the opposite of what you want just to prove you can't force him to do anything. That's where you're headed by playing this game of chicken. I found that out the hard way. I almost lost Jess when I went to Afghanistan."

"Really?"

She sank onto the couch beside him. He told her how he'd missed the signs Jess sent out about needing him around more. He hadn't wanted to see them because he knew if he did he'd have to make changes in his life. He'd have to give up the career he loved. Then he explained about the troubles Reed and Jess had while he was in Afghanistan and how Jess ran away. "I learned something else while I was gone. Teenagers aren't really kids anymore."

"That may be true, but they're not old enough to make their own decisions, either. Ryan has to go back with me. He's not old enough to be on his own."

"Right now you don't have a choice. You can't make him go with you, and you don't have time to convince him. Focus on your mother and getting her help. Let Ryan stay here with me and Jess."

"I don't know if I can bear letting him go."

"You've basically been Ryan's parent. Part of taking on that job means sucking it up and taking a hit because you want what's best for your child."

"Like you gave up your military career."

He nodded.

"My mother never learned that lesson. I always said I'd never make the mistakes she did." Her eyes filled with tears. "I have to let him go, don't I?"

Colt nodded and wrapped his arms around her. He held her for a minute while she cried. Then when she'd gotten everything out of her system, together they walked into the kitchen and he stood beside her as she told her brother she was leaving for California, but he could stay.

Ryan turned to his sister, his eyes wide. "You're letting me live here with Colt and Jess? Permanently?"

Stacy bit her lip and nodded. She was trying so hard to hold it together. "I want you to be happy."

"Thanks." Ryan strode across the room and wrapped his sister in a big hug. "When do you think you'll be back?"

The reality of her leaving and that she might not

return hit Colt head-on. The ache, the pain coursing through him threatened to bring him to his knees. He held his breath and his palms grew sweaty as he waited for her to answer Ryan's question.

The silence stretched. That wasn't a good sign and he knew it.

What had he expected her to do? Say she couldn't wait to come back? That she'd give up her life, her career to see if they could make a go of being a family?

"I don't know. It'll depend on how Mom does. I start shooting my next movie in six weeks, but if she goes into a mental hospital, who knows how long it'll be before I can leave her." She turned in Colt's direction, but she failed to meet his gaze as she nibbled on her lower lip. "Thank you for taking Ryan in. I'll call to discuss the legal issues and support payments."

The last bit of his hope that her going was only temporary, that she'd say she couldn't leave him for good, that she loved him and wanted him in her life withered and died. What she'd just said made it clear that she wasn't coming back any time soon.

"I don't need your money."

I need you. The words hovered in his mind, but he shoved them aside. If she'd give him a sliver of hope, maybe he could tell her how he felt. He could ask her to come back to him when her mother was better, but only an idiot spilled his guts to a woman after she gave him a giant "it's over" signal like Stacy just had.

"I know, but I'm going to help with his support anyway."

He peered into her beautiful blue eyes. He thought Lynn leaving him hurt. That was nothing compared to what he felt now. Lynn had been the love of his youth. Stacy was the love of his life. "When's your flight?"

"Nine-twenty tonight."

He nodded, not sure what to say or do. Should he smile at the woman he loved, say things were fun while they lasted and ask if they could keep in touch via Skype or Facebook?

He wanted her in his life forever, but their lives were so different. He couldn't move to California. He thought about how unhappy Lynn had been when she'd given up her dreams of living in the city for him. He wouldn't make that mistake with a woman again. He loved Stacy, but he had to let her go.

She nodded, as well. Then she walked across the room, kissed him on the cheek and walked out the door.

At least if Ryan moved in with him and Jess maybe he'd see Stacy when she visited her brother. Would having her in his life that way be better or worse than not having a relationship with her? Talk about exquisite torture, and how pathetic was he to consider being willing to accept that?

The deafening sound of the door closing behind her echoed through his silent house.

"Why are you letting her go?" Jess swatted him on the arm. "Do something."

He'd had all could take. "I'm not discussing this." He turned to Ryan. "We need to get your things."

Then Colt headed for the door as well, the teenager trailing after him. When they reached his driveway, Stacy's car was nowhere in sight. His heart sank. Had he really expected her to be sitting in her car waiting to tell him she'd changed her mind?

After a couple of minutes of awkward silence on the

road, Ryan said, "I know you said you didn't want to talk, but you care about my sister. What I don't get is why you're letting her go back to California."

"Give a guy a heads-up before you toss out a bomb like that, especially when he's driving."

"You're avoiding my question."

Damn straight. "I didn't *let* Stacy do anything. Weren't you listening to the conversations she had with you today? She's got a mind of her own, and she made it clear to both of us that her life's in California. Now change the subject."

"There are some things you need to know about my sister, so I'm going to talk, and you're going to listen."

Colt thought about arguing with Ryan, but truth be told he didn't have the strength. It would be easier to tune the kid out.

"Stacy's always been too nice, and our mother's used that and her mind games to keep Stacy under her thumb. Without Stacy, our mom would have to take care of herself. She would have to get a job if Stacy quit bailing her out financially."

"She supports your mom?"

Ryan nodded. "I don't know about right after Dad died because I was a baby, but I do know about the past few years. Mom loves the Hollywood life-style. She spends her days working with her personal trainer, shopping and having three-hour lunches with her friends at four-star restaurants." Ryan told Colt how Andrea lost a good part of the money her first husband left her in a divorce settlement with her second. "Stacy hasn't had much luck getting our mother to live within her means, and she can't say no when Mom comes up short."

Life had forced Stacy to grow up as fast as he had. They'd both had parents who bailed on them. Ones who couldn't cope with life. Colt's father crawled into a bottle and lashed out with his fists. Stacy's mom tried to fill the void with men and a lavish lifestyle.

"Did you ask Stacy to stay?" Ryan asked.

"Not outright, but I hinted at it."

"What did you say? Something like if you want to, you could stay here for a while?"

Pretty much, and hearing Ryan parrot basically what he'd said to Stacy didn't make the words sound any better than when he'd originally uttered them. What woman would take a man up on a botched invitation like that?

"What if she's waiting for you to say you *want* her to stay?"

One thing he admired about Stacy was how she spoke her mind. He never had to guess with her, and since he'd known her, she'd been clear that her career and her life were in California.

"Your sister's not a beat-around-the-bush kind of gal."

"But she's not big on asking for stuff for herself because people always expect her to be strong. Andrea once told her she never had to worry about her because she'll always be all right."

Colt shook his head. "Your mom's a piece of work."

"That's what I've been trying to tell Stacy. When I was younger I used to ask our mom to do things with me, read to me or take me places. She always had an excuse why she couldn't. She was busy. She couldn't leave her husband alone for us to go somewhere for the day. Whatever. I learned to ask Stacy instead. She always had time for me. Growing up Stacy didn't have anyone else to turn to. I think the way she coped was she learned to quit asking."

Life with a father who responded to requests for help with a quick fist and criticism taught Colt to be self-sufficient. What if Stacy learned a similar lesson? What had Ryan just said? Stacy learned to quit asking. What if they'd both been sitting back waiting for the other to open up? Were he and Stacy two people who'd been so overlooked by their families that they'd grown afraid to reach out to anyone for fear they'd end up getting knocked down?

Colt pulled up to the cabin where Ryan and his sister had been staying. If he never told Stacy he loved her and asked her to be part of his life, he'd always wonder what she would've said. Sure it was a risk and he could get hurt if she rejected him, but what if she said yes?

The biggest rewards often required the biggest risk. "Since you're here talking to me like this, I'm guessing you approve of me seeing your sister?"

"That question's so stupid I'm not going to answer it."

He had Ryan's blessing, now he needed his daughter's.

An hour later when Colt and Ryan returned to the house, Ryan went upstairs to settle into the guest room while Colt asked Jess to join him in the living room. He couldn't ask Stacy to be a part of his life unless his daughter supported his decision. When they'd placed the squalling wrinkled pink bundle in his arms almost sixteen years ago, he'd entered into a lifelong commitment.

He'd screwed up when he'd learned of his deployment by not laying everything out with Jess. He'd talked to her, but they never really had a heart-to-heart, compromise and work it out discussion. He may not be Albert Einstein, but he was smart enough to learn from his mistakes. He knew that, but he wasn't quite sure how to start. "I'm sorry I snapped at you earlier."

"That's not what you want to talk to me about. I know something's up because you're acting like you do whenever you've got something to discuss that you don't want to talk about."

"How did you get to be so smart?"

"Good genes." She grinned, looking so much like her mother. He and Lynn may have failed at marriage, but they'd created something incredible in this amazing young woman.

"I'm in love with Stacy."

"I know. You have that same look in your eyes that Uncle Reed does when he looks at Avery. The question is what are you going to do about it?"

His daughter's words nearly knocked him over. She'd grown up so fast. He'd been right when he told Stacy earlier that teenagers really weren't kids anymore. "I want to ask her to marry me, but before I do, I want to make sure you're okay with it."

"What if I said I'm not?"

"Then I wouldn't ask her to marry me, but I won't stop seeing her." He searched his daughter's young face, trying to read her thoughts and then decided to quit guessing. "Are you saying you're not okay with it?"

"She's cool. I like how she makes you happy." Jess's brows furrowed in thought. He braced himself. Experience taught him her looking like that or thinking that hard never led to something he wanted to hear. "What will that make Ryan? My stepuncle? That borders on creepy."

"You may not have to worry about that. Stacy may turn me down."

His daughter laughed until her eyes watered. "Really, Dad? Come on. The woman ran into a burning barn to save you."

Maybe there was hope for him.

Stacy sat in the unforgiving plastic chairs connected like train cars in the Denver airport and realized she'd made the biggest mistake of her life.

She was leaving behind everyone who filled her life with light. Ryan, Jess and, most importantly, Colt. She'd finally found a man she wanted to share her life with, one who'd stood beside her, one who hadn't bailed on her when she needed him or told her she was more trouble than she was worth, and what was she doing? Walking away from him, and for what? A needy, self-centered mother and a career that made a roller-coaster ride look like a smooth experience.

Hardly a fair trade.

Nannette's words hammered in Stacy's mind. *You're not your mother's keeper. You have the right to live your own life.*

As a child she'd lacked the power to do anything about Andrea relying on her as a confidant and a source of financial support. At some point that was no longer true. Since then, by allowing the unhealthy patterns she and Andrea had settled into to continue, Stacy had become part of the problem.

But no more.

She refused to sacrifice her life for her mother any longer. She'd tell Andrea she'd always be there for her, but she wouldn't continue to rescue her. Stacy vowed she'd get her through this rough time with Grant, but then her mother was going to have to learn to stand on her own two feet, to call her own repairmen and live within her own means.

I deserve that.

Nannette had been right. Everyone's life was tough. The giant weight that had been resting on Stacy's chest tumbled off.

Colt had shown her what life could be like, and she intended to do whatever she could to hold on to that. Nothing in her life meant anything if she wasn't with him.

She couldn't leave with things unsettled between them, without telling him how much she loved him. She wanted him in her life. However she could have him. Her hand shaking, she clutched her cell phone and called the man she loved.

When he answered, she plunged forward before she lost her courage. She stared at the floor as she struggled to control her racing thoughts. "I should have said this earlier, but I was afraid to. I'd like us to keep seeing each other even though I'm moving back to California. Once I help my mom through this latest crisis then I can think about the future. I know this is a lot to ask of you because I travel so much for my job and long-distance relationships are hard. I know this isn't the kind of thing people usually discuss over the phone, but—"

"I want to talk about it, too, but do you mind if I sit down?"

Worn, scuffed cowboy boots materialized in her line

of vision and her heart nearly jumped out of her chest. They looked like Colt's, but weren't men in Colorado required by law to own a pair of dog-eared cowboy boots? Her gaze traveled upward until she reached his magnificent face.

This couldn't be real. She was missing him so much she'd started hallucinating. "Am I seeing things or are you really here?"

He shoved his cell phone in his back pocket and then pried hers out of her hand, ended the call and dropped it in her purse. "I'm here. I want to correct a mistake I made earlier." He folded his long muscular frame into the plastic seat beside her. "I never should've let you leave. I love you."

Joy, full and overpowering, exploded inside her. "Only ticketed passengers are allowed at the gate."

A bewildered look crossed his handsome features. "Not exactly the response I expected after my declaration of love."

Finally coming out of her fog, she said, "I love you, too."

His warm, callused hands cupped her face. He felt real. Solid. Tears filled her eyes as he lightly kissed her. Then he slid out of his chair, the plastic scrunching and creaking with his movement, and he knelt in front of her. "You're the best thing that's ever happened to me. Other than with Jess and my brother, I haven't had a lot of luck with family. My father was an abusive bastard who drank himself into an early grave. My mother died when I was twelve, and you know about my marriage, but Stacy, I love you with all my heart. Marry me."

"Yes, I'll marry you."

Colt stood, scooped her into his arms and swung her around as he let out a whoop of joy. Applause erupted around them. She blushed, noticing that they'd drawn a crowd.

"But how do we make things work, practically speaking? I don't know how to do anything but act. Sure, Griffin and Maggie are keeping their careers going, but she's a director and has more control over the projects she does than I do."

"If you can put the breaks on the train you've got barreling down the tracks we can talk about it."

"When I get super nervous I tend to talk a lot."

"I noticed." He set her back on the floor and his knuckles brushed her cheek. "We won't starve if you don't work."

"I won't let you support me."

"I'll do whatever I have to for you to be a part of my life. If that means you going where you need to in order to film a movie, then that's what we'll do, and I'll be here waiting for you. I'll console myself with thinking about how good getting back together will be."

"You'd do that for me?"

"We'll work it out because we're family."

The realization that that's what she, Colt, Ryan and Jess were rippled through her, filling all the empty spots in her heart. She finally had what she'd always longed for. "We are, aren't we?" She smiled, but then asked, "Wait a minute. You never answered my question about what you're doing here at the gate."

He reached into his back pocket, pulled out a boarding pass and held the paper out to her. Los Angeles. Her flight number. She read the information twice, but still refused to believe it. "You're coming to L.A.?"

"You said you couldn't cope with your mother's problems on your own. We'll handle the situation together, and then I'm making sure you come back home with me."

Back home. She liked the sound of that.

* * * * *

Kathleen O'Brien was a feature writer and TV critic before marrying a fellow journalist. Motherhood, which followed soon after, was so marvelous she turned to writing novels, which meant she could work at home. Though she's a lifelong city gal, she has a special place in her heart for tiny towns like Silverdell, where you may not enjoy a lot of privacy...but you never really face your troubles alone, either.

Books by Kathleen O'Brien

Harlequin Superromance

The Sisters of Bell River Ranch

Wild for the Sheriff
Betting on the Cowboy
The Secrets of Bell River
Reclaiming the Cowboy
The Homecoming Baby
Christmas in Hawthorn Bay
Everything but the Baby
Texas Baby
Texas Wedding
For the Love of Family
Texas Trouble

Visit the Author Profile page at
Harlequin.com for more titles.

BETTING ON THE COWBOY

KATHLEEN O'BRIEN

To my editor, Wanda Ottewell, with thanks. Your insight and your understanding mean so much to the stories—and to me.

Chapter 1

Brianna Wright pulled up to the Townsends' elegant Boston Back Bay mansion under a starry black sky, handed her car over to the valet with a forced smile and rushed up the stairs breathlessly. Darn it, she was late. Really late. Ten o'clock. No, almost eleven—thank you *so* much, gridlocked airport traffic!

Now she'd missed three hours of her own party—well, the party her company, Breelie's, had produced, anyhow—and Townsend's fiftieth birthday bash was already in full swing. Music and laughter poured through the open, brilliantly lit windows.

Too much laughter, perhaps, so early? She frowned. The open bar must be getting a workout.

Oh, well. Townsend was a tire magnate, and his millions could cover the liquor tab no matter how high it went. At least it sounded as if the guests were having fun.

She didn't know why that should surprise her—
the parties planned by Breelie's rarely flopped. But
something about this event had always bugged her a
little. Maybe it was just that the "harem" theme had
never appealed to her. That didn't matter, of course.
Whatever the client wanted, he got. Or, in this case,
whatever the client's trophy wife, Iliana Townsend,
wanted, she got.

Bree just hoped Charlie hadn't gone overboard. Not
that she thought he had. As her fiancée and her business partner, he deserved her complete trust. And he
had it…of course he did. It was just that…

She'd been out of town for most of the planning,
which obviously accounted for some of her discomfort. She trusted Charlie implicitly, of course, but…

She did wish he had answered his cell phone more
often this week. When Charlie went dark, it usually
meant he was spending more money than he felt like
justifying over the phone. He trusted his ability to
persuade anyone of anything, but only as long as they
were within the target range of his surface-to-surface
ballistic charm.

As she passed under a faux ogee arch and into the
unrecognizable entry hall, she suddenly froze in place.
She stared, openmouthed, at the glittering, jingling,
splashing, sparkling madness before her.

For an instant, she couldn't decide whether to laugh
or cry.

This was the high-society party she had hoped
would put her event-planning company on the Boston A-list? This…this…*circus?*

What in God's name had Charlie been thinking?
The room writhed with half-naked humanity. Belly

dancers. Sword swallowers. Eunuchs. Champagne fountains, ruby-grape pyramids, peacock-feather fans and tables groaning with bacchanalian treats. Charlie had created an entire fake Persian seraglio, complete with a hundred over-the-hill sultans flirting with two hundred giggling harem "girls."

Bree's temples throbbed, and her airplane-food dinner suddenly turned poisonously acidic.

Damn it, Charlie! She'd told him a thousand times that, in the upscale Boston society event-planning business, reputation was more important than anything else. *Anything.* Even more important than the bottom line.

And, long before this, she'd had a niggling feeling they were getting a reputation for being...

Well, vulgar.

She set her jaw as a trio of belly dancers wriggled by with a tinkle of gold coins in the air and a skitter of gold flickers on the walls. A sword swallower followed behind, ogling the dancers' hips. Behind him—a snake charmer with a real live snake slithering around his shoulders.

Oh, dear God. If vulgarity were an Olympic event, this pretentious absurdity would definitely take the gold.

Her hands tightened into fists at her sides. Charlie might be a genius at coaxing money out of rich women, but Bree was going to strangle him for this.

If she could just find him.

Instead, as she scanned the crowd, the only person she recognized was Bill Townsend, the guest of honor himself. But he didn't look honored. He looked furious. His dark eyes and full lips glowered, and he moved like an angry bull, his bulky shoulders plowing a path through the guests as if they were so many inconveniently placed mannequins. His bushy mustache and eyebrows resembled Tom Selleck more than Yul Brynner, but the scimitar at his side suddenly seemed more lethal than any prop ever should.

Though he passed within two feet of Bree, he didn't notice her any more than he noticed any of the others. He kept up his furious stride until he reached the burbling, three-tiered champagne fountain in the center of the ridiculous room.

Iliana, his forty-five-year-old trophy wife who always looked like a beautifully embalmed twenty-year-old, was nowhere in sight. Had the couple been fighting? *Great.* If the host and hostess ended up having a big row tonight, Bree's party would be remembered for that, not the hours and hours of work she and Charlie had put into it.

An elderly, diffident sultan, whose headdress was bigger than his whole body, approached Townsend, hand outstretched, a "happy birthday" smile on his face. Townsend turned his back on the man rudely. He grabbed a silver chalice from a passing waiter, thrust it under the honey-colored stream, letting the bubbles spill all over his fingers, then knocked the champagne back in one harsh toss.

Bree groaned under her breath. This could get ugly. Where the heck was Charlie? He needed to find Iliana, who might be able to handle her drunk husband. The women were always Charlie's responsibility. He was good with bored trophy wives. He could always pump out an extra squirt of charm and coax them into ever-higher displays of extravagance.

Unfortunately, at the moment, he seemed to be just as absent as the hostess. Bree shut her eyes, trying to swallow her fury. But *really*. Maybe strangling was too good for him.

"Ms. Wright?"

She opened her eyes. A tall "eunuch" stood in front of her, holding a tray of wineglasses. She eyed them carefully, wondering how many bottles they'd run through. If Townsend was already in a foul humor, he might balk at an astronomical liquor tab, after all.

"Everything okay, Ms. Wright?" The eunuch hesitated, looking nervous. Poor guy. She had a reputation, she knew, for being a stickler.

"No. I mean yes, everything's fine." It wasn't this poor guy's fault. He appeared as miserable as she felt. So she propped up her artificial smile, hearing her guardian's voice in her head. Kitty Afton, the Boston divorcée who had taken Bree in after her mother's murder, had believed that cheerfulness was next to godliness. Even in the early days, when surely she knew Bree was heartbroken and traumatized, Kitty had scolded her new protégée for letting her lips lose their pleasant feminine curve. "No one likes a sad sack, Brianna. You'll catch more flies with honey."

The waiter-eunuch nodded uneasily, then moved on. Bree checked Townsend again. He hadn't budged from the fountain. He was refilling his chalice, though his eyes glittered, and a sparkling trail of champagne already trickled from his chin like golden spit.

She couldn't wait for Charlie or Iliana. She'd have to try to handle Townsend herself. Reluctantly, Bree merged into the melee of guests, somehow keeping the smile on her lips.

"Mr. Townsend?"

He turned, the chalice halfway to his mouth, and glared at her over the rim. As he took in her simple slate-blue sheath, his eyes narrowed. "What are you supposed to be? Didn't you get the memo? This is a costume party. You've got to look like an idiot or you don't get in."

She deepened her smile, as if he'd meant it as a joke. But the bitterness in his voice was unmistakable. The drinking was a symptom of a deeper problem… not the cause. She really needed to find Iliana and get things patched up.

"I'm not actually a guest," she explained. "I'm Brianna Wright. My company, Breelie's, is the one you hired to—"

"You're…" He lowered the golden vessel, spilling liquid precariously close to her shoes, but ignoring it. "*You* are Brianna Wright?"

"I am," she said. She'd met him twice, during the initial negotiations, but she wasn't surprised that he didn't remember. He'd spent most of both meetings pacing the hall outside her office, barking at someone on his cell phone.

He shook his head for a minute, and then let out a loud, seal-like honk of laughter. Now, that *did* surprise her. She had traveled in a very uncomfortable, very dressy getup, complete with three-inch heels and panty hose, just so that she would look professional when she arrived. She'd even denied herself the luxury of a nap, so that she wouldn't muss the sleek French knot of blond hair at the nape of her neck.

"You seem amused," she observed coolly, irritated in spite of her determination to remain calm.

"Oh, I am definitely amused, sweetheart." He grinned, showing six very white front teeth surrounded by neighbors far less brilliant. "I really, really am."

She frowned and opened her mouth to respond, but then, without warning, his large hand flicked out and grabbed hers.

"Hey!" She recoiled instinctively from his damp, sticky clutch and the aroma of stale champagne that wafted from his skin. But he had clamped on tightly and didn't let go.

"Come with me, Brianna Wright," he said, turning away from the fountain, tugging her along without so much as glancing back to see if she was willing, or whether she would have to be dragged. "There's something I want to show you."

People were staring at her now, which was saying something, since surely she was the least outlandish spectacle at this particular party. "Mr. Townsend, I really don't think—"

He looked back at her over his shoulder, his eyes suddenly clear and sober. "Your company is in charge of this party, right? Well, there's a problem, and I think you should know about it."

She didn't have much recourse after that, though she did manage eventually to extricate her hand and follow him with a little more dignity and at least the appearance of free will.

The guests seemed to part before them, as if they were just props operated by stagehands pulling levers behind the scenes. Maybe the people smelled danger radiating from their host. Bree certainly did.

When Townsend reached the big central staircase and began to climb, her internal sirens started to go off wildly. Why would he need to show her anything on the second floor? Kitchen, her problem. Buffet table, her problem. Decorations, liquor, security and even valet parking…all Breelie's problems. But her company's responsibilities didn't extend beyond the first floor.

She hesitated, her hand on the polished onyx railing. He hadn't climbed more than four steps when his sixth sense obviously told him he'd lost her. He turned again, and laughed.

"Really, Ms. Wright," he said, his eyes glittering with some secret, inexplicable mirth. The effect was decidedly unwholesome, and a shiver ran down her spine. "I have a houseful of half-dressed concubines. You think I have designs on *your* icy virtue?"

"No," she said. His tone was so dismissive she found herself flushing, which was ridiculous. She'd worked hard to cultivate "icy" and had always considered it a compliment when people described her that way. Better "icy" than half-mad with uncontrolled passions, as so many in her dysfunctional family tended to be. "Of course not."

"Well, then?" He gestured impatiently.

Still, she hesitated. Something about the moment felt profoundly off. Why was he furious one instant, sardonic the next? And why on earth did he want to take her upstairs? Only the bedrooms were up there….

He laughed again, shook his head as if despairing at her naiveté, then abruptly leaned over the banister.

"Ladies and gentlemen!" His voice rose over the chatter, over the bubbling champagne fountain, even over the string quartet in the corner alcove. "Follow me! I have a surprise for you!"

All the faces tilted up toward him, though half the crowd was clearly too drunk to fully process his words and didn't stir. But at least a dozen laughing sultans and belly dancers churned toward the staircase, ready for anything that sounded different and amusing.

Bree wanted to be relieved. Whatever he had in mind, at least it didn't require privacy. That ruled out the most unpleasant scenarios, surely. So why, as the costumed guests surged up the stairs, creating a tidal wave that swept her along, did she have a sudden instinctive desire to turn around and flee?

She didn't do it, of course. That really would have set the gossips buzzing. Instead, she trailed along as Townsend made his way down the wide hall, turning occasionally to put his forefinger theatrically against his lips to shush his followers.

With every step, though, she felt herself retreating deeper into the numb bubble that had protected her from painful situations in the past. In the sixteen years since her mother's murder, she'd perfected the art of plunging her emotions into a frozen state, much like a medically induced coma, even while, on the outside, she appeared utterly serene and confident.

Icy, as she was always being told.

Finally, in front of the last door on the left, Townsend paused. He made one more "shh" gesture to his guests, then crooked his finger invitingly toward Bree, offering her the place of honor beside him. Unseen hands prodded her from behind, urging her toward her host, and before she could react, she was close enough to see the unholy gleam in his eyes.

"Mr. Townsend," she tried again uneasily. But he put his finger against her lips and grinned down at her, like an evil mime. She felt her heart accelerate. Whatever lay behind this door evoked a strong emotion in him. She wished she knew him well enough to interpret that glitter. Was it anger? Or was it glee?

With an elaborate flourish, he reached out for the doorknob and turned it slowly, so slowly it didn't make a sound. Neither did his guests, who obviously had caught the mystery fever and were craning forward in eager, hypnotized silence.

They pressed so fervently that when Townsend finally pushed the door open, Bree almost stumbled across the threshold.

Before her lay a beautiful room, decorated with a champagne-colored carpet and hunter-green bed linens and drapes. The overhead light was off, but a green-and-gold stained-glass dragonfly table lamp cast an amber circle onto the king-size bed, like a spotlight picking out the important actors on a stage.

In that amber circle, something palely pink and subtly obscene jerked and twisted, making rough, breathless, wordless sounds.

For a shell-shocked moment, Bree's mind wouldn't work. She somehow couldn't identify what she was looking at. It wasn't human, surely…that monstrous shape, with too many limbs, white-soled feet rising out of what looked like a tanned and muscled back…

Only when the people behind her began to gasp, and some to titter, did she finally jerk awake and understand. Two or three in the crowd laughed out loud; those more brazen, who had probably known from the start what the "surprise" would be.

With a cry of alarm, the monster on the bed separated into two parts. Charlie, who had been on top, leaped up, grabbing the green bedspread and awkwardly trying to cover himself with it in a pathetic display of selfishness that left his partner completely exposed.

Furiously, the woman on the bed, who was now recognizable as Iliana Townsend, yanked at the bedspread, too. Charlie, whose face was red and pop-eyed with terror, wouldn't let go, and the momentary tug-of-war was such a farce that everyone in the doorway burst out laughing.

Everyone except Townsend himself, and Bree. She suddenly felt dizzy, almost blind with fury. Oddly, she was angrier with Townsend for setting up this humiliation than she was with Charlie for causing it.

She glanced at the man now, wondering how he'd react to the sight of his wife's expensive breast implants bobbing about for everyone to ogle. Wondering if he would find Charlie's egregious lack of chivalry as disgusting as she did.

To her surprise, Townsend was still grinning.

Catching her horrified gaze, he winked salaciously. "Now look at that. Isn't that sweet? In honor of the occasion, my loving wife apparently decided to wear her birthday suit."

More laughter. Scanning the glassy-eyed, half-clad partiers and their mocking host, Bree realized suddenly that she was way out of her depth here. Back home in Silverdell, Colorado, nobody laughed at adultery. Back home, nobody invited an audience to a cuckolding.

Of course, back home, when her father had discovered her mother's infidelity, he had thrown her down the staircase and broken her neck. So maybe this decadent indifference was more civilized, in the end.

But even so, she couldn't understand it. It shocked her, and made her feel slightly ill. Perhaps that meant that, in spite of all the years living here in Boston, all the college education and the designer clothes and the artificially icy poise, she would always be just a Colorado cowgirl at heart.

What a joke…what a long, ironic laugh fate must be having right now, watching her try to handle these Eastern sophisticates—and fail.

Finally the red-faced, guilty cats seemed to find their tongues.

"Bill," Iliana wheedled. "It's not what it looks like—"

"Bree," Charlie called, trying to move toward her, but pinned in place by his lover's death grip on her end of the bedspread. "Bree, give me a chance to explain. She wouldn't take no for an answer—"

"Why, you lying bastard!" Iliana jerked so hard on the spread that Charlie lost his hold. The sudden full-frontal nudity, which cruelly offered everyone the measure of Charlie's shriveled, terrified penis, sent another wave of laughter through the room.

Bree turned her back on the sight. She eyed the others, drawing on every icy ounce of disdain she could muster, and willed them to move away from the door. Slowly, as if repelled by cold waves emanating from her, they did.

Chin high, she walked out. She didn't look back, though she heard Charlie's plaintive call of "Bree! Bree!" behind her, as if he were some kind of frantic cat stuck in a tree he'd foolishly climbed on a whim and now couldn't figure out how to descend.

She kept walking. Down the stairs, through the other guests, who had gone back to their own drinking and flirting, long ago having forgotten that something was unfolding upstairs. Past the champagne fountain, past the pyramids of grapes and the string quartet, still sawing out Mozart to the tone-deaf crowd.

Out to the valet, to whom she handed her ticket calmly. She tipped him a hundred dollars as she climbed into her car because she was so grateful to him for bringing the means to escape.

Protocol required him to feign indifference. She could have handed him a coupon for a fast-food cheeseburger instead of money, and he was supposed to pocket the paper without looking.

But obviously he knew how to sneak a peek surreptitiously. His eyes widened.

"Thank you," he said, shocked into revealing that he'd checked the denomination. "I mean…thank you, Ms. Wright. I hope you had a nice time at the party."

"Yes," she said automatically. She remembered him now. Tim. Tim Murfin. He owned the valet service, and she'd used his company before. He was honest, and he was smart. "Yes, it was a very interesting party."

In her rearview mirror, she saw Charlie racing toward the portico. He was dressed, mostly, though he was still stuffing his shirt into his waistband with rushed fingers. "Bree, wait!"

"Excuse me," she said politely to Tim, and he stepped away from the door, glancing toward Charlie with a furrowed brow.

As soon as the valet was clear, she pulled the door shut and stepped on the gas. She had no intention of letting Charlie reach the car. She wouldn't put it past him to climb onto the hood and splay himself there until she agreed to listen to his stupid excuses.

Nothing he could say could possibly make any difference at all. He'd be busy trying to convince her that he really loved her, that his dalliance had meant nothing. He might even be craven enough to say he'd done it for them, for Breelie's, to keep a customer satisfied.

He would imagine that he'd broken her heart. He'd think, no doubt, that she was hurt by his betrayal, and mourning their lost relationship.

But he'd be wrong. She didn't give a damn about any of that. The minute she'd seen him jump from that bed, ungallantly covering himself and leaving Iliana helplessly naked before all her friends, she'd understood what the real victim of the humiliating melodrama would be.

Not their relationship. Not her heart.

No. She realized at that moment that she'd probably never loved him, not real love, not with her whole soul.

The damage he'd done was even worse than that.

What Charlie had destroyed, by sleeping with their most prominent client, and making a spectacle before half of Boston society, was Brianna's career.

He had destroyed Breelie's.

And she would never, ever, ever forgive him for that.

The front drawing room of Harper House, where Grayson Harper stood waiting for his grandfather, held at least ten red-silk-upholstered seats. He had his choice of armchairs, straight-backed chairs, two divans and one chaise longue. All unoccupied. All antiques, all chosen for comfort as well as beauty.

And yet he stood.

Sitting was something you did when you wanted to make yourself at home. Sitting was relaxed. Unguarded. Sitting made you the patiently waiting beta child to the superior alpha adult who would come stalking in, militarily erect, sneering down at his uninvited visitor.

So, no, he'd stand, thanks anyhow. Gray Harper was no one's beta—especially not his grandfather's. After all this time, he intended to meet the old bastard eye to eye.

Two could play the power game, and obviously his grandfather had made the first move already, keeping Gray cooling his heels down here for as long as possible. He glanced at the ormolu clock on the mantel, which ticked in the deep silence like someone tsking sardonically. The housekeeper, a woman Gray had of course never met, since the old man was too irascible to keep employees for long, had led him into the drawing room at least half an hour ago.

"He's dressing," the woman had said when she returned from announcing Gray. "He says to wait here, and he'll be down soon."

Dressing? Gray smiled with tight lips. His grandfather could have had a new suit of clothes bought, tailored and delivered on foot from the haberdashery on Elk Avenue in that much time.

But patience. Patience. After ten years, what was another ten minutes? He had something to say, and he planned to say it, even if he had to wait all night.

He went to the window and, putting his hands in his pockets, gazed out at the beautifully landscaped view of terraced lawn sloping down to the little town of Silverdell below. The sunset gleamed pink against the thin white spire of the Episcopal church and on the blue-gray rim of mountains in the distance.

Instantly, the sight took Gray back to his youth.

His youth. Not a place he wanted to linger. He squinted, imagining he could see rain on the horizon, even absurdly sniffing a hint of wood smoke in the April air, though the fireplace was cold and still.

Maybe that was why his grandfather was keeping him waiting. Letting him simmer in this ghost-filled room long enough to render him weak.

Frowning, he turned around again.

His grandfather stood in the doorway.

Gray inhaled sharply, startled in spite of having known full well the old man would jockey for an advantage somehow.

"Sir," he said, out of habit more than anything else. Certainly not out of respect.

One corner of his grandfather's thin mouth tilted up slightly, as if he understood the distinction. "Gray."

Another family might have made a drama out of the moment. After ten years of complete silence and absolute estrangement, most people probably would have considered a display of feelings relevant. Shock, recriminations, tears, joy…anything. After all, neither grandfather nor grandson had been completely sure, until today, that the other still lived.

But old Grayson Harper the First would have considered any emotional outburst to be a sign of weakness. And young Grayson Harper the Third simply didn't give a damn anymore.

"I'm sorry I kept you waiting," his grandfather lied. He hobbled into the room, using a silver-tipped cane that Gray had never seen before. He had done the calculations before he arrived, so he knew that his grandfather had just celebrated his eighty-fourth birthday. The old man's hair had been thickly silver as long as Gray could remember, and his face lined, so other than the limp, nothing much had changed.

"No problem," Gray said, matching the tone of fake courtesy. "I'm in no hurry."

"Ah. The luxury of time to kill." His grandfather smiled coldly, putting both palms over the head of the cane and leaning subtly forward. "Still not gainfully employed, then? Or…what is the euphemism these days? Between jobs?"

A pulse started to hammer at Gray's temple, and he took a consciously deep breath. That was cheap bait, a quick piece of dirty chum his grandfather probably tossed out by habit. He wasn't eighteen anymore, and he didn't have to rise to it.

"Exactly," he agreed placidly. "Between jobs."

The older man frowned. He shifted his weight, repositioning the cane. Clearly, his injury, arthritis, gout…whatever necessitated the cane…was bothering him. And yet he equally clearly didn't want to be the first to acknowledge the need to sit.

For one ruthless second, Gray told himself he was glad. It served the old man right. Gray would happily stand here all night, if that meant his grandfather might know even a fraction of the pain he'd caused other people. People like Gray's father and mother.

But the thought died instantly. In the end, it was beneath Gray to torture an old man—it was not his way, in spite of what his grandfather had modeled for him through the years.

So he took the nearest chair. Immediately after, his grandfather settled on the edge of the silk divan stiffly, as if his hip didn't bend correctly anymore. He didn't allow himself a sigh of relief, but the lines in his face eased slightly.

"So." He massaged his palm into the head of the cane, eyeing Gray over it. "What brings you back to Silverdell?"

Just like that. No small talk. No "How are you?" or "Did you marry, have children, stay healthy, make money, buy a house…did you ever forgive me?"

Simply go straight to the point. *Fine*. Again, two could play that game.

"*You* bring me back," Gray answered matter-of-factly.

"Is that so?" His grandfather raised his shaggy white eyebrows. "Not intentionally, I assure you."

Gray shook his head a fraction of an inch. The mean old buzzard hadn't softened a bit, had he? Well, that was probably for the best. His arrogance and unyielding antagonism made Gray's job so much easier. As he'd journeyed back to Colorado from California, he'd wondered what he would do if the old man had grown weak, or senile, or sentimental. He'd wondered what he would say if his grandfather welcomed him home with open arms.

This was much cleaner. Now he could just speak his piece without wasting time trying to be diplomatic. And he could get out of this house before the past swallowed him up and broke his heart all over again.

"Nonetheless, it's true." He gazed at the old man, whose face was tinted a deceptively youthful pink by reflected sunset. "You really are the reason I've returned."

His grandfather frowned, as if he had a sudden gas pain. "Why? Had you heard I was sick or something? Did you hope you could breeze in at the stroke of midnight, butter up a dying man and get yourself written back into my will?"

Gray laughed. "Nope. Hadn't heard a thing. Believe it or not, no one out in California talks about you, your health or your money. Why, *are* you sick?"

"No." More rubbing his palm into the head of the cane, more scowling from under those unruly eyebrows. "I'm old, and my hip isn't what it used to be. But if you're here for a deathbed vigil, you'll have a long time to wait."

"I'm not."

"Well, what, then?" The old man grunted, a deeply skeptical sound. "You don't really expect me to believe the money has nothing to do with it."

Gray leaned back in his chair, smiling. "Oh, the money has *everything* to do with it."

His grandfather's eyes narrowed, but he didn't speak. He simply waited. He obviously refused to give Gray the satisfaction of asking for details.

No problem. Gray had rehearsed this part often enough that he didn't need prompting. He'd been rehearsing it for seventeen years, in fact. Since he was thirteen and filled with impotent fury at being so young, so helpless, so dependent on this tyrant. At being unable to summon the courage to say what ought to be said.

By now, Gray could have delivered this news in his sleep.

"It's one hundred percent about the money," he repeated. "But not your money. Mine."

The expressive eyebrows lifted high. *"Yours?"*

"Yes. You see, I've decided that it's time you returned my inheritance. I've come to tell you that, unless you voluntarily sign over every single penny you took from my father seventeen years ago, I intend to sue you for it."

In the silence that followed, the mantel clock ticked like a time bomb. Gray could hear someone, probably the plump housekeeper, running water in the kitchen, though that part of the house was at least fifty yards away.

Finally his grandfather spoke. "Who told you I took money from him? I'll guarantee your father never said that."

"Not to me. He told other people, who told me. I don't have any proof, of course. But I will get it, if you force me to. And the world will know you stole from your own son."

Finally the old man rose, slowly. Gray watched how he relied on the cane, and wondered whether, without it, his grandfather would be able to stand at all. In spite of everything, pity stirred, and his words suddenly sounded cruel, too harsh for this fragile old man to take.

Gray shut his eyes, annoyed by his own vacillating. This was why he hadn't come back to Silverdell for ten long years. It was just too damn emotionally confusing to feel intense love and intense hatred at the same time, for the same person.

His grandfather didn't seem tormented by any similar ambivalence. He stared at Gray coldly.

"I seem to remember that the last time I saw you I

warned you never to mention your father in my presence again."

Gray nodded. "Yes. You did."

"Still you dare to come here and..." The old lips thinned. "You dare to defy me."

Gray shrugged. "Yes." He glanced through the window, where an olive-green gloaming was overtaking the sunset. "I dare. And yet, as you can see, no lightning bolts have struck me down. The earth still turns."

His grandfather's face darkened. "You always were an impertinent boy, Gray. Too clever by half. I blame your mother for that. Hannah foolishly encouraged you to think—"

But Gray, too, was out of his chair now. "Leave my mother out of this." He took one hard step closer. "You don't have the right to speak her name."

"Perhaps not." Undaunted, his grandfather cocked a sardonic glance toward the window. "And yet...the earth still turns."

For a minute, all Gray's hard-won indifference, his emotional independence and rational perspective, melted away, and he was afraid he might hit the old man. Somehow he held himself in check, though the blood throbbed in his head, and his right hand seemed to have frozen in a tightly muscled fist.

God, this had been a mistake. Just being in this house again scrambled his brain. He had overestimated the distance a few years could put between him and the past. Suddenly, the onslaught of memories was just too much... He saw again, as if it were real, that last night...his father standing there, right there by the fireplace, drinking too much, taking offense at everything old Grayson said...

And his mother quietly weeping, her hand on his father's arm, trying to keep him from finishing the last Scotch. The cold rain sheeting across the windows, the shadows of the elms fighting with the shadows of the fire.

Then the slamming doors, the parting threats and the rain-drenched, curving mountain road...

Damn it. Gray's left elbow began to ache, where the bones had knitted but remained sensitive. It might as well have been days since the accident, not years. He couldn't think straight in this room...this house. Maybe not even in this town.

Why on earth had he imagined that he owed his grandfather a warning? Had he really dreamed the old man might have grown a conscience and would meekly agree to admit his error and make restitution?

Fat chance of that. Old Grayson Harper had never been *wrong* in his life.

Besides, what constituted restitution, anyhow? Had Gray really thought that getting back his father's money could *begin* to restore his losses? Grayson had killed Gray's parents, as surely as if he'd put a gun to their heads. He could fill the Harper Marble Quarry with hundred-dollar bills, and it wouldn't begin to make up for what he'd really stolen from that terrified thirteen-year-old boy.

The boy who had awakened in the hospital the next morning, his arms and legs and ribs broken, his head bandaged and his family dead.

With effort, Gray peeled his fingers away from his palm and pumped them to force sensation to return. He had been a fool to come. Warning? *Ha.* He should have just hired a lawyer, filed the suit and let the fur fly.

"Go ahead," his grandfather said quietly, glancing pointedly at Gray's tense hand. "Do it."

Gray shook his head slowly. "I don't hit people."

"No." The scoffing noise his grandfather emitted was eloquent. "And that's the problem in a nutshell, isn't it? You don't *do* anything. You're just like your father. You drift, charming and completely useless in your expensive suits, trying to get by on your clever one-liners and your smarter-than-thou attitude."

He shook his head, as if to shake away the internal image. "You want money? Try *earning* some! If I'd ever seen you do a lick of real work, hard work, I'd leave it *all* to you. Every goddamn penny. Hell, if I could see you hold a real job for even one month, just four lousy weeks, I'd write you a check for the whole kit and caboodle!"

Dismissive old coot! Gray's shoulders twitched, and he felt his legs burn slightly from the urge to stride out the door. The judgmental bastard was so clueless. He hadn't understood his own son, not for a day of his life. Horrified at Gray's father's desire to be a musician, Grayson had forbidden it entirely, and steered him into a dozen "real" careers, each more ill suited than the one before.

And because, in the end, Grayson couldn't make a successful pig farmer out of a poet, he decided the poet was a slacker and a fool.

Gray hesitated, fighting the urge to lash out and give the old man as good as he had dished. But if he let himself stalk off in a huff, what would he have accomplished? He calmed his pulse and considered what his grandfather had said. If Gray could hold a job, he'd return the money. Surely that was almost as good as an admission of guilt.

Could this be the opening he'd hoped for?

For several seconds, fury warred with common sense. Finally, common sense won.

He didn't really want to bring a lawsuit. It would take forever, and it would cost a fortune on its own. He had no interest in humiliating his grandfather publicly. He wanted only the personal, private admission that the old man had wronged Gray's father—and, in doing so, Gray himself.

He eyed his grandfather narrowly. "Will you put that deal in writing? If I do what you ask…if I hold a 'real' job for four weeks straight without bolting, you'll write a check for every penny my father ever gave you to invest for him?"

The old man squinted at him in return as if he suspected a trick. "Not just any job. A hard job. A dirty job. The kind you turned your nose up at all your life."

Gray wanted to ask him, "What do you know of my life?" The last time they'd seen each other, Gray had been nineteen, reckless, defiant and mixed up as hell. Because he'd refused to come back to Silverdell over his college summer breaks and dig marble in the family quarry, the old man had decided Gray was afraid of real work. Just like his father.

How could old Grayson have been so stupid as to miss the truth? Gray wasn't afraid of work. He was afraid of Silverdell and what madness the memories might create in his heart. He was afraid of what living in this house another summer might make him do to his grandfather.

"Of course," Gray said with feigned calm. "I'll accept a job as dirty and demeaning as you want it to be. The only thing I won't do is take a job at the quarry, or anywhere I would report to you."

The old man worked his lips, clearly thinking fast and hard. "It would have to be here. In Silverdell, I mean. So that I could check on you. So that I could be sure it's not a scam."

"Of course." Gray's smile felt twisted. "I wouldn't dream of asking you to trust me."

If old Grayson recognized the sarcasm, he didn't deign to acknowledge it. He scanned his grandson's face so thoroughly it felt like a scouring.

"Then yes," he said, finally. "If you can hold a real, Joe Lunchbucket job here in Silverdell, one with physical labor and no fancy title, and you can keep it for four weeks straight without bolting, or complaining, or getting yourself fired, I'll write a check for any amount you ask."

Chapter 2

It was two in the morning, and though Bree and Penny had been talking for hours, the conversation showed no signs of sputtering out.

They were ensconced in Penny's suite in Aunt Ruth's beautiful old San Francisco Victorian town house. The sitting area was close enough to Ruth's sickroom to hear her if she called out, but private enough to let them chat in peace. They both still wore their day clothes because getting into pajamas seemed too much of an admission that the night might end.

Bree had been visiting her little sister for three whole days—a true luxury, since ordinarily the entire breadth of the country, and their respective obligations, lay between them.

When the sisters had been split up after their father went to jail, sixty-five-year-old Aunt Ruth had taken

Rowena and Penny into her home. But she'd declared herself unequal to mothering all three sisters. After a tense period in which the state seemed likely to get involved, their mother's college roommate had stepped up. Kitty Afton, a Boston divorcée with no children, had always been fond of Bree, and was glad to offer the teenager a home.

Bree had lived in Boston ever since. She told herself she loved it. And yet, three days in a new place, with a fresh perspective and her little sister's calming presence, had done her a world of good. After the mess with Charlie…

She looked at Penny, suddenly wishing she could scoop her up and take her along when she returned to Boston. Without Charlie, without Breelie's, her "perfect" life in the city seemed hollow. Even the trendy Brighton-area condo she'd snagged a year ago—but never had time to decorate—felt lonely and sterile, and she could hardly bring herself to set foot in it again.

But Penny would never agree to leave San Francisco. Ruth, now in her early eighties, had congestive heart failure and needed full-time care. She really ought to be in a nursing facility, Bree thought, but Penny would never abandon the old lady who had put a roof over her head when everything else in their world had exploded.

So Penny couldn't leave, and Bree couldn't stay… not that she'd been invited. Reluctant or not, she had to get back to Boston and see if she could possibly piece her career back together.

Her plane left from San Fran International first thing in the morning.

So they lingered here, not ready to sleep in spite of

the late hour. Bree had stretched out on top of Penny's small sofa, her head propped on the heel of her hand, and Penny had curled up in the adjacent armchair, sketching her sister as they talked.

"So what's our plan for Charlie?" Penny's face was still bent over her sketch, but her lips curved upward, and her smile could be heard in her words. "Shall we boil him in oil? Or can you think of something more creative?"

Bree laughed. Only Penny could say things like that and still look and sound positively angelic. She was undoubtedly the sweetest person Bree had ever met, but that didn't mean she was saccharine or dull. In her gentle, Alice in Wonderland face, sugar and spice co-existed in complete harmony.

"Boiling in oil sounds fine to me." But Bree yawned as she said it, which showed that, thank goodness, she'd finally lost her bloodthirsty enthusiasm for revenge.

The first day here, she'd spent hours detailing Charlie's sins—which, it turned out, had only begun with Iliana Townsend, not ended there. He had also been cooking Breelie's books for God knew how long, draining the savings to keep himself in cool suits and hot women. When news got out that he'd been sacked, vendors all over Boston practically set Bree's phone on fire, calling to complain they hadn't been paid in months.

It had taken Bree weeks to straighten it all out—and every penny of her personal savings, too. She'd stayed in Boston long enough to finish the last event already contracted…but, as she'd predicted, no one had called to hire her company for anything new.

She had one appointment still on the books, a golden wedding anniversary consult that had been set long before the Townsend fiasco and, miraculously, hadn't yet been canceled. She tried to be optimistic. Maybe, from that small job, she could begin to rebuild the business.

But she'd had a few days of rare freedom, and, so ravaged by resentment and self pity she couldn't stand her own company a minute longer, she'd impulsively booked a plane ticket to visit Penny.

Her little sister was probably the only person on earth Bree could have been completely honest with about how much Charlie's betrayal had hurt. Though she was four years younger than Bree, and five years younger than Rowena, Penny was without question the kindest of the three Wright girls, and the wisest. She was a good listener, and a true empath, with no trace of the schadenfreude most people—especially Rowena—might feel on hearing of Bree's misfortune.

Bree had always thought Penny possessed a touch of magic, though it sounded primitive and superstitious to say so. Maybe she should just say that, in less mystical terms, Penny was a…a born healer. And sure enough, over the days in Penny's company, most of the poison and pain had been drained out of the topic of Charlie, leaving Bree tranquil for the first time in more than a month.

"Yeah, deep-fried Charlie sounds just fine." She let her eyes drift shut. "You know, Pea, maybe you should have been a psychiatrist."

It was a musing, slightly slurred non sequitur that probably proved she had moved beyond tired all the way to incoherent. A thought struck her. She hadn't meant to discount Penny's art. "And an artist, too. I mean instead of being *just* an artist. Obviously you had to be an artist."

Penny chuckled. "You won't think so when you see this picture."

Bree opened her eyes, though she knew nothing in the sketch could change her mind about her sister's talent. Whatever Penny turned her hand to, whether it was oils, pen-and-ink sketches, photography or interior decorating, she ended up creating beauty.

Take this simple, cream-colored room, for instance. The rest of Ruth's house was crowded, lacy, oppressively Victorian. But up here, Penny had designed a cool, clean haven from all that. Without any cliché Western decor—no antlered light fixtures, no river-rock mantels, no bucking-horse sculptures—she managed to capture the essence of their beautiful childhood Colorado home, Bell River Ranch.

How did she do it? More magic, really. The one gorgeous piece of peach-and-turquoise pottery that always made Bree think of a spring sunset. One painting, a sunlit stand of birch trees that could have been trite, but instead was pure poetry. A love seat upholstered in muted silvers, blues and pinks, like the shimmering pebbles in the shallows of Bell River.

"I love this room," she said, another non sequitur. She laughed at herself, realizing she sounded a little drunk, although they'd been sipping nothing but almond-honey tea all night. She climbed up on her knees and peered over the arm of the sofa. "Okay, let me see the picture. If it's awful, though, it's not your fault. Too bad I don't have Ro's problem and get skinny when I'm upset. I bet from that angle my rear end looks huge."

Penny held out the crisp, thick paper with a smile.

"Lucky for you I never got to the rear-end part. I spent the whole time trying to get your face right."

Bree was curious now—and maybe, if she was honest, a little embarrassed. She knew she didn't look her best. She might not have Rowena's problem, but when she wasn't happy her face could look very drawn and hard. She felt hard, since Charlie, and she dreaded seeing that reflected through Penny's eyes.

But when she summoned the courage to look at the paper, the face she saw there didn't look tough at all. In fact, Penny's version of Bree oozed vulnerability. Her blond hair was tousled, and her T-shirt had slid down one shoulder. Her cheekbones were pronounced and graceful, but shadows underscored her abnormally large blue eyes.

She looked wounded, and slightly bewildered, as if she were a child who couldn't understand why anyone would have wanted to hurt her.

She let her hand lower the sketch to her hip. She stared at her sister, frowning. "Is that how I really look?"

Penny raised one shoulder. "Well, you're more beautiful than that," she said. "I'm not good enough to do you justice."

Bree shook her head. "Don't be silly, Pea."

Compliments like that made Bree feel like some kind of criminal fraud. Penny always saw the world through the prism of her own inner sweetness—which was a great beautifier. But right now…

If Bree had really been such a beauty, would her fiancé have been so eager to sleep with a forty-five-year-old married woman made almost entirely of nips and tucks?

Bree held out the sketch so that Penny could see it again. "I mean, do I look this...weak?"

Penny bent forward and studied her drawing with a small frown of concentration. Bree appreciated that she didn't pretend to misunderstand.

"You look very sad," Penny said finally. She glanced up, her brown eyes warm, and smiled to soften the pronouncement. "Which is why we really must toss the bum in boiling oil, first chance we get."

Bree had a horrifying sensation of stinging heat just under her eyelids, and she knew that, if she weren't very, very careful, she could actually end up crying.

Which was unacceptable. "Smile, Brianna," Kitty's voice in her head repeated, as always. "No one likes a sad sack."

"What if it isn't actually Charlie's fault?" She forced herself to meet Penny's eyes. "He says...he says I drove him to it. He says I'm always so critical, so hard to please. He says if I had ever really been the kind of fiancée who helped and supported his decisions—"

Penny snorted delicately. "Oh, for heaven's sake, Bree. Listen to yourself! You're going to believe that lying scumbag? That's the classic technique for abusive boyfriends, you know. Shifting the blame to you, hoping you'll think it's all somehow your fault."

Penny was right, of course. It was the abuser's easy out...*you made me do it.* But Charlie hadn't just been trying to weasel free of the blame. He didn't say those things until he knew the relationship was truly over and he couldn't ever win her back. Problem was, she could hear in his voice, and see in his face, that he meant it. Really meant it.

It was hard to even think back on the contempt in

Charlie's voice as he'd hurled those accusations at her. Harder still, because, deep down inside, she had heard the ring of truth.

"I *am* critical, Pea. You know it's true. I don't know why, but I always seem to be pointing out everyone's mistakes. Especially Charlie's."

Penny was shaking her head. "I don't care if you whipped him with his own belt, mocked his manhood and made him sleep in the root cellar. You still didn't *make* him cheat. You didn't *make* him steal. You didn't *make* him destroy Breelie's. Someone ought to introduce Charlie Newmark to the idea of personal responsibility."

Bree was grateful for the vehemence in Penny's voice, and the loyalty that caused it. But she didn't want to sweep this under the carpet. If she didn't acknowledge her failings, how was she ever going to change anything? If she couldn't get better, she would never be able to put together a relationship that would last.

She didn't want to be alone forever.

"But it's not just Charlie, is it? Every boyfriend I've ever had has said something similar." She flushed as an old, half-forgotten memory came flooding miserably back. The day the sexiest rebel in her ninth-grade class, the boy she'd secretly had a crush on for months, had humiliated her in front of everyone. Wild Gray Harper…he had thought she was cold, prissy and boring…even way back then.

Penny looked at her oddly, and if Bree didn't want to explain that sad old story, she had to recover quickly. "And Rowena," she added. "Charlie might have taken the words right out of her mouth. And Kitty, too—though she sugar-coated it most of the time."

"Kitty was a cross between Pollyanna and a Stepford wife." Penny laughed again, but more softly, as if out of respect for Bree's obvious distress. "She thought it was a sin for a lady to frown, or express a single authentic feeling, or do anything but coddle and flatter the men in her life. I don't know how you stood it all those years."

"She did her best," Bree said loyally. "She wasn't even related to us, you know. She didn't have to take me in."

"I know." Penny's laughter faded away. "That was a dumb thing to say. I'm sorry."

They were silent a moment, remembering, though it was like remembering a nightmare they'd inexplicably all dreamed at exactly the same time. Such horrors couldn't exist in the real world, surely. Their beautiful mother, lying broken and bleeding at the foot of the staircase. Sweet little Penny, so pitiful and bewildered. Penny, who had turned eleven that day, and was unaware that her birthday dress trailed through the blood as she knelt beside the silent body, begging her mother to wake up.

Their father, hauled off to jail for deliberately pushing his unfaithful wife over the railing. A phantasmagoric trial, in which their pathetic, shameful family secrets were trotted out, naked, for all the world to gawk at.

Johnny Wright...rotting in jail for years, so intractably angry. Rejecting the few overtures the sisters could bring themselves to make. Finally dying there of a brain tumor that may well have caused his irrational behavior from the start.

But worst of all was the ripping apart of the sisters, all of them just children, really, as well-meaning social workers, remote family connections and dutiful family friends stepped up, one by one, to offer them a place to live.

Bree shook the memories away. She couldn't let herself drown in them, not after all these years.

She smiled at Penny to show she wasn't angry. They both felt the same grateful loyalty to their respective saviors. Ruth and Kitty weren't perfect, but they'd voluntarily offered the drowning girls harbors in the storm. Ruth had provided stability and an almost cloistered quiet, which Penny's personality had needed. And Kitty, the compulsively smiling divorcée, had, in her own weird, Stepford way, shown Bree how to snap herself out of the trance of shock and grief.

"The point is that they're all saying the same thing," Bree went on. "It's as if they're reading from the same script. They say I am self-righteous, judgmental. I think I know better than everyone else. I'm never willing to trust other people to do things right on their own."

She tucked her hair behind her ear and looked away, over toward Penny's soothing painting of birch trunks. "They can't all be wrong. There must be some truth in it."

Penny didn't respond right away. She tapped her pencil against the sketch pad and ran her lower lip through her teeth softly.

"Well, even if there is…even if you do find it difficult to trust other people…is that so strange, given what happened to us? Why shouldn't you be afraid that people will let you down? Who, in the end, *didn't* let us down?"

And that, too, had the ring of truth. For a minute, Bree couldn't respond. All she had to do was think back, and she could see that the troubles had begun long before the murder. A mother who had always been emotionally absent...a father who couldn't control his jealous rages. Three little girls who practically raised themselves.

There'd been a whole year—Bree realized now that her mother must have taken a new lover—when a ten-year-old Bree had scavenged in the kitchen almost every night, trying to find something to feed Penny. Rowena, as usual, simply hadn't eaten.

One night Bree turned dinner into a hunt for pirate treasure, filling the bread box with carrot "coins" and radish "rubies." She'd felt such triumph, because Penny, only six at the time, had been enchanted. She had never guessed that she feasted on pirate carrots because there wasn't anything else to eat.

"It did something to all of us," Penny went on softly. "Think about Rowena. She was always so angry. She wouldn't get close to anyone for years. At least you try."

Suddenly, in the midst of her stupid self-absorption, Bree realized that Penny's face had grown sad, too. If she'd had any artistic talent, she could have sketched a portrait of Penny that was every bit as melancholy as the one of herself she held in her hand right now.

"What about you, sweetpea?" She lowered her voice, just in case Ruth was awake. "What did it do to you?"

Penny smiled vaguely. For a minute, Bree thought her sister might not even answer. But after several seconds, Penny held out a hand and swept it from left to right, as if to encompass the whole town house.

"It made me cautious. Too cautious. It made me hide out here," she said. "All these years. Here, where the storm can't touch me."

Oh…. Her heart stabbed, Bree stretched across the footboard and took her little sister's hand. She held it tightly, palm to palm, fingers wrapped around the fragile bones and satiny skin.

They really were like two shipwrecked sailors, holding fast to each other for fear the current would sweep them apart and make them struggle alone.

"We'll be all right, Pea. Somehow, we'll figure it out. We'll find a way to put the past behind us, and we'll be happy again. Who knows? Maybe we'll even find a way to be…normal."

She hoped the joke would lighten the mood, but her voice trembled, and it didn't come out quite as humorously as she'd hoped.

As usual, Penny was the one who knew exactly what to say. She squeezed Bree's hand, straightened her spine and gave her a mischievous grin.

"Of course we will," she said, "Look at Rowena! After all those years of being the world's prickliest female, she married her true love, became a stepmother—"

Bree laughed. "To a little hellion."

"Maybe, but he worships the ground she walks on. And she's making her dude-ranch dream come true. Frankly, she's so darn normal it's disgusting."

Bree laughed and let go of her sister's hand. "How

long before she finds a way to screw all that up, do you think?"

"Brianna." Penny frowned. "That's not fair."

Bree shrugged. She loved Rowena, but she didn't trust her. Ro had pushed everyone away for so long, closing off her heart. It had made her cold and selfish, and it had meant that loving her was dangerous. Marriage seemed to have mellowed her, but Bree was too cynical to believe the change was permanent.

Penny set her sketchbook on the end table and lay her pencil on top of it gently. She stretched, yawned and then rested her head on the arm of the chair, her luminous brown eyes gazing, doelike, at Bree.

"Ro seems absolutely blissful," Penny insisted softly. "Everything's going so well. The ranch has its soft opening in about a week."

"I know." Ten days, in fact. Bree kept tabs on the progress of the ranch more closely than Penny could imagine. It was their inheritance, too, and she didn't intend to let Rowena lose everything.

Ro was passionate, sure, but she wasn't good at the long haul. Every week, Bree half expected to hear that her restless, fiery older sister had grown bored, or fought with Dallas, or come down with her old gypsy fever. "Well, I *guess* they'll have the opening…if she doesn't get claustrophobic and run away again."

The silence that followed Bree's acidic comment made her flush uncomfortably. She heard how bitter and unforgiving she sounded. She wanted to take the words back, but that wouldn't be quite honest.

She had tried to forgive and forget, to believe that change was possible. And yet…she still had a rough, scarred-over spot inside her heart where her trust in Rowena used to be.

"I don't know," she said, trying to explain. "It's just that…" But she couldn't finish the sentence. She'd said it all before, and she knew Penny didn't agree.

"Oh, Bree." Finally, Penny smiled. "You know, if you really think you should try to be less judgmental, Rowena might be a pretty good place to start."

Of his almost thirty-one years of life, Gray had resided in Silverdell full time only about five—from the age of thirteen, when his parents died, until eighteen, when he went off to college. Before the accident, he lived wherever his dad's newest doomed venture took them—a horse ranch in Crawford, a pig farm in Butte. After high school, Gray had never come back to Silverdell, not even when he had flunked out of college and his grandfather cut off all funds.

But those five years had been notable for their intense resentment and rebellion. And for the salt-of-the-earth Dellians, they'd apparently been unforgettable. He must have been even more obnoxious than he remembered, because he couldn't find a soul in town willing to hire him to so much as change a lightbulb.

It was only noon, the Monday after his talk with his grandfather, and he'd already struck out at the hardware store, the brickyard and the ranch over at Windy River. Those businesses were all hiring. They just weren't hiring Grayson Harper's black-sheep grandson, who had always been a troublemaker and a wiseass and clearly had condescended to return to Silverdell only so that he could sniff around the old man's will.

But Gray wasn't giving up. In fact, the rejection felt like the kind of challenge he loved. There had to be someone in this town who didn't hold his youth against him. Someone, perhaps, who wasn't a fan of Grayson Harper and might be sympathetic to the orphan who had found himself under his dictatorial thumb.

Crusty old coots like his grandfather made enemies, and all Gray had to do was find one.

Meanwhile, the April sun was climbing up a cloudless turquoise sky, and Gray was hot, tired and hungry. Lunch and another study of the classifieds sounded perfect. Luckily, Silverdell had just about the best barbecue in Colorado.

He glanced down Elk Avenue, remembering that someone had said Marianne Donovan was back in town and she'd opened a café that was pretty good.

She might be the perfect place to start. Not that Marianne qualified as old Grayson's enemy—far from it. Her mother had been Gray's grandmother's nurse, years ago, and the families were still close.

But Marianne had always had a soft spot for Gray, too, the way gentle good girls sometimes did when they met a certain kind of bad boy.

He began walking the main street, noting all the new storefronts, checking for her place. She'd been an instinctively domestic female, even as a teenager, so her restaurant was probably great. Besides, seeing her again would be a pleasant fringe benefit of this visit. She'd been such a nice kid—he had actually found himself being careful with her, treating her with a respect he rarely offered anyone during those angry years.

He almost walked right past it. The place was still

under construction, and the sign hadn't even been hung yet. It leaned against the front bay window, but at the last minute he registered its kelly-green letters in a Celtic script. *Donovan's Dream.*

He backed up and took a look through the cute bay window, which was framed by white Irish-lace curtains draped over a shining brass rod. He spotted Marianne immediately, and smiled to see how little she'd changed. Still fighting those messy red curls and those extra five pounds. Still unable to fully hide the sprinkle of freckles she'd inherited from her mother. Still a well-bred, classic good girl, even though she was his age—pushing thirty.

She was taking someone's order, listening intently to every word they said. But at the same time, her intelligent green eyes were alert to everything going on around her, as any good restaurant owner would be.

Within a few seconds, she noticed him at the window. He expected her to take a minute to recognize him, and maybe another minute to believe her eyes. But she didn't look the least bit surprised to see him standing there. She simply smiled and extended her free hand, beckoning him in enthusiastically.

So…she had heard. Either she was still in contact with his grandfather, or the Silverdell grapevine was as dependable as ever. He nodded, returning her smile, and moved back toward the front door, which opened with a sweet cascade of bells he recognized as the first few notes of "Danny Boy."

She met him at the threshold, holding out her arms for a hug. "Oh, it's so good to see you, Gray," she said. She didn't stint on the hug, and when she pulled back she gazed at him uninhibitedly. "It's been so long. Too long. But you look every bit as gorgeous, you devil."

He grinned. "So do you."

To his surprise, she flushed and self-consciously put a hand to her hair. "Don't be silly. I—" For a moment, her smile faded. "I don't know if your grandfather told you about...well, it's been a tough year. My husband died just before Christmas. And my mother lost her battle with breast cancer about a month later."

Suddenly Gray felt as if he'd been gone a hundred years. Her mother, dead? He'd liked Eileen Donovan very much—and he'd always understood that his grandfather worshipped the woman from afar, his one grand chivalric gesture in a lifetime of rapacious greed and domineering chauvinism.

But Gray hadn't even realized her mother had been sick. That's what happened when you peeled rubber as you sped out of town, then tore off your rearview mirror and chucked it onto the asphalt at the county line.

He frowned. "No. He didn't tell me. I didn't even know you were married."

"Eight years," she said, lifting her left hand, which still wore a simple gold band. She folded her fingers into her palm, as if to feel the comforting squeeze of the ring. "We met in college."

He touched her shoulder. And then, for the first time, he could see that she had changed after all. Her eyes, once as clear as clover, as simple as grass, held depths and complexities and pain. They looked more like his eyes now—although his had been this way since he was thirteen.

"I'm so sorry, Mari. That's a heavy load, losing them so close together."

"Yes," she said simply. "Of course, you understand better than most."

But then, as if she knew he wouldn't want to open that conversation, she smiled again. She hadn't ever been one to wallow in self-pity, anyhow, he remembered. She had wanted their relationship to go further, but when he told her he just wanted to be friends, she'd accepted it like a trooper.

"But enough about me." She tilted a sideways glance at him. "Let's talk about you. For starters, I know exactly why you're here."

"You do?"

"Absolutely. You're looking for a job." She was teasing. He knew her voice well enough still to recognize its notes.

"I am?"

"Yep. But I'm sorry to say we're not hiring today. I've just found an excellent teenage boy who is happy to wash my dishes for gas money, which is all I can afford to pay him."

Gray tilted his head, smiling down at her. "How did you know that I—"

She laughed and put her hand under his arm, leading him deeper into the café. "Everybody knows, silly. Don't you remember Silverdell? They certainly remember you."

"So I've gathered. Most of them have clearly decided they wouldn't hire me if I were the last day laborer on earth."

"Exactly. No fatted calf for you, my friend. In the eyes of Silverdell, you are *not* forgiven."

He raised one eyebrow. "So...what do you think sealed my fate? Switching tombstones that Halloween? Teaching the naked limbo to Mayor Simpson's cross-eyed niece? Or… I know…maybe it was that thing with the moose head?"

"All of the above." Her green eyes twinkled, and she looked more like herself. "Although that moose head…that was plain nasty."

He chuckled. They'd arrived at the one empty table in the restaurant. She pointed to a chair, wordlessly instructing him to sit. Then she grabbed a bright green laminated menu card from its slot in the nearest wait station and placed it in front of him.

"But don't despair, Gray. I happen to know there's at least one person in town who will be completely sympathetic to your cause. And, lucky for you, she *is* hiring right now."

Gray looked up. *"She?"*

"Yep. She. Our newest local entrepreneur. The one person in town whose reputation was even half as bad as yours."

He tried to think. Had anyone around here ever been as reckless and rude as he had? Surely no female. Silverdell women tended to be well-behaved and demure. The cadre of bitchy elder ladies, like that skinny harpy Mrs. Fillmore, insisted on it. No one dared to—

And suddenly he knew. His eyes widened.

"Oh, my God," he said. "Crazy Rowena Wright has come home."

Chapter 3

Bree didn't call ahead to let Rowena know she was coming.

It wasn't that she thought surprising her sister would be fun. Rowena was as likely to be irked by an unannounced visit as she was to be delighted. Bree didn't call because, right up until the last minute, she couldn't bring herself to commit to really, truly going to Bell River Ranch at all.

Every mile along the way, she kept assuring herself she could always change her mind. Drive away. Get back on an airplane and fly home to Boston.

But somehow merely saying that phrase, "home to Boston," made her realize how little she belonged there, even after sixteen years. And so she didn't turn around. She kept driving, from the Gunnison airport toward Silverdell, every minute bringing her closer to the one place in the world she had ever thought of as home.

And the one place in the world she'd ever thought of as hell.

She skirted Silverdell's downtown area, not ready to be seen by anyone she used to know. Instead, she took the loop-around on what the locals called Mansion Street—though maps and strangers called it Callahan Circle. Bell River was the first ranch you encountered as you exited the city limits, so after she passed the elegant old Harper estate she knew she had only about two more miles to go.

Her heart beat faster, and she tightened her fingers on the wheel. Dread...or excitement? She no longer knew.

Man-made structures thinned out the minute she crossed the city line, giving way to open spaces, acre after acre of rolling country greening with spring. The occasional cow or horse gazed placidly at her as she coasted by, and a pair of brown falcons watched her sternly from a fence post, but for those two miles she didn't see another human being.

And then, too soon, the acres that spread out beside the road were Bell River acres. She knew every undulation, every tree, as well as she knew the lines and pads of her own palm. The rippling pastures were achingly the same as they'd been twenty years ago when she'd ridden her bike home from elementary school along this same road.

The same—except better. Much, much better.

She hadn't visited since the wedding four months ago. It had been winter, then—and Rowena had still been in the early, messy stages of renovations, the part of the process where you saw only the broken eggs, not the promise of the omelet.

Now it was April, the time when Colorado clouds began to lift, as if the tent of blue sky actually were being winched up higher and higher each day. The air felt fresh, green with sunshine and sweet breezes.

And the creation of the dude ranch was much further along. The first thing Bree noticed as she turned into the long front driveway was how well the grounds had been groomed. The palsied bristlecone pines on either side of the rickety front fence had been pruned up, as if by dancing masters obsessed with posture. The fence itself had had been replaced with a pair of scrolled wrought-iron gates that stood crisply open, smiling a glossy black welcome.

Muddy patches that once had pitted the fields on either side of the driveway had been converted to smooth carpets of emerald grass.

A few more yards and she got her first good look at the house, set like a jewel in its setting of sparkling white paddocks. It had been freshly painted pale green, with a brand-new hunter-green roof and a wide white porch trimmed in lush hanging baskets of ferns, ivy and lipstick-red geraniums.

Her foot almost stalled on the gas, and the rental car slowed to a crawl. "Wow," she said to the empty car. Rowena had worked a miracle, considering how tight their budget was and how short the timetable.

It was gorgeous. No longer a downtrodden, half-neglected white elephant, but a home. Wholesome, peaceful and inviting. All the things the ranch had never been, even before their mother's death.

Bree determined to make a point of telling her sis-

ter so. Maybe that would help break the ice…get them
off on the right foot. She would show Rowena right
away that she wasn't here as judge, or spy, or critic.
She was here as a friend.

As a sister.

Sister. As if the word were emotionally electrified,
a frisson of fear sizzled through her. It had been a long
time since she'd been comfortable with that word, at
least in relation to Rowena.

She mustn't let herself get carried away. While the
ranch might look inviting, the "invitation" wasn't designed for her. The beautiful scene was, quite literally, a stage set for an ad in a glossy brochure. The
goal was to coax paying guests into booking their va-
cations here.

Her only incontestable credential was her status as
co-owner of the soon-to-open enterprise. Her name,
Brianna Allison Wright, was listed on those thick loan
documents—loans that haunted her every time she
thought about how big the numbers were.

She had every right to show up, with or without advance notice, if only to check on the renovations and
see how her money was being spent.

Besides, about twenty windows overlooked this
front driveway, so she probably had already been spotted. She hit the gas again, pulled around to the back of
the house where a nicely landscaped parking lot had
been created and slipped the car into a space.

Then, squaring her shoulders, she got out.

She left her suitcase in the trunk, though. She still
felt more comfortable having an escape, just in case.
She could pretend she had just stopped by to say hi.

She could say she had a reservation in Aspen, or Crested Butte, or anywhere, to…to do…

Something else. Anything else. In case Ro made it clear Bree wasn't welcome to stay here.

She climbed quickly onto the back porch and made her way to the door, which used to open onto a laundry room, but now, she knew, would lead into the expanded kitchen. She smelled coffee, so she knew Rowena was up, even though it was only a little after eight.

All three sisters had always been early risers. Work on a ranch started before the sun came up, and their father wouldn't have tolerated sleeping in.

Eventually, being early birds had been more than a pattern—it had been in their blood. In all the years Bree had lived on the East Coast, she'd never truly adjusted to night-owl hours. Charlie had often laughed at her, saying they should have called the company "Cinderella's" instead of "Breelie's." What a joke, a high-society event coordinator who started yawning at midnight!

"Watch out! Hey, lady! Watch out!"

Startled out of her thoughts, Bree frowned. The child's shrill voice seemed to be trying to pierce through a cacophony of noise—a hectic tizzy of clucking, barking, screeching, fluttering and stomping. Bree grabbed the doorknob instinctively, as if she might have to flee inside the house, and wheeled around to see what on earth…

Good grief! The area behind her whirled with an onslaught of motion. Inexplicably, about a dozen chickens squawked toward her, frantic and brainless, running into each other comically, stumbling over the stairs as they stormed them, feathers flying. Behind the chickens, a glossy brown puppy galloped in ec-static pursuit. Its long tongue waved like a wet, pink ribbon from its idiotic grin, its soft ears lifted like furry propellers and its gigantic feet churned up con-trails of dust in its path.

Behind the puppy, a boy thundered across the grass, trying to catch up, one hand waving to get her atten-tion, the other recklessly swinging a big straw basket.

It was Alec, Rowena's high-strung stepson. Bree didn't have to look twice. She recognized immediately the mop of thick blond hair and the half devil, half angel charm of the skinny, suntanned face.

"Lady, watch out for the chickens!"

Without thinking, Bree twisted the knob and the door swung open in her hand. She wasn't entirely sure why she did that. She didn't exactly need to plunge to safety behind the refrigerator, or beg her big sister for help. She couldn't possibly think a flock of dithering chickens, a slobbering puppy and a nine-year-old imp posed a significant physical threat.

But, jangled, she did it anyhow—and the result of her actions could have been predicted. The chickens streamed through the escape route the open door of-fered, and the puppy followed joyously, dirt and all.

"Oh, no," she said, thinking they were the most use-less words in the English language, and annoyed with herself for being paralyzed by the ridiculous farce.

The imp pounded up the stairs, pausing just long enough to give her a disgusted look. "Great," he said, staring gloomily through the open door. "Brilliant." Then he took a deep breath and continued the chase inside.

After that, what could Bree do but follow? Maybe she could stop being so fuzzy-minded and help....

But it was too late. In his attempt to catch the puppy, Alec had overturned his basket, and the shining new tiles of the kitchen floor suddenly seemed covered in shining yellow glop, disgustingly dotted with islands of white shards.

Oh, no. He had obviously been gathering the chicken eggs. Judging from the wet mess, his basket must have been full of them. As Bree watched in horror, he slipped in the goo and thudded hard on the floor, face down. The puppy ran two demented circles around him, just enough to get its paws thoroughly coated in raw egg, then streaked off to share the excitement with the rest of the house.

Alec lifted his face, his chin seeming to drip lumpy yellow gore. He narrowed his prematurely handsome blue eyes, and opened his mouth as if to say something heartfelt. But then his jaw went slack. "Bree?"

She smiled weakly. "Hi."

"Alec, what the...?" An irritable male voice boomed from around the corner. The sound was followed immediately by its owner, a shirtless, golden-haired god wearing only a pair of half-buttoned, low-riding blue jeans and a few white tufts of shaving cream missed by a recent razor.

Or, as other people knew him, Dallas Garwood. The sheriff of Silverdell County. Rowena's hunky new husband.

"Why the devil are the chickens in the house?" Dallas's attention was at first focused exclusively on his son, who still sprawled on the floor, wearing a goatee of egg yolk. "Oh, hell, Alec. Is that the eggs?"

"It's not my fault, Dad," Alec protested vehemently. He tried to scramble to his feet, but the slippery floor defeated him, and he couldn't get any higher than a kneeling position. "I totally had it under control, no problem. Then *she* went and opened the door."

She would have paid a king's ransom, at that moment, to fall through a trapdoor in the floor.

But in spite of the extensive renovations, apparently no one had thought to add an escape hatch. She could only wait in mute misery as Dallas frowned, turned and finally saw her. She still stood by the front door, her hand on the knob as if magnetized to it.

His blue eyes, so like his son's, widened. *"Bree?"*

"I'm sorry," she said, though she wasn't sure which part she was apologizing for. For opening the door and letting the livestock into the house, for catching him half dressed or for having the dumb idea to come to Bell River in the first place.

"You...you did this?"

"Well. I did open the door," she admitted. Then she shook her head helplessly. "To be honest, I have no idea what just happened. It's all a bit of a blur."

"I can believe that." To her surprise, he grinned, and then he began to laugh. "Welcome to Bell River, Bree. Around here, the forecast is always sunny with a ninety percent chance of Alec."

Without the least sign of self-consciousness, he crossed the rivulets of egg, avoiding them as much as he could, and wrapped in a warm hug.

"How fantastic that you came. Ro will be thrilled." He turned to his son. "You start cleaning this mess up, Alec. I'll go see if I can corral the circus."

"What circus?" Rowena suddenly appeared on the

other side of the large, walk-in freezer. She was smiling, but she looked exhausted, as if the preparation for the soft opening had worn her out. She was also dirty… a real mess, and at first Bree thought she'd somehow become tangled in the chicken-puppy-egg fiasco.

When Ro drew closer, though, Bree could see that she must have been gardening. Her hands were covered in earth, her cheeks smudged and dirty and the knees of her clover-green jeans were black. About half her long dark hair was clipped back with a green barrette, but the rest was in disarray, wisps clinging to the perspiration on her temples, her collarbone and her damp T-shirt.

"Alec!" Smile fading, Rowena scanned the chaos. Then she turned to Dallas, which led her green-eyed gaze to Bree. Her dramatic eyebrows drew together. "*Bree?* What are *you* doing here?"

The minute she said it, she seemed to realize it had come out wrong, because she bit her lower lip and shot a self-conscious glance at her husband.

"I mean…" She tried in vain to swipe some of the dirty, damp hair from her face. "I'm glad you're here, whatever the reason. I am just sorry you've caught us…in such a state."

Bree shook her head. "No, it's my fault. I should have called ahead, or made a reservation or something. I should have given you some warning."

"Warning?" Dallas laughed, and his easy charm smoothed over what was rapidly becoming a very bumpy conversational road. "To stay in your own home? Wouldn't that be kind of silly? Besides, advance notice probably wouldn't have helped. We always seem to be in crisis mode these days. Although—" he transferred his wry smile to his son "—I have to admit the eggs are a special touch. How about you get going cleaning these up, kiddo?"

"Yes, sir," the boy muttered, his tone just the safe side of polite, but his face sour as he surveyed the chore. He rolled his eyes, then bent forward and plucked a large, curved piece of eggshell from the stew and chucked it into the sink just over his head.

In the distance, the puppy began to bark frantically, followed by the crazed clucking of chickens. Dallas groaned. "I think that's my cue."

He put his arm around Bree's shoulder and hugged her lightly. "See you tonight," he said, as if he took it for granted that she would be staying. "Your suitcases are in the car, I guess. Don't bring them in. Barton will be here in an hour or so, and he'll be glad to do it."

Bree nodded. When she'd been in town for the wedding, she'd met their general manager, a courtly older man named Barton James who used to own a successful dude ranch in Crested Butte. It was probably true that he'd be glad to help. He had come out of retirement because he couldn't stand being idle.

Dallas smiled, as if to reassure Bree one more time that she was welcome. Then he stepped to Rowena and kissed her hard on the lips, apparently not in the least deterred by her dirt-smudged face and sweaty hair.

Bree looked away from the intimacy of that simple touch, and her gaze met Alec's. He rolled his eyes again, eloquently, with all the disgust a nine-year-old could express for the mushiness of adults.

"Might as well get used to it," he said morosely, extricating another bit of eggshell. "They're like this all the time."

Then the doorbell rang.

Rowena pulled free of Dallas's embrace, though she kept one hand against his naked chest, as if she couldn't bear to lose the connection entirely. Her head turned sharply toward the front of the house.

"Oh, my God. Has my interview showed up early?" She glanced at the clock on the stove just behind Alec and moaned. "Oh, no. It can't be. It's not really eight-thirty?"

"It's really eight-thirty," Dallas said. "I'm sorry. I should have warned you it was getting late. You always lose track of time out there."

Rowena had begun brushing her palms together, as if she might be able to whisk away the crusting of soil, but her hands remained shadowed with dirt. She touched her chin, checking for dirt there, but she seemed to realize she was only making matters worse.

"I need a shower. I can't interview anyone like this, but especially not—"

"I'll let him in," Dallas offered quickly.

But Rowena shook her head. "You're half-naked, and you know you two have never really gotten along. Besides, you're on chicken duty."

"I'll do it," Alec piped up eagerly, trying to clamber to his feet, but once again finding it difficult. Apparently even playing butler seemed exciting compared to mopping egg gunk off the floor.

"You most certainly will not." Dallas held up his hands emphatically to freeze his son in place. "You're the most disreputable member of the family right now. And that's saying something."

"I can let him in," Bree heard herself saying. She felt a little like Alec, jumping at the chance to leave the room rather than continue an awkward encounter. But her event-planner side had kicked in, and her intervention was the only answer that made sense.

The doubt in Rowena's eyes wasn't exactly flattering. "Bree, I couldn't ask you to—"

"You're not asking. I'm volunteering. I promise I won't blow your chance to hire this guy, whoever he is. This is the kind of work I do all the time. I'll handle the meet and greet, then dance him around a little, maybe tour the property while you guys pull it together in here."

The doorbell rang again.

"That would be terrific. Thanks, Bree." Dallas nodded toward Rowena, who still frowned, obviously uncertain. "You shower, Ro. I'll get the chickens. Alec will fix the kitchen." He impaled the boy with a sharp glance. "Or else."

"Sounds like a plan." Like any good salesman, Bree took the yes as final. She dropped her purse on the counter and picked her way carefully toward the great room on the other side of the kitchen. "Oh... I guess I should know which job this guy's applying for."

Rowena hesitated. "Assistant social director. Part time. Thirty hours. Minimum wage."

Pretty menial job, Bree thought, to be causing such a stir. So what if he didn't like Ro's grubby fingernails or a little chicken poop in the hall? If he got scared off, so what? Surely qualified candidates for that job were easy to find.

"All right," she said neutrally, determined not to show her confusion. She wasn't here to criticize, remember? She had to stop forgetting that, stop lapsing into her old ways. This was Ro's dream, Ro's decision, Ro's hire. "And his name?"

Rowena blinked, her dark lashes shadowing her green eyes. She opened her mouth, closed it, then blinked again. The doorbell sounded its two-note call a third time, which apparently agitated the chickens, who were closer now, close enough that Bree could hear the flutter of wings above their clucking.

"I probably should know his name, Ro."

"Of course." With one deep breath, Rowena seemed to snap out of her weird spell as quickly as she'd fallen into it. "Actually, you know him, or at least you used to. Remember…remember old man Harper's grandson, Gray?"

Bree frowned. Everyone remembered Gray Harper. The bad and beautiful new kid in town. Part jokester, part heartbreaker—all trouble. The heir to the Harper Quarry millions who had become a local legend when he kissed the money goodbye rather than, as he put it, kiss his grandfather's "arrogant ass."

"Gray Harper? Applying to be your part-time assistant social director? You're kidding, right?"

Rowena shook her head. "Nope. Sorry. Still want to dance him around?"

"I…well, sure," Bree said with a careful smile. No judging, remember? No criticizing. And definitely no being afraid of a formerly snotty teenager who probably wouldn't even remember what he did to her. "Of course."

She left the room, determined to reach the foyer before he pressed the bell again. She smoothed her skirt and checked her hair in the hall mirror. Everything tidy. She'd do fine.

But honestly…what was Rowena thinking?

Gray Harper?

Chapter 4

Just when Gray thought Rowena must have changed her mind about interviewing him, the front door finally opened.

But the elegant blonde knockout who stood there, smiling coolly, wasn't Rowena. No way Rowena could have changed that much, not even after sixteen years, not even after the mellowing experience of falling in love and getting married. Gray considered himself a connoisseur of beautiful women, and even when he was only thirteen he'd understood that Rowena's fiery good looks weren't a product of cosmetics, clothes or hairstyles. She was all dramatic, gypsy bone structure and primal energy.

And, of course, there was the problem of the coloring. She might have dyed her hair, but no way even contact lenses could transform Rowena's flashing eyes, which had been the color of melted emeralds, into this cool pair of iced-sapphire blue.

Cool. Ice.

The words triggered something. He dug around in his psyche for a couple of seconds, then pulled it out: *Aw, heck.* Wouldn't you know it would be one of the guilty memories, one of those inexcusable episodes from his angry years? He seemed to have an inexhaustible supply. Some more rotten than others.

This one really reeked. God, he'd been such an ass back then.

But at least he recognized her now. This was the middle Wright sister, Bree. She'd been his age, so they'd been in the same class, but she hadn't been in his group. She had hung with the student council crowd, the prissy, overachiever girls who had annoyed the heck out of him in those days.

He wouldn't ever have guessed that she'd grow up to be so gorgeous. When their mother was killed and the Wright girls left town, the middle sister had still been in that awkward stage, unsure what to do with anything she possessed, from her thick, nearly white hair to her long, gangly legs.

But she knew now. From crown to polished toenail, she was slick and citified and possessed a distinctive eastern seaboard chic. The look might still be a bit icy—alabaster skin, blue suit to match her violet-bluebell eyes, sleek Grace Kelly French twist showing off expensive pearl earrings. But she somehow managed to pack a visceral wallop, even so.

"Hi, Bree," he said, hoping his surprise—and his more pleasantly primitive reactions—weren't too obvious. "I assumed you probably were a partner in the dude ranch, but I didn't realize you had moved back to town, too."

"Hello, Gray." She smiled politely, all professionalism and poise. "I haven't moved back. I'm just here for a visit, and to help out a little with the soft opening, if I can. Most of the time, I'll be a partner in name only."

"That's a shame," he said. And he meant it. He would have enjoyed spending time with a woman this attractive—assuming she wouldn't scuttle his chances of getting the job.

He wondered if it was even remotely possible that she'd forgotten about…the ice.

He had to laugh at his own wishful thinking. No, it was not even remotely possible she'd forgotten. But perhaps she would want to pretend she had. Her whole bearing announced that she had more than her share of pride.

"I'm so sorry we kept you waiting." She took a step forward, putting one foot onto the porch, which surprised him. They were going out, not in?

Suddenly, from somewhere in the house behind her, a strange, high-pitched noise rang out. He glanced over her shoulder, wondering what on earth could have made such a sound. But her face remained utterly impassive, not even a twitch revealing that she'd heard it.

Man, she was good. He wouldn't want to have to play poker with her. Their gazes locked, and he blinked first. After a couple of seconds, he actually began to wonder whether he had imagined the sound.

She stepped across the threshold, pulling the door shut behind her, and gave him another smile. "Rowena is running a bit late for the interview, so she asked me to show you around the ranch. We're all very excited about the plans for Bell River, and we think you will be, too."

She didn't wait for him to agree, but moved on down the stairs without looking back, taking his cooperation for granted—which made sense, of course. After all, she was the boss lady and he was just a hired hand, assuming he got the job.

Mr. Minimum Wage. Still, Gray wasn't complaining. The view he got while she walked ahead of him was pretty spectacular. It made him think like a college kid…it made the phrase "Boss Lady and the Hired Hand" suggest all kinds of interesting, if idiotic, possibilities.

God, what a sleazeball that made him sound like! Good thing she couldn't read his mind. He had to laugh at himself, proving his grandfather right about how unprofessional and self-indulgent he was.

"One day, son, you'll learn that *real* life is not all about games and girls." Gray's grandfather's face, as he stood in Gray's college dorm on Gray's nineteenth birthday, had been rigid with fury. He'd just realized that Gray wasn't going to cave in to his demands to come home for the summer, not even at the risk of losing the Harper Quarry millions.

The old man never had been able to tolerate being thwarted. He'd run his cold eyes over Gray's expensive suit, and then over the equally expensive red dress Gray's girlfriend was almost wearing.

"If you honestly believe you can make your own way, without the safety net of the Harper name, you're going to have to do a hell of a lot of growing up."

Gray had yawned and gone back to knotting his tie. He and Carla had reservations at nine, and she was eyeing him appraisingly, obviously wondering if he had the starch to stand up to the old tyrant.

So Gray had met his grandfather's gaze in the mirror and grinned. "Oh, dear. Will I have to become like you?"

His grandfather's mouth had tightened. "You couldn't be like me if you tried, you insolent whelp. But, like it or not, if you're going to be poor, you will have to get serious. You will have to get focused. And by God, for once in your spoiled life, you will have to get *dirty*."

Well, the old man hadn't been lying about that, as Gray had soon discovered. But he'd been wrong to assume that getting dirty would bother him. He'd thrived on it, actually, and kept himself so focused that it had been a very, very long time since Gray had found any female special enough to take his mind off "real life."

The subtle stirring of interest Bree Wright had just set in motion...well, frankly, it felt darn nice.

Still, she was talking, and he should be listening. He caught up with her and kept his eyes sensibly on the path as they made their way toward the stables. He tried to pay attention as she detailed the ranch's horsemanship program.

They had built fifty stalls, she explained, because, though they had only twenty horses at the moment, the plan was to increase to fifty head within a year. They also had three ponies for young riders and a "bring your own mount" option for guests who preferred a familiar seat.

"Nice," he said appreciatively as they entered the large, well-designed stables and heard the soft nickering of the animals. He gazed down the wide, clean

walk between the stalls. Half a dozen horses poked
their heads out, and his practiced eye evaluated them
quickly. All excellent specimens, as far as he could see.

Bree didn't seem inclined to take him in any farther, though he was itching to get a closer look. Apparently this was only the nickel tour, skimming the
high points until she could turn him over to Rowena.

Or else she simply wasn't a fan of horses. He allowed himself a quick up and down while she was con-
sulting her watch. That hairdo wouldn't survive five
minutes on horseback, and those high heels had definitely not been bought with the thought of tramping
through sawdust and hay. Maybe more than a decade
on the East Coast had eradicated her inner cowgirl
completely.

After a few seconds, he realized he was still staring at her impossibly long legs, so he yanked his gaze
up where it belonged and said the first thing that came
into his mind. "Are you a good rider?"

She glanced at him, as if surprised by the question,
and lowered her arm, letting her watch fall over the
back of her hand.

"I haven't ridden in years, but I used to be all right,"
she said, but she touched her earring when she said
it, and he had already learned that the gesture was
her tell. The question had made her uncomfortable.
"I was nothing compared to Ro, of course. She was
the horsey one."

He winced, hearing in her voice that she still accepted the childhood labels without question. Big mistake. Labels, he knew all too well, had a way of being
self-fulfilling. He had been "the spoiled brat."

"Really." He tilted his head. "And which 'one' were you?"

Her eyebrows drew together gently. Then she smiled. "I was the prissy one. The ice queen. I thought you might remember that."

Well, that brought the elephant out and plopped it on the table, didn't it? He admired the cool aplomb that allowed her to mention it first. Maybe the episode really didn't bother her as much as it bothered him. Maybe it was easier to live with the memory of having looked foolish than to live with the memory of having been cruel.

"I do remember," he said flatly, without any attempt to make light of it all. Yes, they'd been kids. But even ninth graders bled when they were cut. "I remember that I was an insensitive jackass. You deserved better, and I knew it, even then. It may be sixteen years too late, but I want you to know I'm sorry."

When he had started his speech, she had already begun to exit the stables. At his final word, *sorry,* she stopped walking and gazed placidly back at him, her elegant, symmetrical features half in shadow, half in sunlight.

"Thanks," she said, but he didn't know her well enough to guess whether the simple word was sardonic or sincere.

Truth was, "jackass" might be an understatement. He and his friends had always made fun of girls like her, the ones who were so bloody virtuous and civic-minded, always on committees to organize this and decorate that. But then, that January, just a month or so before her mother's death, she had ratted on his best friend for smoking behind the bleachers.

Irked, Gray had decided she needed to be taken down a peg.

So, inspired by the instructions on one of his grandfather's housekeeper's frozen foods, he had printed out bold red letters on a piece of plain white paper. Then he'd recruited the girl who sat behind Bree in biology to surreptitiously tape it to the back of her shirt.

Caution: Contents Are Frozen. Thaw Before Eating.

She'd worn it for two whole class periods, in which apparently she had no allies. Finally, after school, one of her buddies saw it and yanked it off. By that time, the joke had made its way around the building like a virus, becoming more vulgar by the minute. Even Gray had felt naive when he realized some of the nasty interpretations that could be applied—though of course he pretended to have meant them all along.

"Don't be too hard on yourself, though," she added with a smile. "You had good reason to be rebellious. What happened to your parents…it was so unfair. I didn't understand anything about it that day, of course, but I found out soon enough. When you're furious with life, with fate, with *everything,* it can make you…" She seemed to search for the right way to express herself. "Less than kind."

He nodded. "True. Although in some ways isn't that just a cop-out? People still have choices about how they'll express their anger." He appreciated her generosity, though. "I have to say," he added, "that tragedy doesn't seem to have had a similar effect on you."

Flushing, she rolled the pearl of her earring between two fingers and laughed softly. "That's nice to hear. But then, you've known me all of…ten minutes?

I suspect that the people who know me better would emphatically disagree."

People who knew her better... He wondered whom she meant by that. A husband...an ex-husband? A lover?

Or...he glanced toward the pine-dappled path they'd taken to the stables, and saw Rowena striding briskly toward them, her black hair blowing out behind her in the breeze.

Or a sister?

"Gray!" Rowena met them at the stable door and held out her hand. "Gosh, it's been a long time, hasn't it? But you haven't changed a bit! I would have known you anywhere."

He accepted her warm, welcoming handshake. He would have recognized her, too, of course. Those eyes. Those cheekbones. But he couldn't say she hadn't changed. Though she had been in the eleventh grade the last time they met, and she was now probably nearly thirty-two, a married stepmother juggling family and business, she didn't look a day older. Instead, she seemed, paradoxically, to have grown younger. Softer.

Was that what marriage to Dallas had done for her? Had love really erased all that dangerous tension that had once tightened the muscles in her face and in her body, until she had seemed a hairsbreadth away from exploding?

"I'm so sorry to keep you waiting," she went on. "You've seen the stables, then? I hope Bree has been persuasive. Her mission was to convince you that Bell River Dude Ranch is the perfect place to work."

Bree frowned, as if this was the first she'd heard

of such a mission, but Gray spoke up quickly. "Absolutely. She's made it sound terrific. I'd want to work here even if you weren't the only place in town willing to hire me."

Rowena laughed, but Bree's deepening furrow told Gray that she hadn't been brought in on the joke. When Gray and Rowena had spoken on the phone yesterday, he'd laid everything out frankly, black sheep to black sheep, and asked for her help. In the strictest sense, this meeting wasn't even really an interview, because she'd already offered him the job.

"I was just about to show him where the Phase Two construction will start," Bree said, obviously treading carefully. She pointed west. "We'll be adding a pool and a lodge, just over there. Both of them will allow us to offer many more activities. Your position would be greatly expanded during Phase Two, I'm sure, and—"

Rowena laughed again, reaching out to touch Bree's upper arm gently. "I don't think Gray really cares much about Phase Two," she said. "He'll be long gone by then."

Bree's face went very still, and she twirled her left earring with a studiously careless motion. "Long gone?" she repeated without inflection.

He glanced at Rowena, who nodded subtly, giving him permission to tell Bree the details. "I talked to your sister yesterday, and I explained my situation. I need the dirtiest, most menial job she has, but I need it for only a month. Four weeks, to be exact."

"Only a month?" Bree raised her eyebrows. "And that's because…?"

"Because that's what my grandfather requires, before he'll put me back in his will."

She stared at him a long minute, and the expression in her eyes subtly hardened as she did so, as if she was revising down her estimation of him.

Finally, she turned to Rowena. "You think this is the best decision for the ranch?"

"What do you mean?"

Bree glanced once, quickly, at Gray, then returned her gaze to her sister. "Shouldn't we have employees who really want to work at a dude ranch? At *this* dude ranch? Surely that's in our best interests. And yet, knowing that Gray wants this position for his own personal agenda, and no other reason, you hired him anyway? Sight unseen?"

"Not exactly *unseen*," Rowena corrected, a slight edge creeping into her voice. "We've known Gray for years, Bree. But otherwise, yes. I knew, and that's exactly what I did."

"Why?" Bree's one-word question dripped disapproval.

As Rowena prepared to respond, Gray thought he detected a spark of the old firebrand. Her green eyes narrowed, and they seemed to blaze hot inside her thick fringe of black lashes.

"Because he is willing to work for practically nothing, which is about what I've got left in the budget. Because a month will get me through the soft opening and give me time to replace him. Because he's handsome and smart and charming, and the guests will be eating out of his hand."

"But, Ro, he—"

"I'm not finished." Rowena's syllables were crisp and staccato, and Bree subsided. "Most important, I'm hiring him because no one else will. Because I know what it's like to try to outrun a reputation that got tied to your tail so long ago it feels grafted to you. In a town like Silverdell, that's pretty darned hard to do."

Gray watched as Bree tried to swallow her opposition—a self-control that seemed to be something of a struggle. As complex emotions swept across her classically beautiful features, rendering them infinitely more interesting than perfection ever could, his curiosity was piqued.

Though of course everyone had gossiped about their mother's murder, Gray hadn't really known the Wright sisters very well. Rowena had been older, too sophisticated to bother with a boy like him, and Bree had always seemed too deadly wholesome to be worth his time. The little one…he couldn't remember her name… hadn't registered at all.

Now, though, he sensed layers and textures in Bree's personality that went far beyond "prissy" or "icy" or "dull." And layers between the two sisters, too. Undercurrents both deep and powerful—and touchingly human.

He suspected that, at its heart, this mini-confrontation had very little to do with Rowena's choice for a job as insignificant as the part-time assistant social director…and much more to do with years of unresolved family baggage.

Well, okay, then, maybe he knew them better than he had realized. They all belonged to that sorry club— the children who had survived the unsurvivable and didn't really know why. Or where to go from there.

A large bird, maybe an eagle, landed somewhere high in the pines over their heads, causing the sunlight to shift as the branches swayed. For an instant, the light seemed to catch on two crystal sparkles at the outer edges of Bree's cool blue eyes.

Tears? Gray frowned. Was the ice princess fighting back tears?

She blinked, then, and the illusion disappeared. But he was left with a sudden, inexplicable hunger to know her better, to find out more about her.

A lot more.

And...just his luck. He had only four weeks to do it.

Chapter 5

While Rowena went over the payroll paperwork with Gray, Bree decided to head up to her room and regroup. In the early planning stages, they'd all agreed that one of the upstairs rooms should be set aside for family, always to be left unrented, in case Penny or Bree wanted to visit.

The sister suite, Penny had called it. Because of its size, the space they'd chosen was Rowena's old room. All the upstairs bedrooms had been subdivided to create more guest space. In this one spot, though, they hadn't formed two separate rooms, but one suite with a connected sitting area and a bedroom.

Bree entered slowly. In the old days Rowena had been possessive about her private sanctuary. Her younger sisters had been forbidden to enter without permission, which she rarely granted. Even now, the remnants of inhibition were so strong that Bree felt odd waltzing in as if she belonged there.

Once in, Bree almost imagined she could detect a hint of Balenciaga Paris in the air. Rowena had received a bottle of the expensive perfume from some secret admirer that Christmas—the last they'd ever celebrated in Silverdell.

Ro had pretended to scoff at girly things like perfume, insisting that she preferred natural scents...wildflowers, the wind coming off the river or rain. But Penny, who sometimes crawled into one of her sister's beds after a nightmare, had innocently told Bree that she chose Rowena now, because Ro always smelled of the pretty perfume while she slept. Ro had denied it, but she had clearly felt embarrassed and exposed. She'd been huffy, even with Penny, for days.

Bree knew the smell was only her imagination, of course. Old ghosts were stirring.

She went to the window of the sitting room. It overlooked the back parking lot, but it also had a peaceful view of the misty salmon-and-sapphire-tinted mountain line in the distance, and the view called to her. The physical beauty was shockingly different from anything in Boston, and at the same time it was deeply, hauntingly familiar.

She was still standing there when Gray and Rowena came strolling outside, their paperwork obviously completed. She moved an inch to the right so that the curtain veiled her, embarrassed to be caught watching.

But she needn't have worried. Neither Rowena nor Gray looked up toward the second-floor windows. They seemed completely engrossed in their conversation. Bree couldn't make out words, but occasionally

Rowena pointed to various buildings, as if describing the activities planned on the property. Gray occasionally pointed, too, clearly adding suggestions of his own.

Lots of nodding and smiling, interspersed with laughter. They seemed to communicate awfully well for people who hadn't seen each other in more than a decade.

But then, Gray had chatted comfortably with Bree, too, in spite of their touchy history. Obviously the man possessed formidable people skills. He always had, even in high school, which was probably what had allowed him to be so rough and rebellious without ending up expelled or slapped in jail.

Leaning easily against the driver's door of his white truck now, he suddenly tilted his head back and laughed at something Rowena said. Bree smiled wryly, aware of a quick, supremely female reaction deep in her own body.

Okay, so it wasn't just his people skills that gave him power. He was also dangerously sexy. His body was a six-four, athletic arrangement of rippled muscles and animal grace. She wondered what he did for a living, when he wasn't in Silverdell, trying to vacuum out his grandfather's wallet. Did he do some kind of serious labor? Or did he simply live at the gym?

And his face…she studied it now, trying to pinpoint where exactly its appeal lay. His golden-brown whisker stubble, square jaw and sun-weathered smile lines were all male, hinting at long days on horseback or wielding a jackhammer. But his lush eyelashes, the waves of chestnut hair that tumbled over his broad forehead and those sensually bowed lips belonged in an art gallery, a pirate ship or an eighteenth-century duchess's boudoir.

Above the rest, his intelligent, honey-brown eyes simply said he found the whole question absurd. He was who he was.

Finally, he pulled his keys out of his pocket and beeped open the truck's auto lock. For the first time, Bree actually paid attention to his vehicle. It was nice, a shiny new model, but somehow she'd expected something glitzier. Like maybe a purring silver Jag with a vanity plate that read GRAYT.

He and Rowena hugged goodbye—Bree couldn't help shaking her head at that. When had her prickly older sister developed a warm fuzzy side? Then he climbed into the truck's cab, cranked the engine, executed a deft three-point turn and guided it out of the parking lot and around the house, heading back to the main street.

She wondered where he was staying…and where he would stay, once he reported for work. Phase One of the dude ranch had included creating staff quarters out of the old stable, but she had the impression that, with at least a dozen employees already hired, those bunks were full.

Minutes later, she heard a low rap at her door. She braced herself, assuming that Rowena had come to finish their argument. She moved from the window and shot a glance into the dresser mirror to be sure she didn't look frazzled.

"Come in," she called, trying to sound as benign as possible. She didn't want to fight with Ro. She'd come to Bell River for one reason only…to see if she could start repairing their relationship. The last thing in the world she wanted was to add to the destruction.

But when Rowena entered, her body language was surprisingly relaxed. Bree had always imagined she could see invisible sparks shooting from her sister when she was angry, but she sensed nothing like that now. Nothing but the fatigue she'd noticed earlier.

Apparently Rowena came in peace. Bree hadn't realized she'd been clenching her midsection until the muscles released.

"I showed myself around up here," she said quickly, determined to start right. "Everything looks fabulous, Ro. You've done a masterful job with the guest rooms."

Rowena's smile broadened. "It did turn out well, didn't it? I had a lot of help. Did you know that Cindy Sedgwick got two-thirds of the way through architecture school before she found herself pregnant with twins and had to come home to marry Joey Incanto?"

Bree only vaguely remembered who Cindy Sedgwick was, but she made an impressed face, anyhow. "Cindy designed the rooms for you?"

"Yes, and the new guest cottages, too." Rowena glanced at her watch. "I don't have another interview until eleven-thirty, so I could give you a tour, if you'd like. I figure you might as well see them now, before guests come in and the Trash Clock starts."

Bree chuckled, but to be honest, the joke surprised her. That had been one of their father's favorite lines. He'd always complained that he'd rather postpone buying new equipment as long as he could, because the minute he made the purchase the Trash Clock began ticking, and the new stuff started turning to garbage that would, in its turn, have to be replaced.

Was Rowena really ready to start quoting their father's cranky humor so casually? But then Bree corrected herself. Ro wasn't quoting *their* father—just Bree's. Rowena had found out last year that mad murderer Johnny Wright's DNA didn't match hers in any way.

Zero percent probability that Johnny was Rowena's real dad.

To which Bree and Penny had said...*lucky Ro.* Penny had no hope of a similar reprieve, because she was Johnny Wright's spitting image. But Bree had sent a sample of her DNA off, too, crossing her fingers and saying a prayer.

Her results had been very different. Percent probability of a match? Ninety-nine percent.

Unfortunately, she was the old bastard's daughter through and through, and she'd simply have to live with that. Must be where her grudging, judgmental streak came from, and her difficulty trusting anybody.

But, damn it, DNA wasn't destiny. She was her own person, and if she wanted to be more tolerant and trusting, then she could make it happen. Starting right now.

"I'd love to see the cottages," she said.

For the next hour, her positive attitude was easy to maintain. Four new guest cottages—one that slept six, one that slept four and two smaller units that slept two—had been built as part of Phase One. And each cottage was a perfect jewel.

She loved every detail. She loved their names... River Run, River Song, River Moon and River Rock. She adored their quaint exterior styles, each one unique—some quaint, like fairy-tale storybook cottages, some rustic, like log cabins, and some a hybrid of the two.

And she adored the floor plans, which all included great rooms with big windows overlooking the stunning views. Even the interior decorating was perfect, cozy without being cliché.

Kudos to Cindy Sedgwick. And, of course, to Rowena.

No wonder Ro looked tired. Having staged so many events, Bree understood that every room in every cottage represented about a hundred decisions to make, a hundred details to oversee. She was deeply impressed and didn't pass up any opportunity to say so.

Even cynical Rowena, whose antennae had always been finely tuned to detect empty flattery, was glowing under the effusive compliments by the time they stopped at the last cottage.

"Enough." She smiled, holding out her hand. "I believe you're sincere right now, but one more and I'll start to think you're blowing smoke."

Bree laughed. "Okay. Nothing but insults from this moment on."

She could hardly keep that promise, though. River Moon, built right at the edge of one of the small creek offshoots of Bell River, was a storybook charmer. This cottage, with its round blue door, steeply pitched, sloping roof and climbing yellow roses, would probably be used as the honeymoon suite. Phase Two included marketing the ranch for destination weddings.

They wandered through the adorable rooms, all the way to the sunny bedroom at the back.

"Oh, this quilt is—" But somehow Bree bit her tongue, holding back the word *fabulous*.

Rowena smiled, shaking her head. "I mean it, Bree. Enough."

But the quilt, which had been draped over a Bentwood rocker, *was* fabulous. Bree ran her hand over the intricate blue-and-yellow pattern of entwined hearts. Each cottage bedroom had its own signature antique quilt, the one theme that ran through all four cottages, but this was the most beautiful of them all.

If Bree had wanted to say something less fawning, she might have voiced the one doubt that had niggled at her throughout the tour. Were the interior decorations maybe almost *too* beautiful?

Too beautiful for their tight budget, anyhow.

But obviously she didn't utter a peep about that. She might have reached her limit of compliments, but she hadn't reached the point at which she could dare to express a criticism.

Besides, Ro wasn't exactly a shopaholic. She wouldn't have spent the money if she hadn't thought it was important. Bree forced the worry from her mind, and instead strolled the perimeter of the airy room, drinking in the romance of every charming detail.

"This may be my favorite of all the cottages. That's not a compliment," she hastened to add. "Just a fact. Just a personal preference. The colors…the creek. I don't know, something just appeals to me."

"I thought it might," Rowena said. She lowered herself onto the rocker and leaned her head back against the quilt with a sigh, as if she didn't get to sit down very often these days. "I used the colors from your old room. Remember?"

Bree scanned the area with new eyes. She hadn't noticed it before, but now… Her childhood bedroom had once been painted this exact shade of powder blue, and her canopy bed had been trimmed in bluebell-daffodil patterned linens that she had loved with an innocent, absolute passion. She'd felt like a fairy princess in that room.

"I'd forgotten," she said softly. "I can't believe it, but I'd actually forgotten."

Once the floodgates were open, she felt the memory rush through her. She suddenly saw Rowena and their mother, arguing quietly at the Mill End store in downtown Gunnison. Ro had tucked a bolt of flower-sprigged fabric under her arm with the grim tenacity of a quarterback protecting a football.

Ro couldn't have been more than nine years old at the time, because Bree had been eight when she got her dream room. But the determination on Rowena's face was intense and unshakable, far beyond her years.

"You helped me pick out that print," Bree said suddenly. "You talked Mom into buying it for me, even though it was much too expensive. And I know you couldn't have liked it, really. It wasn't your style at all."

Rowena had shut her eyes, but she was smiling, as if her mind's eye had summoned the pictures, too. "You should have seen the look on your face. Clearly, you were going to curl up and die if you didn't get it. Whether or not *I* liked it was irrelevant."

Bree remembered that. Somehow, her future had seemed to depend on the sweet, feminine flowers in that bolt of fabric. She had believed with all her heart that if her room looked like that she would always be happy. If her room looked any other way, if her bed was draped in any other material, she would be forever unrealized.

Like a rose that never opens, like a candle that won't light.

Of course, she wouldn't have been able to express it—in those terms or any others—back then. But somehow Rowena had intuited all those incoherent emotions, and had been willing to go toe to toe with the grown-ups on Bree's behalf. She wanted to thank her, belatedly. But it seemed silly, after all these years, to make a big deal out of a bolt of fabric.

Still, she suddenly felt a surge of optimism. Rowena had loved her once, and Bree had loved and trusted Ro, too. Completely, without question. She hadn't been afraid of Ro's ferocity, not back then. She had understood that her big sister was a warrior, but they were on the same side of the combat, and Ro fought for her, not against her.

Bree took heart from the memory. If it had been so once, it could be so again. If Bree could just keep from messing anything up...

"Ro, I... I want to tell you that I—"

Out of nowhere, she heard the sound of the cottage's front door opening, and a woman's voice calling out, "Rowena? Are you here?"

Ro opened her eyes and blinked sleepily. "Georgia? I'm back here. With Bree."

Bree cast a questioning look toward her sister, but there wasn't time for Ro to answer it. Two seconds later, a young redhead in a crisp red suit poked her head through the door.

"You busy? I just picked up the banner and I thought you should see it."

Rowena didn't stand up from the chair, which surprised Bree. She just smiled at the newcomer and waved her in. "Georgia, you haven't met my sister Bree, have you? Bree, this is Georgia Brooke, our social director. Other than Barton and me, Georgia is the most overworked, underappreciated person on the payroll."

The redhead, who was more beautifully groomed than beautiful, and who looked, if anything, even more exhausted than Rowena, smiled wanly at Bree.

"We're all tired," she said, her voice proving the truth of her words. For a social director, she certainly didn't project any energy or enthusiasm. Bree hoped the woman could fake it if she had to, when the guests arrived.

"Speaking of which…" Georgia turned anxious, deep-set brown eyes toward Rowena. "Did Gray take the job?"

"He did."

Georgia let out a deep sigh, as if her life had depended upon getting that answer. Rowena obviously noticed the doleful sound and raised her eyebrows. "Hey, shouldn't you be happy? We just hired you a Cadillac assistant for a go-cart price."

"I am happy," Georgia assured her. But she put her hand to her forehead and shut her eyes briefly, as if she felt dizzy, or sick. "I'm just feeling a little off at the moment. Kind of queasy."

Rowena leaned forward in the rocker and eyed her social director closely. "You're not getting the flu, are you? If you think there's the slightest chance, go home. We can't afford to spread germs around the rest of the crew, not this close to the opening."

"No, no." The smile Georgia dredged up, in an attempt to be reassuring, was worse than her frown. "It's nothing like that. I'm thinking maybe the sausage at breakfast was a mistake."

Rowena didn't look completely convinced, but she leaned back again and didn't press. Bree's estimation of the social director went down another peg. She wondered whether Rowena had hired the woman out of desperation, or whether she was an old friend who had played on sentiment.

Something had to account for this...

"What about the banner?" Rowena glanced at the folded cloth in Georgia's hands. "You're happy with it?"

"Well..." Georgia's frown was back in full force. "It looks fine, but when I picked it up the guy charged us twice what he'd estimated. I argued, but he wouldn't budge."

"That's absurd." Bree was so incredulous she spoke without thinking. "If the correct price is on the estimate, he *has* to honor it."

The other woman glanced up, flushing, as if she resented Bree's intrusion. "It wasn't a written estimate," she said, lifting her chin. "We discussed it over the phone. I didn't have any reason to doubt his word."

Bree glanced at Rowena, and she could tell from the tension around her sister's eyes that she was unhappy with this explanation, as well. But, unlike Bree, Ro seemed to be working hard to cover her displeasure.

"Okay. Well, lesson learned. We'll be getting all estimates signed in blood from now on." Rowena smiled. "Let's see this two-hundred-dollar banner, then. I hope it's pretty darn amazing."

Two hundred dollars? Bree opened her mouth, then shut it over the exclamation of disbelief. She couldn't judge until she saw it. Maybe it was fifty feet tall, or lettered in pure gold.

She watched as Georgia unfolded the white vinyl, which read Welcome to Bell River Dude Ranch. It was an extra large, probably the eight by three, simple grommets, black letters in a standard Booker bold italic.

Nothing misspelled or off center, but nothing impressive, either. Not double-sided or custom shaped. No background, no color, no graphics, no special effects or…anything.

For heaven's sake. Even in Boston, where the cost of living was crazy, Bree could have ordered that banner for a third the price.

Not that she would have—not for an unpublicized soft opening, where all the guests would be friends and family…and staying *free*. The thin vinyl wouldn't hold up well enough to reuse during the more important grand opening in June. Maybe if Georgia had ordered it on canvas, or aluminum…

This time, Bree didn't have to force herself to be silent. Even she knew the comments bouncing around in her head shouldn't be spoken aloud.

But her expression must have said it all without words, because Georgia's flush deepened to a splotchy plum color, and her eyes seemed to be watering. Under her deftly applied makeup and chic dress, she suddenly looked like a little girl who found herself in the deep end of the pool and had forgotten how to swim.

She was younger than Bree had initially realized, as well. Early twenties, tops. Looking at Georgia's miserable face, Bree felt something in her chest soften. She remembered what it felt like to be a newbie and to get everything wrong. Breelie's had almost gone out of business in its first year because Bree, still a college senior and overeager to hit the big time, had made every stupid mistake in the book.

It was only two hundred dollars. The dude ranch wasn't going to sink under the cost of one disappointing banner. She put out a hand, smiling at the other woman, trying to think of something encouraging to say.

"Did you plan to hang it on the front gates? The black lettering will look quite nice there, against the wrought iron of the—"

But then, right in the middle of Bree's awkward attempt to console, Georgia emitted a choking sound, stared around the little room with wide, glistening eyes and finally, with a small groan, vomited helplessly.

All over the banner.

Chapter 6

Two hours later, while Rowena interviewed several college kids who wanted jobs on the waitstaff, Bree sat in the beautifully renovated great room with Alec and Barton James.

Though the afternoon had turned chilly, the fireplace in the center of the room was crackling contentedly, and Bree could see what a delightful gathering spot this would be for guests after long days riding or hiking outdoors.

Bree sat on the wide, comfortable sofa, her laptop open, working on her proposal for the golden wedding anniversary party. She'd pitch to the Everlys next week—assuming they didn't call between now and then to cancel. They weren't part of the Townsend set, so she kept her fingers crossed that the gossip hadn't reached their elderly ears.

Over on the wide river-rock-fireplace surround, Barton was trying to teach Alec how to play "Mamas, Don't Let Your Babies Grow Up To Be Cowboys" on the guitar. He'd said it would be fun for them to perform a duet at the opening-night barn dance.

Alec had done pretty well for the first thirty minutes or so. His puppy, a mutt who had turned out to be named Trouble, but who also had turned out to be surprisingly sweet and mellow, slept at his feet.

The boy had a clear, true tenor that sounded charming when mixed with Barton's mellifluous bass. But after about half an hour he'd started to fidget and cast longing glances out the window, and his fingers were too impatient to form the chords correctly.

"Oh, never mind," Barton said finally, propping the guitar on the floor beside him. He ruffled Alec's hair. "I'll handle the music. You just stand there and look adorable. Wear your cowboy hat. And maybe…you got any little rattlesnake boots with spurs?"

Alec glared at the old man as if he were daft. *"No,"* he said, as if that should be obvious. "I have regular boots, like regular people."

Barton didn't seem to hear. He tilted his head and squinted at the boy, apparently imagining the possibilities. "Yes, definitely boots." He nodded, as if satisfied with whatever he had seen in his head. "Silver belt buckle…the works. I tell you, kiddo, all the old cowgirls in the audience are going to eat that stuff up with a spoon."

Alec snorted. *"Gross."*

"Gotta please the ladies, son. That's the first rule of show business. You please the ladies, the menfolk gotta follow. It's kind of interesting, how menfolk don't very often think for themselves. I always say it's because—"

But Alec clearly wasn't in the mood for Barton's cowboy wisdom. "Okay, fine. I'll tell Dad I need rattlesnake boots." He glanced toward the window again. "It's getting dark, and I said I'd help muck the stalls today. I'd better get going."

Barton hesitated. "With spurs?"

Alec groaned. "Yeah. Okay. Spurs."

Over the boy's head, Barton winked at Bree. She lowered her gaze to her laptop, hoping she could hide her smile. Old rascal. He obviously knew Alec would agree to anything right now, if it was the price of busting free. Dallas's son was the outdoorsy type, and his fidgety energy needed an outlet or he'd pop like an overinflated balloon.

Just one of the reasons he and Rowena got along so well, no doubt. Bree could remember that same twitchy tension tormenting her big sister. Ro used to sneak out of the house sometimes in the middle of the night—not to meet up with boyfriends, or drink, or joyride in stolen cars, as most people might think. She just wanted to be outside, because a whole night lying motionless in a narrow bed was more than she could stand.

"Let's go play, Trouble." Alec grabbed his dog, who woke up instantly and licked Alec's face, his tail thumping. He obviously knew the word *play,* and was delighted to be invited.

Ten seconds of sneakers pounding, puppy toenails clicking, and the two of them were gone.

"So what do you think about Gray Harper and this newfangled glamping thing?" Barton had returned to idly strumming his guitar, and he spoke over the music. His tone was pensive, as if he was continuing a conversation he'd been having with someone—maybe himself.

Bree glanced up, and saw that he was looking at her, obviously awaiting her response.

"What is glamping?" She closed her laptop, curious. The word was odd, but it was the connection to Gray Harper that cinched the deal. She had a feeling Rowena wasn't going to tell her much, not after she'd made her disapproval so clear.

"Glamorous camping," Barton said, plunking the guitar strings to accentuate the two words. "It's all the thing these days. Instead of building permanent structures everywhere, a resort'll put up high-end luxury tents, with beds and fireplaces and bathrooms and all that mollycoddle stuff. Rich people pay a lot of money to spend the night in 'em."

She did have a vague recollection of reading something about the concept. Maybe. "But what does it have to do with Gray Harper? We're not planning to offer that at Bell River." She paused, noticing the smile on the old man's face. "Are we?"

"Well, it's a little idea I've been wanting to try," he said. He shrugged his shoulders, as if to say it was no big deal. "I talked Rowena into letting me put one out by Cupcake Creek. Just thought we'd see how it played, you know? I'm a sucker for newfangled things. Keeps me young." He grinned. "Well, keeps boredom from killing me even faster than old age will, anyhow."

"I had no idea." She wondered where the money for such an extravagant purchase had been found. She knew their budget pretty well, and "glamping" wasn't listed anywhere. "Rowena didn't mention it."

"Yeah, well, she thinks I'm crazy, no doubt. But so what? If it doesn't pan out, no sweat. I bought it on a lark. I can always sell it to some other old fool who is itching to try something new."

So Barton had bought it. She mentally apologized to Rowena for even considering the possibility that she'd been hiding expenditures. She really, really had to stop judging everyone as if they were as immoral as that hound dog Charlie Newmark. "And you...you're *glamping* out there now?"

"Gawd, no!" Barton laughed and intoned a few notes of a funeral march. "With these old bones? We're putting Gray Harper out there. He needs a place to stay. We need a guinea pig. So there you go. Everyone wins."

Apparently delighted with his turn of phrase, Barton bent over his guitar and began picking out a new song.

"There you go," he sang, starting off on a plaintive note. "Walking away. I know you think..." He smiled, finding his next line easily. "I'll ask you to stay. But when I'm rid of you, that's when the good life begins. So there you go. *Everyone wins.*"

He ended with a playful wink and a flourish of fingerpicking. Bree applauded softly, laughing as the old man took a small bow. Barton billed himself as the best cowboy poet west of the Mississippi, and she suddenly had a feeling that he might be right.

Alec's littlest-cowboy routine wouldn't be the only thing the old cowgirls would eat up with a spoon.

She started to reopen her laptop and return to her proposal when suddenly, like a grenade tossed into the middle of the easy camaraderie, Rowena appeared, obviously stressed and angry as hell.

Bree frowned, watching Ro's body language, realizing that the sparks she knew so well had finally made an appearance. She wondered what she'd done now.

"Barton, could I talk to Bree privately for a minute, please?" Ro's voice was as tight as the reins on a runaway horse.

"Sure," Barton said easily, slipping his guitar strap over his neck, and sliding the instrument around so that it rode against his shoulder blade. "I can't be sitting here singing all day, anyhow. I've got all kinds of general-managing things to do."

"Thanks," Rowena said, though she didn't seem to notice his little joke. Obviously all her energy was focused on reining in her temper until she and Bree were alone.

Bree waited calmly, refusing to let herself feel anxious or defensive. After that rocky start about the hiring of Gray Harper, she'd bent over backward trying to be supportive. But there was a fine line between bending over backward and allowing yourself to be a doormat. She didn't intend to cross that line, not even for Rowena.

As soon as the front door shut behind Barton, Rowena took a deep breath. "Georgia Brooke just quit."

"What?" That certainly wasn't what Bree had expected her sister to say. "She did? Why?"

"She said it's because of you. She said you made it very clear you think she's not up to the job."

Bree set her laptop aside, stunned. "That's absurd."

"Is it?"

"Of course."

"No, Bree, it isn't." Rowena's eyes flashed. "That is *exactly* what you think. Just because you didn't say so outright doesn't mean your feelings didn't come through, loud and clear. Georgia may be young and inexperienced, but she's not a fool. She sensed your disdain."

Bree knew there was some truth to that, but not enough to account for such a dramatic reaction. If an employee made a mistake, surely they had to expect their employers to be disappointed. Bree hadn't said a single negative word about any of it. If the young woman was so thin-skinned that she couldn't tolerate the idea of a negative thought passing through someone's mind...

Quitting simply wasn't a proportional reaction. If Rowena weren't so tired and stressed herself, she would see that, too.

"I'll talk to Georgia," Bree said. "It probably all seems worse because she's not feeling well. You saw how sick she was. Maybe she's embarrassed about throwing up on the banner. I'll talk to her, and—"

"You can't," Rowena said flatly. "She's already gone. She was in tears. I told her she didn't have to work out her notice if she didn't want to. She didn't want to."

Oh, heavens. "Ro, I really think she's overreacting."

"Maybe she is. I'm not sure what difference that makes. A very nice young woman is still without a job she needed. And I'm without a social director. Good thing Gray Harper isn't as easy to scare off, or I might have lost him, too. I'm sorry my hires don't meet your standards, but do you have any idea how much we have left to do in these next eight days?"

"Not precisely, but I can guess. I do this sort of thing for a living, you know." Bree stood. "So what do you want me to do? If you don't want me to talk to her…"

"I'll tell you exactly what I want." Rowena's shoulders squared tightly. "I want you to find someone to take her place. As you say, you do this for a living. You must know someone who might be interested. Or you can take the job yourself. I don't really care. All I know is…you broke it, Bree. You should fix it."

By the time Bree reached Cupcake Creek late that afternoon, her feet were killing her, and she realized she'd made the typical city-slicker mistake. She hadn't changed out of her regular heels and into boots.

She honestly hadn't thought she'd need them. Cupcake Creek was hidden between two thick stands of woodland, giving it an air of isolated wilderness, but it actually was only about a ten-minute walk from the main house.

So when Barton James, whom she'd sought out after her talk with Rowena, told her that Gray Harper should already be out here, setting up camp, she didn't bother going back to her room. She just headed for the creek.

As she moved through the trees, though, she had begun to doubt herself. Was it possible she'd forgotten the route? Cupcake Creek was only one of many tributaries of Bell River that branched off from the main flow, crisscrossing the ranchland like curious children wandering away from the safety of home. Some were just tiny, shallow fingers of water that died out after a few yards, and others were large and deep enough for tubing.

After so many years, wasn't it possible that she might get lost and follow the wrong stream?

She had just decided to turn around—she was only a few yards from forming blisters—when the trees suddenly parted, revealing the creek, twinkling silver and salmon-pink in the late-afternoon sun. She stood still, hardly breathing, and drank in the familiar sight.

Cupcake had always been the prettiest of Bell River's branches. A placid, curving stream about ten feet wide, nature had decorated the two-foot-deep water with sparkling granite boulders. In summer, riffles of white lace formed where the creek broke around the bottoms of the rocks, and when winter brought the snows, a smooth white frosting collected on the tops.

Bree, who as a small child decided they looked like cupcakes, had given the place its name.

Late afternoon was a magical time out here. Chipmunks chattered, unseen, in the trees, and somewhere she heard the complicated whistling and trilling of a lark bunting. Forgetting her sore feet, she moved closer to the creek, and when she did she finally got a glimpse of the glamping tent.

Wow. Glamorous was the right word. A beige-and-green-striped canvas room erected on a hard floor, the tent looked more like a small house, really. Big enough to stand in, at least twelve by twelve, with several open windows to take advantage of the breeze.

A covered veranda extended the living space, also with a hard floor. It seemed to be set for dinner—Bree saw two chairs and a small table covered with food.

Through the tent doors, which had been snapped into the open position, she spotted a huge bed draped in green linens, rugs on the floor, a potbellied fire-place and a cushioned armchair.

And then she saw Gray, standing beside the bed, smiling as he opened a bottle of wine. She froze in place, shocked by her own body's quick, unmistak-able reaction…a very female, very sexual warmth that flooded her before she could even register consciously how gorgeous he really was.

But he was. Those broad shoulders… Her gaze dropped. And those narrow hips. The easy disorder of his wavy hair, as if someone had been running fin-gers through it. The dimples at the edges of his smile, the sparkling teeth between…

And then she realized he wasn't alone. He was smil-ing *at* someone.

Bree took another few steps to get a better angle. There were two people in the tent. The other was an auburn-haired woman who seemed vaguely familiar, but Bree couldn't be sure… Someone from Silverdell High School, maybe.

Was that how Gray knew her, too?

Probably. But on the other hand, Bree had learned that Gray had left Silverdell right after high school, and this was his first trip back. So, if he'd known this woman in the past, it must have been thirteen or four-teen *years* ago.

Bree shook her head, marveling, trying to dislodge the melting-female reaction and achieve a little wry perspective on the man. He certainly didn't waste any time, did he? She could imagine him flipping through his little black book and coming across a half-forgot-ten number. Then the call. "Hey, gorgeous, remember me? I've unexpectedly happened onto a safari tent for the night. Interested in a little glamp from the past?"

Or maybe it hadn't been like that at all. She had to be careful. She couldn't start assuming that all men were as superficial and selfish as Charlie.

The woman was sitting on the edge of the generous bed, gazing around her as she bounced slightly up and down on the mattress. She said something Bree couldn't hear, then let her head fall back and started to laugh, as if the luxurious setup struck her as funny.

Bree wondered very briefly if she ought to just back away, but she decided not to. Though her hope had been to avoid interacting with anyone she used to know, it was time to revise the plan. Having an extra person here was actually a bonus. Bree needed help, and the more people she could ask, the better.

Besides, it was clearly safer not to be out here alone with this man—not if she was going to go all hot and shivery just at the sight of his sexy hips. The last thing in the world she needed was for Gray Harper to realize she was attracted to him. His ego was already robust enough, thanks. If they had to work together...

"Hello?" She moved forward, calling out loudly enough to be heard, she hoped. "Gray? It's Bree."

Both Gray and the woman came to the tent door, looking curious, but not annoyed. Bree waved, and they both waved back, as if they welcomed the idea of company. Even Gray. She felt a subtle sense of relief.

"Hey, Bree," Gray said as she drew close enough that he didn't have to holler. He had stepped out onto the veranda area. He set the wine bottle on the small table, along with the rest of the food, which looked like gourmet fare...and quite delicious.

But not as delicious as Gray himself, who, as he stepped into the sunlight, almost took her breath away. She felt her neck grow warm, and she was uncomfortably aware that even a witness couldn't completely protect her from this man's incredible sex appeal.

"What brings you all the way out here?" He smiled, then glanced at her feet. "Particularly in those shoes?"

The woman looked down, too, and made a pained sound. "Ooh, ouch," she said sympathetically. Then she smiled. "Don't you remember me, Bree? I'm Marianne Garp. I mean Donovan. I was Marianne Donovan back then. We were in Mrs. Havelock's class together. Ninth grade?"

Bree searched her memory. Now that the woman had emerged from the shadows and the sunlight caught flame-red strands in the auburn curls, her hazy memory began to sharpen.

Oh…yes… Mari Donovan. Of course! Mari had been a quiet, pleasant girl who came from a family so normal they seemed to have stepped out of a Norman Rockwell painting. No one noticed her much, even Bree's student council–honor society types. But then, briefly, around the holidays in ninth grade, she'd become something of a celebrity. Her claim to fame? She had dated wicked Gray Harper for three whole months without, as far as anyone could tell, losing her virginity.

"Of course I remember you." Bree hugged the other woman politely. Of all the Dellians she could have run into, Mari was probably the least difficult. They'd never been close, but Mari had been as quietly kind after the murder—and Rowena's scandal with Dallas Garwood—as she had been before.

Bree remembered Mari and her mother bringing over a casserole, and the two of them standing with Aunt Ruth in the kitchen. Their manner had been respectful, even though the circumstances certainly didn't engender respect for anyone in the Wright family.

While the adults talked, Mari had stood with her gaze cast down, silently compassionate, instead of ogling everything within eyeshot so that she could gossip later about what the murder house looked like.

"Did you come to check out the tent?" Gray waved a hand to indicate she was free to explore the splendor behind him. "Doesn't feel much like roughing it to me. But Barton is certain it's the next big thing, and apparently he likes to stay cutting edge."

Bree nodded, grateful to have something else to think about—something other than the big, comfortable bed she could glimpse through the doorway. "For an eighty-year-old man, he is amazing."

"For a *twenty*-year-old man, he's amazing." Gray laughed. "I have a feeling that, as the Bull Moose at Bell River, he's going to keep us all hopping."

Curious that he should use that expression... Bull Moose. Top screw, it was sometimes called. The boss man on the ranch. Her father had always called himself that. No one back East would have had a clue what it meant.

It wasn't the kind of terminology she'd have expected Gray Harper to use, either. As the pampered grandson of a marble-quarry millionaire, he had never dressed like a rancher, or talked like one. Not even in high school, where all the boys fancied themselves James Dean in *Giant*. Silly hats that swallowed their heads and belt buckles that could blind you from fifty paces. Boots like trophies, proudly constructed of reptiles they had killed themselves.

Gray had his share of affectations, of course. But his had been edgier. More the James Dean of *Rebel Without a Cause.* Careless hair, slouchy jacket and dangerous, haunted eyes.

He had changed so much—at least on the outside. He seemed generally healthier, calmer, more at home in his own skin. His jeans were old and softly molded to his body, not a statement of anything except his preference for comfort and functionality.

The only remnant of the old Gray was this tawdry charade to get hold of his grandfather's money. And maybe the fact that it hadn't taken him more than four hours to get a married woman out here and onto his luxury safari-tent bed.

She bit her lip. Was that fair? Or was it more bitter echoes of Charlie? Mari might be divorced. That her name was now Garp didn't mean anything. She could have changed her name ten times in all these years, for all Bree knew.

Either way, though, she wondered whether Mari understood that, if she got involved with Gray, the whole thing would be merely a one-month wonder.

"Come see." Gray touched Bree's arm, tilting his head toward the tent. "Even I have to admit, it's impressive. On the other hand, I've been staying at the Big Horn Inn the past few nights, so I'm pretty easy to impress."

Mari shuddered comically, although as Bree remembered it, the Big Horn hadn't been so terrible— just ancient, and rumored to have a naked gold miner ghost who ran up and down the halls all night, laughing because he'd finally struck a vein.

"Actually," she said, edging away from his fingertips, which felt strangely hot against her skin, "I didn't come only to see the tent, although it does look very cool. I came because Rowena and I need some help."

His gaze sharpened subtly. "Everything okay?"

"Yes. It's just that Rowena's social director quit today."

"Georgia?" Mari's eyes widened. "I can't believe it! She was so excited to get that job. When Troy broke the engagement, she was really in pieces, but—"

She broke off, wrinkling her nose sheepishly. "I keep forgetting you guys haven't been living in Silverdell your whole lives. Around here, we all still live in each other's pockets. Nothing's private."

For just a moment, Bree's gaze slid to Gray. He was looking at her, too, and she knew what he was thinking. Marianne Donovan might find it warm and cozy to know your neighbors poked around in your trash cans to see whether you finished your peas, maxed out your MasterCard or discarded a home pregnancy test.

But that was because Mari Donovan's trash cans never contained anything sad or embarrassing. For families like the Harpers and the Wrights, all that unrelenting "interest" could sometimes feel more like having the skin flayed off your body in bloody strips.

"I don't know what else has been going on for Georgia, but for Bell River, this is the worst possible time to lose a critical employee, as you can imagine. I told Rowena I'd help find a replacement, but…"

She thought of the dozens of calls she'd placed in the past couple hours. "So far, I'm coming up empty.

I was hoping maybe you knew someone in town who might be a good candidate."

Gray shrugged. "I've only been in town since Friday. I don't know much about anyone local." He turned to Mari. "How is the job market around here? Are there good people hungry for work?"

She shook her head. "Not really. We had a kind of miniboom a few years ago, when the lumber mill located nearby, and then last year two clean-tech companies came, too. I finally was able to find a full staff for Donovan's, but it was a struggle. Hard to open up a restaurant right when a shiny new dude ranch is hiring."

Bree could imagine. "Sorry." She smiled apologetically. "Bad timing, huh?"

"Oh, that's okay!" Mari waved it off. "We're all thrilled for you guys, and for Silverdell as a whole. I just mean the pool of good hires is pretty shallow right now."

Darn. Bree's hopes sank. No wonder Rowena had been so frustrated when Bree had been picky about her choices. She kept forgetting Silverdell wasn't Boston, which teemed with talented, educated, experienced people, young and old, who were hungry for good jobs.

And even in that environment, she had made the colossal mistake of hiring Charlie. She almost laughed, thinking of the irony. Who was she to criticize Rowena, indeed?

Mari bent down to one of the chairs and picked up a sweater she must have tossed there earlier. As she draped it over her shoulders, she shivered slightly. "Getting chilly, which means I'd better head back to handle the dinner rush."

She put her hands on Gray's chest, and rose on tiptoe to give him a peck on the lips. "Don't let the arugula get cold. It's my best dish, and I only brought it because I want some free publicity. I will expect you to tell everyone in town how fabulous Donovan's is."

"Done," he said, and he chucked her lightly under the chin. "Thanks, kid."

She wrinkled her nose. "Kid? I'm not the one sleeping in a tent." Before he could respond, she turned to Bree. "It was great to see you. Maybe you'll get a chance to stop by the restaurant? How long are you staying?"

"Not long." Bree had intended to stay about six days, until right before her meeting to bid on the Everlys' anniversary party. But now, with Rowena so upset, she wondered whether she might have to cut that short. "A few days, at most."

"Aw, too bad. Still, come by if you can. Lots of people would love to say hi, I know. Everyone always hoped things went well for you and your sisters, after you…"

She didn't finish the sentence. Bree nodded, sensing that Mari, at least, believed what she said. Rowena believed it, too. When Bree had expressed doubts that Silverdell would welcome a return of the Wrights to Bell River, Ro had insisted that Dellians were, on the whole, prepared to start fresh, and didn't hold their father's insanity against them.

If that was true—and, judging by the degree of town support the dude ranch was getting, it must be—then Bree and Penny should sail in on relatively smooth waters. Rowena had been by far the wildest of the three girls—the scandalous one who had led the beloved young town hero astray and caused him to get shot in the face. Comparatively, Bree and Penny had been like fully domesticated house kittens: quite harmless.

Bree wondered whether she should leave with Mari. Her instinct to avoid being alone with Gray in this strangely romantic setting was smart. She was far too aware of him, standing there beside her, watching Mari go. Too aware of the scent of him—minty and sweet and very male. And the way his hands looked, one cocked against his narrow hip, the other raised in a goodbye salute. The long, manly fingers. The sharp bones of his wrist, followed by the thick taper of muscle in his golden forearm.

She swallowed. Yes, definitely. She should leave.

But surely she wasn't that big a coward? Her mission wasn't complete. She didn't have a replacement yet for Georgia Brooke—and she still had one more idea to explore.

The two of them watched, and waved, until Mari finally disappeared around the first sharp curve in the wood's path.

"Want a sandwich?"

Bree turned, and saw that Gray stood by the loaded table, surveying the pile of lovely sandwiches. "There's more here than I possibly could eat alone, and it'll hurt her feelings if any goes to waste."

Bree glanced toward the nearest bushes, where a couple of squirrels squatted, short front paws pressed together in mesmerized longing, and stared at the bounty. "I bet you could find plenty of takers."

He followed her gaze and grinned. "Can't feed the wildlife. It's not good for them. Don't you remember the field trips, and the warning signs? Don't you remember poor Mr. Driggs?"

She turned up one side of her mouth. "I remember you tormenting him."

"Exactly." Gray bit into one of the sandwiches, chewed appreciatively, then swallowed. "Poor Mr. Driggs."

He would be unrepentant, of course. And, to be honest, Mr. Driggs had been exasperating. Their English teacher, and a grand pooh-bah Nature Boys master on weekends, he'd spent that year trying to get them to revere the Romantic poets, and to believe that wandering "lonely as a cloud" was the primal pathway to spiritual bliss.

As healthy fifteen-year-olds, they'd naturally had other ideas about bliss.

"They're delicious," Gray said, gesturing one more time for her to help herself to the sandwiches. When she shook her head again, he shrugged and picked up another for himself. "So…what's Rowena going to do about the social-director job? Any chance Georgia will rethink and come back?"

"I doubt it." Bree had called the young woman first, of course. And last. And about a dozen times in between calling every other contact she had in the hospitality industry. But Georgia hadn't answered her phone. "But I was thinking…what about you?"

He paused in the middle of chewing. "What about me?"

"I know you weren't planning to take on a full-time job, but would you consider it? Obviously you were always ridiculously overqualified for the assistant spot."

His eyebrows went up, but he swallowed politely

before he spoke. "Think so? I got the impression you found me…somewhat lacking."

She felt herself flushing. Her pale complexion never hid much. But the sky had taken on even deeper tinges of pink as the sun slid west, so maybe that helped to cover the problem.

"Lacking in motivation, perhaps," she said. "Not native intelligence or ability."

He smiled. "Maybe. But I'm definitely *under*qualified for the social-director position. The only thing I know about parties is how much to tip the bartender."

Something…some hint of amusement lurking at the back of his eyes…made her think he was making a joke at her expense. Once again, she wondered what he did for a living these days. If he was in dire need of an inheritance, he couldn't have spent the past decade sitting around counting gold coins on Easy Street.

Of course, that didn't mean that he necessarily knew a single thing about taking little kids on trail rides, ordering food for barn parties or organizing a horseshoe tournament at a dude ranch.

"You don't have experience, perhaps. But it's not as if you'd have to do heart transplants, or anything. You're smart, able-bodied and you are…you have excellent social skills." She almost said "capable of charming anyone at will" but that seemed too likely to make him laugh. "Those are the only raw materials needed. After that, it's just a matter of picking up the details."

He didn't answer for a few seconds. Instead, he lifted the open wine bottle and poured an inch or two of deep red liquid into one of the glasses. Raising it, he turned the glass in almost imperceptible circles.

"And where would I pick up the details?"

Hope rose like a living thing in her chest. He was considering it. Oh, how she'd love to walk back into Bell River and tell Rowena she'd found a solution!

"Well, I'll be here a few days," she said. "I've got an event-planning business in Boston, so I'm fairly familiar with the process."

"A few days wouldn't be long enough."

She frowned. That faint spark of amusement still gleamed behind his eyes, and it made her uncomfortable, though she couldn't quite say why. "Why not?"

He held his wine up to the sunlight, as if checking for clarity. It glowed ruby-gold, like some magic potion. He tilted the glass to his lips and let some of the wine slide into his mouth.

She felt her insides warming, as if she were the one who drank. She forced herself to look in another direction. The squirrels were still frozen in prayer, still staring at the food, as if they could will it to float their way.

"Why not?" she asked again. "I'd teach you everything I could before I go, and I could leave information behind. And my phone number, of course, for emergencies."

"I'd never be up to speed by then," he said reasonably. "If I don't know what I'm doing, I'd be more of a liability than a help to the ranch."

She frowned. She couldn't risk rescheduling the Everly meeting. If they'd heard the gossip finally, they might seize on any excuse to go with another company. But perhaps she could fly back for the meeting, then return to Colorado a little longer.

"A week?"

He shook his head sadly. "Probably still not enough."

"Well…you tell me, then. How much training do you think you'd need?" She gave him a straight look that demanded he not play games. "After all, we'll still have to be looking for someone permanent. You'll be here only a month yourself…so…"

"True." He gazed at her thoughtfully. "It's hard to set an exact time frame, given how little I know about the job. But I'd say at least…two weeks?"

Two weeks… She tried to imagine being here, living with Rowena and Dallas and Alec, for two weeks. That would take them through most of the first soft-opening week.

She tried to decide whether they'd even want her….

"Two weeks," she repeated aloud, in a voice even she could hear was heavy with doubt.

He chuckled. "You make it sound like a life sentence." Putting down his wine, he reached out and placed his hands lightly on her shoulders. With a subtle pressure, he angled her so that she looked down the creek instead of at the tent.

"Would it really be such a hardship? Spending a couple weeks in a landscape like this?"

Before her, the river sparkled like a sequined ribbon, curving gracefully between the trees until it narrowed and seemed to disappear. The trees shifted overhead, stirring the pink-honey sunlight and tickling the birds into riffs of merry song.

He was right…it was magnificent.

"No, of course not, but—" And then, abruptly, she glimpsed motion, and she realized what he had really wanted her to see. She inhaled softly, thrilled.

Two small otters were playing in the creek. Just

playing, apparently. Without any sign that they had noticed the nearby humans, they slid down the muddy bank, then paddled aimlessly for a few seconds, doubled back and slid down again. Their deep brown fur was soaked, glistening almost as black as their adorable button noses, and their powerful tails propelled them quickly through the water.

In the old days, Rowena had proclaimed that otter sightings guaranteed good luck, and the two younger girls had believed her, of course, as they almost always did. The sightings were rare, even back then, when the three of them had been free to wander these open acres for hours every day.

Maybe some of Mr. Driggs's nature worship had rubbed off, after all, because Bree suddenly felt an almost mystical peace and beauty floating over this spot, like a blessing. Crisp air, pure water, sunlight and the company of squirrel and bird and otter. How long had it been since she'd noticed how much healing power those simple things really had?

She needed healing. And not just from Charlie's betrayal. She might have run away from everything that happened here at Bell River, and covered over the damage—"No one likes a sad sack, Brianna!"—but the underlying wound had never healed.

She'd waited much too long to admit that, even to herself.

"It's beautiful," she said, quietly enough that she didn't disturb the animals. She looked at him. His hands had remained on her shoulders, though his face, too, was turned toward the creek. With his handsome profile rimmed in the colored sunlight, and the five-o'clock stubble tracing the strong jaw... He was beautiful, too. Dangerously beautiful. But surely not really dangerous to her. She hadn't ever been his type, not even when they were teenagers, and not now, either. Marianne, with her red hair and her easy laughter, was far more likely to please him and earn an invitation to share that big, splashy bed.

Besides, Bree could get control of this…this foolishness, which was probably some weird hangover from her youth, an absurd overreaction to his good looks, just because she used to have a crush on him in the ninth grade.

With a little time, that would fade. She would get tougher. After the lesson Charlie had taught her, that wouldn't be so hard.

"Two weeks, then," she said. "Unless you decide that you're ready sooner."

He turned back to her. He smiled.

"Don't count on that," he said.

After she left, and the sun went down, leeching the colors from the creek and sky, Gray felt restless. The tent might be comfortable, but it didn't offer much in the way of distraction from his thoughts.

So he got into his truck and drove into town.

It was only a little after nine when he pulled up in front of his grandfather's house. He killed the engine, but he sat there a while without climbing out, just getting used to seeing the old place again.

French Second Empire, that's what his grandfather always called the architectural style, in his usual self-important way. But Gray's mother had always laughingly referred to it as "the marble wedding cake," and that was the image that had stuck.

It truly was a silly piece of conspicuous consumption. Eight thousand square feet and twenty rooms under a high mansard roof, it would have been little more than a tall, boring white box if it hadn't been for all the frills. Iron cresting on the roof, elaborate cornices and balustrades, window hoods like eyebrows and endless yards of intricately scrolled gingerbread trim. Even the porte cochere dripped curlicues, like something out of a Victorian fairy tale.

Every possible feature was white marble, naturally. It was, Gray had always thought, not so much a home as a three-dimensional billboard advertising Harper Quarry.

The night was turning cold and he hadn't brought a jacket, so finally he got out and headed up the steps to the elevated entry pavilion that projected from the center of the house. Tonight, under the full, silver moon, and wreathed in cold, black sky, the house looked more like a big block of ice than a wedding cake.

He shivered as he touched the frigid metal doorbell.

The same plump, poker-faced housekeeper answered the door. So she was live-in, he deduced. He felt an odd sense of relief. He hadn't enjoyed thinking of the old man rattling around in this marble mausoleum alone, night after night.

Why he should care, he had no idea. Just another of those exhausting ambivalences. One more proof that love and hate remained equipoised just above his heart, like a knife on a fraying string.

"Hi," he said. He smiled, because none of this was her fault. "I'm sorry... I don't think I ever got your name."

She glanced over her shoulder before answering.

"Almeda," she said stiffly, minimally, as if she had a limited ration of words. But then to his surprise she smiled. Well, almost smiled. Stopped frowning, anyhow.

"Almeda. I'm Gray. I'm sorry to call so late. Is my grandfather available?"

The woman hesitated, one hand on the doorknob, the other on the edge of the door, that universally recognized position of impending rejection. The one you used when you'd made the mistake of opening to the salvation salesmen.

"I think he's already retired for the night, Mr. Gray. But if you'd like to leave a—"

"That's all right, Almeda." His grandfather's voice floated out of the darkness behind the woman. "I'll see him. Let him in."

She swung the door open, then let go and backed away to give Gray room to enter. "He's in the library," she said. As she shut the door behind him, she seemed to register his lack of a jacket. "You must be cold. May I get you a cup of coffee? Some hot tea?"

He would have loved to show his appreciation for her friendliness, but he had a feeling his grandfather would dislike the liberty. He probably already had that sour look on his face, just because Gray had dared to ask her name.

"I'm fine, thanks," he said. "I probably won't be staying that long."

She nodded wordlessly, immediately reverting to her usual dour demeanor, then quietly melted away down the dark hall. Gray blinked, trying to adjust to the gloom. Would it kill the old miser to run a few kilowatts now and then?

The library was the second room on the left, just beyond the parlor where Gray had waited that first night. The parlor was unlit, as was the dining room on the right. In fact, the only illumination Gray could see on the entire first floor was an eerie orange light emanating through the open library door.

The light was restless, shifting randomly, throwing strange shadows on the opposite wall. As Gray made his way down the hall, he felt surprised. His grandfather had always read before retiring for the night. Were the old man's eyes still good enough to read by firelight alone?

"Damn it, Gray. Have you forgotten where the library is located?"

His grandfather's tone was crabbed and petulant, as if he resented being kept waiting. Gray took a deep breath.

"No," he responded dryly as he reached the doorway. "Just feeling my way in the dark."

His grandfather didn't rise to greet him, of course. Manners didn't require it, and his leg probably didn't allow it. Gray entered the room with an exaggerated air of indifference, though internally he braced himself for the sight of the portrait.

The goddamn, nauseating portrait.

It had always hung where you couldn't miss it, right between the center stacks of floor-to-ceiling books. And there it hung still.

An impressive, ten-foot canvas, made even more imposing by an extravagantly ornate carved and gilded frame, it was a full-length painting of his grandfather as a young man. Dressed in an elegant brown Western show coat, camel breeches and high, glossy oxblood boots, Grayson Harper the First stood with his broad shoulders squared, his chin high and proud. His thick waves of brown hair lifted slightly in the wind. In one hand, he held a riding crop. In the other, he held the reins of an exquisite black stallion with sleek coat and spirited eyes.

Old Grayson had sat for the portrait when he was twenty-five, and had just made his first million. By then, he'd accepted that his childhood dream of becoming a rancher and horse breeder would never come true. There was just too much money to be made carving up the mountains and trundling blocks of marble down to the hungry towns below.

The picture was his official goodbye, the ten-foot tombstone erected to mark the spot where the rancher dream had died.

But that wasn't what made the portrait stressful for Gray. His problem was that, when he hit about fourteen or so, he found that he couldn't look at the damn thing without a dizzying sensation that he was looking into a mirror.

Every year, the resemblance had grown more pronounced. It didn't matter what he did to his hair, long, short, spiked or shaved. It didn't matter what he wore, or what kind of surly, delinquent expression he twisted his features into.

He was his grandfather's spitting image.

What a cruel twist of fate that it should be Gray who inherited the whole, crummy DNA strand, and not his father, old Grayson's son.

God knew, the old man had tried, forcefully, but always in vain, to make his only son over in his image. But ironically, Gray's father hadn't looked a whit like the old man, and hadn't shared a single trait. He'd hated horses almost as much as he'd hated marble. Gray's father, the sensitive musician, wanted only to be left alone to love his wife, love his son, love his art, but he was never given the chance.

Gray, who after his parents' death hated the old man more than anyone on earth, had inherited it all, from his hair to his jaw to his eyes to his temper. There was no escaping it. He wore the loathsome blood tie like a brand.

And when he realized that he, too, secretly dreamed of life as a rancher, a rider, a breeder…when he realized even that dream had skipped a generation and landed on him like a ton of bricks…that's when he refused to set foot in Harper House ever again.

He would not give the old bastard the satisfaction of seeing his grandson fall in line. He would not obediently take his father's place as old Grayson's dream surrogate.

Did his grandfather really believe he was God? Did he think he could just callously eliminate the disappointing son, simply sweep him off a rainy mountainside like a block of flawed marble, so that he could slide Gray into the slot, like interchangeable pieces in some cosmic puzzle?

Gray gave the portrait a long, frank look as he entered the room, just so that his grandfather would see that it didn't have any power to upset him any longer. Strange to think that, at thirty, he was older now than the arrogant, headstrong young man in the painting.

"Hello, Grandfather," he said politely, turning his

gaze to the old man. He held no book, Gray saw. Apparently he'd just been sitting here, staring into the fire.

Or at his portrait, perhaps?

His grandfather gave him a steady look. "I assume you have news?"

"I do." Gray rested one foot on the heavy brass fireplace fender and extended his hand toward the flames to thaw out his fingers. "I thought you'd like to know I have a job. I start tomorrow."

He cast a glance over his shoulder at the old man. He wondered whether someone might have already told him. Marianne, perhaps? She said not, but she did still visit. She'd openly admitted that.

But age hadn't diminished old Grayson's ability to keep his secrets to himself. "And what will you be doing?"

"I'll be working over at Bell River. Rowena Wright has come home, and she's turning the place into a dude ranch. I'm ostensibly the social director, but the ranch is obviously on such a tight budget that everyone will have to pitch in with everything."

"Social director." The old man made the words sound more vulgar than *gigolo,* or *male prostitute.* "Meaning you'll be teaching rich old ladies to dance and play canasta while you flirt your way into their wallets?"

Gray chuckled. "Occasionally, I suppose, if I'm lucky. Most of the time I'll be building playhouses and digging vegetable gardens and mucking stalls. Oh, and taking packs of snotty six-year-olds on overnight-camping trips."

He stood and faced his grandfather squarely. "I

think, on balance, it qualifies as a dirty job. If you disagree, you'd better tell me now. The four-week clock starts ticking as soon as I report to work in the morning, and I'll expect your written guarantee of our deal, as promised, by the end of the day."

The old man narrowed his eyes, which caught the reflected firelight, making them difficult to read. For a couple of minutes he seemed lost in thought. He kneaded the studded-leather arm of his chair absently, as if he didn't realize he was doing it.

Finally, he nodded slowly. "I suppose it will do. I suppose they were the only ones who were willing to hire you. With a past like theirs, they probably can't be picky."

Gray thought of the companies who had refused to even grant him an interview. He could hear the truth in the old man's voice. He'd tried to make it impossible for Gray to be taken on anywhere in Silverdell. He wasn't above trying to win this thing unfairly.

"Exactly," Gray agreed pleasantly, refusing to be baited. "Two bad seeds in the same pod. That's Rowena Wright and me."

He put his hands toward the fire one more time, for insurance as he headed back out to sleep in his tent. Then he smiled at his grandfather.

"Good night, then," he said. "I'll look for your document by courier? Oh, and just for the record, tomorrow is Wednesday, April twenty-fifth. Four weeks from that date will be Wednesday, May twenty-third. That will be my last day in Silverdell, so I'll expect to see you then. Or at least your banker."

"You'll see me before that," his grandfather responded testily. "I'll expect weekly check-ins and reports on what you've been doing. I also reserve the right to pay unexpected visits to your place of employment, to verify that you are actually there. And actually digging, mucking, snotting, as advertised."

Gray had to laugh. Micromanaging everyone's life, as always. It reminded him so much of the years his grandfather had demanded weekly reports from his teachers, his coaches, his professors, his dorm leaders and academic advisers, all part of the endless power struggle to force Gray to become the kind of scholar his grandfather wanted him to be.

And how had all that worked out in the end? Gray had damn near flunked out of high school, and he had absolutely, irrevocably, deliberately flunked out of college. He'd lost a small fortune on poker games he didn't give a damn about. He'd bought jewels he couldn't afford for girls he didn't respect.

He'd defied his grandfather at every turn, not caring whether he made a mess of his own life in the process.

But the point was…he'd never once considered giving in. He'd never once considered obeying. How sad that the old man hadn't learned a thing from any of that.

"Yes, you should do all those things," he said, still laughing at the thought of old Grayson trying to make Rowena add this to her jam-packed to-do list.

Dear Ms. Wright, please create a "Little Grayson Has Been a Good Boy" checklist for nosy old Mr. Harper.

Mr. Harper would soon learn the difference between the way teachers at elite, expensive private schools responded to a millionaire's demands, and the way Rowena Wright responded to any bastard dumb enough to try to order her around.

"Yes, indeed," he said again, cheerfully, as he strolled out through the library doors. "You should absolutely do that."

Chapter 7

Bree had driven herself half-mad that night. She was unable to sleep, partly because it was so strange being in the family home again. Every groan and creak of old windows, old wood, old tree limbs against the roof… it all sounded slightly haunted. She kept thinking she heard her mother turning her doorknob quietly, as she'd done every night, just to be sure all was well.

But her insomnia also stemmed from constantly second-guessing her decision to stay here a full two weeks. Would she end up regretting it?

As far as the family went, everything appeared okay. Rowena had seemed satisfied, even relieved, when she'd heard what Bree had worked out. Dallas had professed himself delighted. Even Alec had let out a war cry of happiness, and made Bree promise to come see his fort at Little Bell Falls.

Still…she knew that there was one more way this plan could backfire on her.

She couldn't deny it. She was already attracted to Gray Harper. And he wouldn't be averse to accepting any opportunities she offered, however subtle. She'd felt his interest from the start…but it had been fairly open and direct in the gaze he'd turned on her, out by the creek.

Problem was, she knew she was vulnerable right now—or at least her pride was, after Charlie's big public slap in the face. If she and this ridiculously sexy, bored, spoiled, ubervirile male worked closely together, every day…

She could end up making a huge mistake.

Another huge mistake.

Maybe that was something she'd inherited from her mother—a self-destructive preference for bad boys. None of the girls had ever discovered who Moira Wright's final lover had been, though his existence was confirmed by the fact that Moira had been just barely pregnant when she died. The man had never come forward, though, never acknowledged their relationship, never offered to testify against Johnny Wright…so how decent a man could he have been?

And, of course, they all knew how violent and cruel their father had been, though that hadn't stopped him from being shockingly good-looking, openly envied by Moira's acquaintances.

Finally, the mystery man who had fathered Rowena had obviously been someone who couldn't or wouldn't marry Moira, not even when she was carrying his child.

Moira had undoubtedly taken other lovers along

the way, but of the three her daughters knew about, all three were cads…or worse. So Bree shouldn't really have needed Charlie to warn her that a weakness for bad boys was in her blood.

She had tossed and turned until she'd finally given up.

Agonizing didn't help. She was here. She was going to stay and help her sister. So she would simply have to keep a padlock on her emotions.

Bree had smiled as she turned over and shut her eyes, finally seeing the humor in her predicament. She'd already taken a vow of temperance and a vow of silence. Should be easy enough to add a vow of chastity to the list.

Three days later, she had come to realize just *how* easy. Both she and Gray were far too busy, often in different parts of the ranch, or even different parts of the town, to waste time in flirtation. By this morning, just four days before the grand opening, she was too exhausted even to put on makeup, or do anything with her hair but pull it back in a hasty ponytail before she tackled her projects for the day.

Yesterday had been devoted to interviewing the many Dellians who had volunteered to lead special-interest classes with the guests.

Bill Friday knew everything about geology. Archie Stout was an amateur archaeologist. Fanny Bronson was an expert on local artists and writers. Joe Gibson had an idea for wildlife watching, and Bill Miller from the hardware store had a treasure trove of local history that made even a town like Silverdell sound exciting.

So much for Bree not having to face the townsfolk. But the meetings had gone surprisingly well. Everyone had been natural and friendly, and eager to share their expertise—free. She'd said yes to all of them. Then she'd stayed up half the night, all over again, putting together a schedule for classes.

Today would be devoted to the kiddie activities. She'd ordered books and games all morning—paying a fortune to get them overnighted, and wondering how long Georgia Brooke had been sick. Surely this should have been done a couple of weeks ago?

She'd picked out a bunch of music for the sing-along nights, and had emailed a file of lyrics to the local printer for binding and laminating in leaflets the children could hold—leaflets they could wash and disinfect and reuse later.

Now, with barely enough time to pull on a sweater from the community coatroom, and no time at all to find one that actually matched, or even fit, she had to jog out to the old barn to choose the perfect spot to hold Saturday-Morning Horse Tales. Once she decided, she could fax the specs and dimensions to Jude Calhoun, the local carpenter who had agreed to design the seats and stage, and fast-track the order at no extra charge.

By the time she reached the barn, she was slightly winded. She was wearing a pair of Rowena's boots, and her sister's feet were half a size larger, which meant Bree's heel rose up on every step and had to be reseated carefully so that she didn't trip.

As the perspiration met the breeze that blew through the chinks in the barn's sides, she shivered. It was chillier in here than she'd expected. She buttoned the sweater all the way up to her neck, and thanked her lucky stars she'd brought one two sizes too big. It covered all the way down to her knees, and, if she tugged a bit, she could make it drape over her fingers, too.

She gazed a minute, observing the cobwebby corners and wondering if she was brawny enough to shove aside those big pieces of dusty old equipment to see what lay behind. A couple of nooks looked promising, but on the surface nothing was quite perfect.

She unclipped and reattached her barrette, trying to capture as much of the flyaway hair as she could. Maybe better to think it through, before she began muscling things around. She tried to remember what being a kid had felt like. What kind of spot would she have liked at six, or ten, if her mother had wanted to read horse stories aloud?

"Hello, Bree."

She jerked her head up, bumping her crown on a low-hanging beam. A man had just entered the barn, but he stood in the broad, sunlit opening, backlit so dramatically that she had no idea who he was.

"Hello," she said warily. There was something about his voice she didn't like. Some unwarranted familiarity…some undercurrent of sensuality that she registered more with the follicles of her neck hairs than with her conscious mind.

She put her hand in her pocket and touched her cell phone. What was Gray doing right now? How far away was he working? Dallas was downtown, catching bad guys for the rest of the Dellians. And Barton was in the new stables, training the head wrangler.

"It's me, Bree." The man moved forward slowly, hands in front of him, as he might have approached a dangerous horse, or a hissing cat. "It's Charlie."

Her mouth dropped open, and she let go of her

phone. Charlie? A sudden anger rose in her, like a nausea. She wasn't afraid of this weasel. If anything, *he* should be afraid of *her*.

"What the *hell* are you doing here?" She took two hard steps in his direction. "And, more important, how fast can you go away?"

For a moment, as the rude words shot out of her mouth, she could almost see Kitty's shocked face. "You catch more flies with honey, Bree." *Yeah?* Well, you also caught rats, and Bree had caught a doozy.

So to heck with always wearing a smile and making nice. Kitty was gone. Breelie's was probably gone, thanks to this jerk. It was time to get real. Way past time.

"Bree." He somehow made her name two wheedling syllables, which infuriated her even more. Did he really think she was just another bimbo who would melt at the sight of his baby-blue sad-puppy eyes? At the moment, she was far more likely to gouge them out with her fingernails.

If she still had any fingernails. She'd broken most of them over the past three days, opening crates and carrying boxes, stringing lanterns and painting walls and saddling horses.

"Bree," he said again. "Be reasonable."

"I *am* being reasonable. I haven't impaled you with a pitchfork." She blew a strand of damp hair away from her face and narrowed her eyes. "You really should go away, Charlie. Right now, before I change my mind."

He didn't move, the darn fool. He just tilted his head and let his lips soften into a pout. "We need to talk. We have to. You can't just avoid me forever."

"Apparently not."

She thought about asking him how he'd found her, but Charlie had ways. She hadn't entered the witness protection program or anything. She'd just bought a plane ticket like a normal person. Right off the top of her head, she could think of three women who could have been sweet-talked into spilling the beans.

"But that doesn't mean I have to talk to you." Irritated, she ad-libbed the next part, piecing together half-remembered TV dialogue. "In fact, my lawyer expressly forbids it. Until the case is closed, I mean."

She almost smiled as she watched the hostility fall over his face like a shadow, banishing the pout, the sad-puppy eyes and anything else he thought was charming. He was angry now. *Good.* She knew he allowed himself to show anger only when he was trying to hide shame or fear.

She didn't really have a lawyer, of course. She hadn't wanted to pay for a civil suit when she needed all her money to make good on the debts Charlie had racked up in Breelie's name. Plus, she hadn't wanted to risk letting some smitten female juror acquit him, and have him go around forever crowing about being innocent.

But he didn't know that, obviously. His mouth was a tight line of fear masquerading as rage. "You're suing me? For what? For having sex with someone else? Is it a crime to want to make love to a woman who actually has a body temperature higher than an ice cube? Is it a crime to want a lover who actually likes sex?"

Where the devil was that pitchfork? "No, but in your case it might be a hopeless fantasy."

To her grim delight, that was a hit. His face flushed red.

"And it is *definitely* a crime to embezzle from your

employer," she pointed out. "And since I have the paper trail, and the angry suppliers, to prove it, it just seems simpler, in the end, to go that route."

He was quiet for a moment. He stared at her, a pulse in his jaw working overtime. He blinked steadily, as if it were the rhythm of his brains processing.

And then, slowly, the blood receded from his blotchy face.

"You'll lose," he said in a deadly confident monotone. "I had the authority to make every one of those purchases, and you know it. You gave it to me. You were so busy being the big-shot owner that you couldn't be bothered watching the bottom line."

"I was—" She stopped. "I was—"

But he was right, she recognized suddenly, and the realization stole the angry words right out of her mouth.

He was absolutely right. She'd been a fool, giving him so much rope. She should have known he'd use it to hang them both.

It wasn't as if she was blinded by love. She'd long since realized she didn't feel about him the way she should. She kept postponing the moment when they'd have to set the wedding date—not that he was exactly pushing hard, himself.

But she didn't call it off. It was just so much easier to let the relationship glide on smoothly, even if it was going nowhere, than it would have been to grind their engagement to a halt so that she could jump out and get off.

Besides, she had told herself she was being too hard to please. Who, if not Charlie? He was handsome, articulate and the clients loved him. He was also useful. He handled all the boring stuff, like placing orders and balancing the books.

So what if the sex had become almost nonexistent? They were so often at different events, or even in different cities. Even when they were under the same roof, they were exhausted. If lovemaking was a little disappointing, that wasn't unusual. It wouldn't be any different with a different man. That was just how Bree's body worked.

Probably had something to do with her past, but she didn't have the energy to try to figure it out. She poured all her passion into Breelie's, and life was good enough.

Maybe if Charlie hadn't proposed right after Kitty died…

The death had been entirely unexpected—one minute, Kitty was pouring a glass of wine to celebrate the opening of Breelie's. The next minute, an aneurysm burst, and Kitty lay on the floor in a pool of red wine and shattered glass. She'd never awakened again.

That was four years ago, when Bree was twenty-six. Probably, she would have accepted any man who asked her at that moment. It had been such a relief not to have to be alone. That neurosis she *could* trace back to its roots. Ever since the day Aunt Ruth announced that she couldn't take all three girls, and the social worker had explained to Bree that she might have to become a ward of the state, she'd had a horror of being alone.

But she should have forced herself to master it. She should have been tougher, wiser, harder on herself…

She'd been lazy, and she'd been a coward. And she'd paid dearly for it.

"I hope you *do* take me to court," Charlie said, smiling suddenly, as if he smelled the self-doubt that had crept in, knocking out the underpinnings of her righteous indignation. "There's absolutely no chance a jury would convict me. Everyone knows a woman scorned when they see one."

She raised her chin. God help her—maybe she'd inherited her father's temper, after all. Suddenly she saw red, and she wanted to punch him in the nose.

Instead, she forced herself to settle for hurting him back. "A woman scorned? I wonder if they'll still think that's what I am after they get a look at the new man in my life."

Charlie frowned. He looked at her with cold eyes, his gaze moving from her head to her feet slowly. She flushed, remembering the lack of makeup, the messy hair, the oversize sweater...and probably the stable smell as well, since she'd been feeding horses before dawn.

"You're with someone else? Already?"

Why had she made that up? It was childish, more like a teenager than a grown woman. But it would have been humiliating beyond endurance to admit the truth now.

"Colorado is full of cowboys," she equivocated, hoping she wouldn't have to lie outright again. "Perhaps you don't know me as well as you thought you did."

"Either that...or he doesn't know you at all. I'll lay odds you two haven't had sex yet."

She lowered her eyelids. "You'll lay anything, Charlie. You've already demonstrated that."

"Hey, darlin', you comin' up or not? I can't keep the engine revved forever if there's nowhere to drive the train."

The sexy drawl came from the shadowy hayloft just behind Bree's head. Charlie's gaze shot upward, and Bree turned, equally shocked. It sounded like Gray—if Gray had been a sex-crazed cowboy in a 1950s comic book.

Sure enough, a second later, Gray came sauntering to the edge of the loft, looking like someone she'd never seen before. His hair was disheveled, brown waves tumbling in all directions under an oversize cowboy hat she recognized as having once belonged to her father's foreman.

Other than the hat and a smirk, he wasn't wearing much else. No shirt, no shoes, no belt. His jeans technically were on, but they seemed to cling to the lower edge of his hips reluctantly, as if they'd much prefer to slide on down.

He grinned at Charlie. "Sorry to bust up the little confab, buddy, but this gal has a date up here that she definitely don't want to miss."

"Gray." Bree couldn't decide whether to be mortified that Gray had obviously overheard her conversation, or grateful that he'd decided to step into the role of her imaginary cowboy lover. "This is Charlie Newmark. He was just leaving."

Charlie hadn't fully closed his mouth since Gray first spoke. He glanced from Gray to Bree, then back to Gray again.

"*You're* the new boyfriend?"

Gray let his gaze run over Charlie slowly. The very fact that he was above them and had to look down his nose to see the other man made the inspection seem insolent. He held a piece of hay between his sexy lips, and he munched on it thoughtfully.

"Well, that depends on who's asking," he said finally. He pushed the brim of the hat backward so that Charlie could better read his eyes. "And in what tone."

"I'm the *old* boyfriend," Charlie said, though he did dial his voice a couple of notches toward civility.

"Oh!" Gray stretched out the syllable, and his smile broadened. He bent down, gripped both legs of the ladder that had been propped against the edge of the loft and swung himself down to the barn floor without ever stepping on a single rung.

"Nice to meet you, buddy. Tough luck about losing our gal here, but don't feel too bad. The feisty ones are tricky. Some of them just squirt away, no matter how hard you hang on."

While Charlie frowned, clearly trying to decide how to respond, Gray chuckled. He strode up behind Bree and slid his arm around her waist. Surprised, she stiffened, but she didn't pull away. After a second to let her adjust, he tucked her up against him, confidently possessive.

He was playing this role far, far too well. She ought to call a halt to it before Charlie lost his temper. Gray's chivalry probably wouldn't extend to having his nose broken in this impromptu bit of theater.

But she wasn't exactly sure how to slow things down without spoiling the effect. And, to be honest, she wasn't even sure she wanted to. Though she couldn't see Gray's face, the back-to-front connection was deliciously, almost unbearably, intimate. Her shoulder blades pressed into his bare torso, and she could feel his hard, cool touch of the button at the waistband of his jeans as it pressed into her back.

"You sure do know how to drive a guy crazy, darlin'." Gray's voice was teasing. "Were you going to leave me up there all day, just 'a waitin' and 'a wantin'?"

"I…" Someone had forgotten to give her the script. She wasn't as good at improv as Gray was. "No, I was just finishing up some stuff…"

But then he bent his head and skimmed his warm lips against her collarbone. She broke out in ridiculous shivers and couldn't complete the sentence.

"Oh, yeah. That's right, honey." His throaty voice was equal parts absurd and absurdly sexy. "I've got some stuff you can finish up."

Charlie made a rude sound and rolled his eyes. "Good luck with that, cowboy. All I can say is I think you might end up disappointed. Some things look a lot better than they really are, if you know what I mean."

Gray's arm tightened around her waist. He trailed another slow kiss across her neck, all the way up to her ear. Her heart pounded like a jackhammer, and her eyes drifted shut without her permission.

"Yeah, I reckon I know what you mean," Gray said pleasantly. "And all *I* can say is…there's more to riding a horse than sittin' in the saddle and lettin' your feet hang down."

He nudged Bree's hair aside so that he could reach the tender skin at the back of her neck. She felt his mouth curve in a smile, and she knew he was staring at Charlie without ever raising his lips. "If you know what I mean."

Charlie sputtered, but nothing came out. And then, finally, he turned on his heel and left.

Chapter 8

The moment they were alone, Bree made a small twitch forward, and Gray instantly let his arm drop.

He had been walking a fine line, he knew that.

For a while, as he'd listened to their argument, he'd felt his best move was to lie low and never let her guess that she'd been overheard. He'd been up there an hour before she ever arrived because Barton had asked him to clean out the loft.

Bree obviously didn't know that. And, if he was careful, she never needed to know.

As long as she was giving this Charlie jerk as good as she got, Gray was content to remain silent. But then she started letting the bastard get to her. Gray could hear the pain in her voice. The insecurity. The fear that the jackass over there might be right, and the problem might lie in her.

When he heard her tell Charlie she had a new cowboy boyfriend, he had simply succumbed to his impulse. He remembered the moth-eaten old ten-gallon hat he'd set aside in the junk pile earlier. Quietly, he retrieved it, then shucked his shirt and his belt, trading them for the swaggering drawl of the Saturday-morning cartoon cowboys he'd loved as a kid.

After that, he'd simply played it by ear. He hadn't intended to actually touch her, or kiss her neck, but the outrage in Charlie's face was just too gratifying. Still, he wouldn't have gone this far if she'd given him any sign that she wanted him to stop.

Finally, here was the sign. The twitch. So he let go of her. She took a few steps forward, so that she was just outside the barn, where the sunlight could find her. It was as if she needed fresh air after the contamination of Charlie.

He slowly followed. When they were both just beyond the shadows, she squared her shoulders, then turned to face him.

"How long were you listening?"

He shrugged. "Long enough to be hoping you were going to kick him in the groin. I promise you, if there had been a pitchfork among that junk up there, I'd have tossed it down to you in a heartbeat."

She took a deep breath, her blue eyes cloudy. "You heard it all, then?"

"Yeah. I was there from 'Hello, Bree,' which I'm pretty sure was the opening line. It moved pretty fast after that, and I couldn't find a good moment to announce that you had an audience hiding in the balcony."

"I bet that was…awkward." With three tense fingers, she made small circles on her forehead, nodding miserably. "I'm sorry you heard all those—those ugly things. In fact, I'm sorry I said them. I don't usually allow myself to get openly hostile like that. Nasty fights and name-calling are really Rowena's area of expertise."

He smiled. "Well, you're extremely good at it, if that's any consolation."

"It's not." She tried to smile back, but it didn't work all that well. "I was brought up to value restraint. I've seen what happens if people just say and do whatever they want. It might feel good for a minute or two, but there's always a price to pay later." She sighed. "I don't know why I let him get to me."

"Because that's what *he's* extremely good at," Gray observed. "He's the living illustration of the old adage 'the best defense is a good offense.'"

The sound of running came at them from the eastern side of the barn. As they glanced over, Alec raced up, Trouble panting merrily at his side.

"Oh, good, there you are!" Clearly oblivious to any undercurrents swirling in the atmosphere, Alec skidded to a halt, looking sweaty and winded. "Bree, Gray, Rowena says she needs you up at the house."

Bree seemed almost glad of the reprieve. She turned her back on Gray and faced the excited boy. "What's wrong?"

Alec shrugged. "Who knows? Dad was fixing the fireplace, but he's got to go back to the station." He turned to Gray. "That's why Rowena wants you, I guess. That's man work."

"Okay, my little chauvinist in training," he said, laughing. He was surprised that Alec apparently hadn't yet noticed Gray was wearing a cowboy hat instead of a shirt. Maybe in nine-year-old land, that was normal. "Rowena would box your ears for that. But not me. Whenever a real manly man is needed, you can count on me."

Alec grinned, then looked back at Bree. Trouble did exactly the same thing, as if he always mirrored his master's movements. His grin included a lolling tongue, and was punctuated by a noisy sneeze.

"And she wants you, I guess, because she's trying to help the housemaids get fresh linens on the beds." Alec smiled. "But one of the maids is nuts and..."

He chewed his lower lip and apparently decided it would be more fun to let them be surprised. "Oh, you'll see. Come on. Let's go!"

"Okay." Casting a brief glance back at Gray, Bree signed a quick pantomime of shrugging on a shirt and yanking off a hat. Then she followed Alec and the puppy out of the barn.

Gray took a minute to climb back up to the loft and re-dress properly, so the drama was already underway by the time he arrived upstairs in the main house.

Dallas stood by the fireplace of the front guest room, wiping his hands on a rag. Bree and Rowena bookended either side of the king-size bed, each of them deftly tucking a corner of a pale green sheet under the mattress.

In the armchair nearby, one of the white-uniformed maids, a middle-aged woman as fat and pink as a pearl, was fanning herself with a Bell River brochure and talking a mile a minute.

"She was right there, I'm serious, as clear as day, looking just like you or me. Well, looking just like you, of course, Miss Rowena. But it was her. I would know your mother anywhere. I tell you, I nearly fainted."

Gray glanced at Dallas, who widened his eyes with discreet eloquence. He handed Gray a trowel and a bucket of wet mortar.

"Sorry," he said. "We really do have an emergency at the station."

Gray smiled. "Sure you do."

"It's true. It's the answer to a fervent prayer, but it's true." Dallas patted Gray's shoulder sympathetically, ruffled Alec's hair and finally blew a kiss to his wife.

Then, whistling the theme from *The Great Escape,* he disappeared down the stairs.

Gray knelt on the drop cloth by the fireplace, did a quick evaluation of Dallas's progress, then proceeded to apply mortar to one of the remaining cracks. Dallas had been using black mortar, which meant the area would need repainting, too, once the mortar dried.

On the other side of the cheerful, light green room, Rowena and Bree had begun to unfold the bed's top sheet, arranging it carefully on the mattress, perfectly centered and crisp. The maid still jabbered, fanning furiously, as if she was afraid of what would happen if she didn't cool herself down.

"Isamar." Rowena gently broke into the stream of words. "Could you see what she was wearing?"

Rowena's question didn't sound mocking, or even particularly skeptical. Gray flicked another glance at her, wondering whether her staffing crisis was so urgent that she didn't even dare to contradict the superstitious head cases who thought they saw ghosts.

"A dress. Green flowers. Big skirt." The maid groaned and crossed herself with the fan. "Saints preserve me. She smiled right at me. I knew she wanted to tell me something."

Gray groaned inside. But Rowena didn't flinch. She just ran her hand over the top sheet, expertly smoothing out one last wrinkle. Then she picked up a brown blanket and handed one side to Bree.

"It's all right, Isamar. I'm sure it wasn't anything to be afraid of. What else happened? Did she…speak? Did she say anything to you?"

This time, Gray heard a subtle note of melancholy in Rowena's carefully steady voice. He wondered what exactly caused it. It could be any of several emotions— or even all emotions at once.

He tried to imagine how he'd feel if someone told him his mother's ghost walked the corridors of Harper Hall. Mostly, he'd be resentful that such a real and wonderful human being had been reduced to a campfire-ghost-story cliché. But he'd also pity the person who "saw" her, because that person must surely be emotionally or mentally unstable.

At the same time, he knew he'd harbor some tiny, secret, desperate hope that it might, against all reason, be true. Some pathetic desire that the dead weren't really gone forever. That a face so loved, so desperately missed, could really be glimpsed again.

"No." Isamar shook her head so hard her round cheeks ruffled. "She didn't speak. She smiled, and then she was gone."

Gray transferred his gaze to Bree, curious as to how she would react. Just coming back to the house where so much tragedy had occurred must have been difficult enough. Now this…

He assumed that, whether she thought the maid was

batty or just silly, she still would find the discussion disturbing.

To his amazement, she looked completely unfazed. Her expression was so serene, in fact, that he wondered for a moment whether she'd even heard what Isamar was reporting. Did she have earphones in her ears, blocking all sound?

But then Rowena asked her a simple, quiet question: "Can you get the spread from the end table?" Bree nodded with a bland smile and picked up the heavy green-and-brown-flowered coverlet, proving that she must have heard every word spoken in this room.

Rowena and Bree unfolded the spread up the length of the bed, like a synchronized team. When it was perfectly smooth, and they had arranged the large, decorative pillows on top, the bed was neat and elegant. Rowena surveyed it from top to bottom, nodded with quiet satisfaction, then went over to the swooning maid.

Squatting in front of the armchair, she took Isamar's hands in hers. "Why don't you take the rest of the day off?"

"Oh, no, Miss Rowena." Isamar sniffed. "I couldn't. There's so much work."

Rowena smiled. "You're tired. You've had a shock. You'll be paid for the day, but I want you to go on home. Bree will help me finish the rest of the rooms."

It took several more minutes of coaxing, but finally Isamar agreed to call her son to come and get her. Rowena and Bree had to watch her down the stairs, and she insisted on waiting out on the front driveway, rather than in the house.

As they returned to the green guest room, Bree was in the middle of a sentence.

"—we have asked her not to say anything about this to anyone? If people start hearing that we have ghosts, what are the odds the dude ranch will ever be a success?"

Rowena just laughed, as if she quite liked the idea of her mother's ghost floating around, smiling at the maids, and didn't take any threat to the ranch seriously. But Gray wasn't so sure. How many people would risk bringing their families for vacation in a haunted house? Particularly if the gossip ever started focusing on the madness of the father…and whether it might have been passed down to his daughters.

It made Gray angry to think of how fragile the Bell River reputation really was, and how little the Wright women could do to prevent superstitious people from spreading absurd rumors.

But Rowena, at least, seemed quite philosophical, even pragmatic, about the situation.

"I can ask Isamar not to tell anyone, of course. But that's not really going to stop her from telling just one trusted person in deepest, darkest confidence. And that person will tell one person, who will also tell one person. Sooner or later, everyone will know, anyhow. If we've tried to issue a gag order, it's just going to make us seem shady and weird, as if we have something to hide."

Bree lifted one shoulder. "Okay," she said, still projecting an indifference that Gray couldn't quite believe was natural. "Shall we hang pictures in here? Or do you want to do all the beds first, and come back to hang pictures after?"

"Let's do all the beds first," Rowena said. "That way, before it's time to hang pictures, maybe Barton or Gray will be free to help us decide what should go where. They'll hate that, of course, but I'm beyond making good decisions alone anymore."

Pulling his head briefly from the fireplace cave, Gray chuckled. "I can hear you, you know."

"I know." Rowena laughed. "I'm shameless. Desperation will do that to a person. We've got two days until guests arrive, and we've got at least four days of work."

"We'll make it," he said firmly.

And they would. He knew deadlines. The stroke of midnight had a momentum all its own, like a tidal wave, and the wave would sweep everything along with it as it roared in.

He remembered the night he learned that lesson. He'd been about twenty-two, and anxiously awaiting the birth of a prize foal. He had sunk every penny he owned into the stud fee, the stable, the vet and the trainer. Plus, the mare was his favorite horse—he loved her as much as he'd loved any human since the night his parents died.

So she held not only his financial future, but what was left of his heart, as well. He couldn't afford for a single thing to go wrong.

For days he'd driven himself, and everyone around him, half insane with his compulsive need to prepare for every eventuality, to have every particular nailed down, every condition perfect. But once labor began, and it was too late to do anything but guard and guide the newborn into this life, the truth crystallized before him.

All the unfinished details simply didn't matter. You

did what you could, for as long as you could. And then, when the time came, you let the rest go.

"Gray?"

Shaking off the memories, he withdrew from the fireplace again and looked toward the sound of the voice. Rowena had left the room. Only Bree stood there, a few feet from him, her voice as somber as her face. "May I ask you something?"

"Okay." He put the trowel down and gave her his full attention.

"You seem like a relatively sane person," she said.

He smiled. "Guess that depends on relative to what."

He was saner than Charlie Newmark, for instance, who was lunatic enough to cheat on a woman like her. But he was definitely less sane than, say, Rowena's husband. Dallas was a bona fide saint who had never fallen off the virtuous path and never would, even if it were as high and narrow as a tightrope strung between two skyscrapers.

You wouldn't catch Dallas Garwood gambling away his college-tuition money, just to show his grandfather he couldn't be bought. Or stringing half a dozen girls along at the same time in hopes that more attention, more sex, more admiration might finally fill the bottomless hole where his heart used to be.

Dallas would never have spent years refusing to do the work he was born to do, just to demonstrate his independence. Independence from what? Common sense? Happiness?

Bree shook her head. "Not relative to anyone. Just plain sane. Generally." She smiled. "Anyhow, I wanted to know…what do you think about Isamar's story?

Do you think there could possibly be such a thing as ghosts?"

He tried to read her expression. But her face was as impassive as if she'd been carved in marble. He'd like to give her whatever comfort she needed, but he had no idea what she was hoping he'd say.

It had been pretty cut-and-dried for him. In his heart, his mom and dad were both innocent martyrs, loving parents ripped away from the son they would never have abandoned if they'd had a choice.

But for Bree and her sisters, the issue was more complicated. True, if ghosts existed, they might get lucky. They might someday, out of the blue, run into their mother on the stairs.

But they might also run into their father.

Gray decided to be honest. "For a while, when I was a kid, I was pretty desperate to believe there could be. I did just about everything short of joining the spirit world myself, hoping I could find the particular ghosts I was looking for."

There had been a couple of times when he'd considered doing even that. But some remnant of sanity had always held him back. He knew that wasn't what his parents would want. Even if it meant being separated forever, they would have wanted him to live.

"But you never did see them."

"No." He shook his head. "I never did."

He thought he sounded fairly unemotional as he described it—it had been a very long time now, and time did at least give you a layer of numbness.

But her eyes were suddenly shadowed and deep with emotion. "I'm so sorry. When you have to face that someone is really gone forever—there's no hope—"

A small, pained line appeared between her eyebrows. "That must have been...nearly impossible to bear."

He dipped his trowel back into the black mortar, surprised and a little unnerved by the intensity of her empathy. It was as if, for a moment, she'd been able to peel back a corner of his heart and look inside.

And what she saw there, she recognized. She knew, really knew, what he had been through.

It was the strangest sensation. It made him feel more exposed—and at the same time less alone—than he had in many, many years.

He didn't like the feeling.

This wasn't the kind of relationship he was looking for. He had no intention of letting anyone get that close. That door was locked—or at least he had believed it was. He certainly hadn't given the key to her. How could he? He no longer had any idea where to find it, even if he'd wanted to.

Yet, somehow, there she was. And that changed everything.

Until this very moment, he'd been indulging in a fun little fantasy about having a no-strings fling with her while they were both at Bell River.

His only hesitation had been the fear that he might hurt her. He sensed the vulnerability beneath that cool, alabaster surface. It was part of her fascination. He craved a chance to learn what lay beneath those carefully guarded depths.

So he'd promised himself that he'd be very clear about what he was offering. If she was interested, on those terms, they might have a lovely few weeks together. If she wasn't, she could say so, and no hard feelings.

For the first time, though, he saw that this fling he longed for could cut both ways. He could hurt her, yes, as his inability to commit had hurt so many women through the years.

But suddenly he realized it was just barely possible that this particular woman…

That she could hurt him, too.

He felt like a chess piece already out too far on a perilous board when, without warning, someone changed the rules of the game. What now? Which moves was he allowed to make? And what about the other pieces? Where did the danger lurk now?

When his phone rang, it felt like a reprieve. He pulled it from his pocket and read the name there. *Agatha.* Hell. She was…what…three girlfriends ago?

He turned the ringer off and slipped the phone back in his pocket. He glanced at Bree. He could make something up, say he was ignoring a wrong number, a telemarketer, a bore.

But why lie? She might as well know the truth about him, before she started imagining he was some kind of tragic hero she could save.

"That's the only kind of ghost that scares men like me," he said with a brittle smile, tilting his head toward the phone. "The ghost of girlfriends past."

That night, when Gray finally got back to the Cupcake Creek tent, he saw a packet waiting for him, propped against the zippered canvas door. It wasn't thick, but it was obviously official. It bore the return address of the same lawyers his grandfather had always used… Pegram and Quick, over in Montrose.

He tore it open, sat in the deck chair and read it by

the light of the lantern hanging from the highest pitch of the roof.

It didn't take long. For legalese, it was fairly straightforward.

If Gray retained his job at Bell River Ranch for four straight weeks, and if the job included at least 50 percent legitimate manual labor, as defined below, etc, etc, etc, then a new will would be executed, naming Gray as the sole beneficiary of his grandfather's estate.

The only hitch was that the old man had to live for four weeks. If he died before Gray's month was served, his most recent authenticated will would be placed into probate and considered final.

Nothing else. No mention of Gray's father, of course, or of the money old Grayson had supposedly "invested" for him, then had never been willing to release, supposedly because he didn't trust Gray's father's judgment.

And no mention of any of that crap about weekly reports and spot inspections. Maybe the old man had been ashamed to sound so paranoid and overbearing, even to his lawyers, men who were pretty damn overbearing themselves.

After he'd finished reading, Gray sat there on the deck for a long time, the papers draped across his knee. He stared into the shadowy, moon-eerie trees, and listened to the crying of night birds and the occasional splash of something small trying to make its way across the creek.

He ought to feel victorious.

He hadn't been entirely sure his grandfather would actually keep his end of the bargain. Asking for this document had been like playing one final, giant hand of poker, betting everything on the cards that remained facedown, the do-or-die cards. The cards he couldn't see.

He'd placed the bet, though. And, against all odds, he'd won.

He should feel vindicated. Triumphant.

But all he felt was tired. And alone.

And keenly aware that no piece of paper ever printed, whether it had an autographed admission of guilt on it or a string of zeros lined up after a dollar sign, was ever going to make that loneliness go away.

Chapter 9

Suddenly, as if the days disappeared into a maelstrom of frantic activity, it was May first, and the reality of Bell River Dude Ranch was upon them.

Guests began arriving early in the day, several hours earlier than the announced check-in time. Luckily, Barton James had warned Rowena this might happen, and they were ready. They'd set out a brunch in the courtyard between the house and the first cottage. As people trickled in, they dropped their suitcases at the front desk, were handed a map of the Bell River property highlights and then were funneled out to the courtyard, where they ate barbecue sandwiches and hamburgers, and drank milk or lemonade or soda.

Then they had a choice. They could stay put, and bask in the sun, listening to Barton James play cowboy songs. Or they could hike off the calories by following the map to Little Bell Falls, the glamping tent at Cupcake Creek, the rock formations on the eastern perimeter or the Native American message trees on the western slope.

Somehow, the staff made it through the check-in process. By five o'clock, each and every guest had been installed in the correct room, and because by some miracle everyone had the proper number of pillows and towels, and all the hair dryers and telephones and ice machines worked, a brief peace fell over the ranch.

Or so it seemed, unless you were in the barn, helping to get that night's dance ready. The barn doors opened at six-thirty, so for ninety minutes every available staff member scurried about, doing something urgent to the cause.

They hung strands of colored lights, paper lanterns and balloons. They set up tables for the guests and the stage for the musicians, and they lay down the dance floor in lovely parquet squares. They tested the sound system, stocked the bars and checked for spots on the glasses.

The chef, a battle-ax of a woman they called Cookie, who resembled a medieval executioner but created delicacies like a fairy queen, had been snarling through the kitchen all day, and the result was a hundred pastries as light as air, three dozen filets as soft as butter, chafing dish after chafing dish of mouthwatering asparagus and sweet potatoes and endless mounds of salads bursting with color.

At six-thirty, Bree and Rowena stood shoulder to shoulder and, for a moment, held their breath. They gave each other one brief glance, then, while Bree held up a hand signal to the band, Rowena nodded to the waitstaff who stood ready to fling open the barn's huge double doors.

And then the guests began to pour in, and all Bree could do was ride the wave of laughter, eating and dancing that overtook them all.

By ten o'clock, she was exhausted. When she looked up from her last dance to see Gray standing in front of her, holding a glass of iced water, she thought she'd never seen anything so beautiful in her life.

"You are an angel," she said, accepting the tumbler and drinking eagerly. She'd been dancing for two hours without stopping and suddenly realized she must be a little dehydrated.

When she finally got enough, she sighed and pressed the back of her hand to her lips to wipe away the water mustache. "And that is the nectar of the gods."

He smiled. "Time to relax for a few minutes. You've been working too hard. Rowena's going to have Occupational Safety and Health Administration breathing down her neck if you don't take a break now and then."

She nodded reluctantly. "It's been a great way to get to know people, though. There's just so much to learn about the guests if everything is going to run smoothly." She sighed. "It's so much easier to anticipate the trouble spots and head them off if you can."

"Absolutely." He scanned the crowd with a half smile. "For instance, little Mabel Madison... See her over there, dipping her hamburger into her cola? We're going to need to keep her tuckered out. Otherwise, she'll end up burning the place down, or falling out of a paddleboat, or shooting her dad with a bow and arrow."

She laughed. She'd noticed Mabel, too. "She has ten times more energy than any child should. We will have to be careful to keep her away from Alec. That's a chemical explosion waiting to happen."

Gray nodded, agreeing emphatically. He smiled at Fanny Bronson as she danced by, then leaned toward Bree and lowered his voice. "And we're definitely going to have to find Fanny a man. She's been looking at Dallas the way a starving mutt looks at another dog's dinner."

Bree's eyes widened. She had not noticed that. She'd noticed only that Gray himself seemed to be dancing with Fanny a lot. It shouldn't have bothered her—they all had to sprinkle attention on the guests, especially the wallflowers. He was the social director. He was just doing his job.

But it had bothered her anyhow.

He looked particularly handsome tonight, though he hadn't fancied himself up in buckles, bolo ties, big hats and ornate boots, as some of the guys—especially the teenagers—had done. On his body, though, the soft corduroy pants and crisp broadcloth dress shirt were amazing. Especially now that she knew exactly what kind of washboard torso lay beneath that simple button-down shirt.

She had felt an irrational twist of envy, watching Fanny clutch tightly at his shoulders and letting him rest his hand along her waist. The envy was irrational because just a few days ago, at the moment he'd rejected that phone call from an old girlfriend, Bree had vowed she would not allow herself any more fantasies about Gray Harper, who she strongly suspected had serious issues with commitment.

The past few days had been so busy, and he'd been so completely professional and helpful, that she'd almost been able to make good on that vow.

But tonight felt different, as if the gala atmosphere of the opening made it okay to relax the rules a little. Even Rowena had let her guard down and had been warm and sisterly all night. A logical leap from that to saying it was okay to flirt with Gray, but Bree was too happy to split hairs right now.

"Barton is going to be great with the tween girls," Bree noted, eager to change the subject from Fanny. She pointed toward the elderly man, who was waltzing a ten-year-old girl across the dance floor. The girl, who had been hanging sulkily along the buffet table half an hour ago, giggled irrepressibly, pink cheeked and bright eyed.

"Yep." Gray grinned at the sight of the mismatched pair. "And how about Dallas? His brand of saintliness seems tailor-made for wallflowers of a certain age."

She'd noticed that, too. Her charming brother-in-law had been dividing his time between two elderly spinster sisters with striking, if fading, beauty, and killer line-dancing skills. Right now he stood between them, listening attentively, as if there was nowhere on earth he'd rather be.

"Rowena doesn't dance much?" Gray glanced toward the far corner, where Ro stood with half a dozen guests who were looking at a display of horse portraits.

Bree smiled. "Her mission is like ours. She's doing reconnaissance for tomorrow. By tomorrow, she has to be ready to match each guest with a mount, and apparently that's tricky."

Gray smiled. "Because of the inverse fantasy-reality ratio?"

"Exactly." Bree wondered, not for the first time, whether he might, in "real" life, work at another dude ranch somewhere. He seemed very familiar with the ins and outs of things—in spite of his earlier contention that he needed a lot of training to get up to speed.

She'd realized within the first couple of days that he needed her "training" like he needed more sex appeal. But by then she was too invested in the soft opening to even consider walking away.

On the other hand, he wasn't quite sunburned or callused enough to be a full-time wrangler. So maybe he was just a quick study. But, for whatever reason, he clearly understood that as Ro tried to match a horse to each guest, she'd be working mostly from instinct. Apparently, what people expressed a desire to ride didn't always dovetail with what they had the talent, experience or disposition to handle.

"So everyone seems to have a niche here tonight." Gray's voice had a teasing lilt. "But you, on the other hand…"

Bree raised her eyebrows. "I what?"

"You attract them all. Old or young. Rich or poor. Married or un. There isn't a male in this barn tonight who doesn't want a place on your dance card."

She chuckled. "You should talk."

"I notice you play favorites, though. There's one guy who has been getting more than his share of your attention."

"You mean Alec?" She'd danced with Dallas's son four times—she noticed she was the only one who ever said yes more than once. Sometimes Trouble insisted on trotting right out to the dance floor with Alec and getting in the way. However, even when Trouble stayed on the sidelines, basking in the attention of the dog-loving crowd, Alec had a tendency to stomp on his partner's feet.

"No. I mean Matt Gordon."

"Oh. Yes, that's true."

Gray must have been paying closer attention than she'd guessed. She had given a lot of her time to a guest named Matt Gordon, a sixty-five-ish man, neither handsome nor ugly, neither bold nor shy. Just quiet, self-contained and—though she couldn't pinpoint how she knew this—very, very sad.

She wasn't sure exactly how Matt was connected to the Bell River family-and-friends list. Though everyone invited to the soft opening was handpicked by some member of the staff, she didn't remember the name from the roster she'd seen initially.

But here he was. And she knew a hurting soul when she saw one.

"I like him," she said. "And I get the feeling he needs cheering up. I'm on a mission to make him smile, sometime before this night is through."

"I fear that mission may be doomed to failure. Matt's wife died two months ago."

She frowned. "How do you know that?"

"He told me. We ran into each other at the bar, and we talked for a few minutes."

"That's strange," she said, feeling oddly disappointed that the man hadn't confided in her. They had talked far more than "a few minutes," and she had genuinely liked him. She'd thought the feeling was mutual. "I wonder why he didn't tell me."

He looked at her, his expression matter-of-fact. "Probably because you're trying to make him smile."

"What on earth does that mean? What's wrong with trying to make him smile?"

He hesitated a minute, then shrugged. "I think you may be missing the more important question. What's wrong with being sad?"

She started to laugh, as if he might be making a joke. *What was wrong with being sad?* What kind of question was that?

But his expression remained completely serious. Her smile faded.

"It seems pretty self-explanatory to me," she said, mildly defensive. "No one *wants* to be sad."

"No," he agreed. "What most people want is to be accepted for exactly who and what they are. What most people want is the freedom to be honest and genuine and not to have to pretend to be anything they're not."

She flushed slightly. Gray was being kind, but he wasn't sugarcoating it, either. Her efforts were wrongheaded. What Matt Gordon really needed, Gray was telling her, was a safe place in which to work through his feelings—not rush blindly to change or deny them.

Intellectually, she could hear the power of that concept. With her conscious brain, she knew Gray had touched on something profound. The freedom to be honest, with yourself, and with others, too. The freedom to stop pretending. That would, absolutely, be the greatest imaginable gift one person could ever give another.

And yet, while her brain understood, her heart and her subconscious reflexes, which obviously drove her behavior, didn't have the slightest idea what that kind of freedom felt like.

"No one likes a sad sack, Bree."

As always, Kitty's words were close at hand. But Bree's need to cover the truth went much further back than that. Other voices, other memories, cautioned her against the danger of honesty, as well.

She could hear her father raging at Rowena. "Say anything like that to me again, you little bitch, and they will be the last words you ever utter under this roof."

She could see her mother at the family dinner table, a smile plastered on her face, but the eyes above the smile as empty as a doll's. Sometimes, while her husband talked, Moira's eyes slid away, focusing on something in the middle distance that only she could see. Her real life, maybe, playing out somewhere else, while her body sat propped up in a chair at home, nicely dressed and smiling.

And then, most painful of all, Bree could see Penny, who had crawled into Bree's bed because their father's angry voice had awakened her. Those liquid eyes staring up at her. "Are you scared, too, Bree?"

And Bree's own voice, answering with a steady certainty she'd never genuinely felt, never once in her life. "Of course not, Pea. There's nothing to be afraid of."

She had no idea how to explain any of this to Gray, who was watching her now with dark eyes. Those memories seemed out of place here, anyhow, under the cheerful colored lights, with the music playing and the guests dancing, and the new dream of a dude ranch being born.

No one wanted a sad sack at a barn dance. Already she felt the urge to simply smile, to make light of it all, to smooth past the moment before she ruined Rowena's party.

"Bree, do you understand what I'm trying to say? You don't have to pretend with me. Whatever you're feeling, it's okay." Gray touched her arm. He started to say something else, and then, abruptly, his touch tightened, and a scowl descended over his features.

"Oh, *hell* no. No way, buster."

She looked to the back of the barn, following Gray's gaze. A spotty teenager was making a beeline for them, his eager eyes locked on Bree. She recognized him as a boy she'd danced with a couple of hours ago.

Gray laughed. "See what I mean? I've been waiting for hours to get a chance to talk to you, and this kid is not going to spoil it now."

Without warning, he grabbed her hand and tugged her toward the doors, which stood open to provide fresh air and easy movement. Tossing an apologetic smile toward the teen, Bree hurried along after him, dodging balloons and waiters with trays of soda, her full skirt rippling behind her.

He didn't pause to speak to anyone, though several people clearly would have liked to say hello. He kept going until they reached the doors, and then he pulled her another ten feet, until they were all alone in the moonlit darkness.

Just outside the barn, where they still could hear the music, he stopped under the overhanging branches of a live oak strung with colored lights.

He didn't let go of her hand and she didn't ask him to.

Her heart pounded a little faster, as if their exit had been in full flight instead of merely a speedy walk.

He glanced over her shoulder, checking to be sure they hadn't been followed. No one else shot through the doors.

"We've eluded them," he said with a playful smile. "At least for now."

She was still too breathless to speak, so she settled for a nod. She wouldn't have known what to say, anyhow. Out here, being this close to him was ten times as intimate and unsettling as it had been inside the barn. She felt, all of a sudden, as awkward as if they'd just closeted themselves in a bedroom.

Without a trace of any similar self-consciousness, he leaned back against the oak tree trunk and watched her for a long moment in silence. Then, with a light forefinger touch, he slowly traced the ruffle at the scooped neckline of her full-skirted, poet-sleeved peasant dress.

"I can't say I blame them, though," he said softly. "What man doesn't long to dance with the gypsy queen?"

The compliment went through her with a lovely warmth, like a sweet cocktail. She'd ordered this dress from a catalog last week, expressly for tonight, secretly thinking he might like it. Though she'd paid far too much, when it arrived she'd been thrilled. A soft blue cambric, its smocked waist made her look tiny, and the yellow satin ribbons threaded through the neckline and cuffs turned her hair the color of daffodils.

He brought his hand up and touched the matching yellow ribbon she'd wound through her complicated French braid. It had taken her an hour to create that effect, and suddenly it all seemed worth it.

"You know you're driving every man here crazy tonight. Including me."

Bree laughed, trying to cover the tension his touch always seemed to set off inside her. "Well, I'm one of the few single women in the room over fifteen and under fifty, so it probably doesn't really mean much. Still, it's fun to be popular."

For a minute, she thought she saw disappointment on his face. Would he call her on the glib, artificial response? Would he insist on an answer more "genuine"?

And what would she do if he did?

Before he could say anything, though, the band launched into the first few notes of a slow song. Gray smiled and, tightening his fingers around hers, he tugged her softly toward him.

"I think this one is mine," he said.

Perhaps, she thought as they came together, this was one way of being honest. She wanted to be in his arms, and he wanted her there. The dance was just their excuse.

She felt stilted at first, but after a few seconds she began to relax against him. Once she did, their bodies fit easily, as she had known they would. He put his arms around her waist. She put hers around his neck, turning her face into the warm, pulsing column of his throat.

They didn't talk, and she was glad. All her consciousness was focused on cataloging the details of him, filing them carefully away in her sensory memory. She might need them...for when one, or both, of them were gone.

His clean, profoundly male scent, with hints of spice and lime and sea breezes. The startling baby softness of his hair tickling her fingers. The strong, steady thump of his heart and the answering nervous skitter of her own.

The graceful power of his thighs as they slowly, almost imperceptibly, moved against hers, creating fire as easily as if her bones were kindling and her skin had been glazed with kerosene.

She began having trouble breathing normally. Everything was tightening inside her, and every new touch brought a shimmer of beautiful pain. She made a soft sound, a sort of choked whimper she was unable to control.

When he heard it, his hands tightened on her hips. And then they pressed slowly, tilting her into him, one excruciating inch at a time. Her muscles coiled in on themselves, and her heart raced helplessly.

"Gray." She lifted her face, fighting to pull air into lungs that seemed to have stopped working altogether. The colored party lights illuminated his dark, liquid eyes, and she clung to them with her gaze.

He bent his head to hers, shutting off the light. He kissed her.

The cold night air, the sad music. The press of light against her closed lids—green, then blue, then green again. The smell of climbing roses and nearby horses. All of it mingled with the magic of Gray's mouth until the kiss was not something they *did,* but rather something they *were.* Their lips moving together, wet and hot and urgent, was as much a part of the night as the rustle of oak leaves, or the smell of Bell River on the breeze.

It went on forever…there was no need to pull back,

no need to part. She breathed him instead of air; she beat with his heart instead of her own.

But at some point the sounds of the night changed, and she sensed that people were coming out of the barn. Gray lifted his head, and as the cool wind touched her lips again she opened her eyes. His gleamed at her, like pools of honeyed moonlight.

"Bree! We've been looking for you!"

It was Alec. Of course it was. Alec, her own personal Jiminy Cricket, the inescapable alarm clock for her sleeping conscience.

Bree took a deep breath, arranged a smile on her swollen lips and turned toward the little boy and his ever-faithful puppy. "Hey, kiddo. What's up?"

"You've gotta come back inside. There's going to be a dance contest, and I need you to dance with me. Will you? You've gotta say yes, Bree, because everyone else said no."

Behind her, Gray smothered a laugh. She glanced at him once, as if to say, *so much for honesty!* He shook his head softly, but he added a wink to show her he understood.

And then his cell phone rang. He glanced at it but didn't answer. He thumbed it off and slipped it back into his pocket. He didn't seem to feel the need to mention who it was.

And just like that, the spell vanished. Whatever magic had held reality at bay was gone, and the regular world came washing over her like cold rain.

Well, of course he understood. He understood that he could have her whenever he wanted her, with just a flick of his fingers. Just as he could have almost any female he wanted.

Maybe that was really what his little speech had been about. *Gray,* not Matt Gordon, was the one who needed the freedom to be exactly what he was. To feel only what he genuinely felt. No pretense, on his part, that this was more than sex. And therefore, no false expectations on her part. She could never say he'd led her on....

Really, she was a walking cliché. Hadn't she predicted, from that very first night, that she'd fall into this trap? She had known from the start that she wasn't up to resisting an expert like Grayson Harper.

She was no gypsy queen. Thirty years old, and she was still just another silly girl who got romanced in the shadows after the dance. And he was merely another bored playboy who knew that a girl with yellow ribbons in her hair was asking to be kissed.

She almost laughed at the soap-operatic predictability. If Gray wanted to know what she was *genuinely, honestly* feeling right now, she just might have been prepared to tell him.

She felt ridiculous. She felt like a fool.

And she felt weak, because despite everything, she still smoldered with a yearning to be back in his arms.

But he didn't ask. So she turned and took Alec's hand. "Come on, Trouble," she said, and they went back into the barn.

She slept, because she had to. The first full day of activities would be a killer, even at the best of times.

But she woke early, and she sent a dozen emails to people she had overlooked in her first, frantic efforts to find a new social director for the ranch. She sent them to near strangers, and complete strangers, to friends of friends and friends of enemies.

Then she placed a few more calls. She followed up on the people she'd called in the first round, just in case they'd changed their minds, or been laid off, or their companies had been swallowed up by volcanoes.

She grasped at every straw she could find. And came up empty again.

Once, she thought she might be getting a callback from one of the people she'd contacted. But when she answered, it turned out to be the Everlys.

Surprise, surprise. They wanted to cancel their appointment to discuss the anniversary celebration. They'd decided to go with another company.

When she hung up, she was actually too emotionally stunned to think straight. She sat cross-legged on her bed, her laptop open beside her, holding her cell phone in both hands and glaring at it, as if she'd like to strangle it for letting her down.

"Useless piece of—"

Belatedly, as she started to toss the cell toward the foot of the bed, she realized Rowena was standing in the doorway, fully dressed in crisp denim jeans and a white blouse, looking as fresh as a marsh marigold.

Bree stopped the hurl midmotion, the phone awkwardly extended, as if she was handing it to her sister.

Her heart sank as she recognized that look on Ro's face. It was barely repressed anger. She straightened her back instinctively. "Good morning," she said awkwardly.

"If you're that desperate to leave," Rowena responded in a clipped, cool voice, "just go."

Drat. She'd heard enough—maybe all of it. Bree felt

very much the guilty little sister suddenly, sitting here in her silk pajamas. She hadn't even combed her hair before starting this scouring of her contact list. She pushed a tangled lock away from her eyes and tried not to get defensive. That always escalated the trouble.

"I'm not desperate to leave, Ro. I just know that the clock is ticking for Gray. You'll need someone to replace him, and I'd like to help with that."

But it wasn't an entirely honest answer, and, in spite of whatever tensions lay between them, they knew each other too well. Rowena could tell it was, at best, a half truth.

Her face tightened. After last night's camaraderie, this regression to mistrust and misunderstanding was almost physically painful to Bree.

She even considered, briefly, telling Ro what was really behind her desperate dialing.

But what could she say? The truth? The truth went something like this: "I've inherited the worst of both of them, Ro. I'm as weak as Mom, and as crazy as Dad. I'm falling for another guy who is going to break my heart, and, even though I've got nothing to go home to, I need to get the heck out of here before I do something dumb."

She couldn't lay herself bare like that. She wanted to trust Rowena, but she had years of doubt to overcome. It would take more than a week to do that.

Rowena shrugged. "Well, just don't think you have to stay because you think we're desperate. We'd find a way to make do."

"I know you would, Ro."

Bree could hear the injured pride in her sister's voice, and a part of her wanted to just stand up and ask Rowena for a hug. She thought of how freely Ro seemed to dispense physical affection these days. To Dallas, to Alec, to Barton...even to Gray and the rest of the employees at the ranch.

But it had been so many, many years since Bree had felt close enough to ask. So she settled for answering the unspoken question. "I've been staying because I'm enjoying being a part of it all, not because I dream that I'm indispensable. I have seen you in action, and I know you can handle anything."

Rowena frowned, as if to dismiss empty flattery, but Bree wouldn't let herself be dissuaded. This part was the truth, the whole truth, and she needed to get it said.

"I'm serious, Ro. I didn't expect to, but I've learned to love the ranch, and I am very grateful that you've let me be involved. In fact, I'm afraid that when I do have to go back to Boston and resume my old life, it's going to feel..."

What was the right word? Empty? Lonely? False? Meaningless and sterile and forlorn?

All of the above?

Suddenly, her throat grew painfully tight, and she wondered whether she'd be able to finish the sentence at all. Ro was looking at her, head tilted, a strange, searching expression in her fierce green eyes.

Bree coughed self-consciously and forced herself to go on, though she chose her words from a less emotionally loaded vocabulary.

"I'm sorry. I'm just afraid it might be...difficult."

From around the corner, she heard the sound of Dallas's voice calling to Alec. Rowena glanced in that direction, and when she looked back at Bree, her face was composed and neutral once again.

"We can sort all that out later, I guess," she said, her voice neither harsh nor gentle, revealing little. "Right now, you'd better get dressed. We've got about thirty hungry mouths to feed."

Chapter 10

For almost a full week now, though Bree had stopped talking about leaving Bell River any time soon, Gray knew that she'd studiously avoided letting herself get stuck anywhere alone with him.

He found her inaccessibility frustrating. More than frustrating. But his own feelings were a little too murky to sort out, so, even as the days passed, he didn't make any real effort to circumvent her wishes.

He still physically desired her, fiercely. That wasn't the murky part. In fact, ever since the kiss, the *desire* part of the situation had been crystal clear. He thought about her, about the feel of her body against his, the taste of her mouth, the smell of her hair, the heat of her response to his touch…and he thought about those things pretty much every minute he was awake.

And, more and more frequently, she played a starring role in his dreams, too.

So no. He definitely wasn't confused about the physical part. He wasn't even confused about whether she wanted the same thing. He knew the signs, and he saw them everywhere. Fifty-foot billboards. Big, screaming neon blinkers.

The chemistry between them was off the charts. If they ever did make love, it would be amazing.

The emotional part, though—that was where he kept tying himself in knots. Every time she walked by him, all sleek and cool and regal, pretending not to see him, he was like a pile of dry brush in a lightning strike. He'd burst into flames from the inside out, just from wanting to pull that perfect hair from its perfect clip and feel it tumbling messily over his fingers.

It was like torture. So he'd tell himself he was just going to have to go caveman and make it happen.

But then he'd start remembering all the wrong things. The haunted look in her blank face when the maid had reported seeing her mother's ghost. How easy it had been for that asshat Charlie to make her doubt herself. How, when she was with Rowena and Dallas and Alec, she always seemed to be sitting just beyond the lamplight, so isolated by something he couldn't define. So alone it made him ache…

And then he'd remember how startling it had been to catch her looking inside his heart, so easily, almost inadvertently, as if she'd just stumbled onto it lying there at her feet, open and waiting—when he'd been so sure it was locked away and utterly unreachable by mortal man.

Then, before he knew it, he would have changed his mind. No caveman. No hair over his fingers, no kisses in the shadows. He'd carefully count the days until May twenty-third. Another nineteen. Eighteen. Fifteen.

Two weeks now. Just two weeks more, and then he could leave with a clear conscience. After that, if she sat with pain bruising the skin around her eyes, with ghosts at her shoulder and the light always just beyond her reach...well, then at least it wouldn't be Gray's fault. He wouldn't have to carry the guilt around with him like a boulder for the rest of his rotten life.

Their luck ran out that Wednesday, though. It was the night of the Bell River First Annual Costume Party Cookout. The elaborate event had been weeks in the planning, but planning could be coordinated by email and text and telephone. Tonight, for the first time since the barn dance, they'd have to actually work side by side for hours.

This was one of Bell River's rare adults-only events. One of the college kids on the waitstaff had been temporarily elevated to "children's director" for the night, and she and a few other part-timers would keep the kids entertained with movies and popcorn, with sleeping bags so that the parents could have a little unencumbered fun.

Gray had taken responsibility for the games, decorations and physical setup. Bree was in charge of costumes. They'd never quite found a time to discuss what he would go as, so he'd just told her to pick something, and he'd wear it.

At five o'clock he presented himself at her office to receive his wardrobe.

Foolishly, he had decided that her choice would tell him something about what she was thinking. If she gave him something cheesy, the costume equivalent of the studly cartoon cowboy he'd played for Charlie's benefit, then he'd assume she was trying to make light of the whole thing—to defuse the tension by turning it into a joke.

If she assigned him a character who was foolish, or dull—like a smelly moonshiner, or an aproned green-grocer—then she probably still felt vulnerable. She wanted to be absolutely certain he couldn't tempt her, no matter what he said or did.

If, on the other hand, she gave him a more traditional cowboy-hero look, if she was willing to let him play it straight, then maybe she was still open to the idea that they might...

He shook his head, listening to his convoluted logic. Or maybe he was completely full of bull chips.

Probably she just assigned the costumes first come, first serve, according to size and sex. Undoubtedly she would let the guests have first choice, and the staff would have to settle for the scraps.

"Hey, there," he said as he opened her office door and looked around. "Ready for me?"

"I am," she said. She was kneeling in front of a steamer trunk full of brightly colored items—some clothes, from the looks of them, but also hats and scarves and gloves and jewelry, shoes and umbrellas and bags. "Come on in."

He waited a minute or two while she continued rummaging, and finally she turned, her arms full of red, white and blue things he couldn't quite identify.

"Your costume is going to be really fun," she said with such bright determination that he instantly knew exactly how untrue that statement was.

And he also knew that he'd been right all along.

Her choice of costume was definitely going to tell him something about her frame of mind.

Just not necessarily anything good.

He eyed the brightly striped red-and-white shirt she lay on the desk, followed by gigantic blue denim jeans and a tomato-red cowboy hat.

"I'm going as a Western Uncle Sam?"

She laughed. Not a natural sound. "No, not Uncle Sam."

He raised his eyebrows and guessed again. The stripes were enough to blind you. "A cowboy umpire?"

"No," she said, smiling as she continued to lay out pieces. Red elastic suspenders. Some pancake-makeup sticks. Oversize brown hobo shoes. A lasso. An absurd blue flower attached to a pin.

"No, no, not an umpire," she said again, growing more visibly nervous with every item she deposited on the desk. She cut a sidelong glance at him, as if trying to gauge how close he was to figuring it out…and how he'd react when he did.

But of course he already had figured it out. He knew even before she added the clincher: a large, round, honking red rubber nose.

He tried not to, but he couldn't stop himself. He burst out laughing.

She gave him a quizzical look. "You like it?"

He nodded. "I love it," he said emphatically.

She still looked a little anxious, as if his reaction made no sense. She probably had no idea why her choice pleased him so much. She probably never dreamed that she'd just told him everything he needed to know about how she felt.

And it was exactly what he'd been hoping to hear—

masochistic fool that he was. She'd just reassured him that he was not alone in his torment. She still wanted to make love to him so badly she could hardly trust herself to be in the same room with him.

Not unless she neutralized his sex appeal in every way she could.

Actually, this *was* going to be fun.

He was going as a rodeo clown.

Bree stood at one end of the great room and surveyed the sea of cowboys, bank robbers, sheriffs, dancing girls, cardsharps, gunslingers, gold miners, Annie Oakleys, John Waynes…and one completely uninhibited rodeo clown.

The party was a smash success, and she was flying high. Rowena had even come over a little while ago and hugged her so hard she practically spun her around.

Twenty guests and ten staff members, and somehow she'd come up with a unique costume for every one of them. A few of the choices had been obvious… no-brainers. Dallas, of course, had to be the Old West sheriff. No one but Rowena could do justice to Annie Oakley. Barton James was a little harder, if only because there were so many options for him. He looked exactly like Gregory Peck, so all those Gunfighter and Big Country movies came to mind. But he was also the perfect cowboy crooner, so she was tempted to go Gene Autry or Tex Ritter.

Finally, she let him choose, and he went with Gene Autry, which was the simplest costume ever—essentially Barton's own clothes, his guitar and a huge white hat.

After that, she made her way down the list, one by

one, until she got to the last two—her own costume and Gray's. It had been tempting, so tempting, to cast him as a gunslinger. He would have been mouthwatering in a long brown leather duster and high boots, with that sexy gun belt hanging low on his narrow hips. But even imagining it made her feel a little woozy, which was a very bad sign. If she was already swooning over a mental image, how would she stand a chance of resisting the real thing?

She had a weak moment for herself, too, when she opened the delivery of the saloon-girl costume. The satin gown was a gorgeous peacock-feather blue, with black fringe sleeves that shimmered if you so much as breathed, and a complex bustle that pinned back with a cameo brooch. She would have loved to show up in that, and see how strong Gray's willpower really was.

But they'd both been so careful ever since the night of the dance. Clearly, he was as reluctant to complicate things as she was. The saner, wiser route was to give the costumes to other people....

And so that's exactly what she did. Fanny Bronson got the saloon-girl gown, which Bree thought should earn her some extra brownie points, especially since Fanny had spent the past week flirting shamelessly with Gray every chance she got.

Bree assigned herself the schoolmarm costume. Drab olive green, which made her skin look sallow. Shapeless, buttoned all the way up the throat and down to the wrists. She even added a pair of glassless granny glasses and a severe bun at the nape of her neck for good measure.

She gave the marvelous gunslinger duster to the only other male who had the body to pull it off—

little Mabel Madison's dad, Jimmy. He deserved it, Bree thought, for surviving five years as Mabel's father without running away and changing his name.

In the end, she decided to give Gray the rodeo clown. It was almost criminal to hide his good looks in an absurd costume like that, but it was the only way she could feel even remotely safe tonight. Face covered in white pancake makeup, nose bulbous and honking, feet flopping and suspenders snapping...surely even she could drive thoughts of sex from her mind while he was looking like that.

Ha. Wrong.

For starters, he still looked fantastic. The suspenders outlined that washboard chest, and the white makeup just seemed to accentuate his elegant bone structure and sensual mouth. He wasn't the least bit subdued by the foolishness of the costume. Quite the contrary, it seemed to bring out an effervescence, a vitality that was positively magnetic.

He'd been surrounded by women all night. Laughing, fawning women who clearly found his every word hilarious. Women who wanted to "play with" his suspenders. Women who wanted to squeeze his nose or sniff his big blue flower.

Or, after a few glasses of wine, make risqué jokes about the significance of the size of his feet.

But that was okay. If the clown costume couldn't save her, a perimeter of possessive women served the purpose just as well. She settled back, let Dallas bring her a glass of wine and proceeded to simply enjoy the success of the party.

Right now, Barton was singing a set of Gene Autry songs, and had just launched into a particularly plaintive rendition of "Red River Valley," when suddenly the white face of her favorite rodeo clown appeared in front of her.

"May I have this dance, schoolmarm?" He held out his hand and made a deep, courtly bow. "I know I'm just a lowly rodeo clown, but you mustn't blame me for that. Blame the costume gods, who cursed me with this nose, this face…"

She laughed. "Cursed? I've been watching you, clown, and, if anything, you owe the costume gods a prayer of thanks. I'm not sure you've ever been more popular."

"Still." His painted smile didn't obscure the intensity of his gaze. "Dance with me."

She shook her head. "Schoolmarms don't dance. They have their reputations to protect."

"I will protect you," he said quietly. "Dance with me."

"I'll dance with you, Gray!" Fanny Bronson came wriggling over, her fringes shimmying. She gave Bree an arch look. "Saloon girls don't worry about prissy things like reputation. Saloon girls know how to show a man a good time."

For a minute, Bree thought Gray might reject the other woman. He regarded her coldly, though the painted smile hid his sober face—or at least Bree hoped it would hide it sufficiently to fool someone as tipsy as Fanny.

"She's right," Bree said brightly. "Schoolmarms are always on duty. Always working."

She stressed that last word, hoping he would remember that he, too, was supposed to be working, and Fanny was the task at hand. Fanny might have been drinking just enough to cause a scene if he didn't handle this deftly.

"She's right, Mr. Clown." Fanny turned, presenting her backside to Gray, and shook her bustle coquettishly. "Saloon girls just want to have fun."

When he didn't respond, Fanny backed up a few inches and wriggled harder. And then a few more inches. And a few more. As she backed him toward the punch bowl, Gray stepped neatly out of the way and took her arm, trying to guide her to safety, as well. But she was apparently feeling feisty, and insisted on remaining on her original, doomed trajectory.

Consequently, she ended up doing her shimmy right over the punch, with the lowest layers of the bustle dangling like fat blue spatulas, stirring the chunks of pineapple clumsily.

"Oh," she cried out, realizing her mistake. She tried to correct her course, but she came within an inch of losing her footing and falling, bustle first, into the bowl.

At the very last second, Gray caught her as she tumbled, saving her from the humiliation and discomfort of spending the rest of the evening picking slivers of cut glass out of her rear end.

She collapsed into his arms, laughing. She decided that his chivalry deserved a kiss, and was endeavoring to plant one on him when Rowena suddenly showed up with an elderly man in tow.

"Gray?"

As Gray continued to politely stiff-arm Fanny, the way an experienced parent might keep at bay an infant fascinated by a pair of shiny glasses, he looked over at Rowena. Bree, who had already realized who the old man was, watched Gray's face, and even through the makeup she could tell the instant he recognized his grandfather.

The old man's face was almost as white as his grandson's. He scornfully raked his piercing gaze over Gray's costume, from the red nose to the hobo shoes. And then he did the same to Fanny, who still flirtatiously wrestled with Gray's blocking arms for the right to reach his lips.

"Hello, Grandfather," Gray said casually, as if this was no surprise at all. His tone held no undercurrent of apology, either for his idiotic costume or for the tipsy, lovesick female in his arms. "It's nice of you to visit, but I'm afraid I'm working right now."

"Working? This is what you call a job?" Old Grayson Harper paused, then added a deeply disgusted sound that said more than any real word ever could.

As if he hadn't heard it, Gray simply nodded. "Yes. This is what I call a job. So perhaps, if you don't mind, we could talk tomorrow instead?"

The old man had already begun to walk away, leaning heavily on his cane. At Gray's words, he paused, his back stiff and unyielding.

"I don't think that'll be necessary," he said over his shoulder, turning his head only a fraction of an inch. "As far as I'm concerned, there's nothing left to say."

Rowena followed Gray's grandfather toward the front hall, tossing Bree a grimace as she passed. Gray seemed to have forgotten the old man as soon as he was out of sight. He had finally pinned Fanny's hands without hurting her, and had forced her to meet his eyes and focus on his voice.

"How about if I get you some coffee, Fanny?" His

voice was surprisingly gentle, as if he really were dealing with a child. "Otherwise, you're going to feel like
the devil in the morning. You have an early riding
lesson, don't you? You wouldn't want to miss that."

Bree watched as Fanny's artificial bravado seeped
out of her like helium from a broken balloon. She
sagged in his arms and didn't resist when he softly
led her to a chair and arranged her on it.

"I already feel like the devil," she said, reaching up to massage her head where the comb of her
feather headdress attached to her scalp. She dragged
the feather out unceremoniously and sighed with relief. "Ouch."

Bree had expected Gray to chase his grandfather out
to the parking lot, hot to defend himself. But instead,
when he seemed fairly certain that Fanny wasn't going
to topple over in her chair, he headed toward the buffet table, clearly making good on his offer of coffee.

So the old man was just going to swan in here, insult
Gray—and insult Bell River, too, really—then swan
out again, uncontested? Indignation rose in her, fiery
hot. She heard the front door close behind the old man,
and she knew she could catch him. His cane made him
slow, and her outrage made her fast.

Even so, she almost missed him because he hadn't
bothered to park like a normal person. He'd simply
had his chauffeur idle his gleaming limo a few feet
from the door. By the time Bree made it to the porch,
he was about to climb into the limo, while his young,
shapely female chauffeur silently held the door for him.

"Mr. Harper," Bree called. "Mr. Harper, wait a minute."

The old man turned, frowning. She tried to run

across the porch, but her long schoolmarm dress, with its sprigged green flowers designed to look as if they'd been repurposed from a feed sack, flapped around her ankles, slowing her down. So she gathered the hem up in one hand and jogged down the steps to the waiting limo instead.

"I'm sorry," old Harper said, looking at her down his long, elegant nose that she suddenly realized looked so much like Gray's. "Have we met?"

"We're meeting right now," she said, catching her breath. "My name is Brianna Wright. This is my ranch, and your grandson is my employee."

He raised one silver eyebrow. "My condolences, Ms. Wright."

She narrowed her eyes. "Very funny, Mr. Harper. But I'm not out here to see which of us can be the more bitingly sardonic. I freely concede that, by virtue of having ten times more experience and a hundred times more arrogance than I do, you'd win that contest every time."

Something reluctantly appreciative gleamed behind the old man's eyes as he studied her face. "Perhaps you underestimate yourself, Ms. Wright. Perhaps not *every* time."

She frowned, but he held up a hand. "We'll let that pass. Your comment does beg the question, though. What *are* you out here for?"

"It's simple. I'm here to tell you that you're wrong. You're one hundred percent wrong about Gray, and you're wrong about this job."

"Really."

"Yes, really." She felt herself flushing. She was already sick of his snarky tone. Why couldn't he just have a normal discussion, instead of using every syllable to convey his superiority to, and authority over, mere mortals like her?

"Does he know you're out here?"

"Of course not. He's already forgotten you were ever here."

"All right." The old man shifted his weight again and grasped the door of his limo for balance. "But please, don't take all night."

Fair enough. She inhaled deeply, registering how cold the night air was, especially for an old man with joint problems, and began.

"The social director job is all about making sure the ranch's guests have a good time. Basically, that means fourteen-hour days, every day. Ten of those hours are spent building, cleaning, planning, painting, hauling, assembling, ordering, accounting and then pitching in for any other area that's short-staffed. Which, around here these days, means every area, from the horse stables to the vegetable garden, from the backed-up plumbing to the busted chain saw."

The old man blinked, cleared his throat and shifted his weight on his cane, all body language designed to encourage her to get to the point.

So she did.

"The other four are spent at the event itself. While you're there, your job is to pretend you're having more fun than a barrel of monkeys, when actually every muscle in your body is screaming and you would gladly trade your left foot for one uninterrupted night's sleep. You have to be interested in, and kind to, all the guests. *All of them.* Even the mean ones, the boring ones."

She narrowed her eyes. "Or, in Gray's case, the drunk ones who just want to have sex with him on the lazy Susan."

The old man laughed. *Good.* That meant he hadn't tuned her out. He was still listening.

"And I promise you, Mr. Harper. Those last four hours are a heck of a lot harder than the ten you spent mucking out stalls and snaking out toilets. But Gray handles them all with an amazing degree of diligence, skill, commitment and compassion."

The chauffeur hadn't moved a muscle during any of this. Bree glanced at her, wondering whether the old man hired only hearing-impaired mutes so that he wouldn't get any annoying backtalk or gossip from his staff.

"That's a very impassioned defense of my grandson," Harper observed placidly. "Do you mind if I ask…are you, perhaps, one of the drunk ones who wants to have sex on the lazy Susan?"

Out of the corner of her eye, Bree thought she might have seen the chauffeur's lips compress, as if smothering a smile.

"Yes," Bree enunciated clearly, smiling when the old man's eyes widened. She finished the sentence slowly so that there was no mistake. "I *do* mind."

"I see," he said dryly. "The question was actually rhetorical, Ms. Wright."

"But my answer wasn't." She made an irritated, tsking sound between her teeth. "What's wrong with you? Why do you find it so hard to believe that Gray is working his behind off at this job? As we all are."

He shrugged. "He has about fifteen million reasons to lie about it."

Well, that just capped it. She was tired of being rational with this pigheaded old fool. *Sorry, Kitty,* she said mentally. Apparently, ladies do lose their tempers. And it felt just fine, actually. Apparently, it was becoming her favorite new bad habit.

"You know what, Mr. Harper? I suddenly think I can see why your grandson hasn't spoken to you in so many years. You're one nasty piece of work."

He drew his head back, as if offended. "Ms. Wright, let me assure you that—"

"No. You let *me* assure *you.* Two things." She put her forefinger out toward his chest, punching the air for emphasis. "First, your implication that we would conspire with him to defraud you of your millions is damn insulting. And second, your theory that we would hire a useless slacker at a time like this, just to help him steal your money? That you'd even consider it possible shows a profound ignorance, both of the demands of a dude ranch, and of the kind of women my sisters and I are."

She gathered up her ugly dress and prepared to go back upstairs and into the house.

"One last thing. I don't ever want to see you at Bell River again. If you are struck by another urgent need to humiliate and harass your grandson, you'll have to do it somewhere else."

Chapter 11

It was going to be a long afternoon, so Gray grabbed a third mouthwatering biscuit from the basket in the kitchen as he headed out to join the Junior Explorers Expedition. As he passed Cookie, who was fiercely dicing onions for dinner, he managed to land a loud, smacking kiss on her cheek.

Her net-covered head reared up, and her thick black eyebrows dived toward each other. "No!" she growled, waving her very sharp knife in the air to express her displeasure. "No kissing!"

He grinned, holding up the biscuit and lowering his eyelids in dreamy ecstasy, a wordless explanation of why he'd been unable to restrain himself.

"You're a goddess," he said as he backed away from her toward the door. He pushed it open and loped down the stairs, glancing at his watch. One-fifteen. They should have left fifteen minutes ago.

He stuffed the rest of the biscuit in his mouth and concentrated on his clothes. He'd just managed to get his shirt buttoned and tucked in when he spotted the collection of children lined up behind the barn.

Most of them had taken off their backpacks, dropping them onto the grass. They all seemed bored and fidgety, and Mabel Madison had already started writing something in the grass with small, carefully arranged pebbles and stones.

As he drew closer, he saw what she'd accomplished so far. H-E-L. He chuckled, wondering whether she was preparing to curse or send an SOS.

Bree stood in front of the kids, looking adorable in pedal-pusher jeans, white sneakers and a blue-and-white-checked shirt. She'd pulled her hair into a fifties-style ponytail that bounced when she moved and caught the afternoon sunlight as if about half its strands were twenty-four-karat gold.

In one hand she held a clipboard and in the other a pencil, which she aimed toward the children as she counted them off.

"Seven, eight, nine...and ten. Good! Everyone is here." She took a deep breath. "Still."

When she caught sight of Gray, she frowned slightly. "Have you seen Rowena? We're already running behind, and the schedule is pretty tight if we're going to get back before dark."

"Sorry." He held up his hands, pointing his thumbs toward his chest. "Looks as if I'm Rowena today."

A couple of little girls giggled, apparently finding that pretty funny. He joined Bree at the front so that they could talk without every word being overheard. Alec was in the group of ten, and Rowena had been especially adamant that the boy mustn't be allowed to worry.

"She was a little under the weather this morning," he said quietly. "Nothing serious, but Dallas put his foot down, said she can't go anywhere today. I got drafted to take her place."

Her frown deepened, and she tapped the pencil against the clipboard nervously. "What's wrong? God, I hope she hasn't caught whatever Georgia Brooke had."

He lifted one shoulder to say he had no idea. Well, he had ideas, but not the kind you bandied around in public—especially when one of the members of the public was Alec. The kid was already watching them with hyperfocused, squinted eyes, as if he was trying to read their lips.

Just in case the little scamp actually possessed that skill, Gray angled his torso to thwart him. "A minor stomach bug, I gather. She seems fine, except apparently she puked earlier. She insisted she was good to go, but Dallas…well, he was doing the Dallas thing." Gray smiled. "You know the Dallas thing."

She shook her head, but she was smiling, too. "Definitely."

She bent down and put the clipboard into her backpack, then zipped the pocket shut. Standing straight again, she smiled at the children. "Okay, explorers! Let's get this show on the road."

The cheer that went up from the kids was so heartfelt you'd think they'd just been rescued from man-eating tigers or won a trip to Disney World. Mabel kicked her stones and did a stomping, twirling happy dance.

Apparently, fifteen minutes was a very, very long time to a kid.

As they started hiking, moving fairly quickly across the flat, landscaped ranch land that lay closest to the home and outbuildings, Bree filled him in on the four-hour trip's itinerary. The theme today was tree scarring.

Yesterday, the kids had attended a session led by Barton James, who told them all about the Ute Indians, and the special trees they'd left behind as they traveled through Colorado. They'd seen slides of peeled-bark trees, where the bark had been stripped, probably for medicinal or ritual purposes, and prayer trees, pine saplings that had been roped to the ground so that they grew with a distinct "elbow" bend, and message trees, on which the Ute had carved symbols into aspen trunks, telling stories of their history.

No documented scarred trees had ever been found on Bell River property, though the children were excited at the prospect of discovering the first. Barton had been smart, though, and taught them how to identify other types of scarring, like fire, lightning and animals, so that they wouldn't come home frustrated by failure.

The kids had already eaten lunch. So the plan was to hike, in roughly half-hour-long segments, until three, when they'd stop for a snack and a nap. Then they'd take a slightly different route home, arriving back at Bell River just before six.

"Sorry you got roped into it," Bree said, glancing over her shoulder to be sure the stragglers weren't falling too far behind.

He smiled. "I'm not."

She didn't meet his eyes. "It's a long day, though. The whole idea is to keep the kids occupied while the grown-ups go white-water rafting, and bring them home as tired as their parents will be. But I have a feeling you and I are going to be dead on our feet by the time it's over."

"You can't scare me," he said, still smiling. "The weather's perfect, the scenery's gorgeous and I get to spend an entire afternoon with you. I couldn't have designed a more perfect situation if fate had asked me for a blueprint."

She did look at him then. Her gaze was surprisingly frank. "I got the impression we were trying to avoid spending a whole lot of time together these days."

He had to admire the way she came at the subject head-on. She was getting her confidence back.

"That's part of what's so perfect," he said, smiling. "With ten sets of curious, prying, *tattling* eyes as chaperones, we aren't likely to do anything dumb."

Bree didn't get a chance to respond. Mabel's older brother, Michael, came up at that moment, his normally pleasant face pursed up like a prune.

"Mabel says she has to go to the bathroom." He scowled down at his feet. "I don't know why I have to tell you. She should talk for herself. She's six now, not two."

Bree touched the boy's shoulder sympathetically. "Little sisters are a lot of trouble, aren't they? I know all about it. I've got one...and I am one." She gestured toward Michael's friends, who were walking together just ahead. "You go have some fun. I'll talk to her."

His face unkinked, and he shot her a grateful smile. "Okay. Thanks. But...just so you know, she doesn't really have to go. Not this soon. Mabel can hold it like forever. She's just trying to get attention. Dad says it's a girl thing."

A girl thing? Surely even geeky Jimmy Madison, who Gray remembered dimly from high school, hadn't said anything as dumb as that. The kid must have misunderstood. But it struck Gray's funny bone anyhow, and he had to exert a conscious effort not to laugh.

He had to hand it to Bree, though. She kept a straight face like a pro.

"Thanks for the heads-up," Bree said evenly, neither buying Michael's evaluation of his sister nor rejecting it. "I'll check it out."

The boy nodded, then sped off to catch up to his friends, as if he'd done the best he could do to prepare her, but now the battle was hers.

Bree turned once, to give Gray a soldier's salute, then she found her way to Mabel, who was sulkily walking just to the right of the path, kicking every stone she encountered.

Gray watched the pantomime that followed with amused appreciation. Bree obviously adopted a neutral position first, just in case the crisis was real. Then she asked Mabel to produce her biodegradable toilet paper from her backpack, and she pointed to the thick stand of trees off to the side.

Mabel's face darkened and tightened, and she folded her bony arms over her chest. Bree didn't look the least fazed. She simply plucked out the simple map Mabel had in her pocket—each child had been given one— unfolded it and then pointed to something not far from where they were.

Gray had spent too many years playing poker in

order to infuriate his grandfather, and he understood perfectly what was going on. Bree was calling Mabel's bluff. If the little girl had a problem, step over there and deal with it. If she didn't, then stop fussing and wait until they reached the cabin that was clearly marked, and only about twenty minutes away.

Mabel snatched the map back, refolded it, shoved it in her pocket, then churned her legs faster so that she got ahead of Bree quickly and never looked back.

Slowing down, Bree fell in line with Gray, and when they were at a safe distance, her pent-up mirth came out in smothered chuckles.

"Oh, my dear heaven, she's a pistol. I've never felt sorry for Jimmy Madison in my life, but I do now. Do you remember him?"

Gray nodded. "I think so. Chess club, right? All logic and box thinking. A real rule follower." He watched Mabel storming up the path, kicking at stones, some so big it was a miracle she hadn't broken her toes. "Man. He probably doesn't know what hit him."

Bree's laughter had spent itself, and her face had settled into an oddly pensive expression.

"Still…" She watched the fuming little girl kick her way up the hill. "Maybe it will serve her well later in life."

"What will?"

"All that spunk. All that defiance. Maybe, when she grows up, she'll never be afraid to say what she means, or stand up for what she believes in. Maybe, when she's a grown woman, no one will ever be able to make her doubt herself."

She seemed to realize she'd let the conversation grow too serious, because she shook off the philosophical air and grinned. "But what am I saying? *When* she grows up? I guess it's more like...*if* she grows up."

He laughed. But he suddenly realized he owed Mabel a thank-you. She'd just provided the opening he'd been waiting for all morning.

"Hey," he began casually. "Speaking of feisty, kick-ass females..."

Bree, who had been silently counting the heads in front of them on the path, making sure all the children were in sight, glanced toward him curiously.

"What about them?"

"My grandfather called me last night."

It might sound like a non sequitur, but she would understand. And, of course, she did. Her pace slowed momentarily, then recovered almost at once.

"Did he? And what did he want?"

"He wanted to tell me about this...this feisty, kick-ass female who got hold of him as he was leaving the costume party Wednesday night. Apparently, she grabbed him by the scruff of the neck and shook him till his teeth rattled."

Bree kept walking, her gaze steady on the path ahead, a half smile playing at her lips. "Ah, the angry-female-as-rabid-dog metaphor. Classic. Did he happen to trot out the phrase 'uppity broad'?"

"No. No, come to think of it, I don't think he did."

She gave him a quick, sidelong glance. "The b word?"

He pretended to search his memory. "Nope."

"Really." She tilted her head quizzically. "I guess he warned you to steer clear of her, though?"

"Actually, he told me I was one lucky fool to have someone like that fighting on my side. He said to be sure to tell her that she'd been very persuasive, in her own eccentric, rabid-dog way, and, because of her, he had no intention of reneging on our deal."

She relaxed then, and let a smile spread across her face, all the way to her beautiful eyes.

"Good, then. Good for him." She caught Gray's gaze. "And good for you, too, I suppose. Just twelve more days of prison here, and you're a wealthy man."

He nodded. "It would seem so."

They walked in silence for a few minutes after that. She was probably thinking about how much she disapproved of his deal with his grandfather.

But he was thinking something else entirely.

The time had gone by so fast.

When he'd initially shown up at Bell River, asking for a job, a month had seemed an eternity. A luxury of weeks. And he had known, from the very first day, that he wanted to spend that month as Brianna Wright's lover.

He hadn't even felt any particular urgency about seducing her. It had seemed inevitable, like something that would simply happen on its own, the way a piece of perfectly ripe fruit might just drop from a tree and land in your outstretched hand.

When, on that first day, Barton James asked him to test-drive the lavish tent, he'd jumped at the offer. The luxury of true privacy. A romantic setting. It was exactly what he needed. What *they* needed.

That's how sure he'd been. He didn't just assume... he *knew* Bree would come to his bed.

And he knew she'd be happy there. He would make certain of it. He'd belonged to the Bachelor Club long enough to know that was the most important mission—if only because a woman who had been happy in your bed never could bring herself to be quite as bitter when the time came for her to leave it.

Uncomplicated physical pleasure in the moonlit tent, beside the sparkling creek, serenaded by birdsong. What could be more natural?

So he'd launched his plan to make sure she stayed around a couple of weeks, ostensibly to "train" him. From there he'd figured it would be a cinch to make the two weeks turn into four. He had planned to make it a month she'd never forget—and never regret.

But then, like an idiot, he'd gone and let the whole thing get…complicated. And now, more than half the time they could have spent in each other's arms was already gone, never to return. Twelve days. That was all he had left.

If he didn't stop overthinking this act that should be so simple, so ancient, universal and pure, he would wake up one day soon and discover it was too late. He'd shake her hand as he left Colorado. Or maybe he'd kiss her—yes, of course, undoubtedly he would kiss her.

But, either way, they would part as friends.

Just friends.

But no. No, no, no, no.

Something inside him rebelled at the very sound of those words. Already the phrase was a lie. They might not have made love, but they were far, far more than "just friends."

"We're here," Bree's voice suddenly called out merrily. "This is our first stop!"

For a minute, Gray felt disoriented, as if his thoughts had been the true reality and she'd just dragged him into a meaningless, intrusive dream.

In front of them, ten heads turned, ten small faces smiled. "This is it?"

"This is it! Time to get out your journals, everyone."

As the children eagerly complied, digging through their backpacks and pulling out small, spiral-bound books, Bree smiled awkwardly at Gray, her gaze suddenly uncertain.

"Everything okay?"

He wondered whether he looked as crazed as he felt. He couldn't seem to think straight. All he knew was that he couldn't let this happen. Every hour they lost, every minute they continued as "just friends," seemed like a crime.

And yet, what could he do about it? Scoop her up and carry her deep into the trees? Make violent, pagan love to her while ten little nature explorers wandered the forest fearfully, calling, "Ms. Wright? Ms. Wright? Where are you?"

"Gray, are you okay with this?" She knit her eyebrows. "We promised them we'd break into two teams. You'll take five, and I'll take five. They're excited about the prizes. For the team that finds the most trees. Didn't Rowena tell you?"

"Yes," he said. "No. Hell, I don't know. It doesn't matter. I'll take five. I'll take them all. Just promise you'll come to me tonight."

She tilted her head back, her blue eyes wide. *"What?"*

"We need to talk, Bree. We can't go on like this." But then, like a schizophrenic arguing with himself, he shook his head firmly. "No, that's not the truth. We don't need to talk. We need to be lovers. Come tonight. I've been a fool. We've lost too much time already."

"Gray, I—" She twisted her earring nervously and

lowered her voice so that the children couldn't hear. "I can't talk about this now. I can't *think* about this now."

"Well, I can't think about anything else."

She shook her head again. "We have to. The children are counting on us."

Damn the children, he wanted to say. But his blood was finally cooling, and sanity was starting to hover at the edges of his brain, the way dawn shows up at the edges of night. He glanced toward the nearest kids, a seven-year-old girl and her six-year-old brother, both of whom wore impossibly tiny pairs of glasses. They bent solemnly over their books, dutifully printing their names in slow, unsteady block letters on the first page.

They really were counting on the grown-ups, though they didn't even realize it. They trusted so completely they had no idea trust was even involved.

"I know," he said. He tried to look normal, tried to *be* normal. "I do know, Bree. I'll behave, I promise. But you should know, it's taking every ounce of willpower I have not to sling you over my shoulder and ravish you in the woods."

In spite of everything, she smiled.

"Ravish me? Remember that feisty, kick-ass lady your grandfather told you about?"

He laughed. "Clearly. That's why I'm in a ravishing mood...."

She shook her head helplessly. "Honestly, Gray, you are im—"

"Ms. Wright? Ms. Wright?" Mabel Madison appeared out of nowhere and began tugging insistently on the tail of Bree's shirt. "Ms. Wright, where's the cabin? You said there would be a cabin, with a bathroom and a door and a roof."

"There is, Mabel," she said, bending down and smiling patiently at the furious little girl. "It's right over there." She pointed west. "See?"

Gray looked, too. And he saw it immediately...a small brown cabin, with a bedroom...no, he meant to say *bathroom*...and a door and a roof.

For one last, irrational moment he pondered whether there was any way, any possible way...

"For heaven's sake! *Forget about it!*" Bree's voice was stern, but when he looked over at her, wiggling his eyebrows, her eyes were alight with mirth.

"I'm serious, you impossible beast. Just put the whole thing out of your mind instantly."

"I can't!" Mabel's eyes widened. Apparently no one had ever talked to her like that before. Her voice rose to a near-hysterical pitch. "I can't forget about it, Ms. Wright! I'm going to pee my pants!"

Bree and Gray looked at her, and then at each other, and then, though they knew Mabel would have no idea what caused them to do so, they both broke down in nearly silent, helpless laughter.

Mabel made a low, growling sound of utter frustration. Gray considered trying to smooth things over, but obviously it was too late. The little girl scowled fiercely at him. And then, as if he'd left her no choice, she kicked him in the shins.

Somehow, Gray made it through the endless afternoon. The countless rest stops, the eternal search for marks on trees, the snacks, the naps, the questions, the noise. And always the tantalizing glimpses of Bree in the distance, her ponytail bobbing and gleaming, her body as lithe and easy in the woods as a forest fairy.

Sometimes, when he didn't see her for long stretches, he could actually stop obsessing about her and start to enjoy the moment. The kids were cute, especially his five. Alec had insisted on working with his aunt, claiming kinship. And after Mabel attacked Gray, she suddenly was terrified to be around him, apparently for fear he'd decide to exact revenge.

So Bree had ended up with both the little devils, and Gray had caught the lucky draw. He felt guilty, especially when it occurred to him that Bree might have engineered the arrangement because she doubted his ability to focus at the moment.

She needn't have worried. He was doing fine.

Sure, every hour or two, he glared up at the sun, which still gleamed high and round in the sky, like a pure gold poker chip, the kind you got when you hit the once-in-a-lifetime jackpot.

Sink, damn you.

He'd bark the command in his head, though he would like some credit, thank you, for being sane enough not to say it aloud.

Just call it a day, for God's sake. SET.

Naturally, the sun didn't respond any better to autocratic demands than humans did. But gradually, one degree at a time, it lost its hold on the glassy blue dome of the afternoon. It began to slide slowly down the western sky, like an egg yolk on a well-greased pan.

As the air began to cool, the shadows stretched longer and the landmarks grew more familiar, signaling their approach to Bell River's ranch house. Gray felt his temper subside. Festering, stagnant frustration was replaced by a freshly flowing rill of sparkling anticipation.

Not long now.

She hadn't ever promised she would come, of course. He hadn't forgotten that. But she would.

Surely she would.

Belatedly, he threw himself into helping his team accumulate points. Even as twilight approached, and good trees grew more difficult to spot, he found the long, vertical scars of a lightning strike and the curved gouges of animal claws. He even became a momentary hero when he located a heart with the initials MW+BB carved in an aspen, then checked the rules and discovered that nothing said the scarring had to be old.

When they reached the last rest stop, less than half an hour from home, he and his team found a small, charming glen already blooming with early columbine and conveniently furnished with a cluster of fallen logs arranged like a sectional sofa.

They had been sitting down for no more than five minutes, happily tallying up their impressive finds and laughing at Michael Madison's knock-knock jokes, when suddenly Bree appeared at the edge of the glen.

Gray's gaze went straight to her, of course. But for once she didn't send the usual buzz of longing through him. This time the sight of her created a tiny needle of fear. Some unnatural microexpression, or some physical detail that didn't fit… He couldn't pinpoint how, but he knew that something was seriously wrong.

He stood. "Carry on," he told his five, copying his earlier merry tone perfectly, though his mood had already done an about-face, based on nothing more than the fact that Bree stood before him and he didn't feel the instinctive urge to smile.

He made his way to her quickly. "What is it? What's wrong?"

Mutely, she shook her head, but he knew she didn't mean, "No, nothing's wrong." The shake was just an instinctive denial. It was her mind rejecting whatever it was that had happened.

"Bree." He put his hands on her shoulders, shocked by how cold they were. Her eyes were very wide, their blue depths tinged with a peach light from the setting sun. "Tell me. Whatever it is, we will fix it."

"I can't find Alec." She pressed her hands together, as if she needed to hold on to something. "He's gone."

Chapter 12

Funny, Bree thought, though she knew that wasn't the right word. Funny how, once something huge happened in a certain spot, you could never go there again without feeling at least an echo, an aftershock, of whatever you'd felt before.

It was like a kind of haunting, when you thought about it.

The spot she had been standing in when she realized Alec was not with the others…now that would always been one of those places for her.

She'd been looking down a pretty, violet-sprinkled ravine when one of the kids had casually said, "Where's Alec?" And even before her conscious mind could react, her subconscious had begun to scream.

Yes, yes, it howled. *That is what I've been trying to tell you. We haven't heard Alec do anything, not talk, or laugh, or make silly monster sounds, for a very long time. Something is terribly wrong.*

So, over the next thirty horrible minutes, whenever anyone—everyone—asked her where was the last place she definitely remembered seeing Alec, she had simply responded, "He was with us when we left rest stop number two, but he was not with us when we got halfway to rest stop number one. That was between 5:30 and 5:45 p.m." Between the moment went everything was all right and the moment when everything turned black.

Thirty minutes, she knew now, could be a lifetime. Thirty minutes to imagine every hideous accident that could have happened. Every rattlesnake, black widow, scorpion or puma he might have encountered unprepared. Every psychopath who might have followed when he wandered off to check out a bird or fossil. Every petit mal, or grand mal, or so-far-unidentified allergy to macaroni and cheese or bee stings that might have stopped his heart, or his lungs, or his brain.

Thirty minutes to imagine facing Dallas and Rowena with the news. Thirty minutes to imagine their pain...

Only two things kept her from falling apart during those harrowing thirty minutes. One was the determination to be a helpful part of the search, not another hysterical female to comfort. The other was Gray, whose calm competence was immensely reassuring. As far as she could tell, Gray never for a single second considered the possibility that Alec would not return, safe and sound.

And at the end of those thirty minutes, just as Rowena and Dallas arrived at rest stop number one, the staging area, Alec came sauntering into view.

For a split second, when she saw his thatch of blond hair coming toward them in the gloaming, Bree thought her knees might simply give out on her. She put one hand out blindly and somehow Gray was there. He took her reaching fingers and chafed them softly so that the blood moved through them again. Then he rested her hand on his arm and looked at her with a one-sided smile.

"Told you," he said. "I'd go throttle the kid myself, but I'm pretty sure Rowena will do a more thorough job of it."

Bree watched numbly as Rowena first nearly smothered Alec in a hug that went on for what seemed like hours. Then she pulled back and took the boy's bony shoulders in her hands.

"What on earth were you thinking, Alec Garwood? Of all the dumb, thoughtless, immature things you could have done! Do you have any idea what you just put your aunt Bree through?"

Alec cast a glance toward Bree, looking absolutely miserable. "I'm sorry, Rowena," he said. "It was an accident, I swear. We got so close to my fort, and I wanted to check on it. But turned out some animal must have gotten into my stash of candy, tried to eat the whole thing. What a mess." He glanced up at his dad. "I'm sorry, Dad, really. But it's actually pretty disgusting what a half-digested Tootsie Roll looks like. I *had* to clean up, didn't I? And then before I knew it, it was getting dark."

Dallas shook his head. "Don't you be telling *me* you're sorry, son. I wasn't scared, because I know you.

But Aunt Bree hasn't seen what a little escape artist you are, and she was really, really worried."

Alec might be an escape artist, but he wasn't a coward. Bree had to admire the pluck that made him come over to where she stood, with his shoulders back and his chin up like a man, even though his face was slack with embarrassment and guilt.

"I'm sorry that I frightened you, Bree," he said with a simple humility and a lack of aggressive defense that was very appealing. "I didn't mean to. I honestly *never* mean to upset or scare people or mess things up. The problem is, I never start out feeling like I'm doing anything bad or dangerous. If I did, I wouldn't do it, you know?"

It was a bit convoluted, linguistically, but emotionally and logically, he was on solid ground. Basically, yes, she did know. She bent down and gave him a kiss. "I think I understand," she said. "Mostly I'm just glad you're not inside a puma's belly right now, being digested for his Friday dinner."

Alec's blue eyes lit up. "Gross. Is that what you thought happened to me?"

"That was just one of the things I considered," she said. "It wasn't even the worst."

"No?" He wrinkled his nose, fascinated. "What *was* the worst?"

"Alec," Rowena interrupted firmly. "Enough."

"Oh, well." He sighed. "Anyway, I'm pretty sure pumas would rather eat deer and elk and stuff. Maybe raccoon."

Dallas laughed. "And I'm pretty sure you taste like raccoon. God knows you smell like one. Come on.

I'll take you home and hose you off with some Purple People Eater."

Alec smiled up at Bree. "That's what we call the purple gunk Dad cleans machinery with. He's just kidding, though. You can't use it on people or it rots their skin off."

"Lovely," Gray said.

"Yeah, it's really strong. But you never know…he hasn't seen the stuff that got on my shoes. It used to be Tootsie Rolls, I guess, but it's something else now, that's for sure." He shuddered, screwing up his mouth, as if just imagining it made his face pucker. "It might be a while before I buy those again."

Dallas came over and, laying his palm flat on the crown of his son's head, steered him toward the clearing, where he had parked his truck. "It'll be a while before you buy anything again," he observed. "It's hard to go shopping when you're grounded."

"Aww, man…"

Alec's voice dwindled as the pair moved out of sight. Bree looked over at Rowena, wondering what she could possibly say. Rowena had been wonderful, defending her in front of Alec, but she could only imagine how little faith she could have in Bree now.

Gray's hand was still warm and bracing against her arm. She smiled at him, then extricated herself softly and walked to where Rowena stood. If a nine-year-old boy could make an honest apology without any attempt at a cover-up, then surely she could, too.

"Ro, there's nothing I can say that makes this any better, but I want you to know how sorry I am. I wouldn't have put Alec in danger for anything in the world—nor would I have risked giving the dude ranch a bad name. I let you down, and it's just by the grace of God that everything turned out all right. I don't have an excuse. I just lost track, pure and simple."

Rowena was staring at her, almost as if she didn't recognize the language Bree was speaking.

She tried again. "I know the ranch will recover from this more easily if I'm not around, so I'll leave as soon as possible. I don't guess there's any way to keep the story from getting out, but—"

Rowena extended her hands and took Bree's shoulders, much as she had taken Alec's when she really needed him to focus and pay heed to what she said.

"Bree. Listen to me, honey. This wasn't your fault. Alec is... Alec is special. He's a free spirit. When he needs to get loose, not even one of Dallas's jail cells could hold him. If this is anyone's fault, it's ours, because we should have warned you."

"But, Ro, I—"

Rowena shook her head, sighing. "I can't even tell you how many times *we've* lost track of him. That's not hyperbole. I mean literally, I don't want to tell anyone how many times because one of these days someone will call social services and tell them what bad parents we are."

Bree laughed, and Rowena did, too, but darkly. "Dallas says he decided long ago that all he can do is teach Alec as much as he can about how to handle himself in a crisis, then hope for the best. And pray. Or drink. Or both."

"What about those chips they put in dogs these days?" Bree grinned at her sister. "At least that way when he gets out, you could track him down."

Rowena shook her head. "You think you're making

a joke, but Dallas approached the vet about getting the chip. A year or so ago."

"And?"

"Well, he was an officious little guy. Stuffy, can't really think outside the box, Dallas said. Apparently, he got a touch self-righteous." She winked at Bree. "We use a different vet now."

For a minute Bree's vision fractured into a hundred tiny white, iridescent stars. That wink, that slow, sassy, green-eyed cat wink, came straight from the old days.

The *old* old days, before tragedy struck the Wright family, before the daughters were split up and deposited in different parts of the country. It even came from a time when they had seemed almost like twins. Before Rowena's one year of age difference magically seemed to turn into three or four, or ten. It came from back when all three sisters were allies, fighting shoulder to shoulder against a world that didn't seem to care.

It was a good thing Kitty had taught Bree never to cry—*no one likes a sad sack, Brianna*—because she was suddenly so flooded with gratitude and relief that she could feel it racing through her like a cresting river, searching for an outlet.

Most of all, of course, she felt profound relief that Alec was safe. But she also was deeply relieved that Rowena didn't judge her harshly for what had happened. And grateful that Rowena still cared enough to give her that old wink, here in the new life. Grateful that Rowena had been strong enough to stop Bree from killing the dude ranch idea before it was born, just because she was skeptical, or fearful, or jealous... or whatever the heck was really wrong with her.

And Gray...

She was grateful for Gray, too. For his strength and his support, for his patience and his sense of humor, and his...

"Do you want a ride home?" Rowena was yawning, and Bree suddenly remembered that her sister had been sick this morning.

"No, thanks, I'm happy to walk. It'll work off some of the tension I built up while I was worrying. And speaking of worrying, are you okay? When you couldn't come on the tree hunt today, I wasn't sure what to think."

Rowena ran her fingers through her hair and yawned again. "You should think your sister is married to an overly protective Old West lawman who is going to have to learn a few things about women. If he wanted a wife who would retire to her bed all day every time she feels a little woozy, he made a wrong turn somewhere along the way. He ended up in the twenty-first century instead of the 1850s."

Gray laughed, holding up his hand. "I think this is where I come in, ladies," he said. "I remember something about a spunky, feisty, kick-ass..."

Bree's chest tightened, either with excitement or with anxiety. Something about living in Silverdell made it difficult for her to tell the two apart, she'd discovered.

"Are you leaving?" She tried to keep her voice neutral, but her tight throat still drove the tones up two or three notes. "I know it's been a long day. I guess you're pretty tired."

"Not terribly," he said with a smile that made her toes tingle. "How about you?"

"Not terribly..." Her voice was markedly less confident than his. "I mean, if you were in the mood, I might be up to…"

When her sentence died out uncomfortably, Rowena rolled her eyes, chuckling. "Well, over here in my part of the forest, I definitely *am* terribly tired. So, since I'm the one with the car, I'll just say good night and leave you to figure out who is up to what."

Bree smiled. Impulsively, she went over and held out her arms for a hug. This wasn't something Rowena used to do, so it wasn't a familiar motion. After only a fraction of a second's hesitation, Rowena accepted. She moved into Bree's embrace and hugged her without holding back.

One more time, the crystalline stars formed in front of Bree's eyes.

"Have fun," Rowena whispered as their cheeks met. She pulled her head back and touched Bree's flyaway, sun-streaked hair with gentle, almost maternal fingers. "And don't forget what the wise women say."

Bree smiled. "What do they say?"

Rowena cast a quick, meaningful glance in Gray's direction. "That a lady rarely gets a second chance to make a magnificent mistake."

"Are you hungry?" Gray wasn't sure what the maids had left in his tent's minifridge today, but they always brought something simple and delicious. A loaf of Cookie's homemade bread, perhaps, along with some fresh fruit, maybe a couple of tarts or custards from the dessert tray. They restocked his water bottles, and presumably they also checked the liquor cabinet, although he hadn't had any reason to tap that yet.

They did everything but leave mints on his pillow—and they probably would have added that touch, too, if it hadn't been for the problem of attracting too much attention from the local wildlife. Apparently, this culinary pampering came standard with a glamping package, and Barton had wanted to be sure Gray got the full experience before he rendered his verdict.

For the first time since he got here, Gray was glad he had something to offer. Bree's face was dangerously pale under the blue moonlight. Her eyes were glazed, as if she was on the verge of either waking up or passing out. She looked half done in.

She shook her head politely, though. "I don't think I'm very hungry," she said. "But thanks."

Wrong answer. Of course she was hungry. They hadn't eaten since the child-size snack of Bing cherries and cheese crackers at three o'clock. It was almost nine now.

She probably had no idea what she felt, physically or psychologically. The afternoon's drama overload obviously had temporarily cauterized her nervous system.

She'd been the one to suggest coming to the tent—he wouldn't have mentioned it again for a million dollars, given how the day had ended. But now that she was here, she seemed slightly bewildered, as if she couldn't imagine why she'd thought it was a good idea.

With her arms crossed, her hands gripping her elbows, she hovered just outside the tent, watching him. She leaned against the buttoned-back door's aluminum brace, but she kept her toes behind some invisible line, as if crossing the threshold could have profound, near-mystical consequences.

"I'm just not very hungry," she explained, as if she wasn't sure whether she'd already said that.

"Well, I am," he lied.

She was getting fuzzier by the minute. She needed to eat, and she needed plenty of water. She needed to sit down, and she needed to clear her mind.

If she didn't, he was going to end up slinging her over his shoulder today, after all. Only, unlike in his fantasies, he'd be hauling her like a sack of dehydrated potatoes right back up to the main house, where Rowena could boss her into accepting some familial TLC.

No way in hell Gray was going to seduce a woman in Bree's state.

First rule of Bachelor Club: you do not touch females who are weepy, crazy, high or drunk. Second rule of Bachelor Club: you *do not* touch females who are weepy, crazy, high or drunk.

Right now, Bree's decision-making skills were as impaired as those of anyone in those categories. Essentially, she *was* drunk—in her case, drunk with fatigue and the aftereffects of adrenaline shock.

He unlocked the door to the small refrigerator and checked its contents. A round of crusty Armenian bread and a chocolate mousse topped with fresh strawberries. He pulled them out, balancing the bread on his forearm, and grabbed a couple water bottles with the other hand. "Maybe we could share something small. Just sit for a while and shake off the day."

She didn't say yes, but she didn't say no, either. She was staring at the king-size bed that suddenly seemed to obscenely dominate the interior space. She had a small line between her eyebrows, as if something about it bothered her, but she was having trouble processing exactly what.

Shaking his head, he returned to the door and

smiled down at her reassuringly before nudging her out of the way with his elbow.

"Let's sit outside," he said. "It's a nice night."

She nodded vigorously, as though she wanted to stress what an excellent idea that was. She took one of the deck chairs under the awning and lowered herself into it with a long, groaning sigh that undoubtedly sounded a lot more sexual than she realized.

"Do you mind if I take off my shoes?" She extended her feet and stared down at her sneakers disapprovingly. "They're so dirty and so uncomfortable."

She smiled over at him, lifting her eyebrows playfully. "But at least they don't have puma puke on them, right?"

He chuckled, wondering whether she was already feeling better, just from sitting down in the fresh air, or whether approaching delirium made her witty.

"Of course not," he said. He twisted the cap off a water bottle and handed it across the small table that divided their two chairs. "Make yourself comfortable."

She groaned again as she freed her slim, pale feet, first from the shoes, then from the white ankle socks beneath. She reached down and massaged her arches, closing her eyes and dropping her head back in an ecstasy of relief.

The tightening in his groin was instant and painful. His college fraternity had owned porn videos that were a hell of a lot less erotic than the uninhibited self-pleasuring she was administering to her feet.

Bolting back his water, he forced himself to look somewhere else. Apparently Bachelor Club needed a few more rules.

When she finished, she sighed. "Oh, that's better,"

she said. She glanced at his shoes. "Don't you want to take yours off, too?"

He smiled through his tightly clenched jaw. "Later, maybe."

She'd finished almost half her water now. Maybe time to add some food. He broke off a piece of bread and extended it.

"Try this," he suggested casually. "It's Cookie's Armenian bread. Pretty fantastic."

She seemed to have forgotten she wasn't hungry, because she accepted the chunk of bread with a simple thank-you and began munching on it instantly. She ate slowly, savoring every crumb.

"It's heavenly," she said, almost as if she was talking to herself. With a deep sigh, she turned her gaze into the middle distance. She did not seem to be looking at anything in particular. It was more as if…as if she rested her tired eyes on the night's peaceful beauty, like a pillow.

And it was beautiful. The purple-blue sky was star-studded and clear, the air clean and cool. The creek glittered silver in the moonlight, curling through the darkened landscape like a spangled ribbon that had slipped from some celestial gown.

He broke off another hunk of bread and shared it. And then another, until most of the loaf was gone. She shifted, pulling her feet up and cupping her toes in her palms, as if the night air had begun to sting their nakedness.

The movement was completely different from anything she'd done since she got here. Though she still didn't speak, and she still gazed into the darkness,

Bree's silence, and her stillness, had taken on a new quality.

A quality of...

Awareness, that was the only word he could think of. Where twenty minutes ago she had been vague, as insubstantial as a ghost, drifting just beyond her physical body, now she had returned to this moment and this place.

She once again inhabited her own skin. She knew where she was. And she knew why she was here.

An owl called somewhere beyond the distant ponderosa pines, a cold and haunting sound. The temperature was dropping fast, and the paper-thin aspen leaves, always the first to notice, had begun to whisper about the rising wind.

"Are you cold?" he asked.

She nodded. "A little."

"Do you want to go home?"

For a minute she didn't answer. Then she shook her head. "No."

"You can do whatever you want to do," he said. "I hope you know that. If you've changed your mind, or if you didn't even realize what you were saying in the first place, it doesn't matter. If you want to leave, I'll take you home immediately."

He sat very still as he waited for her answer. He told himself that he was ready for whatever she decided. He told himself that if she wasn't able to come to him tonight without doubt, and leave him tomorrow without regret, he would rather she never came to him at all.

But he was lying. He was saying what civilization required him to say—but it simply wasn't true. He had been driven half-mad with this unquenched thirst, and, on some deep, terrible level, he'd become more beast than man.

He wanted her on *any* terms. No matter what she said, what she felt or even what she did, he couldn't stop wanting her, any more than he could stop wanting air to breathe just because it was too cold, or too hot, or too filled with smoke or fire.

Every muscle in his body had been stretched unbearably taut from day after day of that helpless desire. If she walked away now and left him here with no relief, he thought the agony might finally break him in two.

Still…she hadn't given him an answer.

And then she stood, slowly, putting her bare feet onto the cold deck carefully. She turned toward him, and with two deliberate steps she closed the distance between them. For however long that took, he didn't breathe.

When she stood before him, she smiled softly. "I want to stay," she said.

He'd expected relief, expected his muscles to unclench and the pain between his legs to subside, just a little, just until he could sweep her into his arms and carry her into the tent.

But instead he felt a cruel twisting of the rack, a new and terrible cascade of fire that pinned him where he was. She had placed her palms on his knees and begun to push softly. He had no power to resist her, and his legs parted. She sank gracefully to her knees, her dark blue eyes locked on his as she descended.

"Bree." His voice was the only part of him he owned, the only part he could control. He felt as if unseen cords bound him to the chair, his hands, his shoulders, his ankles, his straining, burning thighs...

And all his helpless struggle to stand, to protect, to resist, only drove the fire higher. She touched the button of his jeans, working it open, and he felt an arcing pressure on his spine, as if the bones would crack.

"Bree. No." And still he couldn't stop her.

She dragged his zipper down, then peeled back the cloth that had been confining him. He pulsed helplessly, desire coursing through every nerve ending like an unblocked river, swelling him, inflaming him, until, when she closed her lips over the tip of him, he had to bite back a cry.

He was lost....

But somehow, at the final instant—with some instinct that must have been more powerful than life itself—he found the strength to hold back.

He breathed rhythmically, with intention, with a terrible, unnatural control. With his will alone, he created a microscopic invisible sheen of numbness between his skin and his nerve endings, and it helped him to endure the hot, sweet fire of her slow mouth....

For a while. For a very little while. Within minutes—seconds—the magic numbness began to wear off, and he felt himself falling.

He touched her silken, golden hair.

"No," he said softly, though even his vocal cords were on fire. "Not yet. I want more than this."

When she released him, he had to bite back a groan of relief. He stood quickly, pulled her to her feet, then lifted her into his arms and carried her, as he'd dreamed of doing so many times, into the waiting shadows of the tent.

Chapter 13

He was disappointed, as she had known he would be.

When their lovemaking was over, she lay on her side in his big, luxurious bed and wondered what she could have done differently.

Should she have faked it, the way she used to do with Charlie?

It had seemed wrong, somehow, to erect that wordless lie and place it forever between them. Every time she'd faked a climax with Charlie, she had loved him a little less. Not because she thought it was his fault—she knew it wasn't—but because every lie was one more wall erected between them.

Perhaps he couldn't see the walls—from his side they probably were invisible, made of transparent glass. But on her side, they were solid, and growing thicker every day. Eventually, the distance they created between them muffled all honest communication and cut off any hope of true intimacy.

Eventually, it was as if Charlie maintained a relationship only with the pretend Bree, the fake Bree—and the real, frustrated woman who feared she was somehow inadequate…that woman was walled up in the soundproof glass prison she had built for herself.

Ironic, that she had been willing to live like that with Charlie, a man she had assumed she would marry—and yet had refused to risk the same with Gray, a man who, in twelve short days, would exit her life forever and never look back.

She turned her face to the pillow. She couldn't try to sort all that out now. She was so tired. And she was so sorry that, no matter what else she had done to delight him, his pleasure had been canceled out by that last, disappointing thirty seconds, when he finally realized that she would not, or could not, let go.

That, in spite of his perfect body, his experienced technique and his endless patience and generosity, they still would not end it together.

They would not share the moment of final surrender—the one everyone read about in books, the one that proved two people belonged together because their bodies spoke the same mysterious language, and their souls flew like birds, like angels and heroes and gods, on simultaneous currents of bliss.

It had been too late for him to hold back, but she had seen the dark surprise that altered his face when he realized he flew alone.

And she'd felt the kindness, the apparently inexhaustible generosity that made him reach out for her again, as soon as he could find the strength. She'd stayed his hand, nudged his lips back up to her own lips, asking him to settle for a kiss instead.

"I'm fine," she had said. "It was beautiful, and I'm fine. Really."

He had raised himself on one elbow and looked down at her for a long time with an inscrutable gaze. His hand had slowly stroked her damp skin, from waist to hip, across her rib cage and up again. He had traced his fingers lightly over the soft pink tip of her breast, as if the truth lay there.

"I don't think you are," he had said finally. Then he had smiled, that sweet, sexy smile that made her heart flop helplessly in her chest, and lowered his lips to her neck. "But we can fix that, sweetheart, I promise."

"No, really." She had smiled, too, though her effort felt strained. She couldn't put him through that all over again. She couldn't put herself through it. It wouldn't work. And besides, it wasn't necessary.

"I'm really fine. Just…a little tired, I think."

And now she lay in the dark, wondering whether it would have been easier, in the end, just to go on pretending. Why didn't he believe that she had loved every minute of it? Why couldn't he accept that a woman like her, a woman whose body just wouldn't cooperate with that kind of ultimate surrender, could still be moved to feel pleasure, even joy, when she touched a man who excited her, who made her breath come faster just to look at him?

She was still a woman. She felt passion. She longed for the hot pressure of him inside her, filling her almost to the edge of glorious pain. What woman would not thrill to a lover as masterful as Gray Harper? The magic, knowing fingers on her skin, the clever lips brushing fire into every secret nerve ending and creating shimmers that crossed her body in waves of light.

Tonight, for a moment, she'd almost thought she could give in, surrender and let her body do what ought to come naturally. For a minute, she'd been filled with light, and she'd thought, *yes, this is why a woman should never pretend.* Because allowing yourself to wait, no matter how exposed and awkward you feel, is the only chance you'll ever have to make things better.

How could any lover ever help her find her way to the real thing if she kept pretending it had already happened?

In the end, she'd pulled back, the same as always. The miracle hadn't come through, but even that moment of hope had been exciting....

And if there could be another moment, and another after that...maybe someday...

But even if it never happened, she could still experience a deep and transporting satisfaction in lovemaking. Just a different kind. Her kind. Her ultimate pleasure would come from seeing his, if only he could accept that it was no failure for him to reach that pinnacle alone.

She would thrill to his thrill. Could she ever convince him that was enough?

And would she even get another chance?

Though she lay there for hours, listening to the melodic murmur of Cupcake Creek as it surged across long, thick downed logs and frothed softly at the undersides of its mounded rocks, she never did find an answer to any of those questions.

After all these years, she hadn't really expected to.

Eventually, Gray's hand softened on her thigh.

His breathing changed, and she knew he had finally surrendered to sleep. She eased free of his hand and climbed quietly out of the bed. She dressed in the dark and, looking back at the tent only once, she carefully made her way back to Bell River by moonlight.

When Gray's cell rang before dawn the next morning, he didn't even check the caller ID. He was 100 percent certain it had to be Bree.

"Hey," he said thickly, smiling half into the pillow and half into the phone. "Why did you sneak away like that? I wasn't finished with you."

The awkward silence on the other end was his first clue. *Hell.* He pulled himself to a sitting position, covers bunching everywhere, and brought the phone down where he could belatedly check the number.

Harper Hall.

He chuckled wryly, scraping his hair out of his forehead with his fingers. *Wonderful.* Always helpful to play to your stereotype.

He put the phone back to his ear. "Sorry. Got you confused with a really nice dream I had last night." Another silence. "Grandfather? What, have you fainted from the shock of hearing that I have a love life?"

"Mr. Gray?" A woman's voice spoke haltingly into the phone, sounding bewildered. "I don't know what you mean when you say all that. I am calling you, not Mr. Harper. I am Almeda."

"Almeda!" Feeling absurd, he put his hand on his face and scrubbed hard. He needed to get some blood flowing to his brain, damn it. He wasn't thinking very fast this morning. "I'm sorry. I was—I thought you were my grandfather, and I thought I was playing a joke on him."

"Oh, I see." She didn't seem to think it was very funny, though. And all of a sudden his brain woke up, and he felt a chill pass through him that had nothing to do with the cold, misty Bell River morning he could see through the windows of the tent.

Why was his grandfather's housekeeper calling him at dawn?

Or ever?

It had to mean only one thing. Something was wrong with his grandfather.

"Almeda, has something happened?"

"Yes." She sounded immensely relieved that he finally understood. "Yes, that is why I am calling. Mr. Harper…" She tried again. "Mr. Harper, he…" She choked on something that sounded like tears…but how could it be? Could she actually care about the old coot? Old Grayson always used to say, with a perverse pride, that everyone he'd ever employed had probably wanted to stab him in his bed.

No "probably" about it. Even as a teenager, Gray had known it to be true.

"Almeda, has he been hurt? Do I need to call an ambulance?"

"No," she said. "It came already. It took him to the hospital. They say they think he is having a heart attack. They say—"

She broke off again. Gray kept the phone to his ear, but he'd left the bed and was yanking clothes out of the wicker chests and setting them on the dresser. Jeans, sweatshirt, underwear, socks…where the hell had he put his socks?

"They say it could be bad."

She had finally swallowed her tears and found her voice—and then it was as if she couldn't seem to stop the words from pouring out.

"Oh, Mr. Gray, you should go. The things he says to you... They are not his real feelings. You should go now."

Oh, who the hell cared about socks? Gray jammed his feet into his tennis shoes and grabbed his keys from the dresser.

"I'm on my way," he said.

Gray had about a million reasons why he would never, ever consider living in Silverdell again, but Silverdell Memorial Hospital had to be right up there at the top of the list.

That's where they'd brought him after the accident. He'd spent two months inside its white-walled prison, locked in a vicious, unresolvable battle with the doctors and staff.

In his eyes, they had seemed like monstrous machine people, devoid of logical thought, guided only by their knee-jerk, one-size-fits-all, dogmatic conviction that every human being should live. Including Gray.

He had violently disagreed. And, when he discovered the extent of his injuries, he figured God did, too.

But the doctors toiled on, clearly believing they knew better than God. And, in the end, they'd held all the cards—all the IVs and resuscitators, all the burn salves and body casts and traction apparatus. All the skin grafts and miracle drugs and needles and antidepressants and shrinks.

He'd had no choice. And so he had lived.

His chest turned to iron for a minute when he first walked through the double doors and approached the information desk. Then he took a deep breath, told both the panic and the memory to go to hell, and his chest opened again.

He'd learned, long ago, that you had to nip that crap in the bud, or you'd end up in a straitjacket, eating your food through a straw.

"I'm looking for Grayson Harper. He was brought in by ambulance an hour ago, maybe? Possible heart attack?"

The reception clerk had that constipated look that told him she was going to require all kinds of paper-work proof, including social security numbers, patient IDs and maybe a secret decoder ring, before she coughed up any information about his grandfather.

"Look, I'm his grandson. I'm his only living relative. If you'll just tell me what floor he's on, or whether he's still in the E.R.—"

"Gray!" Out of the corner of his eye, he spotted Marianne Donovan, who had been sitting by the far door. "Gray, I was waiting for you! Almeda said she'd already called you and you were on your way."

She rushed up, her cherry-red coat folded over her arm, and smiled at the battle-ax behind the desk. "It's okay, June. I'll tell Gray what he needs to know."

As she drew him off to the side, he realized he felt a little less tense already. Marianne wouldn't be smiling like that if the old man were dead. And if his grandfather had made it this far, he was unlikely to kick the bucket now. Gray happened to know for a fact that the doctors here never let anyone die on their watch.

"Was it a heart attack? Do they know yet?"

She shook her head. "From what I can tell, they think this one was a false alarm. Maybe really bad indigestion, or maybe stress related. But apparently when they ran the tests they saw some things that raised some red flags. Bottom line, they think he may have had other heart attacks, and—"

Gray frowned. "Attacks? As in more than one?"

"Yes. They say there may have been quite a few over the past few months. Or years. Who knows? He's not admitting anything, and obviously he never got help. So they're going to keep him awhile and do a whole barrage of tests."

Gray laughed. "I bet he's loving that."

"He's giving them fits." She sighed. "They wouldn't have told me, either, you know, if I'd just shown up and asked. I only know any of this because I rode over in the ambulance with him. Almeda called me right away, and I live so close, so—"

"Hey." He shook his head and smiled. "It's fine. I'm glad you were there for him. It's not as though I'm going to waltz in after all these years and be jealous because he's got a new best friend."

She nodded a bit ruefully. "Anyhow, he's in fine fettle, denouncing everything and everyone, and generally making himself odious all around. That seems to be what he does when he's frightened or hurt."

Gray laughed, and then regretted it when he realized how bitter he sounded. "Excellent strategy. Can't imagine why it never works."

She reproved him with her eyes, but that was all.

"Anyhow, he said he wanted to talk to you, if you showed up." She sighed again, even more heavily, as if the two of them exhausted her. "Heaven only knows what kind of nasty thing he wants to get off his chest. Are you willing to risk it?"

Gray considered. "Sure," he said finally. "I'm already here. What do I have to lose?"

She raised her eyebrows, as if to say he shouldn't underestimate his grandfather in a rage, but she need not have worried. Gray had never underestimated exactly how toxic his grandfather could be, and he wasn't likely to start now.

Mostly, he just wanted to get it over with...so that he could return to Bell River, and Bree. On the way to the hospital, when he'd had no idea whether his grandfather was going to live or die, he'd put all personal issues out of his mind with little effort.

But now, as the slow elevator crawled to the third floor, the doors repeatedly trying to close, then opening again as people wrestled their way on and off with gurneys, wheelchairs, crutches, flowers, medicine carts and IVs, Gray found his mind straying back to last night.

He'd really taken a hit to the old ego, that was for sure. There he was, in the middle of one of the most amazing sexual experiences of his life...

No, not *one* of the most. *The* most. Brianna Wright turned him on, moved him, body and soul...like no one he'd ever known. Ever.

Her beauty was only part of it, although when he finally took her clothes off he almost couldn't breathe. Beauty was the nursery-school word for what she had. She was magnificent, like some timeless work of art, all alabaster symmetry and transcendent grace. Her proportions, from simple things, like the ratio of her breast to her waist, or her waist to her hips, to more profound things, like the relationship of all that to the ratio of everything on him, were impossibly perfect.

If he'd been a poetic man, he might have said that she seemed to have been designed to resonate with the secret spiritual harmonics that regulated everything in the whole damn universe.

So there he was, resonating all over the place, ready to erupt into a brave new world where he finally understood the meaning of life and love and birth and death, and why the rainbow is made of colors and the flowers bloom in the spring...

And in the middle of all that he'd suddenly realized that Bree had, in return, received...absolutely nothing.

Nothing. Except maybe a level of sexual frustration that must have been the equivalent of an undetonated atom bomb.

He leaned back against the elevator wall and shut his eyes. *Well done, Harper.*

She'd led him to Olympus and turned him into a god.

He hadn't even been able to lead her to one average, garden-variety orgasm.

"Gray? Hey. Are you okay?"

He opened his eyes and saw Marianne's mildly irritated face staring at him.

She scowled. "That was a strange look. What on earth were you thinking about?"

He smiled.

"Just something I've got to take care of later," he said.

And he would. That was a disaster he never intended to repeat.

It wouldn't be difficult. Even last night, she'd been

so close. He might have been half-crazed with his own desire, but he always registered things like that. She'd been all the way up at the top of the wheel, strung tight and only half conscious. And the wheel was still spinning and sending off sparks.

He knew that spot. It was the sweet spot, the place where it suddenly all got so easy. Where, if she wanted to, his lover could just stay forever, right on the edge, like a bird on a wire, letting the electricity move through her in shivering waves that never quite set her free.

Or...

He could let her fall. He could adjust the angle, or the pressure, or the pace, by even one degree... He could lean down and take her nipple in his mouth, completing the circuit. He could let his thumb graze the tiny, throbbing nub just above where he filled her. Sometimes all he had to do was say her name and she would suddenly lose all control, cry out and shatter in helpless pieces around him.

Bree had been there, he was sure of it. She had been in that sweet spot, over and over. By all the rules that governed the human body, she should have shattered...

And yet she hadn't. And he suddenly resented all the hours that stood between him and the moment, tonight, when he would be able to set that right.

"Don't put your fierce face on already, Gray." Mari was frowning at him again, looking troubled. "Don't go in spoiling for a fight."

He laughed. Was that what he looked like? Like he was spoiling for a fight? He'd have to work on that before tonight.

"I'll be good," he said meekly.

She stopped before a closed door. "He's got a private room, of course."

Of course. Who would put up with him?

She knocked politely, and in response a gruff voice barked, "What *now,* for God's sake?"

She backed away, putting her hands up as if to say she'd had enough for today. "He's all yours," she said. Then she squeezed Gray's hand. "Seriously. Good luck. I hope it goes all right."

"It'll be fine," Gray said. "And even if he tries to beat me senseless, I'm in a hospital, right? They'll save me. They'll probably put me in the adjoining room."

She laughed and turned to leave. At the last minute, as she turned the corner that would take her out of sight, she waved a hand over her shoulder in a playful goodbye.

Okay. His turn now. Time to get this done.

Squaring his shoulders, Gray opened the door.

Chapter 14

His grandfather was sitting up in the room's one chair, undoubtedly violating doctor's orders. He was hooked up awkwardly to a couple of machines that clearly were intended to service a patient who was expected to be lying in the bed.

His face was thin, his nose hawkish, as he glanced up from the brochure he had been perusing. Gray read a few words upside down. Some patronizing little lecture about the benefits of exercise for heart conditions.

Well, stop the presses.

Apparently his grandfather had the same reaction. He tossed the pamphlet onto the bed tray. "Talk about belaboring the obvious," he said acidly. He folded his bony hands in his lap. "So. You did come. Who called you? Marianne?"

"Does it matter?" Gray sat on the edge of the unused bed, if only to show himself that he could. He didn't have any lingering horror of these nasty slabs of plastic torture. "I came."

"Of course you did. You don't want me to die before your month is up, and I have a chance to write a new will. You were probably afraid that I'd keel over prematurely, leaving everything disposed of as it was before."

Gray smiled coldly. "Terrified."

His grandfather didn't seem to have a response, which surprised Gray. Already, after just a couple of weeks in Silverdell again, he'd fallen back into old patterns, and had expected the rhythm of insult-deflect-insult-deflect to continue ad nauseam.

Silence, unless it was a pointed silence created to be its own form of insult or deflect, didn't really fit the pattern. This silence felt more…impotent.

And yet, it stretched on. Old Grayson fiddled with the belt tied at the waist of his robe, then with the piece of tape that held his IV needle in place on the back of his hand.

Gray noted the purple bruising around the ropy blue vein and wondered if they'd had trouble inserting the needle. Then he wondered why he cared. If there had been trouble, it was probably caused by his grandfather's refusal to cooperate.

But as the seconds ticked on, and the old man didn't seem to be able to focus well enough to hold a conversation, Gray felt a small current of sympathy drift into the ocean of cold antagonism that was his normal emotional state around his grandfather.

Grayson's age was finally catching up with him. Though he had always seemed omniscient, omnipotent and immortal, he was, in the end, merely a human being. He couldn't fight nature forever. Being too stubborn to admit you'd had heart attacks wasn't really the same thing as not having them. Just as being too stubborn to *die* from a heart attack wouldn't really be the same thing as continuing to live.

But if he admitted to physical weakness—or even, God forbid, to cognitive decline—then who *was* old Grayson Harper the First? If he wasn't a force to be reckoned with, a powerhouse to be placated, a lacerating wit to be feared…then what role was left for him to play?

Guess that was the final downside of living your life as an unmitigated bastard. When you stumbled, who had any incentive to help you to your feet? If you'd populated your world with people who wanted to stab you in your bed, when the day came that you were too weak to defend yourself, one of them would do it.

"Marianne said you wanted to talk to me." Gray kept his voice neutral. He'd promised Mari that he'd be good. On the off chance that his grandfather didn't actually have plans to be vicious, Gray would be smarter not to goad him into it. "What did you want to say?"

Slowly, his grandfather raised his hand to scratch the side of his neck. Gray was shocked to see a tremor in the fingers, a tremor so strong the old man had to start twice before he could manage to lift high enough to reach the spot.

"Would you like some water?" Gray wasn't sure what water would do to help, but some atavistic instinct took over, and water was all he could think of to offer.

His grandfather shook his head, waving away the pitcher with that same trembling hand. It was almost as if he didn't notice the tremor. As if it had been with him a long time, and had become a part of his life.

How long? How long did it take to accept something like that?

Gray knew it would be almost impossible for him to *ever* adjust his mental image of this man. In his head, his grandfather would always be about sixty-five, as vigorous as he was ruthless, as sharp intellectually as he was unforgiving and unkind.

"I wanted to tell you something," his grandfather said suddenly, as if he'd just heard the question. "Something about your father."

Gray shot a glance at the old man, who was staring down at his bedroom slippers. His scalp was as pink as a baby's butt beneath his thinning silver hair.

"Well, I'm not sure I want to hear it."

The old man lifted his head and fixed a glittering eye on Gray. "I'm sure you don't. But that doesn't mean I shouldn't say it. Perhaps I should have told you years ago. Maybe you wouldn't have turned him into such a saint. Saints are…tricky. They loom so large. Makes it difficult to put them in perspective."

Gray felt suddenly very tired. "Is this a joke? You think I canonized my father because of anything *you* said? I can't remember you praising a single thing about him, ever in your life."

His grandfather nodded. "I'm sure that's true. I was very disappointed in my only son, and I may have been too harsh."

Gray laughed. "*May* have…"

His grandfather pretended not to hear that.

"However," he went on, "you are bright enough to

see that there are two routes to sainthood, only one of which is to be beloved and praised for great works."

Gray took the bait. "And the other is...?"

His grandfather shrugged. "The other is to be a martyr."

Gray didn't respond. He saw, of course, what his grandfather was getting at. But so what? What did this have to do with anything?

"Your father drank. Not like a normal person drinks. He drank too much. You know that, even if you don't admit to yourself how big a problem it had actually become."

"Of course I know. I also know *why* he drank."

His grandfather made a dismissive snort. "He drank because he was an alcoholic. People don't become alcoholics because they hate their fathers, Gray. Otherwise, half the world would be drunk all the time."

The old man smiled without mirth. "They become alcoholics because they have something on their DNA strand that makes them susceptible to addiction. Your father had that something."

Gray felt the familiar defensive anger rising in his chest, but he didn't let it come out in words. Instead, he tried just to sit with it, and let it be, for now. Perhaps that was because some sliver of honesty told him the old man wasn't lying about this.

Take Gray himself. He hated his grandfather. For a few years there, he'd hated the whole bloody world. And yet, he'd never turned to booze or drugs. He would have, if they had seemed appealing. But they didn't, so he didn't.

Because he clearly did not have that *something*...

He thought of the portrait hanging in the library,

and how it had always felt like a prophecy of doom. He had been created in the mold of his despised grandfather—and shared almost nothing with his beloved father.

How ironic. The twist of fate he'd hated the most might, perversely, have been what saved his life.

"All right," he said. "He was an alcoholic. What is the significance of that? Are you trying to say that makes it okay for you to have let him get behind a wheel? You knew he was drunk. You knew he was upset, unstable, incapable of good judgment. And any fool could see the weather was dangerous."

His grandfather didn't deny it. In fact, he nodded, his eyes shut.

"So why the hell didn't you lock the door and throw away the keys? I'll tell you why. Because you *wanted* him to die."

When he started that short speech, Gray had been talking to the wall, but when he got to the last line he turned, wanting to hurl the final words right into the old man's face and watch the blood drain out of it.

To his shock, his grandfather's face was already bloodless, and twisted in a rictus of pain so hideous that it was almost impossible to witness the change without a rush of instinctive pity…without a reflexive urge to do whatever it took to make agony like that subside.

"Don't," the old man whispered through those painfully twisted lips. "You can say I killed him because I didn't stop him. You can say it was my fault because I didn't prevent him from leaving."

A small, beaded strand of what looked like spittle clung to the edge of the old man's lips, and Gray realized suddenly that his grandfather's face had contorted so hideously, not in pain, but because he was trying not to weep.

"I know you think that, so say it." His grandfather raised his voice harshly. "*Say it, damn you.* I say it, too, every day of my life. But you *will not say* I…"

Suddenly, the tears spilled, slowly tracking the gaunt furrows of the old man's sunken cheeks. The spit he couldn't swallow dribbled piteously down his chin. Even so, he balled his palsied hand into a fierce fist and raised it menacingly toward Gray, as if to say he'd kill him if he had to.

"You will *not,* you bastard. Do you hear me? You will not say I *wanted* him to die!"

"So…" Bree paused dramatically, aware of the five young bodies leaning forward intently, wondering what the angry matador would do to the bull who refused to fight. Then she smiled. "They had to take Ferdinand home."

"Home?" One of the little girls who had come to today's Saturday-Morning Horse Tales gasped with joy, followed by a spontaneous burst of applause from her four friends, all arranged on the colorful padded benches in front of Bree.

Bree let the celebration continue a minute or two, getting a kick out of the beaming faces. Then, as the girls subsided, she read the last line or two of the book about the bull who loved to smell the flowers just quietly.

When she closed the final page, the youngest member of the audience, five-year-old Teegan Ross, stood up impulsively and began to dance.

"I love Ferdinand the Bull!" She spun herself in circles until she got dizzy and had to plop back down on her violet-polka-dotted cushion. Even then, she folded her hands, prayerlike, under her chin and shivered fervently. "I love him *so much*."

What a cutie! This was only the second Horse Tales session, but Bree could already tell it would be one of her favorite rituals. She was already making plans for next week. She and Rowena had agreed that each story time should have at least one horse story, so…maybe "Misty of Chincoteague" next time?

She'd have to double-check the ages of the children expected—they'd have a whole new group by next week.

Right on the hour, one of the part-time kids' counselors, a pink-cheeked sweetie named Rose, appeared at the barn door, ready to collect her charges. As they bustled out, kids began telling Rose all about Ferdinand, and asking if they could have some time today to sit and smell flowers just quietly.

Bree tidied her books away, then pulled out the supplies to sanitize the cushions. Ideas to improve the event tumbled around in her mind.

Maybe they should build up a lending library of children's books, so that the ones who were inspired by Horse Tales time could let it carry over…

Or maybe in winter, when the barn was cold, they could—

Winter?

What was she thinking? She wouldn't even be here for the *summer* season. Much less the fall. The winter was just a dream, still rough sketches on a drawing board. Rowena was still crunching numbers nightly, trying to decide if they could afford to offer skiing lessons, and what effect sleigh rides and sledding and fires in every hearth would have on the insurance.

One more story time. That was the extent of her hands-on involvement. Then she'd go back to Boston. Gray would go, too—home to wherever that meant for him, doing whatever he really loved. Eleven days now. A week from this coming Wednesday, he'd win his bet and be on his way.

She took out her phone to see if he had tried to call. He hadn't.

But surely he would soon? Maybe she was simply feeling mellow from breathing kiddie-joy fumes for the past hour, but she couldn't quite believe he would tire of her after only one time.

The fretting she'd done last night seemed kind of silly now. She hadn't broken down all her lifelong barriers. That would have been asking too much. But he had brought her so much further than she'd ever gone before.

She'd been so *close*.

It might not seem like much to anyone else, but she knew it was practically a miracle. She had been so close that for the first time she believed it might be possible, someday, to just let go and let it happen.

She didn't know if it would take two seconds, or two years. She didn't even know whether Gray would be willing to be patient long enough.... But she knew that, for the first time, she didn't just want to give up and run away. She knew she couldn't pretend it didn't matter to her.

It did matter. Deeply. She wanted things to change. She wanted that icy place inside her to melt and disappear. And for the first time she believed it actually might. And, even though the whole concept still embarrassed her—even frightened her, in a way—she desperately wanted to try.

She glanced at her phone again and decided that if he hadn't called by the time she got off duty, she was going to call him. Or maybe she'd just hike down to the tent. Skip the phoning step, save time…

She laughed, listening to herself. Who was this edgy, buzzing, shameless hussy—and what had she done with the ice maiden?

She'd never felt this way about sex with Charlie. Not even close, not even in the earliest days. At the time, she'd assumed it was because she was in mourning for Kitty. When that never wore off, she reluctantly had to accept that she'd probably gotten her "Contents Are Frozen" label the old-fashioned way—she'd earned it.

Not anymore, though.

The Bree who lived in Boston and the Bree of Bell River Ranch were like two different women. The question was…which one was the real one?

Oh, please… The prayer came without conscious thought. *Let it be this one.*

Through the open barn door, a picture postcard advertising the beauty of Colorado spread out before her. Green pastureland, where glossy, healthy horses cantered lazily under a warm sun. Tidy white paddock fences with clusters of blue flax growing at the base of the posts, as if they'd been decorated for a garden party. In the misty distance, silver mountains stuck up like stony knuckles, giving the impression that the whole happy valley was cupped in the protective palm of some silent giant.

Like a huge, natural rush of wind or wave, love for this exquisite land swept into Bree—almost too much emotion to contain in one body. Impulsively, she twirled herself in happy circles, understanding now why Teegan Ross had needed to dance off her joy.

Suddenly, she felt the vibration of her cell phone, and she froze in place, eagerly digging it out of her back pocket. *Gray,* her mind whispered, even her thoughts sounding breathless.

But it wasn't Gray. It was Dallas.

"Hey, Bree," His voice was warm, as always. He had never hinted that Rowena's ambivalence about Bree had created any in him. He always treated her like family.

"Sorry to have to ask, but is there any chance you can handle the pony rides this afternoon? Ro's not feeling great. I suggested Gray first, but she says he got held up in town. And I can't come in till about four because I'm stuck at the office."

"Of course," she said immediately, but it worried her that Rowena was still feeling bad. She'd looked healthy enough last night, although naturally they were all living in a constant state of fatigue. "Is everything okay?"

"Everything's fine." Dallas would say that anyhow, of course, but he had a very comforting way of making it sound sincere. "She's worn herself out over the past few months, that's all. You know how Rowena is when she's determined—she only has the one speed."

So true. Rowena's passions had "all out" and "off." Nothing in between, like "sensible" or "lukewarm." She'd been in all-out mode for about a year now.

"So maybe this is just her body telling her brain who's ultimately the boss here. If she won't voluntarily slow down, it'll make her do it." He sighed. "She's way too bullheaded for her own good."

Also true. But he didn't sound truly critical. Bree could hear that, even though he worried about his wife, he admired her independence and drive.

Oh, lucky Ro—to have a man who understood her so well and yet seemed to love her flaws as much as he loved her virtues.

"I'll be happy to take the lessons. As long as you're sure there's nothing seriously wrong."

He laughed. "Nothing seriously wrong."

Out of nowhere, a thought occurred to her. Once it did, she was shocked that it hadn't occurred before.

"Dallas." She tried to think how to say it. "Is it possible that…well, that maybe there's actually something seriously *right,* instead?"

He didn't skip a beat. Even if she was a bit dense, obviously the idea wasn't coming out of nowhere for him.

"I just don't know yet, Bree," he said with disarming honesty. "But I sure do hope so. If it turns out to be…" He trailed off for a minute, as though lost in the implications of the whole amazing possibility.

Finally, he laughed. "Well, I'll keep you posted. I can't promise you'll be the *first* to know, because once we tell Alec, he'll be shouting it from the rooftops, and all western Colorado will find out at approximately the same time."

When they hung up, Bree felt even more restless and unfocused than ever, and yet oddly buoyant, like a helium balloon tugging free of its string. She needed to do something, anything, to work off all this emotion. And—no offense, Teegan—she'd like it to be more useful than simply twirling in place.

What she really wanted was to do something for Rowena. For years now, Bree had been so pinch hearted, so grudging as a sister. Even as her heart began to unfurl, she still didn't quite know how to express her feelings freely.

She wanted to do something to show Rowena how much she cared. And now, if there was a baby on the way...

She gathered her things and headed out of the barn. She should get some lunch before the pony lessons. But she couldn't really think about food, or ponies, or anything but how happy she would be for Rowena if it turned out to be true....

A child would be such a gift—a child who was Rowena's own in every way. It would ground her, give her roots. She would have an unquestioned, unconditional bond with another human being, something she had never really known.

It had been so hard for her, growing up under the cloud of Johnny Wright's inexplicable rejection. Bree knew that Ro had always felt as if she didn't quite belong, but she'd never known why. Not until she found the picture that made it fall into place—the picture of her mother's long-ago lover.

Rowena had found the picture quite by accident—actually, Dallas's son, Alec, reportedly was the one who had unearthed it from the secret spot where Moira Wright had hidden it. The photo showed Moira with a mystery man. Rowan…his first name, that's all they knew about him. His first name, his tall, lanky body covered in bulky ski clothes and a smile on Moira's face that spoke volumes.

That smile, and the date written on the back of the picture, about eight months before Rowena's birth, had been enough to open a floodgate, and a million questions had poured through. Before long, Rowena's need to know had been greater than her fear of finding out.

She had sent off samples of her DNA and Johnny Wright's—and the verdict had been unequivocal. There was a zero percent chance that Rowena was Johnny Wright's biological daughter.

Rowan, the man at whom her mother turned that dazzling, unfamiliar smile, had undoubtedly been Rowena's real father.

And that meant he would be Rowena's child's real grandfather.

He might still be alive, and if he was, he would be the child's only surviving grandparent, on either side. He would hold the answers to some of the most important questions of the child's life. Not just what name to write on the "Grandfather" leaf of the baby book's family tree, but more profound questions, too.

He held answers that would speak to who the new baby really was, what kind of people he came from and who else in this world shared his blood and had his back.

All the answers that, if they had come sooner, might have filled the angry, confused and empty spot inside Rowena's heart.

And suddenly Bree knew what she could do for her

sister. Well, she couldn't do it herself, but she could hire someone who could.

She could track down and identify the handsome, smiling, athletic man in the photo. She could find the mysterious Rowan.

Chapter 15

After clearing his absence with Rowena, Gray had spent the day in town. Most of the time, he camped out at Donovan's, where Mari had unofficially dedicated a small back booth for his use the past couple of weeks. The space was a real help. He made a lot of calls and processed a lot of paperwork there, taking care of things back home.

Thank heaven for laptops, smartphones and digital signatures. And for Mari's unquestioning acceptance of his right to privacy.

It wasn't as easy having two full-time jobs as one might think, especially when they had to be kept entirely separate—even entirely secret, if he wanted to get dramatic about it. He had a whole new understanding of how slick those bigamists you read about had to be, keeping two sets of unsuspecting families in different towns.

And how tired. Frankly, he couldn't imagine why they thought it was worth it.

But today he wasn't tending his secret double life. He was trying to figure out what to do about his grandfather. He'd finally cleared the privacy hurdles by hanging around in the hall after the old man kicked him out of the room and refusing to go away until the doctor showed up for rounds.

Then he put his grandfather more or less on the spot. In the doctor's presence, he got the old man to agree, although not without a lot of snide asides about "deathbed vultures," to add Gray's name to the list of people who could be consulted.

A short list indeed. Disturbingly short. Before Gray was added, Marianne and Almeda had been the only names on it. Gray was shocked. Back when he was a kid, his grandfather had been a big mover and shaker. Where were all the hangers-on that sick old rich people were supposed to be surrounded by? His grandfather's isolation was apparently almost absolute.

Not that Gray had any intention of getting sucked into the situation. Wasn't much he could do from a five-hundred-mile distance, and living any closer than five hundred miles from Silverdell was unthinkable.

But neither could he walk away without making sure old Grayson had a network in place to provide basic care.

Which meant he had approximately eleven days to find some nurses, home-health aides and the like. Maybe a part-time maid to help Almeda keep up with that drafty old marble mausoleum.

He was exhausted by the time he trudged back to the tent. The toughest work he'd ever done, either at this ranch or any other, was ten times easier than a day spent wrangling with doctors and hospitals.

It wasn't fully dark yet as he arrived, but the moon had risen in a blue twilight. Maid service had, as always, left the bedside lamp on, which made the tent glow like a big block of amber against the silver sparkle of the creek.

Something out here was oddly healing. The tumble of water over rocks was a soothing sound, and the minute he heard it, that strung-tight feeling between his shoulders disappeared.

Rowena had asked everyone their thoughts on maybe putting in a spa so that the ranch could offer massages and facials and all those other TLC services people splurged on while vacationing. He hadn't weighed in, not being the herbal-wrap type, but suddenly he thought this might be a good spot for it.

"Gray? Is that you?"

A dark shadow unwound itself from the other shadows under the awning. Little by little, it turned into a slender female body, which stretched like a sleepy kitten, arched and yawned softly.

Bree. Instantly, the strung-tight feeling reappeared, but slightly farther south. He reached the deck just as she made it to her feet. Without saying a word, and certainly without asking himself whether it was the smartest move, he dropped his laptop onto the other chair and then scooped her into his arms.

Their kiss went on...and on. Her mouth tasted like violets in the rain. And her skin felt like satin...if satin had been struck by lightning and glowed hotly gold, the sizzle of electricity trapped in its threads.

It was intoxicating, and every stroke of his lips over

hers led to another, until, where she pressed herself against his chest, he could feel her heart skittering wildly. He knew then, that he had to pull back. He'd thought about her on and off all day, of course—and by lunchtime he'd decided that they must talk things over before they mindlessly tumbled into bed again.

But with her heartbeat already racing like that, and his own body fired up and straining, he didn't have a chance of staying sane enough for talking. Not if he didn't slow down now.

He lifted his head sluggishly, with tremendous effort, as if breaking a magnetic pull. He couldn't get more than a few inches, but it was a start.

"Hi, there," he said belatedly. His lips felt thick, as if words didn't come as naturally as kissing. "I missed you today."

She smiled, and he saw that her mouth, too, had been slightly inflamed, distended by the intensity of the kiss. Her pale pink lipstick smeared just beyond the beautiful bow of her upper lip. He had to fight the urge to plant one more kiss there, to cool and soothe its sensitive flesh.

But there wasn't anything cool about him right now. Every inch of him, lips included, was on fire, and all another kiss could do was burn them both.

"Are you hungry?"

She smiled. "No. I ate with the guests, and then I came out here to bring you some of the apple cobbler. It was amazing. I hated for you to miss it."

He glanced toward the small table, where a pretty white pleated bowl sat, filled with something rich with red and gold and cinnamon.

"You came all the way out here to bring me apple cobbler?"

"Of course." She tilted her head, biting her lower lip even as she smiled. "What other reason could I possibly have?"

The gleam of her perfect white teeth against that swollen red lip almost undid him. He had to look away, just to be able to keep from scooping her up all over again.

But she clearly had expected him to. And when he didn't, she tensed slightly. "Gray?" She put her hand on his arm. "Was I wrong to come?"

He shook his head. "No. Of course not. It's just—you know what I *want* to do. I want to take you to bed right now and make love all night, until neither of us can remember our own names."

"Um." Her fingers were hot, twitching slightly against his skin where she held his arm. "I think that's a brilliant idea. Why aren't we doing that?"

He wasn't sure he remembered anymore. The plan that had seemed rational, even imperative, while he sat in Donovan's this afternoon now seemed as silly and useless as planning to follow a child's scribbled map to find imaginary buried treasure.

Still…he retained just enough clarity to understand that his brain might possibly be more trustworthy sitting alone at Donovan's than it was out here, with Bree's slim, pink-tipped fingers shooting electricity through his system.

They *did* have to talk. His conscience required it.

He'd thought back on last night's sex and realized that there'd been something slightly off from the start, when she'd immediately assumed they should begin, not with mutual foreplay, but with her pleasuring him alone. And then, throughout the night, her body had yo-yoed cruelly between acute responsiveness, almost to the point of surrender, followed by a sudden withdrawal that short-circuited the sexual current and sent her back to square one.

And then, even when he'd been ready to tend exclusively to her, to focus solely on bringing her the release she needed, with no distractions, no fears that she was neglecting to take care of him, she had rejected the suggestion outright. She seemed not to fully register how much she needed to finish what they'd started. When he touched her, she hummed like a live wire, but she pretended that was no big deal...that it was simply, somehow, her normal.

He wasn't a psychologist. But he had a very strong suspicion this was more than just exhaustion or an off night. He wanted to probe a little, maybe try to understand what fears were in her way and how he might be able to help her overcome them.

If he could possibly make sense of this without embarrassing or frightening her, he wanted to try. If he couldn't...

He didn't want to think about what he'd do if he couldn't.

"I just think we should talk a little first. There are so many things we don't know about each other."

"Like what?"

"Like...almost everything." He smiled. "And at the same time, nothing in particular. It's only that we skipped some of the steps involved in most relationships."

"Even relationships like ours?" Her eyes were shadowed, but quite steady as she met his gaze. "Twelve-day relationships?"

He reached out and touched the swollen bud of her lower lip with his forefinger. "Do you really think relationships are measured only in days?"

She hesitated. And then she shook her head, her lips sliding slowly an inch left, then an inch right, grazing his fingertip with a velvet warmth.

"Then let's go sit by the creek and talk," he said. He let his hand fall, tracing the curve of her neck, the sweet line of her collarbone. "No agenda. We'll just talk about whatever comes to mind. It's still early. We have plenty of time."

She smiled ruefully, and he knew what she was thinking. Eleven days was all they had—and by no measure could that be considered *plenty*. But unless he wanted a repeat of last night's inexplicable, unresolved finale, he had to get answers to some very delicate questions.

He ducked into the tent for a minute and grabbed a blanket and a couple of sweatshirts, in case it turned even colder.

"Let's go," he said as he came out. He extended his hand. She was ready. She took it without hesitation and let him lead her down the short, rocky path overgrown with grasses until they reached the edge of the creek.

They found a smooth spot where the grass was low, the ground fairly level. He spread the blanket, and then he stretched himself out on one side, leaving plenty of room for her to take the other. She waited a couple of minutes before joining him, standing instead at the water's edge, watching its gently sweeping current move silver ripples like cargoes of sequins toward the purple horizon.

Finally, she came to the blanket and sat, then lay on her side next to him. She pulled her knees up a little and tucked her hands under her cheek. Their faces were only a few inches apart.

"What kept you in town today?"

He felt his shoulders stiffen instinctively. He stretched them, consciously working out the tension. Funny, he hadn't considered that she might ask him tough questions, too. But if he wanted honesty from her, he was going to have to offer some in return.

"My grandfather was taken to the hospital this morning," he said as matter-of-factly as he could. "They thought he might be having a heart attack."

"Oh." Her eyes were liquid, blue-black in the darkness. "I'm so sorry. How is he? Is he going to be all right?"

"I think so, for now, anyhow. As it turns out, it was a false alarm today, but they think his heart has been damaged by other, earlier attacks that he never sought treatment for."

"Oh, dear." She blinked thoughtfully. "He's stubborn?"

"Very."

"Is that part of the problem between the two of you? That you're both stubborn? Are you too much alike, do you think?"

He smiled. "Me, stubborn?" But she didn't rush to assure him it wasn't true, so he just shrugged lightly. "Maybe. I contend that he's the real problem, of course, and that I'm simply being firm and fair in the face of his pigheaded arrogance. But no doubt he thinks the same thing about me."

She nodded. "No doubt." She shut her eyes for a moment, as if she was focusing on something she saw in her mind's eye. "Family relationships are so fraught with dangers, aren't they? And I don't mean just things like what my father did. He was insane—they say the brain tumor that killed him might have been affecting him a lot longer than we knew. I mean even in normal families. It's always the people we love who hurt us the most."

"Well, who else has the power?" He thought of how, ultimately, it had been easy to develop a genuine indifference to the morons who had spread some of the worst rumors about the accident that had killed Gray's parents. Creeps like that idiot Farley Miller, the ferret-faced little kid who thought he was a big deal just because his father owned the hardware store. Indifference was easy because Gray didn't actually give a rat's ass what Farley said or thought about anything.

But ever reaching the point that his grandfather's insults would bounce harmlessly off his skin like rubber bullets? Wasn't ever going to happen.

"And besides," he added, "I think the whole notion of 'normal' may be an illusion. Have you ever known anybody who was really normal, once you scratched the surface? I haven't."

"I guess not." She shook her head slowly. Then a small smile lit her face. "But I've definitely known some people who were a whole heck of a lot more 'not-normal' than others, if you know what I mean."

He rolled over on his back and stared up at the stars so that he could begin to get to the point without making her feel cornered. "What about Charlie? How normal was he?"

She didn't answer at first. Then she sighed. "It's hard to be sure. If a person does rotten things while they're involved with me, isn't there a possibility it's my fault, not theirs?"

He turned his head briefly, gave her a very direct look, then returned to perusing the stars. "No."

She chuckled softly, clearly appreciating the absolute certainty of the word. "Well, in that case, Charlie is a rotting fish corpse with legs, and if he's normal I think I'd rather move to Mars."

He liked that, and he smiled, though he remained on his back. She was still on her side, watching him. He could feel her gaze touching him softly—on the jaw, down his arm, across his chest. He tingled everywhere he imagined her eyes, and when she reached the spot between his legs, he turned his head.

She was staring exactly there, her lips parted slightly, her eyes sparkling slivers under her lowered lids. He felt himself stiffening, as if her gaze had actual pressure.

"How long were you with him? Was he the love of your life?"

A beat of silence.

Then she reached out and put her hand on his hip. "Gray, what is it you really want to know? Are you asking me if sex with Charlie was better than the sex I had with you? Because if that's what's bothering you, you should stop worrying. I came closer to…to letting go when I was with you than I had ever imagined possible."

He turned back on his side so that he faced her

again. He'd been wrong. Artificial physical distance didn't help, not when the conversation was getting so emotionally naked.

To make this work, he needed to be closer, not farther apart. He needed to touch her while they talked. He reached out, put his arms around her waist and gathered her in. It wasn't sexual—her knees still were tucked against her stomach and grazed him just above the belt.

But it was intimate. It was united, and that was what they needed right now.

"Close doesn't count, Bree," he said softly. "Not in sex. If anything, close is worse. Close hurts."

"I know." She was so near now that when she tilted her head in slightly, their foreheads touched. She rested there, as if the connection soothed. "I learned that last night. But…you have to understand. Close is a big step for me."

Overhead, the shadow of a long-legged bird passed, stirring the air rhythmically with a soft whuffle of beating wings. As if in response to the sensual sound, Bree's fingers kneaded his shoulder softly, and then she restlessly shifted her knees.

"Close is progress," she said. "Close could be…hope."

He could feel the tension building in her even now, and every instinct told him to start over, try again and just keep loving her, learning her body, teaching her to trust him—and herself—until whatever stood between them collapsed and floated away.

But he wasn't quite arrogant enough to be so sure he could overcome absolutely every bad possibility in the world. And if he pushed, and pressed, and insisted, and exhausted her, and still failed…wasn't it possible that he'd do far, far more damage than she'd already endured?

"Bree, what happens? Do you know? When you realize that you're not going to be able to...let go...what does it feel like? Is there something I do—or say? Do you remember something else? Some*one* else?"

She shut her eyes, but she shook her head. "I don't know. Everyone tells me it has to be connected to my mother's death, but I have no idea how. There was no sexual abuse in the family. My father didn't—hurt her that way. They were arguing, and he pushed her. She fell down the stairs and broke her neck. He may not even have intended to do it."

"What were they arguing about?"

"She..." Bree's voice suddenly grew thready, and he tightened his hands on her back, as if he could silently remind her that he was holding on. "She had a lover, and he found out. He was furious. I think her infidelity was a problem...a problem they'd had before."

She was trembling suddenly, not on the surface, but somewhere deep inside, below the fragile bones and satin skin. He knew, instinctively, that this must be the dark place....

Of course it was. Could it be any more obvious, when you thought about it? Her mother had surrendered to passion, to lovers, to the comfort and thrill of illicit affairs. And she had been punished for it.

She had, essentially, been executed for the crime of sex.

Maybe that was an absurd layman's oversimplification. He was no psychiatrist. But how could such a situation not have created a twisted logic in her daughter's mind? Sex equaled danger. At least the kind of sex that was purely for pleasure. Duty sex, cold, oblig-atory marital-responsibility sex…that might be safe. But passion? Desire? Abandon?

Too dangerous to consider.

"Did you ever talk to a therapist?" He'd take her to one this minute if he thought it could set her free. Not so that he could have the pleasure of using her body—that was out of the question, no matter what else hap-pened tonight.

But he'd do that, or *anything,* if he thought it would make her happy.

"Every week for more than four years," she said in a dry tone. "Kitty was a wonderful woman, and she did her best to make sure I wasn't scarred by what hap-pened. And the therapists were good. They helped me come to terms with a lot of things."

"But four years…that means you stopped when you were only eighteen or so? Did you even have a clue, that early, that you would find it difficult to—"

"No. But I sought my own doctors when I got en-gaged to Charlie. They gave me anti-anxiety pills. They tried lots of things, actually, and so did I, for a while. But eventually I just decided it wasn't worth all the fuss. Charlie and I hardly ever—" She smiled. "Well, I figured I just wasn't all that attracted to him. He is a rotting fish corpse with legs, after all."

He reached up and traced her smile with his fingers. He loved her smile. Out here, it caught the moonlight, and it lit her entire face.

When his fingers reached the bow of her upper lip, she kissed them softly. "You, on the other hand…"

He felt his breath come faster. "Yes?"

"You are..." She gave him a look through her lashes. "*Not* a rotting fish corpse."

He shook his head, smiling. Then he put his hands around her waist again and tucked her as close as their knees would allow him to bring her.

"I want you to spend the night with me, Bree. The whole night. No slipping away in the darkness. Will you do that?"

"That's why I'm here," she said simply.

He knew, though, that she still didn't understand. He hoped he could find the right words. Ducking his head, he sought her gaze and held it.

"But I'm not going to make love to you. Not tonight."

"You're not?" Her voice was small, like a child's, and her eyes were dark.

"No. We both need peace tonight, far more than we need sex. I don't want to bring those old shadows into the tent with us. No talk of letting go, or surrender, or 'coming close,' or any words that are really synonyms for failure and fear. No memories of other struggles or other people. Just the two of us, easy together. And sleep."

She touched her hand to his hair. He took a deep breath. "Can you do that, Bree?"

"I can try," she said.

Chapter 16

In the end it was easy, so much easier than she could have imagined.

He gave her a heavy sweater to wear, and she slipped it on before sliding her jeans off. Without awkwardness, he donned sweatpants and a T-shirt. After she climbed into bed, he fed the wood fire in the small black stove that vented through the roof of the tent, until gradually its crackling warmth overcame the chilly night air.

Then, for a long time, they simply lay in the luxurious king-size bed, with soft, downy quilts and blankets and pillows to keep their body heat close. They talked about the silliest, most irrelevant things. Movies, books, trips they'd taken that went nightmarishly, comically wrong, sights that had been magical and unforgettable. They talked about Bell River, and she told him about having hired a private investigator to identify Rowena's biological father.

She even told him about Charlie. They were tired by then, a little punch-drunk, and had reached the point at which everything seemed hilarious. When she described Charlie jerking the sheet off the bed, desperately and futilely trying to cover himself at the expense of his ladylove, Gray had laughed out loud.

"Well, at least now I know where the rotting-fish-corpse image came from," he said. And realizing he'd hit on a truth even she hadn't consciously seen, Bree began to giggle so goofily she actually couldn't breathe, and he had to reach out and grab her hand to make sure she didn't slide off the side of the bed.

It was nonsense, more like being best friends who felt free to be ridiculous together. With sex off the agenda, there was no need to be self-conscious, to worry about how you looked, or whether you said or did the "right" things.

You could simply say the things that were true.

And then, deep into the night, he offered her answers to questions she hadn't ever felt free to ask, like where he lived—northern California—and what he did for a living—he worked on a ranch that bred horses.

He even told her about how he'd avoided the whole ranch-cowboy life for years just because he knew his grandfather longed for him to take that route. He said it had taken him far too long to wise up to how incredibly self-destructive that had been.

"I was late catching on because I was blinded by my anger. But I finally understood that if I made my life choices merely to annoy my grandfather, I was still letting him control me. I wouldn't have real independence until I stopped caring what he thought—good or bad. So I decided to follow my gut, which led me straight to the ranch."

Bree mulled that over, nestled in her warm cocoon of downy blankets and soft sheets. So that explained why he was such a natural at Bell River. He really was a cowboy, not just the playboy heir to a marble-quarry fortune.

But it just made the mystery of the money even more inexplicable. She blinked heavily, feeling her tiredness overtake her. She wondered whether he'd waited this late to share anything meaningful because he'd *wanted* her to be too drowsy to be terribly analytical or ask persistent follow-up questions.

But if he had, he'd chosen the wrong tactic. Actually, she would have been much more diffident if she'd been fully awake. Exhaustion always hit her a little like liquor. She didn't think all that clearly, but she had very few inhibitions about sharing her muddled thoughts. It had driven Charlie crazy.

"Can that really be true, though?" She yawned. "That you entirely stopped caring what your grandfather thinks, I mean. If you had, I don't believe you'd be here."

"Here? You mean in Silverdell?"

"At Bell River." She shut her eyes, letting the words free-associate, since she was far too tired to be entirely logical. "The thing is, I don't believe you're really after the money. I've spent a lot of time around people who are money crazy, and they're obnoxious. Really. Just awful. They're nothing like you."

He chuckled. "It's a lot of money, Bree."

"I know." She forced her eyes open. "But still…"

She yawned again, and her eyes insisted on shutting. "I just can't believe that's what brought you here. Not entirely, anyhow. You're here because some tiny part of you wants to fix things between the two of you."

"Nope."

"Yep." She snuggled deeper under the covers, reaching out her hand to touch his shoulder, enjoying the hot-velvet feel of his skin over the rounded muscle. She just let her palm curve around it, fitting as if it belonged there. "You know how I know?"

Almost absently, as if he, too, did it without thinking, he put his hand over hers. It felt so warm. Strong. And safe. Her body was relaxing, her mind drifting even further away on this unmoored, king-size dream craft with downy, billowing sails.

"How do you know?"

"I know," she said thickly, "because I've done the same thing. Last year I came to Bell River, and I said it was about money. About Rowena spending too much or something. But really, way down deep inside, I just wanted to be around her, because maybe then we would work it out."

"And did you?"

She laughed, realizing her example was dumb. But it was the best she could think of when she was drifting so far above the conversation, above the tent and the creek and the whole of reality, really.

"Nope. I made a giant mess of it. But that's not the point. The point is, I wouldn't have come just for the money." She squeezed his shoulder. "And neither would you."

Maybe he answered her. Maybe he told her she was dead wrong and didn't understand him one bit. But if he did, she didn't hear it. She had suddenly realized how good it would feel to let herself sink into sleep, just let it happen without a fight, and it did. It felt wonderful, the most peaceful feeling she could remember for a long, long time....

She must have slept for hours, because later, when she heard an anguished cry nearby, sounding exactly like a lost child, she woke from a very deep sleep with a start, terrified by the sound.

"It's okay." Gray's voice was soothing in the darkness. He sounded gentle, quiet, but as if he'd been wide awake the whole time. "It's just an elk."

An elk...yes, of course. How could she have forgotten that sound? She pushed her hair out of her eyes, trying to orient herself.

Sometime while she slept, she must have shifted, because she realized she was spooned against Gray, the solid wall of his torso behind her back, and his knees tucked in the hollow behind her own. His strong, warm arms were wrapped around her waist.

The elk cried out again, eerie in the deep, echoing night, which seemed to press blackly on the tent.

"It's all right," he said again. "I won't let anything hurt you."

She fuzzily considered that promise for a second or two...but not for long. On some very primitive level, she already knew it was true.

She wriggled back against him so that their bodies were a perfect fit, and not even a tiny black sliver of night could slip between them. Then she made a small, contented sound, hoping he knew it meant she believed him. It meant a lot of other things, too, but she was too blurry-minded to sort out what they were, or how to say them.

She purred one more time, tugging his arms tighter so that they encased her in warmth. And then, blanketed in bliss, she slid effortlessly back into sleep.

By Friday, she'd spent six nights with him in that big, wonderful bed. Not all of them had been as easily platonic as the first. Sometimes the comfort touches deepened, or strayed. Sometimes they kissed, because it seemed impossible not to.

Always, she felt the slow coiling of desire, low in her midsection, as her body readied itself for more. But his willpower was amazing. Though she knew he wanted her—he had no way to hide it—he never allowed either of them to reach the point of no return.

Only once did it seem that his iron control might weaken.

On Tuesday, the new guests had arrived, and she and Gray were busy in separate parts of the ranch. By the time they made it back to the tent, they were exhausted, which should have made restraint easier but didn't. Apparently it took a lot of unseen energy for him to hold the fire back.

Somehow, he held on then, too. He was just as charming, just as entertaining and intimate as ever, until it came time to actually sleep. Then he positioned himself with his back to her, a little farther over. And for the first time she didn't wake in the night to discover she'd spooned herself against him.

He hadn't been kidding when he'd said he thought they should wait. Wait for what, exactly, though? He'd said only that he had to be sure she was ready.

She had no idea how he would judge that, or whether she could make any promises. But she understood. She was, in her own quietly frigid way, still too mixed up—she could sense that he saw her as impaired. Or at least her emotions were. He wasn't the type to want to feel that he'd taken advantage. He clearly would rather not get tangled in her issues and end up feeling guilty for something that should have been purely fun.

So, though the awareness of desire was always present, he never let it get raw, or even disagreeable. It was more like a sense of always being plugged in, with the current flowing, potent, but for the moment harmless.

Sometimes a hum, a flutter, a pulsing, a warmth… but never an ache. Never pain.

The only really painful part was watching their days tick down.

On Friday, she found herself with a few free hours now that Rowena had hired more staffers. Three part-time children's counselors, half a dozen part-time wranglers and a full-time woman named Maura who would function as receptionist, reservationist and concierge had all come on board in the past few days. Maura, particularly, had been a coup. She had come out of retirement to take this job, and had decades of experience, making her easily the most useful employee in the place. Up to and including the Wright sisters themselves, who were still neophytes, and struggling to learn as they went.

Gray and Dallas were busy climbing around on scaffolding this afternoon, with hammers and nail guns and all kinds of tools they loved to play with. Rowena had accused them of being glad the contractor was running behind schedule for getting the arts and crafts building finished.

That way, he'd needed to call for help.

The upshot of all these changes was that Bree felt a little lost, as if she wasn't really needed anywhere. She wandered into Rowena and Dallas's wing and poked her head into the room they'd set up as a home office.

Rowena sat at her computer, staring at something on the screen.

"Need any help with anything?" Bree plopped herself on one of the chairs nearby. "Amazingly, I'm free until the bonfire tonight."

"No…" Rowena seemed distracted. "I'm just writing back to Bonnie. Though when, or even if, she'll check email again, there's no way to tell."

"Is she okay?"

"She says she is." Rowena chewed on her thumbnail. "I sure hope so."

Bree hadn't known Bonnie very well—she'd met her only a couple of times. Bonnie used to do some housekeeping work for Rowena, back before they decided to launch the dude ranch project. Though she'd apparently been a bit of a mystery woman, she and Rowena had become very close friends.

Some shadowy personal problem had forced Bonnie to disappear, though, right after Rowena and Dallas's wedding. Dallas's younger brother, Mitch, had gone with her, as protector and friend…and probably lover, too.

They'd been gone almost a year now, and Rowena clearly felt no closer to knowing what the problem was, or how to help her friend. Bree had seen how much it upset Ro, and she wished there was something she could do.

If only the private investigator would call with news. She tried to be patient. It had been only a few days, but maybe he'd get lucky....

"Honestly, Bree, there's no emergency right now." Rowena closed the email and seemed to make an effort to be more cheerful. "Maybe we're getting the hang of it, or maybe this group is just easier." She sighed. "Lord knows *everything's* easier without Mabel Madison around."

Bree laughed. "I'm sure Gray feels safer now that she's gone. What a holy terror! You should see the bruises on his shins."

Leaning back in her desk chair, Rowena wriggled her eyebrows as if Bree had said something dirty. "No thanks. I'll leave that to you."

Bree rolled her eyes, and Rowena chuckled, clearly enjoying herself.

"Okay, seriously, if you're feeling that you must martyr yourself, Alec will be home from school in—" Rowena glanced at her watch "—two hours. If you could keep him out of my hair while I talk to the insurance guy at three, that would be fantastic."

"Sure. I want to add a couple of tables to the Horse Tales area. I'll make him help me paint them."

"Good." Rowena picked up a stack of unopened mail. "Between now and then, why don't you use the time to get some rest?"

"I'd rather be busy." Bree grabbed a superhero figure that Alec had left on the desk and made it wave its sword at Ro. "I'm Action Brianna. And I'm not tired."

Rowena grinned. "You're not? After spending all

these nights at the tent? I'm sorry, sis, but sounds as if there's something you guys aren't doing right."

Caught by surprise, Bree felt herself flushing. Ro was joking, of course. She had no idea how close to home the joke had hit. And, while the sisters had made great strides during this long visit, Bree still wasn't ready to confide things this intimate to Rowena.

Or to anyone. She didn't know what was really happening with Gray. Their relationship, whatever it was, was fragile and utterly unique, at least in her life. She wouldn't even have known how to describe it.

Rowena didn't seem to notice Bree's hot cheeks, thank goodness. She had inserted the letter opener into the first piece of mail and slit it open. As she glanced at the letter inside, she moved on to another topic.

"Okay, well, maybe you can help me decide where to put the spa."

"Are we definitely getting a spa?"

"Yes." Rowena smiled. "We're definitely getting one *someday*. I'd love to build it as part of Phase Two, but it all depends on how much it costs. And that depends, to a large extent, on where we decide to put it. So what do you think? We've narrowed the location down to Cupcake Creek, where Gray's tent is now, and Little Bell Falls."

Bree shuddered. "Oh, not Little Bell Falls!"

"Why not?" Rowena lowered the mail to her lap. "What's wrong with Little Bell? It's beautiful out there."

"It's creepy." Bree thought about the heavily treed spot, with its horsetail waterfall appearing out of nowhere and its unnaturally round, disturbingly deep, plunge pool at the bottom. "It's too remote, anyhow.

Do you think the guests will want to make a trek like that just to get a massage?"

Rowena's brow creased. "Are you sure you're remembering the spot correctly? It's really not *that* far. And it's not a bit creepy. How long has it been since you've seen it?"

Bree tried to remember. She couldn't.

"A very long time," she admitted. "I never liked it, so I didn't go there the way you did. I bet it's been twenty years."

"Well, then." Rowena looked smug. "You clearly haven't given it a fair chance. So there you go. That's what you're going to do with your spare time."

Bree gave her sister a sour look. It was strange, because she couldn't put her finger on exactly what the problem was. But she knew from the tightness in her gut that she definitely did *not* want to go out there.

Maybe she was just partial to Cupcake Creek, for obvious reasons, and resented any other location even being considered.

"Ro, it's clear as day that you've already decided you prefer Little Bell Falls, so what's the point in my going?"

Rowena had already found one of the maps they gave arriving guests, pulled it open and had begun sketching out a special, relatively convoluted back route to get to Little Bell. The longer she had to keep sketching, the more absurd it seemed.

"Ro, look how far you're having to draw that line. That's what I mean by 'too remote.' That's what anybody would call too remote."

Rowena held out the map, and Bree saw that she was wearing her dreaded stubborn look.

In spite of her reluctance, she had to laugh. "Oh, the horrors of being the younger sister," she lamented. "You're so sure you're the boss of me."

But exactly like in the old days, Rowena was not moved. "Just check it out. It's got charm. It's got moving water, a great view of the mountains, ancient trees and absolutely everything needed to make the guests feel they've been transported to another world."

"Well, they have. You have to get a passport, two airplanes and a Native American guide merely to find your way out there."

"What on earth is *wrong* with you?" Rowena scowled. "It's gorgeous. Don't you remember the columbine everywhere? The goldeneye? The bluebells?"

That did sound familiar. Something in Bree's chest tightened at the mention of the wildflowers, but she still couldn't place any particular memory that caused such a negative reaction.

"Okay. Fine. I'll go look at it. Although you know it'll cost more to put it way out there—"

"Go," Rowena commanded. This time she had picked up the letter opener again and pointed it at Bree.

And so, out of a lifetime's habit—and a growing curiosity to find out why she had such an irrational dislike for the spot—Bree went.

Chapter 17

It took her twenty minutes to find the place. Though Ro's directions were great, she got lost twice—her subconscious still resisting the visit, perhaps?

Finally she spotted the gigantic, spreading live oak that Rowena had drawn on the map, aware, obviously, that the monstrous tree would be the most noticeable landmark for miles.

Even the tree gave Bree a chill. Something felt unnatural about a tree that had outlived several generations of Bell River owners and would undoubtedly outlive her, too. And every year it grew bigger, stretching its limbs out horizontally, and sometimes in fantastically twisted shapes, until it looked like a gigantic, deformed brown spider, crouching there by the plunge pool, waiting…for something Bree couldn't name.

The hiss of the falls bothered her, too. Partly because it sounded deliberately hostile, like the sound a snake makes to warn you to stay away. But also because the sound was so loud you just knew it might be covering other sounds.

Even more disturbing sounds.

It wasn't until she glimpsed the bluebells growing on the western edge that things began to fall into place. But the minute she saw them, she froze in her steps.

It was early for bluebells. She wasn't sure how she knew that, but she did. Bluebells weren't usually out, at least here by the falls, until mid-June, at least.

And then, as if the falls had suddenly roared to life and started racing toward her like a malevolent tidal wave, she was suddenly flooded with a memory so vivid, so powerful and so terrible...

For a minute she thought she could no longer breathe.

She felt herself going down onto her haunches, as if the pressure of it forced her toward the ground. She clutched some kind of small plant, as if it could keep her from being swallowed up by the earth, or falling off it. But the plant bent, too, crushed either by her or by the memory's dreadful weight.

She shut her eyes, spinning, dizzy. She didn't want to remember.

But she did...

She was about six. It was June. She was mad because she wanted to pick some bluebells for her dollhouse garden.

But there weren't any bluebells near the house. The only ones she'd ever seen were at Little Bell Falls.

She wasn't allowed to go that far alone, and usually that wasn't the kind of rule she ignored. She was always aware of what happened to Ro when she disobeyed an order, and it scared her. Ro didn't care, but Bree wasn't as brave as her big sister. She didn't like getting in trouble.

But today was about the tenth day in a row that her mother had hardly even come home to sleep. That wasn't fair.

So she'd saddled up Tommy, her paint, and hooked a wicker basket over the saddle horn. She needed something to carry the bluebells back in. Then she'd bumped Tommy's sides softly with her heels, and they'd cantered down to the falls.

She was only a little afraid. She didn't really think she was taking a very big chance. She didn't see how she could get caught.

She didn't have any idea where her mother was. She was too young to even consider the possibility that she *ought* to know things like that. Mom was just *Somewhere Else. Somewhere Having Fun.*

It never, ever occurred to her that *Somewhere Else* was Little Bell Falls.

Even now, more than twenty-four years later, she still had no memory, none at all, of what the man with her mother had looked like. He had been just a naked, white body without a face.

But why didn't he have a face? Had his face been obscured by a tree limb?

Even without a face, he had looked like a bad man because he was naked. Everyone, even her mother, had told her that if a man ever tried to make her look at his private parts, or touch them, he was a very bad man, and she should tell on him.

But she *couldn't* tell on him, because her mother

was naked, too. Bree had no visual memory of that, just a memory of trying to hold in her reeling mind the confusing certainty that her mother was outside where people could see her, where this naked man could see her, and she had no clothes on.

Bree was so dumb she didn't even know she should run away, quick before they saw her seeing them. She just stood there, with the small twigs at the end of the oak tree branches scratching her bare legs, and heard herself make a whimpering sound.

Rowena called it Bree's spoiled-baby sound. Bree wished she could tell Ro that this time *she* wasn't really making it. It seemed to be making itself, using her throat and voice without her permission.

Her mother must have heard it because she turned her face toward the sound. She looked mad and embarrassed, and scared, too. Like when she took a bath at home and forgot to lock the door, then jumped when Bree came in, as if it was Bree's fault she hadn't guessed her mother needed privacy.

For a minute, her mother's eyes searched the big tree. And then, when she saw Bree and their gazes locked, she seemed to go crazy, as if she was having a fit, an epileptic fit, or a conniption fit, maybe, like Ro always said people did.

Her mother began pushing at the man's chest, using the hard, bony part at the bottom of her palms. And she started this awful, embarrassing scrabbling with her feet, as if she wanted to stand, but the man's big white legs were in her way. His legs were between her legs....

Bree couldn't look at it anymore. She might be watching her mother die right this very minute, or choke, or have a heart attack, or something. And she didn't want to see the man's face, but he was getting up, getting off her mother. He was going to turn around, and then she would see everything she wasn't supposed to see....

She ran back to where Tommy was standing, quietly eating grass, not even knowing what had happened with her mother. She had started to cry, and she almost fell down when she tried to get on Tommy's back.

But she made it, because she was too afraid to fail. And when she got the reins in her hand, she dug her heels into his sides. She must have dug hard, way too hard, because he started to run. He galloped faster than she'd ever gone, faster than she was *allowed* to go.

He knew the way home, so he just ran. When he tried to jump over Cupcake Creek, she fell off. She hit her head on the bank and it hurt, a lot. She got very wet, but she didn't pass out. She just lay there, crying, in the hot June sun, until her mother, who was now dressed normally and all alone, found her there.

Her mother picked her up, kissed her and hugged her and cried a little bit, too, though she didn't mention what had happened to make them both cry. Bree knew, right then, that her mother was never going to explain.

And she didn't want Bree to ask.

When they got home, Tommy was already waiting by his stall, looking as if he felt bad for knocking her off.

Bree forgave him. She was glad Tommy was okay because that meant there was nothing that would have to be explained to Daddy. She hadn't even torn her dress.

And so no one ever mentioned it again.

* * *

She had changed, Gray thought. She looked…
somehow…indefinably…

Different.

Okay, moron. That wasn't specific enough to mean
a damn thing.

From his post by the back porch, where he handed
sing-along booklets to each person who came out, Gray
watched Bree. She moved around the bonfire, projecting almost as much warmth as the fire itself. She chatted with the guests, laughed at their jokes, squatted
reassuringly to get on level with their shy children.

But she'd always been an accomplished hostess.
That was her career. So what was actually different
about tonight?

Well, for one, she appeared more confident. Less
self-conscious, and yet at the same time more *uncon-*
sciously sensual. It was as though, for the first time in
her life, she was wearing a skin that fit.

Blue moonlight in her hair, auburn-and-pink bonfire flames reflecting against her arms, golden sweater
over her jeans…she looked like stained glass come
to life.

Real, hot-blooded life. Yes, that was the difference—he'd guessed it from the start. The difference
was the level of heat she sent out. She didn't move like
an ice princess anymore. She moved like a woman who
had fully and finally thawed.

Oh, really? How *convenient.*

Probably this was just his libido talking, doing a
masterful sales job, hoping to weasel its way around
his determination to keep from exploiting a damaged,
vulnerable woman.

Naturally, the libido had been counting the days—just as the rest of him had. Every inch of him heard the clock ticking and knew he was running out of time. Five days from today, his bet with his grandfather came to an end, and he'd be on the next plane to Monterey.

So could he trust what his so-called "instincts" were telling him? Wasn't it just a little too opportune that somehow, in the twenty-four hours between the agony he'd endured all night last night and *now,* she had somehow cast years of emotional chains aside and been born again as sexual fair game?

The last guest came down the steps, and he handed out the booklet with a sense of relief. He felt the magnetic pull of her all the way across the backyard, and it had been practically splitting his body in two.

He made his way over to her with minimal detouring—if anyone was far enough away that it was plausible he couldn't hear them over the crackle of the bonfire, he just shrugged sadly, put his hand to his ear in the universally recognized sign for "too loud" and moved on.

Even so, three people snagged him. By the time he reached her, she was sitting next to Barton, who had his guitar out and had started to play.

She smiled at him....

Come on, boss, his libido taunted, *are you imagining* that? That sock in the solar plexus? She might as well have reached out her hand, struck a match and held it to his central nervous system. He was instantly on fire.

She glanced ruefully at the seats around her, which were filling up fast. Barton, still strumming, raised one eyebrow at Gray and grinned. "If you think I'm gentleman enough to give you my seat, son, you're mistaken. You snooze, you lose."

Gray laughed, even though he didn't much feel like it. He glanced at her other side. Great. It was Alec, who had about as big a crush on Bree as Gray did, even if he had a much purer heart about it. His only dream was to buy her a horse of her own. He thought that might convince her to stay at Bell River.

Well, sure, Gray's libido observed nastily. *That's Alec's only Bree-dream because he's nine. It's easy to be pure of heart when you're nine.*

Alec scowled. "No way, Jose," he said without even waiting for Gray to say a word.

He glanced at Bree. She was laughing softly. But Gray smiled back, undaunted. He'd be darned if he was going to let an old man and a kid take his woman from him. He shrugged, as if to say "they made me do it," and then he sat in the grass right in front of her, with his back against her knees.

For a second, she seemed startled. No one else was sitting that close to the fire. He dropped his head back across her thighs and smiled at her upside down. Rowena and Dallas obviously already knew—and frankly, he didn't give a darn who else around here discovered they were a couple.

She laughed out loud, gazing down at his mischievous grin. But a second later she ran her fingers through his hair, slid them around to his ear and tugged on it gently. He had to take a deep breath. Who knew the earlobe was connected directly to the…other parts?

"Come on back here, you idiot, before you go up in smoke." She softened her legs just a little, so that he could wedge his torso between them. He was tall enough that he could rest his elbows on her kneecaps, and he did, mostly for the excuse to dangle his hands down the sides of her legs and stroke the underside of her knees with secret fingers.

He must have looked particularly comfortable and content, because, before long, husbands and wives, moms and kids, even brothers and little sisters had arranged themselves the same way. He gave Bree another upside-down smile.

"Yeah, you're a trendsetter," she said, her tone affectionately mocking. For punishment, he stroked the sensitive flesh behind her knee until, with slightly unsteady fingers, she batted his hand away.

A few minutes later, Barton launched into his signature version of "Red River Valley." The crowd stilled, listening to the elegant baritone sing the plaintive words about love and loss…about the man who was leaving the valley and the heartbroken girl who had loved him true.

Everyone knew the song, of course, so when Barton called for support, the guests responded. First just a few, the best singers who weren't afraid to stand out. Then, on the easy chorus, everyone sang along, even the children.

It should have been a mess. Gray could hear the boys whose unpredictable octave-changing squeaks announced that they'd officially hit puberty. He could hear the very old, whose sweet tones quavered. And of course the tone deaf added their own special harmonies. But in spite of all that, the effect of those gathered voices rising into the cool, crisp air was pure magic.

Three songs later, Gray eyed Barton suspiciously.

Every single tune had been sad, every one about the pain of leave-taking, the heartbreak of saying good-bye.

Was Barton trying to tell him something?

On the other hand, maybe it was Gray's own hyper-awareness of his impending departure that made the choices seem deliberate. "On Top of Old Smokey" was a pretty standard campfire song, and so was "Down in the Valley."

But then came "Shenandoah," which clearly belonged on the East Coast. And finally...

"Jamaica Farewell" at a dude ranch in southwestern Colorado? *Come on, Barton. Give a guy a break.*

When the old man caught Gray shooting him that questioning glance, he grinned, admitting everything, and obediently switched gears. "The Bear Went Over the Mountain," "Puff the Magic Dragon" and "I've Been Working on the Railroad" brought the tempo up and finally got the tears out of everyone's eyes.

But right in the middle of the laughter and fun, in response to some signal only she could hear—or some vibration only she could feel—Bree tensed, and she began digging in her jeans pocket for her phone. When she found it, she looked at the screen, then almost fell over her own feet, and Gray's, trying to extricate herself from the bench.

She managed to stay erect, and hurried away, answering as she went. "This is Bree," he heard her say in a voice as tight as a guy wire.

He got up, too. In case she needed him.

It had better not be the fish corpse calling. Not now, and not ever again. The story of harem boy's birthday-party sex scandal had seemed funny that first night because she'd told it with charm and humor. But the more Gray thought about the humiliation she must have felt, the more he wanted to see how Charlie Newmark adjusted to life as a eunuch.

He made his way across the spotlighted lawn to where Bree had found a shadowed corner in which to take the call. He made sure she saw him, for support, but then he hung back out of earshot, in case she really needed privacy.

The call didn't last long. She paced as she talked, her golden hair and golden sweater moving in and out of a shaft of moonlight like a looping dream. He tried to read her face, but all he could be sure of was that she felt tense. Whether with excitement or with anger or fear, he couldn't make out from where he stood.

Behind him, Barton had begun "Loch Lomond." More goodbye music...

Before the short, sad song was over, Bree had returned. Her eyes were shining, and his heart relaxed. Whatever it was, it was good news.

He waited, not wanting to ask. If she didn't volunteer, he'd just have to live with the question.

"That was the investigator," she said, her voice low and breathless. She glanced toward the campfire, as if she wanted to be certain Rowena was safely out of earshot.

He was surprised. That possibility hadn't occurred to him. It seemed too soon, either way. Bree had offered the man very little to work with, so definitive answers seemed unlikely after he'd worked on it less than a week. But surely no decent detective would have thrown in the towel so quickly, either.

"Oh, Gray." She clasped her elbows with her hands, as if to hold herself safely together. "He's found Rowena's father."

Bree sat in her suite until almost midnight, waiting for the guests to retire to their rooms and cottages. It took a while, because the campfire had been such fun, and because the spring weather was so lovely: no chilling wind, no rain, no frost, nothing to drive them indoors.

She'd sent Rowena a text message earlier.

Have you got a minute to spare later? I'd like to talk. Just us.

Rowena's answering text had been typically brief.

K. Front desk. Not till midnight. At least.

Trying to be patient, Bree watched from her window, holding the thick, sealed manila envelope the detective had delivered immediately after his call. She thought of Gray, waiting for her in his amber-lit tent by the creek, and hoped he understood why she had to do this first, no matter how long it took.

The parking lot, seen from her window, bustled with activity for a while, as robe-clad guests darted back out to grab the last paperback books and pill cases they'd forgotten earlier. But gradually the cottage doors stopped opening, and the area slipped into a trance, a misty film creeping across the windshields of the sleeping trucks and minivans.

One by one, the cottage lights went out. Even the

scent of the bonfire finally disappeared, though it had lingered the longest, without its usual stiff breeze to fly away on.

Surely, she told herself, the coast was clear now. The ranch seemed to have curled up on its moonlit green hills and closed its eyes for the night. Its silence was broken only by the occasional hoot of an owl, a nicker now and then from the stables and the half-heard murmur of Bell River in the distance.

Even so, she waited another half hour because Rowena had asked her to.

Midnight. At least.

At twelve-fifteen, her patience ran out. Easing her door shut behind her, she moved noiselessly down the stairs. The silence was almost eerie, actually.

Then she heard a creak just below her. The skin at the back of her neck prickled, and for the first time ever she considered the possibility that she might see her mother on these stairs, just as the housekeeper still insisted she did, every day.

If Moira Wright were ever to materialize, wouldn't it probably be now? Now, when Bree was carrying her mother's deepest secret in this envelope, prepared to deliver the truth that might finally set Rowena free?

For a chilled second, her feet stilled, and she grasped the railing for balance. She realized, with a swooping sensation of suddenly being hollowed out, that she really didn't know how her mother would feel about what she'd done.

If the ghost could appear, would she be happy? Grateful, even? Would Moira be relieved to know that Johnny Wright couldn't hurt anyone anymore? That it was safe for Rowena and her biological father to find each other at last?

Or would her spirit manifest as a nightmare, blocking Bree's passage and declaring herself betrayed? Moira had kept the secret of Ro's real paternity her entire life. She'd carried it with her, as the cliché went, to the grave. Would she consider it a sacrilege for Bree to disturb the shadows now?

Oh, for heaven's sake. Bree gripped the envelope tighter and ordered her legs to continue down the stairs. She didn't believe in ghosts. Period. She had too much respect for the dead to believe any such thing. Why would unchained spirits, who had the universe at their command, feel the slightest desire to float around earth, ringing bells and tipping tables and dispensing cryptic advice that would be mostly misinterpreted or overlooked?

She reached the bottom of the steps without incident, of course. *No ghosts.* For better or worse, the people who got left behind were on their own.

Just as she rounded the corner to the registration desk, her cell phone beeped again.

GD sprinklers busted. Meet shed instead?

That was fine with her. More privacy out there, anyhow. Though…she did wish she'd brought along a sweater. Even on gorgeous spring nights like this, sometimes the bottom fell out of the thermostat and the temperature would plummet to near freezing in the blink of an eye.

But she didn't feel like traversing those stairs again, whether it made sense or not. So she just went on outside, around the western wing of the house, and headed for the utility shed.

When she got within a few yards, she heard Rowena cursing. Her feet froze one more time, which made her smile. Truth be told, she was still far more intimidated by Ro in a mood than she ever could be by the prospect of encountering a ghost.

"What the Sam Hill is *wrong* with you?"

Oh, that's why the cussing was so loud. Bree had forgotten that the timer, and the valves, were all situated on the outside of the shed. Rowena stood just a few feet away, flashlight in one hand and a screwdriver in the other, staring at the still-locked green timer box.

"What's wrong?" Bree looked over Rowena's shoulder sympathetically.

"Everything. First the sprinklers didn't come on when they were supposed to, and now I can't even check the timer. The blasted screw is stripped."

Oddly, Ro's voice sounded almost on the edge of tears, and she smacked her screwdriver against the edge of the plastic box three times hard, not for any apparent purpose except to vent some intense frustration.

Bree wasn't sure what to make of the overreaction. This sprinkler thing wasn't likely to be a big problem—not the kind that cleaned out their cash reserves or shut down the ranch for days, anyhow. Ro handled tougher things than this without blinking, every single day.

But in the cold beam of the flashlight, which wandered around as Rowena yanked at the box and eventually ended up right in her face, Bree could see circles of exhaustion under Rowena's eyes.

Maybe, with one thing and another, Ro had just run into one problem too many.

When Bree saw her sister start to slide her nails in the groove of the timer-box door, ready to pry it open, she put her hand out. "Hey. Want me to try?"

As if Bree's question brought her to her senses, Rowena stopped. She took a deep breath. Squaring her shoulders, she slid the screwdriver into her pocket and looked over at Bree.

"No, that's all right. I'll either bust it open with my bare teeth in a minute, or I'll calm down and call someone in the morning." She smiled wanly. "You said you wanted to talk. What's up?"

For no good reason, Bree felt suddenly nervous, as if she were in fifth grade again and it was her turn to perform in the oration contest. She had a little speech ready—she'd had plenty of time, up there in her room, to think about how to deliver her news. But, as little speeches so often did, it seemed too stilted and synthetic when it came face-to-face with the moment.

"I have some news," she said. She shifted the manila envelope to get a better grip. She felt, out of nowhere, as if she might drop it.

Rowena's gaze cut briefly to the envelope. "I hope it's good news."

"Yes, it is. I mean, *I* think it is. I hope you do, too."

"We won the lottery?"

Bree smiled. "Not exactly. But it is pretty exciting, anyhow. You see, I wanted to do something, something really special, to thank you for being so nice about… about my coming here. I didn't get off to a great start, but you gave me a second chance, and I wanted you to know how much I appreciated that."

Oh, dear. She had fallen back on the little speech, and it sounded just as bogus she'd feared it would. Ro had twisted her mouth sideways and started to frown, as if she thought Bree wasn't making much sense.

So Bree tried again. "Anyhow, I know you've been so busy...so caught up with the ranch, and with starting your life with Dallas and Alec, and...well, with everything, that you've hardly had time to think about yourself."

"Don't tell me—" Rowena raised her eyebrows quizzically "—you bought me a pedicure."

Bree laughed. As if she'd ever do that. Rowena had never needed to resort to such superficial trappings of beauty. She'd laughed at the girls who thought you could hook a guy like a fish just by dangling shiny hair extensions and acrylic nails in front of his face. And even if you could, she'd pointed out, why would you want a boy dumb enough to fall for all that?

"No," Bree said. She knew that the joke was Ro's way of telling her to get to the point, so she just inhaled hard, and did so. "What I did was...well, I hired a private detective. Remember you emailed me the picture you found of Mom—the one where she's on the ski slope with Rowan?"

She waited for Rowena to agree, or to nod, or make any sign at all to indicate that she was following. But, oddly, her sister didn't say a thing. She didn't even blink.

There was nothing to do but push forward. Get to the part that qualified as good news.

"Well, I gave it to the detective, and I asked him if he thought he might be able to identify the man in the picture. He wasn't very optimistic, at first. But I got a call from him tonight. And he did it, Ro. He actually did it." She held out the envelope. "He found out who your father is. This is his report."

In the silence that followed, Bree could hear her own heart thumping. What was wrong? Why was Rowena staring at her like that? Why did her face suddenly look, not just tired, but hard?

And why didn't she accept the packet?

"I—I didn't open it, Ro. It's still sealed. I thought you should be the first one to learn whatever it is he found."

Rowena laughed at that. The sound echoed into the still night harshly, like the sound of a wild bird. Still laughing, she reached out two fingers and plucked the envelope from her sister's hands.

But she didn't even look at it. She let it hang slackly at her side, never taking her flashing green gaze from Bree.

Bree's skin went clammy with fear.

"Well, that's very generous of you," Rowena said, the wild laughter still coloring the edges of her voice, making her sound like a stranger. "It actually occurred to you that I might want to be the first to know?"

"Yes. Of course." Though she wasn't sure how it happened, Bree was suddenly teetering on conversational ice skates, sliding all over the place, unable to find traction. "I assumed that…well, of course you would."

"I see. But it *didn't* occur to you that I might like to be the one who decided *when* I should know? Or even *if* I should know?"

"*If* you should know?" Bree shook her head, bewildered. "But of course you would want to know."

"Why 'of course'?" As she moved forward into the moonlight, Rowena's green eyes gleamed like animal eyes. "Because *you* think I should? Because, as always, Bree knows best?"

Bree flinched. And then, as comprehension finally dawned, she felt a terrible sinking in her chest. Like a comic-book character with the proverbial lightbulb going on over its stupid, stupid head, she finally, belatedly understood what she had done.

Of course Rowena would see this as interference. She would see it as bossy, prissy Brianna Wright at her most controlling.

Because…*dear God*…that's exactly what it was.

"Ro, please, really. I… I guess it was dumb, but that's honestly not what I was—"

Her sister held up her hand, the one that had accepted the envelope. She glanced at it, as if surprised to discover she still had it.

"Don't bother, Bree."

She let the envelope fall. At the same instant, the angry fire in her face abruptly blinked out. It was as if the flame had been lit temporarily by a powerful spark of emotion, then guttered quickly, unable to maintain the intensity required to sustain itself.

In place of the anger, the old, exhausted look returned. Moonlight was not kind to the blue-black circles under her eyes, the white, tense skin around her nose, the jagged, too-thin cheekbones and the haggard lines around her wounded mouth.

Bree's heart ached as if someone had stepped on it with boots, twisting, to make sure it had been fully extinguished. She'd seen that beautiful, tragic face so often in her life. Even, during their lost years, in her dreams. Like a body with no protective skin, Rowena wore her pain on the surface, for everyone to see.

But this time Bree had put it there.

Like a bad joke, somewhere a mechanical click sounded, followed by a sibilant *whoosh, swish*...and then the sudden appearance of rising sprinkler heads, spraying tiny fountains of moonlit mist everywhere.

But neither of them reacted. What were a few drops of water right now? Bree couldn't tell whether Rowena even knew. She gave no sign that she felt the light spray that sparkled on her face like tears.

"You know, I really thought you'd changed," Rowena said flatly, no rise or fall in the monotone of her voice. "But you haven't. Maybe you can't. You still think you know better than everyone else, don't you? Especially me. I haven't made a decision in my entire life that you approve of."

Bree put out her hand, which had acquired a faint sheen of moisture. Her shirt had begun to grow subtly heavier on her shoulders,

"Oh, Ro, that's not true. Sometimes I've said things that I—"

But Rowena cut her off again, wearily. "You know, it doesn't really matter anymore. I've learned to get along pretty well without your approval, through the years. But you should know that this time...this time you've gone too far. This was..." Without finishing the sentence, Rowena held up the detective's report. Bree could see that Ro had squeezed the thick envelope so hard she'd torn the paper.

But that was only possible because she'd been dangling the envelope all this time right where it took a direct hit from the misting spray.

The paper was growing darker, softening, taking on a sodden, ruined look.

"Ro." Even now, Bree couldn't bear to see the treasure lost, the ink letters running together to obliterate the name. It was all she could do to refrain from reaching out and grabbing it from her sister's hand.

Rowena shook her head, slowly, as if she was too tired to do anything very fast.

"You really should have stayed out of this, Bree," she said. "It wasn't your decision to make. It was *mine*."

Chapter 18

Gray had been waiting so long, sitting on the deck with his computer propped on the arm of the chair, that he'd read all today's reports, and then caught up on all the other reports he'd been inadequately skimming for the past three weeks.

The three-ring circus that was horse breeding—foals that had been born this past January, mares that were already carrying the foals that would be born next year and the purchase of new breeding stock for future foals—generated more paperwork than anything else he'd ever done. If he wasn't a little bit crazy, and in love with every trivial detail about horses, he would have pitched the computer in the creek hours ago.

At least the work had made the time pass a little more quickly. He closed the laptop, stretched to loosen the kinks in his shoulders and then glanced at his watch. One-thirty in the morning. He stood, stretched again and decided to walk down to the water's edge to get his blood moving.

He had no intention of going to sleep. He refused to believe she wasn't coming, sooner or later.

It was one of those preternaturally quiet nights, when the wind seemed to have blown into some other corner of the world. The creek was as still as a painting of water. Even the gauzy moonlight didn't bend or refract or twinkle, as it usually did where it touched the creek's surface. It might have been a lifeless strip of silver foil bisecting a hard pane of black glass.

Lifeless. That was how he felt. Not dead, but too still. A picture of a man, a video indefinitely on pause. Waiting for Bree to arrive so that real life could begin again.

He put his hands in his pockets, trying to banish a nagging feeling that something had gone wrong. When Bree had first told him about hiring the P.I., he'd felt a twinge of foreboding.

Would Rowena really be as excited about this as Bree obviously believed she would? Would she really welcome anyone poking around in her personal business—even her own sister?

He hadn't ever known Rowena intimately, but he had one intensely vivid memory of her that made him wonder...

After Moira Wright's murder, Gray's grandfather had insisted that the two of them go to her funeral. Gray had protested vehemently. He thought the idea sucked.

He knew firsthand how much drowning people hated being patronized by people who weren't. Hated even being *looked at* by them, as if they were the two-headed boy in the circus, and the normal people could pay their fifty cents and ogle them all day.

The not-drowning people had two reactions to the drowning ones. Only two—each as loathsome as the other.

One was a lascivious curiosity. *Ooh, I wonder what that's like?* The other was a smug certainty that they'd earned their own good fortune. *Oh, thank goodness that's not me...but then, I know better than to*—insert appropriate tragedy-attracting behavior here—*at least I know better than to drive drunk. At least I know better than to marry a madman.*

He didn't fit in either category, and he didn't want the Wrights to think he did. But his grandfather had insisted, and Gray was only in ninth grade, old enough to make the battle ugly, but too young to win it. And so they went.

Sometime during the service, a woman had commented on the little sister's bloodstained dress, apparently shocked, as if Emily Post simply wouldn't approve.

Gray had felt like snorting. *Idiot.* As if Emily Post would be fine with the rest of it, with the adultery, and the murder, and the orphaned little girls...as long as the funeral clothes were clean.

Rowena must have heard the comment because, though she'd been staring down at the ground almost the entire time, she suddenly lifted her head and stared straight at the stupid woman.

Gray would truly never forget the set of that bony, Greek-tragedy face. Haughty, pointed chin and blazing eyes, lips curled with contempt, nostrils white and flaring. If looks could kill, he'd thought, and he'd liked her then. She had guts. She had pride. Too much pride, but as far as he was concerned, that was better than not enough.

Rowena seemed much happier now, mellowed by marriage and by a fulfilled life at the dude ranch. But he knew, unfortunately, that pride never really went away—it was like a river that sometimes dived underground and sometimes branched off into new directions, but rarely really disappeared for good.

He felt guilty now, wondering if he should have said something. Shared his worry that Rowena was too complicated for Bree to take any of her reactions for granted.

But Bree had been so excited, so happy to have this great surprise in the works.... He hadn't wanted to burst a single bubble that night because they had needed every one.

He turned around, scanning the trees. What was happening back at the main house?

It was almost two before he heard her footsteps on the deck. He climbed back up the creek bank and reached the tent just as she finished scanning the room, and turned around again, looking bedraggled and oddly lost.

"Oh, there you are," she said softly. Her eyes were shadowed and dark, and every inch of her body language was written in the code for pure distress. "I'm sorry... I'm sorry I'm so late."

Without a word, he crossed to her and took her in his arms. "You're here now," he said. Her shirt was wet, and so, he realized, was her hair. He pulled wet strands of the golden silk from her pale cheeks. "What happened?"

"Ro thought the sprinklers were broken," she said, apparently taking his question literally. "They came on all of a sudden, while we were standing there."

But he didn't care about the wet clothes. "I mean, what happened with Rowena?"

She looked at him, her face momentarily blank. She shook her head, but he couldn't be certain she was conscious that she did it.

"I've made such a terrible mess of it all." The expression on her face broke his heart. "I thought I had learned my lesson, but I was so wrong. She thinks I haven't changed a bit. She believes I disapprove of everything she's ever done."

"But you don't," he said.

"I know. But I keep doing things that make her feel...unloved. And now I've done it again. Why on earth did I think it was all right to meddle in anything as personal as that? Why couldn't I see that it was her life, not mine? Her father, not mine? Why didn't I respect her decision to do nothing?"

He tightened his arms around her. "Because you love her. You can't be happy unless she is."

Strange. He'd never been able to come up with a working definition of love before—probably because he hadn't ever been sure it existed anywhere on this earth, now that his parents were gone. But suddenly it seemed like the most obvious thing in the world.

"You love Rowena, and you always will. That makes her happiness your business. And you thought connecting with her real father would make her happy."

"Well, I was wrong." She tried to smile. "And I've

paid such a high price for my selfishness, Gray. I was on my last chance with her. I'd been so unforgiving for so long, so judgmental. This was my last chance to make it up to her."

"No," he said, on instinct rather than experience. He knew all too well how intractable stubborn pride could be. But not Rowena's, surely. Not to the point that she'd permanently reject her sister.

"Yes, it was," she repeated with certainty. "And I threw my last chance away because I wanted to be the hero. I wanted to be the one who showed her the right path to take."

"I don't believe that. Whatever she said tonight, Rowena loves you, too. And when you love someone, there's no such thing as a last chance. There's always one more. *Always*."

He wondered, actually, whether he really believed the corny, mawkish phrases he'd just uttered. These weren't sentiments that had ever passed his lips before.

But so what? Even if they weren't true for him, it was different for the Wright sisters. For them, it was true. They loved each other, and they *needed* each other. They'd survived the same unspeakable shipwreck, and they bore the same scars. Their psyches were littered, no...they were *mined*...with the same dangerous detritus.

No one else on this earth, except those three, could ever say, "I understand how you feel" and be telling the absolute truth.

Not even Gray.

Bree looked at him, and though he still saw worry and regret in her eyes, he didn't see...

He didn't see fear. The change he thought he noticed earlier tonight…a lifetime ago, at the campfire… was still there.

"You're a very kind man," she said thoughtfully.

He shook his head vehemently. He would walk out of this tent, this ranch, this city, this state, in only four days. He'd be leaving her behind, collateral damage in the mindless determination to escape his grandfather—and his memories.

And he wasn't even going to try to stop himself.

"I'll be gone in four days, Bree. You know damn well I'm anything but kind."

"You've been very kind to me. These past few weeks…your patience, and your friendship, and your faith in me…" She blinked, and swallowed hard. "It gave me the courage I badly needed, courage to face some old demons. And I did. Thanks to you, I did."

He frowned. "Don't be ridiculous. Your courage has been with you all your life. What you've been through would have broken most people. But it didn't break you. It didn't even make you hard, or selfish, or cruel. I wish I could say as much for myself."

She smiled up at him. "Maybe I should say it for you. You're a very kind man, Gray Harper."

"And you're amazing, Brianna Wright." He meant to be sincere but lighthearted as they exchanged compliments. Instead, his voice sounded oddly thick. Why did this feel as if they were already saying goodbye? He had four more days…. "You're amazing, and beautiful, and good. Don't you ever lose track of that."

For a minute, she just let her head come to rest against his chest. Her ear was pressed against his heart, and he wondered if she could hear what the erratic beat was saying.

Then she lifted her head. Her clear blue eyes searched his.

"Will you please make love to me, Gray? I think it's time. I think we've waited long enough."

For a minute he could hardly speak. He burned, instantly, but he had trained himself not to feel it. He was terrified to let go of that control. It had been so difficult to achieve and, once peeled away, he knew he'd never be able to get it back.

"Bree." He met her searching gaze. "Is that really what you want?"

"What I want, and what I need." She took a deep breath. "I'm ready, Gray. I've learned a lot about myself today. Some of it was very hard, and some of it breaks my heart. But none of it changes the fact that I want you. I want to be in your arms when I finally... stop being afraid."

He tried to find his moral compass...he tried to find true north, where honesty stood out clearly from lies and wrong never could pass for right....

Where was it? Where was the line he mustn't cross? He had seen it so clearly just yesterday. He'd seen it in her sad eyes, her anxious smiles. But tonight the line seemed to be moving, shifting, evaporating beneath this new confidence he felt in her.

She was even more erotic now, with this new light in her eyes, this new certainty in her voice, than she had ever been, even that first night, when he had turned to putty in her hands.

Even more beautiful, even more impossible to resist. He had to breathe shallowly because even deep movements of his diaphragm put pressure in places that were already about to explode.

"If you're just upset about Rowena…if you're just dreading being alone…"

"I'm not. I am upset about her. And I do dread being alone. But that's not why I want to make love to you."

"You don't have to do this. You don't have to do anything. You know that, don't you?" He touched her face. "I'm here, if you want me here. There's no price to be paid for that."

She groaned, tilting her cheek into his hand to deepen the touch.

"Gray," she said, her voice tight, thready with her rapid breaths that exhaled warmly against his palm. "Gray, please. Stop talking and make love to me."

After that, it was too late. He couldn't have stopped himself from touching her unless he'd been ready to stop his own heart from beating. He kissed her first, but she had no patience, and her hands went everywhere. Their mouths clung, but the mad rush to discard clothes, to reveal and discover and explore every inch of naked skin, made the kiss loud with panting and laughter, all probing, primitive wetness and heat.

They fell onto the bed, giddy, needing air but unwilling to part long enough to breathe. She tried to touch him, but he couldn't have survived it, so he laid her back against the pillows and used everything he possessed to make sure she was far too distracted to try again.

He used his lips, his tongue, his fingers, his voice. He even trailed his hair across her breasts until she cried out, begging for something firmer, something hotter. He suckled her till she was pebbled and panting, and then he let the wetness grow cold before closing over her again with a heat that shocked and made her arc upward in small jerks of uncontrollable fire.

He kept her loud, rewarding every cry, every whimper, every groan that proved she wasn't holding back a thing. He made her laugh even while she screamed. He made her tell him what she wanted, and then he gave it to her, and more, too.

Finally, because he couldn't wait any longer, he slipped his hand between her legs, and then the shock was his. She was open and ready, desperate with pulsing moisture, moaning with swollen heat.

"It's going to be wonderful," he whispered. "It's going to be as beautiful as you are."

She twisted under his hand, and he smiled, feeling that tiny, half-bursting, delicately engorged pearl trying to throb itself into his hand, where it might find release. He carefully folded back the skin in which it was nestled, like pink petals opening around a treasured seed.

He placed his hands under her hips so that she was cantilevered against them, her pelvis tilting up just enough for him to see clearly the damply throbbing spot he'd laid bare to the moonlight.

Later, he thought as he lowered his hungry mouth to the spot. Later, they would start again, and he would fill her body with his body, her heart with his heart.

But right now, he was going to give her the crazed, spinning bliss she'd been waiting for for so long. He lowered his head, took the pearl gently, so gently, between his lips and pressed his tongue against her.

Just the warm tip of his tongue, burrowing into the secret, pink and painfully erect nub. She whimpered once, a shocked and helpless sound.

And then, nothing, nothing could have stopped what followed.

She was half-mad with it, writhing, her limbs jerking and breaking out in cascades of rippling shivers. Between his lips, a series of endlessly contracting spasms pulsated against his tongue.

When she started to calm, he started again, catching her unguarded, and the pulsing never fully stopped between one orgasm and the next. She cried out, over and over, sometimes his name, and sometimes just animal vocalizations of release. Her buttocks bucked against his hands, her legs wrapped themselves around his shoulders and her hands tugged frantically at his hair, until finally her muscles gave out, the shivering ebbed and her head fell back limply against the pillow.

Later, he thought, laying his cheek against her satin thigh. Later, they would start again.

When she woke, she woke him, too, and this time she made love to him, just as she'd wanted to do that first night.

And with all the times after that, they eventually lost track of whose turn it was, until it was just bodies, and sensations, and joy.

Around the time she felt dawn stirring the shadows with its golden fingers, she knew she couldn't stay awake a minute more, not even to feel his magic hands on her skin.

At the moment, he lay across the bed, glorious in his nakedness, his head against her belly. She touched his hair and wished that she could tell him how beautiful this night had been. If she never made love again in her life, she would live a fully satisfied woman.

But she was too tired for words. She tugged tenderly on his hair, trying to urge him up to his own pillow. He must be tired, too.

He came, understanding her unspoken signals so well—as he had done all this marvelous night. He kissed her once, softly on the lips, and then he lay on his side, watching her as she drifted into sleep.

She smiled. She wanted to tell him he could sleep, too. He needed rest, and there were no more monsters to guard her from. But she couldn't think of those words, either.

Finally, she just whispered, "I love you, Gray," through her half-sleeping lips.

She felt his hand go very still against her breast. Forcing her eyes open just enough to see his profile in the gloamy dawn, she smiled.

His eyes were wide and very dark.

Oh, dear, she thought, although she couldn't really find any true sense of alarm. She knew what he must be thinking. He was afraid she was trying to hold on to him. He thought she was clinging…trying to make him feel so guilty, perhaps, that he would stay?

She could fix it. In the morning, she told herself, she would explain. She knew he would leave in four days, and she had always known it. She regretted nothing. She would change nothing.

She loved him, that was all. In the morning, she'd explain that the declaration didn't come attached to strings. She could make him understand.

Several hours later, when her cell-phone alarm finally did rouse her from the half-drugged, blissful slumber, she raised up on one elbow.

Something was different. Blinking to clear her tired

eyes, she slowly scanned the strangely empty, brightly sunlit tent.

Birds were singing outside, and the creek was luffing in a fresh morning breeze. Between them, they filled the tent with music. But other than that, and the luxury furnishings provided by Barton James—and of course Bree herself—the tent was empty.

Gray's things were gone. All of them.

His computer and papers and phone were gone. All of them.

His clothes, his coat, his watch and shoes were gone, too. All of them.

One last hope crossed her mind. Perhaps he'd left a note. He might have been called to his grandfather's hospital room, or…

She raised up again, checking the chair, the desk, the little wooden platform on which his suitcase had once been stored. The surfaces were bare. All of them.

Then she saw the note lying across his pillow. She picked it up, registering that her fingers felt cold and a little numb. His handwriting was bold and black against the pure white.

It was perfect. And so are you. Never forget that.

Never? She stared at the black masculine slashes. It wasn't a cruel note. It obviously had been meant as a kindness, a touch of soothing ointment to put over whatever wound his departure might leave behind.

Never was the word she hated, the word that told her exactly how long he would be gone. Never was such a vast, echoing word. Such a final word.

Never meant forever.

She dropped back against the pillow, holding the sheet to her naked breast and trying to understand.

Last night she told him that she loved him. And now, this morning...

Gray Harper, who would have been a millionaire in four short days, was gone. All of him.

Chapter 19

She was scheduled to lead the Saturday-Morning Horse Tales, so thankfully she didn't have time to brood. She'd slept till the last minute—she hated to think what would have happened if she didn't have a strict habit of always setting her own alarm, never relying on anyone else to wake her. She barely had time to grab a shower and still make it to the old barn by ten.

The hour didn't go quite as well as last week's, but what else could she have expected? Last week, she'd felt so at home here, growing more relaxed around Rowena every day, and excited at the possibility of seeing Gray again that night. She'd been brimming with enthusiasm, delighted by the children and turning over a hundred ideas to make everything better.

Yeah. Great ideas, like hiring a private investigator to poke around in Rowena's personal affairs—then taking the information and offering it to her sister, gift-wrapped, and expecting a pat on the head.

What a difference a week made!

Today, Gray was gone with no goodbye. She had taken two giant steps backward with Rowena, if she hadn't destroyed their chances altogether.

And she felt like a hopeless interloper at Bell River. Or, even worse, she felt like the disagreeable relative who had invited herself over, and who was barely endured out of duty until she finally got the hint and took herself home in a huff.

Small wonder she was a little short on the enthusiasm and delight.

Still, she tried not to let the children notice, and she was relieved when, the hour over, Rose showed up to escort the kids to their next adventure. Today, they'd go bird-watching.

She was moving systematically through her cleanup routine, had just shelved the books and dragged out the cushion cleansers, when a long, lean shadow moved into the rectangle of sunlight formed by the open barn doors.

Her heart skipped a beat. That was Gray's outline, right down to the wave of hair that lifted up with the hint of a cowlick at the hairline, then tumbled sweetly back down onto his forehead.

"Well? Is it true?" The shadow entered the barn, and the movement alone told her it wasn't Gray. Her heart slumped back into its previous sluggish pace. It was Gray's autocratic grandfather, leaning heavily on his cane and scowling down his aristocratic nose. "Is it true that he's run away?"

She spritzed cleanser on the first cushion and began

wiping it down with rougher strokes than usual. The old man really got under her skin.

"Gray is a grown man, Mr. Harper, so he doesn't have to 'run away' from anything. He leaves however and whenever he chooses. But if you're asking whether he's gone, the answer is yes."

She finished the cushion, tossed it in the pile and began another, all without meeting the old man's gaze.

He made a small, disdainful sound. "So. He left you, too. I wonder why."

And he'd just have to go on wondering. Bree certainly wasn't going to indulge in a cozy little sit-down so that she could fill him in. Besides, surely he knew better than anyone why his grandson didn't want to spend an extra minute in Silverdell.

"It's usually a matter of his having been asked to do something boring," he said sarcastically. "Like real work. I gather he's commitment-phobic, as well, though. I hear that no one woman has ever lasted a full month with him, so don't take it personally, Ms. Wright."

She set her bottle, rag and gloves on the table. Then she walked right up to the old guy and stood toe to toe with him. He had really, really picked the wrong day.

"I'll tell you what I take personally, Mr. Harper. I take it personally when I tell you not to set foot on Bell River land, but you decide to ignore me."

He smiled, and she had to steel herself not to see echoes of Gray. "I didn't ignore you," he explained reasonably. "I overruled you in an emergency. There's a difference."

"Not much," she countered. "But if you'll excuse me, I'm expected in the kitchen."

"No, you're not." He smiled again. "I was just in the kitchen, talking to your lovely brother-in-law, Sheriff Garwood. We're old friends. He told me you were probably out here, and that you'd have an hour or two before your next scheduled session."

She started to flush, but forced herself not to. "My excuse about the kitchen was a conversational nicety, Mr. Harper. Like when the person you're talking on the phone to says, 'well, I won't keep you.' You're not supposed to believe it's true. You're supposed to understand you've been politely disposed of. I told you that last time you came around that I wouldn't listen to you denigrate Gray. I won't listen now, either."

Harper's face darkened, and she was reminded uncomfortably that he had been in the hospital only yesterday.

"No? Are you really still determined to defend him? Even after he *disposed of* you, too? Even though he clearly played you for a fool every bit as much as he played me?"

Bree clenched her jaw. She wasn't going to let this angry old man draw her into a fight. He clearly needed someone to agree that Gray was an evil, selfish bastard, and thought that maybe the woman who had been left behind might be in the mood for a little fickle-lover bashing.

But he was dead wrong.

"I regret nothing about my friendship with your grandson, Mr. Harper." She held her chin high. "*Nothing*. Gray is a remarkable man. In fact, I would go so far as to say he's amazing. I'm even more impressed now, because I can see that he had to develop his integrity on his own, without any role model to follow."

"Amazing?" The furrowed face drew back slightly, incredulous. *"Integrity?* I would laugh if it weren't so pitiful. I know you've been sleeping in that ridiculous tent with him, but still…sex is one thing. This misguided loyalty is another." He shook his head, as if she'd disappointed him. "I wouldn't have thought you'd be so easy to dupe, Ms. Wright."

She returned his gaze icily. Obviously, he was trying to sting her, and was waiting for her to squeal. She wouldn't give him the satisfaction.

He tried again. "I don't know how you feel about my grandson, Ms. Wright, but you need to understand this. He doesn't know how to care about anyone. Maybe it isn't his fault. Things happened to him when he was very young, and those things may have damaged him beyond repair. But please. Don't romanticize him. He is far from amazing, I assure you."

She gave the old man a hard, level look. "So *that's* where he gets those ideas about himself."

He frowned. "What are you talking about?"

"He says those same things about himself. Apparently, you've taught him well. But maybe you need to ask yourself how well you really know your grandson anymore, Mr. Harper. Ask yourself why you think he's incapable of love. Is it simply because he doesn't love *you?"*

He banged his cane on the ground, an imperial gesture, as if to command that she watch her tone. But the barn floor muffled the sound, and his action had no power here.

"Here's one important difference between you and me," she went on. "When my relationships don't work out, I'm learning to take responsibility for my part in the failure. If I love someone, but they don't love me back, I won't any longer automatically assume it's because they're bad people, or because they don't know how to love."

"If you love someone?" Harper slumped suddenly, bending over his cane as if the effort to hold himself upright was too great. "*Love?* Damn that selfish boy. It went that far? He made you fall in *love* with him?"

The truth was, when she spoke she hadn't been thinking only about Gray. She'd also been thinking of Rowena, and her mother, and maybe even her father, too. She'd been thinking about all kinds of love, and all kinds of heartache.

And what it took to make a relationship last over the long haul. For the first time in her life, she felt she was beginning to understand how much work went into that.

It took the courage to face life squarely, not to run away when it got scary, not to dodge hurtful truths or deny even the memory of old traumas. It took honesty and self-awareness and the ability to live with uncertainty and risk.

But most of all, it took mercy and compassion. You had to be willing to forgive the people who hurt you, and, even more challenging, you had to be willing to forgive yourself.

Even in his eighties, old Mr. Harper clearly hadn't yet been able to do any of that. She wished she could make him see how impossible it would be for him to bring about any real changes when he wouldn't admit that he might be part of the problem. She'd been stuck in that rut for far too long.

"*Made* me fall in love?" She shook her head sadly. "I think you're still missing the point."

"Is that so? And what would the point be?"

"Love can't be mandated. It has to be earned. In a hundred ways, Gray earned mine. If I didn't earn his, then I just have to live with that. Maybe I can even learn from it. But if I lash out, if I try to ease my pain by blaming him and trying to devalue him…"

She stared at Harper intently, wondering if any of this was getting through. She hoped so. She had suddenly glimpsed, with a raw clarity, exactly how much agony, loneliness and guilt lay beneath his surface fury.

Just as fear and insecurity had always lurked below her own judgmental, icy crust.

"Then can't you see, Mr. Harper? Lashing out doesn't make him change his mind and decide he ought to love me after all. All it does is prove how right he was to walk away."

Apparently, Gray had somehow notified Rowena that he was quitting, because when Bree hustled out to referee the after-lunch horseshoe contest that should have been his task, it was already covered.

Arkansas Muldoon, one of the older men who had signed on as part-time waitstaff, had already been drafted to fill in for Gray.

Actually, she was relieved. Most important, if Rowena already knew, at least Bree didn't have to break the news.

But she was also relieved because, while horseshoes ought to be a sleepy time-waster, around here it got surprisingly competitive. The last set of guests had nearly come to blows once over a fine point in the rules—a problem that Arkansas, a six-foot-three former NFL quarterback, would be far better qualified to squelch.

She thanked Arkansas for helping, then glanced up toward the house. The back-porch swing and wooden rocking chairs were all swaying under the weight of a dozen or more guests who'd gathered to watch and cheer.

"You don't happen to know where Rowena is, do you?"

Arkansas stared at his stopwatch, obviously having been warned about how seriously the thirty-second tossing rule was enforced by the players. "No, sorry. She's gone, I know that. I saw her drive off in the car."

"Foot foul!" Ethan Shipley stood beside his opponent, sweet, freckle-faced Chad Bartlett, who was Dallas's deputy and an overall good guy. Shipley thrust out his arm, finger pointing at the ground as dramatically as if he needed to make the gesture visible for a worldwide television audience, like a football referee. "Dead shoe!"

Chad backed up, eyeing Shipley as if he were a volcano about to erupt, and extended a conciliatory hand.

"No problem," he said, stepping off his pitching platform. "It's all yours."

A few catcalls from the audience on the porch seemed to indicate the foul wasn't quite that cut-and-dried. Though Bree had been going to ask Arkansas about Dallas's whereabouts next, she saw that this wasn't the right time to distract him. She smiled to let him know she understood.

He winked back before jogging over to the contestants. "Now, boys, let's take this slow..."

With a little help from Barton, she finally found Dallas out in the east field, a chain saw on the ground beside him and a sawhorse beside that. Sometime over the past few days, a large oak limb had fallen, crushing several feet of paddock fencing. He'd clearly been working on the repair a long time, judging from the sweat around his T-shirt and the wood chips in his hair.

She'd brought out a bottled water, which he took gratefully. "Sorry to interrupt," she said.

He laughed. "Interrupt away." He drank half the bottle in one swig. "In fact, if you could manufacture a bank robbery or something requiring the sheriff's immediate presence in town, I'd be seriously in your debt."

"I'll work on that." She smiled. "I was just wondering if you knew when Ro would be back."

"No. Sorry. I've been out here all day. I know yesterday she talked about picking up some light fixtures for the arts building." He took another drink, then bent to set the bottle on the grass. As he did, he glanced up at her thoughtfully. "But today the errand didn't seem high on her list. She acted a little down. I take it you guys haven't patched things up yet?"

Bree shook her head. "No. That's why I wanted to find her. But to tell you the truth, I don't think she's all that interested in patching things up."

"Sure she is."

Bree raised an eyebrow. "You didn't hear her last night. She was furious."

"Still. I know Rowena. She wants to make up,

all right. She's just not very good at *admitting* she wants it."

Bree hoped he was right. "I'm not sure what she's told you about it, but I want you to know I meant well when I asked for the search. I see now how dumb it was, but I got caught up in the excitement of surprising her. I hadn't even considered the possibility she might not want to know. I thought that, especially if there was a baby on the way…"

Dallas put one hand on the sawhorse and wiped his brow with the other.

"About that," he said quietly. "Since you asked me before, you should know. There's not."

She blinked. She heard him, but the news didn't really sink in, not in the first instant. "There's no baby?"

"No." He shook his head, as if the fact needed corroborating. "She just found out for sure—which is probably why her emotions are so intense right now. I think she was hoping. Entertaining the possibility. Just as you and I were."

"Does she know that I—?"

"Of course not." He smiled, but it was a poignant smile…a rarity for this sunny man. "You know how proud she is. She wouldn't want anyone to think she wanted something she can't have."

"Can't have?" Bree's heart thumped. "Is there any reason to believe she can't….?"

"Of course not. Not in real-world facts. But in Rowena-world fears…" He let that dwindle off.

Bree understood. "She hasn't ever really believed she deserves to be happy. And she's so ridiculously contented now, with you and Alec, and the ranch. So I guess she's always waiting for the other shoe to drop."

"Exactly." He hesitated a second, absently brushing sawdust from his forearms. Then he seemed to decide to simply say what was on his mind. "I hope you understand that her anger about what you did…well, it has very little to do with you, or anything you supposedly did wrong."

"Of course it does." Bree appreciated the effort to console her, but she wanted to be honest with herself. "I shouldn't have interfered. It's a lesson I'm having a hard time learning. I'm not very good at accepting people as they are and not trying to change them."

"Well, that's for you to say, I guess." He smiled again. "But you should remember that Rowena's fear of rejection runs deep. She's spent a lifetime trying to beat other people to it—rejecting them before they can reject her."

Bree nodded. "Our father… I mean, Johnny…"

"Yeah." Dallas's face darkened. "I sure would have liked just five minutes alone in a room with that bastard." Then one side of his mouth ticked up wryly. "But she doesn't need me to do her dirty work. Now that she knows the truth, she could handle it with her own five minutes."

"True." Bree had to chuckle. Ro wouldn't have laid a finger on Johnny, but she'd have flayed his skin right off his body anyhow, using only her whips of words. "That's why I felt so sure that, if she could connect with her *real* father, she'd jump at the chance. To have him accept her, show that he wants her, after all those years of—"

"But what if he didn't?"

Bree frowned at Dallas's quiet interjection. "Didn't what?"

"Didn't want her. Didn't accept her."

"Oh."

The simple sentences opened up a void at Bree's feet, as if the ground she'd thought she was standing on had been merely a clever illusion. She wondered, suddenly, if this was how Rowena had felt when she learned her whole childhood had been a lie.

"But he would want her. Of course he would." Her mind backed away from the emptiness instinctively, as if she were scrabbling back from a near fall off a high cliff. "It's obvious our mother never told him. He never even knew he had a child—"

"I agree," Dallas said mildly. "But it's not enough for *us* to be sure. She isn't. And, after a lifetime of rejection, can't you see how terrifying it is to risk facing another one? And this time it wouldn't be from an angry bully who resented having been tricked into accepting another man's child as his. It wouldn't be from a madman with a brain tumor scrambling his judgment. It would be from her own flesh and blood."

Of course Bree could see. Terrifying, indeed. She shivered, in spite of how balmy the spring afternoon was and how brightly the sun was shining on the green pasture, picking out the pink-and-yellow wildflowers that had sprouted up as May wore on.

"In spite of that, I still believe she'll come around eventually." His voice was low and thoughtful. He, too, gazed into the middle distance, as if the peaceful day bolstered his optimism. "She's not the type to run scared forever."

Bree smiled. Once more, she felt a twinge of envy that her sister had found such a wonderful life partner who saw her clearly and cherished everything he saw.

She wondered whether any miracle like that could possibly be waiting around some corner in her own life.

Or whether she'd just met her miracle. And lost him.

"How about you?" Dallas tilted his head, suddenly, surprising Bree by looking at her with a quiet intensity, almost as if he knew the direction her thoughts had taken. "It's been a rough couple days, hasn't it? First Ro losing her cool, and then…"

She flushed.

"I heard about Gray." Dallas shrugged, as if that was enough to say. "Are you doing okay?"

She thought of the anchor that seemed to have been hooked to her heart, making it ride low and heavy in her chest.

"I'm fine," she lied. Then she scrunched up one corner of her mouth and decided to be honest. "Or I will be, soon enough. He never pretended he was going to stay when his four weeks were up, so I don't have any complaints. I may not be as tough as Rowena, but I'm not likely to curl up and die just because he left a few days early."

He nodded. "Yeah. That's what I thought. You Wright sisters are a mighty formidable posse." He picked up the chain saw, smiling at her over its big chain of metal teeth. "If you ask me, Gray Harper is a damn fool. And if I ever see him again, I'll be happy to tell him so."

Chapter 20

Bree didn't think of herself as a woman who operated on instinct much of the time. She'd always been too walled off, too frozen inside, maybe, for instincts to stand a chance.

But today, her gut was making itself heard in no uncertain terms. She wanted to find Rowena, and her gut said that Silverdell Memorial Cemetery was the place. Bree hadn't visited in years, but she had heard Ro make a few comments—about reminding the city to keep the grass mowed or the litter collected—that indicated she no longer avoided the site.

Set out of town by a few miles, and a long hike up into the ponderosa pines of Sterling Peak, the cemetery had been around at least a hundred years. Up high, angels and lambs and clasped hands made of marble joined with heartbreaking verses to memorialize the dead. But as the plots moved down the hill, the dates grew more recent and the tombstones simpler.

"Moira Wright, beloved mother" was among the newer graves. But no longer the newest, Bree noticed as she parked her car—right next to Rowena's.

This once, her gut had been telling the truth.

She opened her door and got out, glad she'd tied her hair back in a ponytail. Up here, the wind blew stronger, bending the heads of purple asters and yellow potentilla bushes—and even ruffling the bouquets of plastic flowers that were slowly fading under the hot spring sun.

She could see Rowena sitting on the small marble bench that overlooked Moira's grave. The detective's manila envelope lay in her lap. It had dried since the sprinkler's soaking last night and once again shone gold in the sunlight.

For a minute, Bree couldn't force herself to go any farther. Her feet simply wouldn't start walking. The last time she and Rowena had been here together had been the day of the funeral. Penny had swayed groggily between them, her brown eyes wide and uncomprehending. Drugged by the doctor almost into catatonia, she still had refused to remove her party dress, with its terrible red trimming of blood.

That was the last time they had been safe inside their sisterhood. Bree's eyes stung, remembering.

Why had the grown-ups, with their unassailable "logic," decided to split them up? They had needed each other—desperately. They had needed the security of knowing that this one bond, at least, had not and could not be broken.

They would have been better off begging crumbs

from neighbors until Rowena or Bree, or both, had been old enough to get jobs and take care of Penny.

Together, they might have been able to survive intact. But once they'd been so clumsily separated, like conjoined souls subjected to a botched amputation, they'd been forever deformed.

Somehow, Bree had to find the words to make Rowena forgive her so that they could work toward becoming whole again.

But what if it really was too late?

Rowena had obviously come here to commune with her mother, to ask her what she should do about the man whose name lay in the envelope. And maybe Moira would give her an answer. She and her firstborn had always been so close.

For the first time, no pang of envy pinched Bree's chest when she remembered how forgotten she'd always felt. Everyone had paired up so neatly. Moira and Rowena. Penny and their father. But Brianna stood alone.

She'd always understood that their father preferred Penny because she was no threat, always gentle, always the peacemaker. But now, finally, Bree also understood why her mother's obsession with Rowena had been so absolute.

Moira had wrapped her heart around Rowena like a bandage, trying to protect her from Johnny, trying to make up for the father, the real father, she'd never allowed her daughter to know. That didn't mean she didn't love her other daughters, too. It meant only that she felt she had injured her eldest daughter and wanted to set things right.

Oh, Mom, she thought with a piercing pity. *You must*

have been so lost. I'm lost now, too. Please help me find the words. Please help me get this right.

The wind picked up suddenly, and it seemed to carry a whisper on its back. A woman's voice, as gentle as a cool palm on Bree's hot forehead.

Don't be afraid, Brianna. I love you very much.

Startled, Bree glanced around, her heart racing even as she felt incredibly foolish. She knew full well the words weren't real, couldn't be real. It had sounded like her mother's voice. But of course she was alone, except for Rowena, who, fifty yards away, had not moved a muscle since Bree arrived.

It must have been the wind breathing in the pines, or sighing across the old mining scars that mottled the sloping hillside.

Or the overwrought nerves in her own psyche, thrumming in response to her thoughts, summoning up the words she wanted to hear. An auditory hallucination.

Or, more simply put, a plain, vanilla case of wishful thinking.

But whatever the source, the sound had relaxed the anxious place inside her and thawed her fear-frozen feet. The tall iron gates were never locked, so Bree simply walked in.

Though tall, still-unmowed grasses muffled her steps, Rowena must have heard something. When she was within a few gravestones of her sister, Rowena turned.

Her green eyes sparkled with tears. But when she recognized her sister, she smiled, like sunshine breaking through clouds. She smiled as though she'd just received the answer to a prayer.

"Oh, Bree," she said, her voice trembling with intensity. "Can you ever forgive me? I've been such a terrible fool."

By Thursday, everything was falling into place so well that Bree sometimes caught herself playfully indulging the fantasy that some supernatural hand really might be directing the sails of her life after all.

Isamar, the housekeeper who had continued to see ghosts for the past month, assured her that Moira's spirit was still smiling. But then Rowena reported that Isamar also occasionally "saw" the ghost of Pippi Longstocking, and no one could convince her that the little girl was a fictional character and thus really didn't qualify to haunt anyone.

Okay, so Isamar was a little teched, as the other maids said, on the subject of the paranormal. It didn't matter. Bree knew that her "supernatural hand" idea was just a lovely piece of make-believe, but it made her smile all the same.

That day in the cemetery, Rowena had asked her to stay at Bell River permanently, either as the social director or just as family. She didn't want them ever to be separated by so many miles again.

Though the offer was a dream come true, Bree had briefly asked herself whether the memories—both of the family tragedy and of the joyous days with Gray— would be too difficult to live with.

Very briefly.

Ten seconds later, she'd accepted Rowena's offer, hugging her sister and laughing, with waves of joy washing through her. She wanted the social director job. She loved the work, as she hadn't loved her event planning business in a long, long time.

She and Rowena, Dallas and an ecstatic Alec—with Trouble, of course, putting his two cents in occasionally—had held a family meeting and worked it all out. River Moon would be her personal cottage—Rowena had to admit that, subconsciously at least, she'd designed that cottage as a home for Bree all along.

Now they were all hip deep in plans for the summer season, which would open in just a week. June first to September first, seven-night minimum…and they already had enough bookings to make payroll, which amazed and thrilled them. Not to mention how much it thrilled the bank that had said yes to the business loan in the first place.

The soft opening had generated so much goodwill— all that word-of-mouth publicity had more than paid for itself. Bree thought about calling Georgia Brooke and apologizing for being such a judgmental grouch that first day. Two-hundred-dollar banner? She would gladly have doubled that, now that she knew how all-important the good first impression had been.

Rowena was still not ready to open that envelope from the detective, but as she had sat on the marble bench in the cemetery that day, explaining why she needed more time to think, Bree had not uttered a single syllable of protest. She still hadn't. It was Rowena's life, and Rowena alone would decide when, or if, she was ready to reach out to her father.

Amid all these gifts, there was only one dark spot left in her heart. Bree actually felt a little spoiled, a bit childish and ungrateful, to realize that she still wasn't completely happy.

Though she knew it was pointless, she still carried the anchor of Gray's memory hooked to her heart. She still dreamed of him at night—and saw his shadow fall in every sunlit doorway, always throwing itself between her and the perfect joy she knew she should be feeling.

Once she would have said it was impossible to fall in love in four weeks. Now she knew she'd fallen in love with him the first day. The moment he touched her shoulders and turned her toward the creek so that she could watch the otters playing in the water, her body and her heart had belonged to him.

The fact that he clearly didn't want them was apparently irrelevant.

She tried to be mature. *Patience,* she told herself. Time really did heal things that seemed irreparable. A year ago, she wouldn't have believed she and Rowena could be so close...and yet they had found their way back to each other.

Once she would have said she could never live in Bell River again. She would have said that no one could live in this doomed structure and be happy.

And yet here she was, feeling *home* again for the first time in sixteen years.

Someday, she'd think of Gray without heartache. Someday, she would stop feeling a burst of painful electricity through her nerves whenever she saw a long, lean cowboy walk down Elk Avenue, or watched a brunet wrangler saunter into the barn.

Someday. But not today.

Today, she was interviewing for the position of assistant social director, and every single candidate fell short, simply because they weren't Gray. They didn't have his laughing eyes, or his teasing voice, his soft brown hair, strong hands, easy grace and smoldering…

Oh. Groaning at the flame of longing that burned rapidly through her, from chest to pelvis, she put her head in her hands. She had to stop this. She was going to make herself ill.

She sat like that for several minutes, trying to collect herself. Her new office had been carved out of a back room in the recently completed arts-and-crafts building, and it smelled of new paint and unpacked boxes.

She didn't have a lot of furniture yet. Just a desk, a chair, a computer and a lot of empty filing cabinets waiting to be stuffed with the mounds of documents, contracts, bills of lading, applications and correspondence that now stood in two-foot piles all over the room.

Just thinking about the mess made her head feel heavier, and she kept it in her hands. It was ironic, really. She dared to be picky about her job candidates? What a joke! The applicants probably got one look at this mess and decided she'd be a hellish, disorganized boss, impossible to work for and chronically unprepared.

Not to mention a little scatty. Sometimes, when one of Bell River's taller cowboys passed the window, she'd get a far-off look in her eye, and it would take three tries to make her focus on the interview again.

So, who was next…? She couldn't face shuffling through the papers to figure it out. She rubbed her eyes with the heels of her hands and tried to remember. She'd seen three…no, four…

"Ms. Wright? I'm here about the position?"

Great. Now she'd been caught half napping, or whatever you called it when you daydreamed about having the best sex you'd ever dreamed of having... but never would again.

She sat up with a smile, trying to look bright-faced and professional.

And found herself looking into the laughing hazel eyes of Grayson Harper the Third.

He stood in front of her desk, dressed in denim jeans and a white dress shirt, with his cowboy hat held in front of him, two-handed and humble.

But his grin wasn't humble. His grin was all Gray.

"I've come about the position?"

Without the anchor to hold it down, her heart felt as if it was trying to lift its way out of her chest. She held it in with deep, careful breaths.

"I'm afraid I don't have you on my calendar." She moved papers around blindly, just for show. "Perhaps we should start with...um...what position, exactly, are you applying for?"

He tilted his head. "Well, that depends, I guess, on what you're looking for. Because whatever that is, that's the one I want."

So he had come intending to be charming. She bought time by looking at the papers again, though she barely registered a single word. Her conscious mind was trying to put the pieces in the right places and figure out what this could possibly mean.

But all the primitive, subconscious, instinctive parts of her were smiling, and trilling, and bouncing for joy.

Who cares what it means? He's here.

But she had to care. Didn't she? She had to protect her heart from being broken all over again.

Didn't she?

"Mind if I sit?"

She shook her head.

"Thanks." With an exaggerated display of diffidence, he pulled out the chair and sat, resting his hat on the edge of the desk. She picked up her pen, as she'd done with all the other applicants, and tried to think what her first question should be.

Continuing the charade seemed silly, but even if she abandoned it, she couldn't be truly authentic, could she? She couldn't just burst into tears, or start beating his chest, weeping, "Where *were* you, damn it? Where did you *go?* Why didn't you say goodbye?"

And she certainly couldn't jump into his arms and say, "I don't care where you've been. Just make love to me, right now, before I lose my mind."

All of that…out of the question. Humiliating, to have such a storm raging inside her…especially considering he'd been gone only five days.

Five days that had felt like five years.

So she'd have to say something civilized, something poised and unruffled. Something like, "It's good to see you, Gray. How have you been?"

Which was every bit as artificial as the applicant act.

And less likely to allow her to ask the questions that mattered. So she held the pen over her notebook and glanced up at him.

"Perhaps you should tell me about your work experience. Have you ever worked on a ranch before?"

"I have." He held up his hand to tick off the dates. "My first job was a cattle ranch in Texas. I was there two years. Then three years at a ranch in Wyoming, where they also bred horses. The past eight years, I've been in California, on a ranch that breeds quarter horses."

She raised her eyebrows. "No experience on a dude ranch?"

"Well, very little. About three weeks."

"I see." She had to fight the urge to correct him. *Not three weeks, Gray.* Twenty-four days. Just four days short of his allotted time.

She rotated the pen through her fingers, picking her words carefully. "Why such a short time? Did you not find the work…compatible?"

"Oh, *very.*"

"So…" She made a meaningless note on the paper. Her fingers on the pen weren't as steady as they should be. "It's customary to ask…why *did* you leave your last job?"

He touched his hat, pinching the dent in the brim. Then he gave her a look so direct she felt her cheeks burn. "It's a long story. Before I bore you with it, I'd like to be sure you're really…interested."

She raised her chin. "I'm listening. I have half an hour before my next interview, so take your time."

"Okay." He settled back in the chair, crossing his ankle over one knee. The gesture outlined his strong legs, from the long, graceful thigh to the soft boot that cupped his lean, elegantly muscled calf.

An invisible coil inside her midsection tightened, and she looked back down at her paper.

"Actually," he said, "the answer is long because it's not just one simple answer. There are many parts to it. I'll start with the easiest—and that was that I couldn't keep the job because I'd taken it under false pretenses."

She shot a glance up at him. "False pretenses?"

"In a way. You see, I didn't tell the truth about who I was, or where I come from, or what I really wanted."

"Go on."

"I let it be assumed that I was just a ranch hand somewhere and fairly hard up for money. I implied that I'd taken the job because I wanted to be reinstated in my rich grandfather's will."

"And that wasn't true?"

"Technically, it was. I do work on a ranch. And I did make a bet with him that I could keep the Bell River job for four weeks. If I could, he had to put me back in the will. If I couldn't, he had the right to disinherit me, and I would never mention it again. So the part about the job being my way back into the will was all true."

"What part was a lie?"

"I did want him to give me the money, but not because I was particularly hard up for it, as I let everyone assume. I wanted him to acknowledge that he owed it to me. I wanted him to admit that he'd taken money from my father, supposedly to invest for him, but then refused to give it back because he didn't approve of my father's lifestyle and wanted to be able to control him."

She thought of old man Harper and decided it wasn't impossible to believe this.

"All right," she said. "So now are you back in your grandfather's will? Did your plan work?"

"Not really." He shrugged. "Unfortunately, when I spent time in Silverdell, and with my grandfather, I began to doubt the black-and-white version of events I'd clung to ever since my parents died. I didn't want to let go of that comfortable old story, that my father was a martyr and my grandfather was a beast. But being home again brought back memories that just didn't line up with such a simplistic version. I had to recognize that my father had problems, serious problems. My grandfather didn't handle them well, and that's an understatement. But even so..."

She could hear tension in his voice. She didn't speak. Empty platitudes wouldn't help, and because she didn't know the characters involved, she had nothing else to offer.

"In the end, I saw that they were probably both made up of a little bit of the martyr and a little bit of the beast." His smile was slightly twisted. "As most people are, I suppose. As I am myself."

She nodded. Her own homecoming had been a relearning of the past, too. Abandoning the old thinking was surprisingly difficult.

"I'll probably never untangle the whole truth of what happened to my father's money, but I knew I no longer wanted it. Somewhere along the way, I saw how empty that victory would be. Getting the money back wouldn't vindicate my father. My father is dead, and beyond caring. And so I had to leave."

"You didn't tell your grandfather, though." She thought of old Harper's fury the other day. "You didn't explain to him why you were leaving."

He shook his head. "He wouldn't have believed me. He's a stubborn old coot, and he sets a lot of store by his money. So of course he assumes everyone else does, too. He would have accused me of merely choosing another route to weasel myself back into his good graces. He'd have thought I was switching to the flattering-toady route, feeding him empty hypocritical words because it was easier than working hard."

He chuckled. "And that would have got my dander up, and we would have been right back where we started. So I just left, before the four weeks had elapsed, so that he could see I had voluntarily forfeited the bet. When I left, I didn't think I wanted to have a relationship with him. All I knew, or all I was willing to admit to myself that morning, was that I didn't want him to be able to accuse me of being what he calls a 'deathbed vulture.'"

She heard the small added clause... *All I was willing to admit to myself that morning*...

"Have you changed your mind since?"

He smiled. "Well, you see, that brings me to the more complicated part of the whole mess. There was a woman."

"Ah." She tapped her pen on the paper, hoping it looked like detached amusement, but aware that, at least to her, it sounded jittery and uncomfortable. "There always is."

"You see, I met someone who insisted that what I really wanted, though I wasn't admitting it, even to myself, was another chance to work things out with my grandfather. I wanted to understand him and make him understand me. I wanted to forgive and be forgiven. The money, she said, had always been merely my excuse to put myself back in his life long enough to do that."

She was the "someone," of course. She remembered the night she'd told him that. He had seemed to laugh it off. It had never occurred to her that the thought had taken root...and might somehow have changed his course.

"And...?"

"And sometime over the past few days, I began to see that she might have been right. When I leave here, I'll go to Harper House, and see whether any of that is possible."

"I see. I guess the only part I still don't understand is—" she bit her lower lip "—why you had to leave in such a hurry. Without…time to really say goodbye."

"Well, that's where the explanation gets really complicated. Or maybe…maybe it's almost ridiculously simple. I left because I was a coward, and a fool."

"A coward?"

"Yes. The thing is… I don't have long-term relationships. When I was just a kid, I decided that caring about other people was simply too damn dangerous. I almost didn't survive the loss of my parents, quite literally, and I didn't intend to risk ever feeling like that again. Caring about anyone at all seemed risky. Love—" He shook his head. "Love seemed like something only an idiot would consider, like standing too close to a bomb that's already ticking. So I keep my relationships light, and I am always honest about what I am willing to give. Every affair I ever entered into had an end date, stamped and officially announced, even before it started."

She nodded slowly. He had been honest. She'd never had any reason to fault him there.

"So this woman…she was supposed to be another short-term affair. Good times, fun, no hard feelings when it was over. But then…then, one night, she told me she'd fallen in love with me."

She lowered her gaze to the pen. "Obviously that was a big mistake."

"Yes, it was. But only because I was, as I say, a coward and a fool. Predictably, I panicked. I could see that, for the first time, my carefully constructed walls were in danger of being breached. She had a way...a way of suddenly getting close, and making me feel things I wasn't comfortable feeling."

"So you ran."

"I ran. It's what I do. But this time, something went wrong. I hadn't been gone forty-eight hours before I realized it was too late. I couldn't run away this time. Because she was already inside me. She was already in my head, and in my heart, and in my dreams. I hadn't left her behind in Silverdell at all. I'd brought her with me. And the pain I was so afraid of feeling? It was already inside me, too."

She realized she was holding her breath. She tried to loosen it, but her chest felt too tight.

"Do you understand, Bree? There was no point in running anymore, no point trying to protect myself, trying to prevent getting hurt. I wasn't *in danger of* caring. I wasn't *in danger of* falling in love. I had already done it."

Little fireworks had begun to detonate inside her. But it seemed impossible. She wondered whether she might be dreaming, or whether, in some terrible way, he was teasing her, or just being nice. Or trying to get his job back for reasons of his own...

On some deeper level—the detonating-fireworks level—she knew those doubts were absurd. But...the old cliché "too good to be true" seemed to make sense in a new and concrete way.

She took a shaky breath. "And how does she feel about you?"

He let his gaze slide over her face. "She loves me,

too. She doesn't trust me, and she doesn't really trust herself. But she said she loves me, and I believe her." A slow smile tugged at the corners of his mouth. "That is…unless she said it as the result of a sexually induced endorphin high. You see, the sex was pretty phenomenal, so I suppose it might have been that."

She raised her eyebrows, flushing all the way down to her collarbone. "Oh, really? That's smug, don't you think?"

"No. It's actually an understatement. The sex was amazing."

Amazing…the drumbeat in her belly sounded those three syllables slowly, over and over, as heat gathered. But she couldn't give in to that yet. There was still one piece that didn't seem to fit….

"Something you said, right at the beginning…about taking the job under false pretenses. You said you let people assume you were 'just' a ranch hand. You let them assume you needed the money. Are you saying you *don't* need the money?"

"I'm not saying I have sixteen million dollars in my hip pocket, if that's what you mean." He smiled easily. "But I am saying that I won't go hungry, even now that I'll never inherit the Harper millions. The ranch I work on is my ranch. The horses we breed are my horses. I have five hundred acres and fifty employees. I'm doing just fine."

She tried to take it in. She was happy for him, of course. But five hundred acres of horse ranch in California, a thriving breeding business…

Even if he had been serious when he said that he loved her…how could they ever have a real relationship? There was no way he could do that kind of work from Colorado.

And how could she leave Bell River and Rowena, now that she'd finally found them again?

He frowned. "Actually, I thought you might take that news a little better. Surely, when a man declares his love for you, it's preferable to learn that he's solvent?"

"I—" She shook her head, abandoning the job-interview pretense. "I'm not sure I can absorb all this. I'm not even sure how much of what we're saying is serious, and how much of it is just a game and…"

"The part about my loving you is serious." His gaze was dark on hers, and yet its depths seemed to reflect a banked fire that made her breath come faster. "Deadly, forever serious."

"I—" Her tongue tangled on whatever had been supposed to come next.

"But you're right. The rest of it is a game—and I hope the rest of our lives will be, too. I want to make you laugh, Bree. I want to fill your life with so much sunshine that you forget what darkness looks like."

She felt a strange stinging behind her eyelids. Surely she wasn't going to cry, was she? Not when he was talking about sunshine and laughter.

"We've both been through enough," he said, his voice intense and determined. "Too much sadness, too much fear. I want us to put all that behind us. I want our future to be filled with fun, and work we're passionate about, with sex and joy. And love."

She shook her head, afraid, so afraid, that in a minute she'd wake up. Or he would. "But what future? A future…*where?*"

He looked at her as if confused. Then he laughed.

"Here, of course. Do you think I could have failed to see how important Bell River is to you? I've just spent the past twenty-four hours negotiating with Rowena and Dallas. As long as you and Penny agree, it looks as though Gray Stables will be setting up its breeding operations here on Bell River land. I'll rent about a hundred acres on the western slope."

She widened her eyes. Rowena had known for twenty-four hours that Gray was coming back? When she saw her sister next, she was going to...

Kiss her.

Suddenly, her heart was pumping a gold-shining liquid through her veins, and she wondered whether, if they turned off the office lights, she might glow in the dark.

And then the thought of being alone in the dark with Gray just made her heart pump the magic liquid faster, and she heard her breath coming fast and shallow.

She picked up her pen, trying to create space for air. "It sounds as if you're significantly overqualified for the assistant social director position, Mr. Harper. Why would you be interested in such a menial job?"

With a slow smile, he stood, then made his way around the desk until he reached her chair.

"Because," he said softly, "I'm hoping that, once I'm back in the Bell River family, I can, slowly but surely, work my way up the ladder."

He put out his hands. She took them, and he tugged her slowly to her feet. She wondered if her gold-shining limbs could hold her erect, or whether they would simply melt under her.

"And what job do you have your eye on?" She kept

her interview expression in place. "Where do you see yourself in, say, five years?"

"I see myself right here," he said, pulling her closer, and then closer, until their bodies melded from chest to knee. "Beside you. Inside you."

She made a soft sound without meaning to. He kissed the edge of her mouth, as if to catch the whimper, and then slid his lips around to her ear.

"Of course, by then we'll have to fight for our privacy," he said, "because we'll have two children and a dog. And maybe another on the way."

She shut her eyes, shivering as he tugged on her earlobe. "Another dog?"

He laughed, and the vibration passed through her like a tiny, hot earthquake. "How about two children, two dogs, three cats…do you like cats?…four horses *and* a baby on the way?"

She smiled. "So this ultimate title, the one you're climbing the ladder to reach…it's zookeeper?"

He lowered his lips, letting them hover tantalizingly over hers. "The title I want is *husband,* Bree. It's *lover.* Your lover, your partner, your friend. If you'll allow me to be all those things to you, it will be the title of the luckiest man in the world."

If she'd allow it? Torn between laughing and crying, she nodded, unable to trust her voice. With a low growl of triumph, he finally lowered his mouth to hers and kissed her with all the fire she'd thought she'd lost forever.

She had just surrendered to the shivering joy, and had let her hips move, finding the rising heat between his legs, when she heard someone knock on her office door.

She groaned, but he ignored both knock and groan, instead teasing her lips open wider with his tongue. And then she, too, ignored everything but that dark, wet place where they were joined.

"Bree?" The door creaked open. "Bree, your three o'clock interview is—"

A beat of silence, during which Gray continued to assault every sense Bree possessed. Whoever knocked had better leave, because Bree might just fracture into a thousand pieces right here, right now, standing up....

And then she heard a small chuckle from the threshold. *"Oh."*

Finally, the sound of the door closing. And Rowena's laughing voice speaking to someone unseen.

"I'm very sorry, Mrs. Brimley. It appears as if that position has just been perfectly—and *permanently*—filled."

* * * * *

SPECIAL EXCERPT FROM

◆ **HARLEQUIN**

SPECIAL EDITION

*Tamara Owens is supposed to be finding the person
stealing from her father. But when she meets prime
suspect Flint Collins—and his new charge, Diamond—
she can't bear to pull away, despite her tragic past.
Will Flint be able to look past her lies to make them a
family by Christmas?*

*Read on for a sneak preview of
the next book in The Daycare Chronicles,*
An Unexpected Christmas Baby
by USA TODAY *bestselling author Tara Taylor Quinn.*

How hadn't he heard her first knock?

And then she saw the carrier on the chair next to him. He'd
been rocking it.

"What on earth are you doing to that baby?" she exclaimed,
nothing in mind but to rescue the child in obvious distress.

"Damned if I know," he said loudly enough to be heard
over the noise. "I fed her, burped her, changed her. I've done
everything they said to do, but she won't stop crying."

Tamara was already unbuckling the strap that held the
crying infant in her seat. She was so tiny! Couldn't have been
more than a few days old. There were no tears on her cheeks.

"There's nothing poking her. I checked," Collins said,
not interfering as she lifted the baby from the seat, careful to
support the little head.

It wasn't until that warm weight settled against her that
Tamara realized what she'd done. She was holding a baby.
Something she couldn't do.

She was going to pay. With a hellacious nightmare at the
very least.

The baby's cries had stopped as soon as Tamara picked her up.

"What did you do?" Collins was there, practically touching her, he was standing so close.

"Nothing. I picked her up."

"There must've been some problem with the seat, after all…" He'd tossed the infant head support on the desk and was removing the washable cover.

"I'm guessing she just wanted to be held," Tamara said. What the hell was she doing?

Tearless crying generally meant anger, not physical distress.

And why did Flint Collins have a baby in his office?

She had to put the child down. But couldn't until he put the seat back together. The newborn's eyes were closed and she hiccuped and then sighed.

Clenching her lips for a second, Tamara looked away. "Babies need to be held almost as much as they need to be fed," she told him while she tried to understand what was going on.

He was checking the foam beneath the seat cover and the straps, too. He was fairly distraught himself.

Not what she would've predicted from a hard-core businessman possibly stealing from her father.

"Who is she?" she asked, figuring it was best to start at the bottom and work her way up to exposing him for the thief he probably was.

He straightened. Stared at the baby in her arms, his brown eyes softening and yet giving away a hint of what looked like fear at the same time. In that second she wished like hell that her father was wrong and Collins wouldn't turn out to be the one who was stealing from Owens Investments.

Don't miss
An Unexpected Christmas Baby *by Tara Taylor Quinn,*
available November 2018 wherever
Harlequin® Special Edition books and ebooks are sold.

www.Harlequin.com

HARLEQUIN®

S P E C I A L E D I T I O N

Life, Love and Family

Save **$1.00**

on the purchase of ANY

Harlequin® Special Edition book.

Available wherever books are sold,
including most bookstores, supermarkets,
drugstores and discount stores.

Save $1.00

on the purchase of any Harlequin® Special Edition book.

Coupon valid until December 31, 2018.
Redeemable at participating outlets in the U.S. and Canada only.
Limit one coupon per customer.

52615971

Canadian Retailers: Harlequin Enterprises Limited will pay the face value of this coupon plus 10.25¢ if submitted by customer for this product only. Any other use constitutes fraud. Coupon is nonassignable. Void if taxed, prohibited or restricted by law. Consumer must pay any government taxes. Void if copied. Inmar Promotional Services ("IPS") customers submit coupons and proof of sales to Harlequin Enterprises Limited, P.O. Box 31000, Scarborough, ON M1R 0E7, Canada. Non-IPS retailer—for reimbursement submit coupons and proof of sales directly to Harlequin Enterprises Limited, Retail Marketing Department, Bay Adelaide Centre, East Tower, 22 Adelaide Street West, 40th Floor, Toronto, Ontario M5H 4E3, Canada.

5 65373 00076 2   (8100)0 12386

U.S. Retailers: Harlequin Enterprises Limited will pay the face value of this coupon plus 8¢ if submitted by customer for this product only. Any other use constitutes fraud. Coupon is nonassignable. Void if taxed, prohibited or restricted by law. Consumer must pay any government taxes. Void if copied. For reimbursement submit coupons and proof of sales directly to Harlequin Enterprises, Ltd 482, NCH Marketing Services, P.O. Box 880001, El Paso, TX 88588-0001, U.S.A. Cash value 1/100 cents.

® and ™ are trademarks owned and used by the trademark owner and/or its licensee.

© 2018 Harlequin Enterprises Limited

HSECOUP04505

Looking for more satisfying love stories
with community and family at their core?

Check out **Harlequin® Special Edition**
and **Love Inspired®** books!

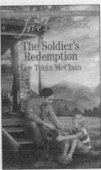

New books available every month!

CONNECT WITH US AT:

Facebook.com/groups/HarlequinConnection

**ROMANCE WHEN
YOU NEED IT**

HFGENRE2018

Looking for inspiration in tales
of hope, faith and heartfelt romance?

Check out **Love Inspired®** and
Love Inspired® Suspense books!

New books available every month!

CONNECT WITH US AT:

Facebook.com/groups/HarlequinConnection

Facebook.com/HarlequinBooks

Twitter.com/HarlequinBooks

Instagram.com/HarlequinBooks

Pinterest.com/HarlequinBooks

ReaderService.com

LIGENRE2018R2

Love Harlequin romance?

DISCOVER.

Be the first to find out about promotions, news and exclusive content!

f Facebook.com/HarlequinBooks

Twitter.com/HarlequinBooks

Instagram.com/HarlequinBooks

Pinterest.com/HarlequinBooks

ReaderService.com

EXPLORE.

Sign up for the Harlequin e-newsletter and download a free book from any series at **TryHarlequin.com.**

CONNECT.

Join our Harlequin community to share your thoughts and connect with other romance readers!
Facebook.com/groups/HarlequinConnection

HARLEQUIN®

ROMANCE WHEN YOU NEED IT

HSOCIAL2018